Praise for Laura Elliot's
GUILTY

"Intriguing from start to finish, with meaty characters and unrelenting suspense." —*Booklist*

"The level of suspense is kept high throughout *Guilty*, and those who enjoy stories that just can't be put down will love this psychological thriller." —Bookreporter.com

"*Guilty* is one gripping psychological thriller with a well-constructed plot and realistic and believable characters... Incredibly thought-provoking, it'll make you question everything." —Novel Deelights

"I was gripped from the first few pages and found myself hooked on a rollercoaster ride up to the last few pages...I read it in pretty much one sitting, I just needed to know how the book was going to end." —Donna's Book Blog

"*Guilty* was such a great book. It was filled with so many twists and turns...It was well written and definitely made you want more with every page turn." —Oh My Lit

"A mesmerizing psychological thriller...[that] will leave you completely fulfilled with a flawless ending. *Guilty* is the first novel I have read by Laura Elliot and it will NOT be my last. I found *Guilty* to be impossible to put down, the characters are intoxicating, and the story is compulsively addictive." —Books and Smiles

ALSO BY LAURA ELLIOT

The Wife Before Me

GUILTY

LAURA ELLIOT

GRAND CENTRAL
PUBLISHING
NEW YORK   BOSTON

Copyright © 2017 by Laura Elliot
Cover design and illustration by Emma Graves
Cover copyright © 2020 by Hachette Book Group, Inc.

Grand Central Publishing
Hachette Book Group
1290 Avenue of the Americas
New York, NY 10104
grandcentralpublishing.com
twitter.com/grandcentralpub

Originally published in 2017 by Bookouture in the UK
First U.S. mass market edition: March 2020

Grand Central Publishing is a division of Hachette Book Group, Inc.
The Grand Central Publishing name and logo is a trademark of
Hachette Book Group, Inc.

The Hachette Speakers Bureau provides a wide range of authors for
speaking events. To find out more, go to www.hachettespeakersbureau.com
or call (866) 376-6591.

ISBN: 978-1-5387-0139-3 (mass market)

Printed in the United States of America

OPM

10 9 8 7 6 5 4 3 2 1

To my one and only beloved sister, Deirdre Mullally.
Thank you for your love, support and enduring friendship.

PROLOGUE

The night has laid claim to Cherrywood Terrace. Street lamps pool the pavements and burglar alarms wink from the walls of slumbering houses. A chink of light escapes between old Mr. Shannon's bedroom curtains. He never sleeps at night, or so he tells her, staying awake with crosswords and books of poetry in case death comes calling in the small hours to catch him unawares.

In the room next door her parents are sleeping. Her father's faint, rhythmic snoring is the only sound to break the silence as she rummages through the clutter at the bottom of her wardrobe. From deep in the toe of a boot she has outgrown, she removes a phone and reads the last text she received. The one she has ignored until now. The challenge is clear. It's dangerous, high-risk, reckless, unnecessary. She doesn't have to take it on yet, even as she repeats these words to herself, she feels a coiling excitement, the giddy fever of knowing she can do it— will do it—and no one will ever call her a coward again.

She shoves cans of spray paint and a torch into her backpack, along with the phone. Better change her trainers for boots. Turnstone Marsh will be swampy in places. She pauses on the landing. Madness, she thinks. Why am I doing this? But anger has pushed her this far and it remains the barb that drives her down the stairs.

Out on the terrace she hesitates and looks toward a house on the far side. She was there earlier, silently entering and leaving the same way. She shrugs the memory aside and walks swiftly to the end of the terrace where a pedestrian lane provides a short-cut to Turnstone Marsh.

It's darker here. Her footsteps sound too loud. The wind tosses her hair as it tunnels between the high walls on either side of her. She sees it flailing in the shadow cast before her and pauses, afraid she is being followed. All is silent when she looks back. No footsteps behind her, none coming toward her. She reaches the end of the lane and crosses the road to the marsh.

Bells of white bindweed flutter like specters in the roadside hedges and she hesitates, torn between the desire to return home and burrow under her duvet and the need to continue on and complete the challenge. She climbs an embankment and jumps down on to the spongy grass. The humps and hollows of the marsh are familiar to her. This is where she used to ride her mountain bike when she was younger, but her surroundings look different now, eerie and threatening. She takes the torch from her backpack and sweeps it over the jagged outline of Toblerone Range. She remembers the struggle to cycle to the top peak, then the exhilarating ride across the humps. The thrill of descending without stopping or falling off. Now, she is facing an even bigger challenge and she is anxious to complete it before her parents awaken and discover she is missing.

She follows the path by the river. The ground is firmer here, safer than walking along the grassy trails. At the end of the marsh, she crosses Orchard Road and stops outside the

haunted house. The gate is padlocked. She shines her torch
along the boundary wall and finds a gap where the bricks
that have broken away provide her with a foothold to climb
over.

The outside walls of the house are covered in graffiti. Last
year, the front door was removed and used for a Hallowe'en
bonfire. At the entrance, the smell of mildew forces her to a
standstill. She asks herself once again why she has taken on
such a senseless dare. It's white-knuckle, crazy stuff. A man
died in this house. Seven days dead before he was discovered
by the postman. His ghost could be waiting inside, ready to
wail at her when she steps over the threshold. Even if ghosts
don't exist, there will be rats watching her, waiting to bite.

She turns to leave, then changes her mind. She must go
forward if she is to reclaim her position with The Fearless.
She climbs down the steps into the basement. In the beam
from her torch, she sees old, moldering furniture, rusting pots and pans. She almost trips over a horse's saddle.
Slashed open, its fleece, scraggy as a crow's nest, spills from
the interior. She takes the cans of paint from her backpack.
The walls are already covered in graffiti, stupid swirls and
squiggles and angles and curses. That's just vandalism. She
believes graffiti should have a purpose. It should make a
statement. A protest against authority, particularly parents
who've forgotten what it's like to be young. She positions her
torch on the floor and sets to work.

It's done. She videos her art with the Fearless phone. The
cover loosens and flaps against her hand. Impatiently, she
pulls the phone free and films the junk strewn across the
basement. This will add atmosphere to her video. Paws skit-
ter across the floor. She sprints toward the stairs.

At last, she's out in the open. The fresh air feels damp
on her skin and she can breathe freely again. The anger that

gave her the courage to complete the challenge turns to relief but she feels regret, also. She has broken a promise she made to someone special. She pushes this stab of guilt aside and argues with herself that friends are more important. Belonging matters. And she will be back in the circle again—right in its center—after tonight.

A briar snags her jeans. In the darkness, it feels as if a hand has gripped her ankle to prevent her escaping. She bends and pulls at the material, swears softly as the phone slips from her hand into the long grass. By the light of the torch she finds it. The cover has fallen into a patch of thistles. Prickly leaves sting her fingers as she tries to pluck it free. She leaves it there, anxious to be gone from this spooky, derelict site.

She clambers through the gap in the boundary wall and jumps down on to Orchard Road. Once outside, she videos the gate and the exterior of the bleak house where the ghost of Isaac Cronin roams through the moldy rooms.

She presses record on her phone and shouts, "A message to The Fearless. It's done. No one can ever call me chicken again." She spins across the road, giddy with triumph and a story she is longing to tell. The moon pearls the sky, shining coldly and mercilessly down on the last exhilarating moments of Constance Lawson's young life.

PART ONE

CHAPTER ONE

Day One

It began with a phone call. Still sleepy, Karl Lawson reached for his mobile on the bedside locker, surprised to see his brother's name on the screen. Justin never rang in the morning. An early riser, he was usually on the M50 by now, hoping to reach Junction 9 before the peak-hour traffic slowed everyone down.

"Is Constance with you?" he asked before Karl had a chance to speak.

"No," he replied, the abruptness of Justin's question snapping him fully awake. "Why on earth should she be here at this hour?"

"Has she been in touch with you this morning or last night?"

"I haven't seen her for a few days. Why? Is something wrong?"

Justin hesitated, as if choosing his words with care. "She's not in her bedroom. I thought she might have called over to talk to you."

"Talk about what?" Karl left his bed and crossed to the window, from where he had a view of his brother's house. Justin's car was still in the driveway.

"Things were a bit fraught here last night," Justin admitted. "And she usually runs to you when she thinks we're trying to clip her wings."

Fraught was probably a euphemism for blistering fury, Karl thought. He was familiar with the rows Constance had with her parents. She was the eldest of three and often complained that her upbringing had been a dress rehearsal for the siblings coming up behind her. Justin was right in thinking she could have confided in him but not on this occasion.

"Was it a bad row?" he asked.

"Apart from telling us we'd ruined her life, no worse than usual," Justin replied. "But that's neither here nor there at the moment."

"What was the row about?"

"Does it matter?"

"If you thought she'd come straight to me then, yes, it does matter."

"We're not allowing her to attend the Blasted Glass concert."

"Ah, for God's sake, Justin, you can't—"

"We discussed it with the other parents." Justin cut across his protests. "We all agreed that the girls are too young… and they *are*. You should have asked our permission before you told them you had those tickets."

"I'd no idea there'd be a problem. They've been looking forward to that gig for weeks."

"I don't want an argument about this," Justin snapped. "Right now I need to find her or she'll be late for summer camp."

"Have you phoned her friends?"

"Jenna's already done so. They've no idea where she is. They texted each other last night about the concert. Hate rants about parents, I should imagine, but Constance never men-

tioned anything about where she was going this morning...
or if she planned to go out during the night." Justin's voice
sharpened, as if the latter possibility was too dangerous to
entertain.

"*Night*? Constance would never go out at night." Even as
he spoke, Karl knew this was untrue and the alarm he sensed
behind his brother's questions added to his disquiet.

"What about the riding-school?" he asked. "Doesn't she
help out in the stables when she's on her school holidays?"

"Not without telling us... usually," said Justin. "But you
could be right. I'll check there. It's either that or she's training in the park with the Harriers."

"I presume you've rung her mobile?"

"She left it on her bedside locker."

"Then she can't have gone far. That phone is like an
extension of her right arm." Karl's feet were cold against the
wooden floor but the chill that ran through him came from
an uneasiness that, as yet, had no direction.

"I'll check the beach," he said.

"Why the beach?" Justin sounded surprised.

"If she's out riding, that's where she could have taken the
horse. She's just working off some teenage angst. We'll find
her quickly enough."

After they ended the call he sat on the edge of the bed and
checked his texts. Three days since he had last heard from
Constance.

Have you got the tickets, Uncle Karl?

I have indeed, he'd texted back.

*And backstage passes to meet the band. You owe me,
kid. Big time.*

What was wrong with Justin and Jenna, he wondered as he pulled on a T-shirt and jeans. Constance had been a fan of Blasted Glass ever since Karl introduced her to their new music. The fact that he could get free concert tickets for her and her friends had been an added bonus. He imagined her disappointment last night, her anger over her parents' decision.

He heard Sasha's door opening, the soft patter of her feet on the landing.

"Daddy . . . Daddy." She ran across the bedroom, two Dora the Explorer heads waggling on her slippers, her Dora dressing gown flaring behind her as she jumped into his arms.

He hoisted her on to his back and they descended the stairs, singing the Dora theme song at the top of their voices. She held his neck in a strangle-like grip until he lowered her into an armchair and put on a DVD.

"Ten minutes, that's all," he said. "Then you have to get dressed for summer camp."

Sasha ignored his warning, her attention already focused on the screen. Having moved seamlessly from the Teletubbies to Barney then on to Dora, her latest phase showed no signs of abating.

Nicole was still in her nurse's uniform when he entered the kitchen. She looked tired after her night shift in Emergency.

"Rough night?" He kissed the top of her head.

"Chaotic, as usual," she replied. "But no dramas." She plunged the handle on the cafetière and filled the kitchen with the smell of freshly brewed coffee. "What's new in your world?"

"Justin just rang." He accepted the cup of coffee and drank it standing up. "Sounds like Constance is in trouble."

"How so?"

"She'd a row with her parents last night."

"Not another one?"

"This time she's letting them cool their heels. She wasn't in her bedroom when Jenna checked earlier."

"That's not like Constance." Nicole sat down on a kitchen chair and yawned. Mascara smudged the skin under her eyes and wisps of blond hair feathered her cheeks.

"She's thirteen," Karl replied. "Testing the waters."

"I'm surprised she's not here. You're usually her first port of call when there's trouble on the home front."

"That's what Justin thought," he replied. "But not on this occasion. I know you're tired but can you hold the fort for a short while longer? I told Justin I'd drive around, see if I can find her. I'll be back in time to bring Sasha to summer camp."

"Go on, then. I'll get her dressed. I suppose she's watching Dora again."

"Need you ask?" He pulled the hall door behind him and glanced across the road toward his brother's house. Justin had already left for the stables.

The morning traffic was beginning to build as Karl drove through Glenmoore. Once past the village and on to the coast road, it eased. It was still too early for the dog walkers but a few joggers were already in action. Karl parked his car on North Beach Road and walked down the wooden steps to the beach. Coral clouds stippled the sky and a cormorant, surfacing from the sea, flapped its wings as it landed on a rock. It was going to be a hot day.

Apart from a shoal of dead jellyfish glistening on the sand, the beach was deserted and unmarked by any indentations from horses' hooves. He walked toward a formation of rock that curved naturally into a sheltered cove. Nicknamed Ben's Shack as a tribute to the teenager who had organized the first beach party there, this was where the young people from Glenmoore gathered in the summer. The Shack parties had been a rite of passage for him and Justin during their late teens: bonfires blazing, guitars playing, bottles clinking, weed and sex; a potent mix. Justin had met his wife, Jenna, who was also a Glenmoore local, at one such party. They often reminisced with Karl about those nights, laughing ruefully and vowing to lock their children in towers rather than allow them anywhere near Ben's Shack.

Karl entered the cove, expecting to find dead embers and bent beer cans. The sand was clean. Clearly no beach parties had taken place there for a while. The uneasiness he had felt since his brother's phone call lessened as he walked back to his car.

Justin rang. Constance was not at the riding-school and he was driving to Glenmoore Park in the hope that she might have decided to run with the Junior Harriers.

Nicole was stretched on the sofa when Karl returned home and Sasha, dressed in jeans and a Dora T-shirt, was snuggled against her as she watched her DVD.

"No luck," he said. "I'm sorry I took so long."

"Do you think we've any reason to worry?" Nicole hugged Sasha closer.

"I'm sure she's fine," he replied. "I'll call over to Jenna and see what's happening."

"I can drive the kids to summer camp."

"No, you won't," he said. "It's way past your bedtime. I'll pick up Matthew and Lara, and come back for Sasha."

Justin's car was still missing from the driveway. Karl unlocked the front door and entered the kitchen, where Jenna was speaking on Constance's phone.

"She wouldn't leave the house in the morning without telling us where she was going," she said to Karl when the phone call ended. "She loves helping out with summer camp and she should be getting ready to leave right now. I'm worried something's happened to her."

"Nothing's happened to her," Karl reassured her. "She's sulking somewhere, probably regretting running away but afraid to come home in case she's in even more trouble."

Jenna stared at the mobile screen, as if she expected a message to flash into view and solve the mystery of her daughter's whereabouts. "I'm making my way through the names in her address book. I'd no idea she knew so many people."

The kitchen door opened and Lara, her younger daughter, flounced into the room in her nightdress.

"Where's Constance?" she asked.

"She's just gone out for a little while," said Jenna.

"But she didn't give me a cuddle."

"Here's one now." Jenna scooped her up in her arms and hugged her. "Constance will give you all the cuddles you want when she comes back." She buried her face in the little girl's hair, her voice muffled. "It's time to get dressed for summer camp." She handed the phone to Karl. "Will you ring a few of those numbers while I'm upstairs? Someone has to know something."

"Will do." Karl took the phone and hit the number Jenna pointed out to him. It continued ringing and he was about to cancel the call when a youth answered.

"Yo, bitch. What's up?" The voice was young and brash.

"Is that Lucas O'Malley?" Karl asked.

The youth's sharp intake of breath was followed by a pause. When he spoke again his tone was more muted. "Who's that?"

"I'm Constance Lawson's uncle. Is my niece with you?"

"No. Why do you want to know? Is something wrong?"

"Hopefully, nothing's wrong. She's gone off without her phone and her parents are trying to contact her."

"So, why ring me? I hardly know her."

"Are you in the habit of calling strangers 'bitch'?"

"It's a term, man. It don't mean nothing."

"If you see her tell her to ring her parents immediately."

Karl was ending his fourth call, and was no nearer to finding out anything about Constance's whereabouts, when Matthew, his nephew, rushed into the kitchen in his tracksuit and trainers.

"Has Constance *really* run away?" he asked as he shook cereal into a bowl.

"Of course not," Karl replied. "She's probably with her friends."

"She's *always* with her friends." He spooned Rice Krispies into his mouth and swallowed noisily. "She hates living with us. That's what she said last night. Girls are *so* stupid. They're always crying about something."

Karl left his nephew musing over the shortcomings of big sisters and escaped into the living room to ring the next number. He kept looking out the window, convinced Constance was going to rush through the gate, sheepish, apologetic, her ponytail swinging, horrified that her friends were being contacted.

When Jenna came downstairs with Lara, he ushered the little girl and Matthew into the car, and stopped at his house to collect Sasha.

Cars were arriving and leaving the campus in Glenmoore College, which served as a summer camp during the holidays. Matthew had joined the football camp and Karl dropped the girls into the arts and crafts room. He made his way to the field behind the school where the track and field camp was located, hoping to see Constance among the volunteers. No sign of her anywhere and Justin, obviously sharing the same hope, was already speaking to the coach. It was clear from the slope of his shoulders that Constance had not turned up. Nor had she been seen at the train station, the shopping center or the cafès in the village, he told Karl as they walked back to their cars.

Jenna had finished checking the names on Constance's phone when they returned to the house.

"I know it's too early to call the police." Justin slumped into a chair and rubbed his chin. "But I'm afraid to let it go on any longer."

"Getting the police involved at this stage seems like a drastic step," said Karl. "She's only been gone a short while."

"This *is* drastic," Jenna replied. "It's ten o'clock and we've no idea how long she's been missing."

"Did her friends mention anything about a dare?" Karl asked.

"A dare?" Justin sat up straighter. "What do you mean?"

"Constance did something stupid a few weeks ago." He hesitated, aware that they were watching him intently. "She begged me not to tell you. She was afraid of how you'd react—"

"Cut the crap and tell us what happened," Justin snapped.

The brightness had gone from the morning. Karl was conscious of this dulling as he began to speak, a thumbprint smudging his future, but he was unaware that the familiar whorls and lines of his life would never be the same again.

CHAPTER TWO

"Ben's Shack," he said. "Three weeks ago, I picked Constance up from there." He saw his brother wince and look sharply across at Jenna. Apart from that exchange, they remained silent as Karl told them about the phone call he had received from Constance. She had rung him in the early hours when Nicole and Sasha were sleeping, and he was downstairs working on his laptop. Hearing her slurred, disjoined sentences and gulping sobs, he had decided the caller was playing a practical joke. A drunken teenager randomly tapping digits. He was about to end the call when he recognized her voice.

"Uncle Karl...help me, Uncle Karl...*please* help me."

"Just calm down." He tried to make sense of what she was saying. "Take it slowly and tell me exactly what's going on."

She had left her house after her parents had gone to bed and was at a party in Ben's Shack. The party was over and she was alone on the beach. Her house key had fallen from her jacket pocket and disappeared into the sand. She begged him to collect her and bring his spare key to her house with him. He mustn't tell her parents. She would run into the sea if he brought them with him. She sounded hysterical, capable of carrying out her threat, and Karl, unable to tell if she was drunk or drugged, or both, drove to the beach to pick her up.

He had cut across the sand dunes, following a well-worn track through the marram grass. The tide was out and wet sand gleamed in the moonlight. Ben's Shack was deserted but the glowing embers of the bonfire led Karl to her. She was huddled behind the rocks, the smell of vomit on her clothes, her eyes luminous, her gaze disoriented.

"I'm sorry...sorry...*sorry*..." She had blubbered apologies into his neck as he carried her from the beach. She was feather-light in his arms, her stick-like legs dangling. She made him think of an overdressed rag doll, her short skirt rucked above her thighs, a glittery top stretched across her small breasts. A sprite child, perched on the cusp between capricious, dangerous immaturity and budding sexuality.

Back in his car, he had listened while she attempted to explain what had happened. She belonged to a gang called The Fearless. They were an exclusive group who dared each other to undertake different challenges. Painting graffiti on walls, egging the front doors of teachers' houses, water-bombing passing cars, using a fake ID in a pub to order a vodka and Red Bull, breaking into graveyards and lying on tombstones to take selfies...her voice shook as she listed the various challenges the members had undertaken. She became evasive when Karl demanded the names of the gang. Membership of The Fearless would be taken away if a member revealed anyone else's identity or refused a dare. Constance had been challenged to take a naggin of vodka from her parents' drinks cabinet and gate-crash Ben's Shack.

She held up her phone to show Karl the video she had taken at the party. Flames from a bonfire leaping upward. A young man sitting astride a rock, playing his guitar. Two girls dancing together, bodies touching, arms raised, holding bottles. The gang on the beach had been at least five years older than Constance. She admitted that she'd videoed them from behind the rocks, too frightened to mingle with them. She had taken selfies of herself drinking the vodka but admitted she had only drunk it for courage. The night had ended on an even more dismal note when she lost her keys and threw up over the sand.

"For God's sake, Constance, I always thought you were a sensible girl." Karl had been outraged by her recklessness. "What are your parents going to say when they find out?"

"Please don't tell them, Uncle Karl. *Promise* me you'll never tell them."

"We're not arguing about this," he had replied. "I have to tell them. Anything could have happened to you tonight."

"I rang you because I knew you'd understand." She was terrified, sobbing, pleading…please…please…*please*. She would do anything he asked if only he would keep that night a secret. "They'll ground me for forever if they find out. You've no idea what they're like. They're *so* strict. They don't remember what it's like to be young. Not like you do."

He told her she must leave the gang. She cried some more but, before he drove her home, he had wrung the promise from her. Cherrywood Terrace had been deserted when he braked outside her house.

"Thank you, Uncle Karl, you're the *best*." She flung her arms around him and kissed his cheek. "I just wish you were my dad." She stumbled up the driveway, then turned and waved before closing the door behind her.

Over the following weeks, Karl checked that she had kept her promise. She insisted she was no longer in the gang and he had taken her at her word. Now, as he faced her parents, and watched their agitation grow, the burden of what she had confided to him fell like a stone between them.

"Our daughter got drunk, gate-crashed Ben's Shack and you never thought to let us know." Jenna sounded more astonished than angry.

"It was stupid of me. I know that now," Karl replied. "But Constance promised it wouldn't happen again. I trusted her. We've all had similar experiences when—"

"Not when we were thirteen." Justin slammed his fist into his other hand. "Jesus Christ, Karl, I can't believe you never told us." The edginess in his voice echoed with past recriminations. The tone was always there, lying below the surface, ready to rise when, as now, he expected to hear the worst from his irresponsible younger brother.

"She was frightened of what you'd say—"

"Your first responsibility was to us, her parents." Jenna stared angrily at him. "If Constance is in some kind of trouble I'll never forgive you."

"This isn't the time for a row." Karl tried to placate her. "I searched the beach because I thought there might have been another party last night. It was a shot in the dark and I was wrong. But she could be involved in another challenge. Check her texts—"

"I've already checked them," said Jenna. "There's no information that can help us." She showed Karl the texts. Constance had been angry, ranting about her parents and her disappointment over the concert, but there was nothing about The Fearless or the reckless challenges she had described. He checked the photographs in her gallery, the dates they were taken, but was unable to find the video Constance had shown him.

"She must have deleted it." He handed the phone back to Jenna. "Her friends have to know something. You should ring Tracey and Gillian again. They must be members of the gang."

"If they do know something, they won't be able to hide it from the police." Justin stood up and shoved his arms into his jacket. "I've wasted enough time. I'm going to Glenmoore Garda Station to report her missing. Come with me and tell them what you know about these so-called challenges."

✦

Coffee was brewing in the police station when they arrived and the guard on desk duty had poured a mug for himself. It cooled by his elbow as he took details from Justin. After a short wait, they were brought into a back office where a heavyset woman with short, brown hair introduced herself as Sergeant Moran and asked them to be seated. She fired questions at Justin. Did Constance have a boyfriend? Was she in the habit of staying out late? Had she shown signs of withdrawal, a loss of interest in school? Had there been a row at home?

"Sort of," Justin admitted.

"There's no such thing as a 'sort-of' row with a thirteen-year-old," the sergeant said. "What was it about?" If her grim expression was any indication, she must also be the mother of teenagers, Karl thought. His apprehension was increasing every time she glanced at him.

"She was annoyed because we refused her permission to go to a rock concert," said Justin. "She went to bed at about eleven but we only realized she was missing this morning." He turned to Karl. "You tell her why you thought Constance could be on the beach."

Sergeant Moran listened impassively as he repeated what he knew. "This could easily be a similar escapade," she said when he finished. "We'll do some preliminary checks with the emergency services and talk to her close friends. Once we've reviewed the situation, we'll be back in touch with you. In the meantime, continue the search and contact us immediately if you've any further information."

Nicole was in bed when he returned home. He debated waking her but decided to let her sleep.

He rang his office and spoke to Barbara Nelson, his deputy editor.

"Everything's under control here," she assured him when Karl explained what had happened. "I'll look after things until you come in."

He swallowed, his throat suddenly dry. "I don't know what's going on, Barbara. It's so unlike Constance to wander off without telling her parents."

"She'll be back soon," said Barbara. "I ran away from home when I was fourteen. Can't remember why now. It was either my bulimic phase or else the shoplifting episode." She laughed. "Those teenage years, Karl. Who'd want them back? Give me the midlife crisis, anytime."

"You could be right." Her cheerfulness lifted him briefly. "I'll talk to you later."

Unable to stay in the house, he left a note for Nicole and drove to Glenmoore Woods. The trees formed arches above him and the sun flickered through the high crowns as he called Constance's name. The woods had been his playground when he was a boy. He had known its distinctive terrain but, today, everywhere looked the same. No markers to distinguish one tree-lined path from another. What would Constance have done here? Met someone? A boy perhaps, and kissed him in one of the loamy hollows? Karl poked a stick through the undergrowth in the hope that he would find something, a scrap of clothing, a hairslide, a shoe, anything that would give him a clue that she had walked this way. The rustle startled a bird from the undergrowth, its wings almost brushing his face. She would never have come here, he

realized. He was just wasting time; yet he continued comb-
ing the woods until Justin rang. An immediate police search
was being organized. Sergeant Moran wanted to question
Karl again and would be calling Justin's house shortly.

The sergeant looked even more intimidating in her yellow
hi-vis jacket. Her presence seemed to suck the air from the
living room. She was accompanied by a younger policeman,
who introduced himself as Garda Finnegan. Constance's
friends had been questioned, she said. They had denied any
knowledge about a dare and insisted they had never heard
of The Fearless. The photo galleries on their phones had
been examined but nothing linked to the images Karl had
described.

The young guard took notes as Karl told them what he
knew about The Fearless. His information was sparse and
sounded more outlandish each time he repeated it. A garda
family liaison officer arrived shortly afterward. Shauna
Robertson's expression was confident yet kindly, her voice
trained to soothe distraught families. Matthew and Lara
would have to be interviewed. The questioning would be
sensitive, Shauna reassured them, and done in the presence
of their parents. If journalists made contact, their queries
would be handled by the Garda Press Office. Sensational
reports could frighten Constance and make it more difficult
to find her. The guards left shortly afterward, taking Constance's mobile phone and laptop with them. Jenna's terror
was barely contained as she accompanied them to the front
door.

Neighbors came to their gates, puzzled by the sight of a
squad car on Cherrywood Terrace. The news was spreading. A missing child; soon the tremor would become seismic. They gathered in the kitchen, hugged Jenna and Justin.
Everyone kept insisting there had to be a rational explanation

for Constance's disappearance. No time must be lost in finding her. They spoke too fast, as if they were afraid a pause would allow doubt to settle and ferment.

The doorbell rang again. When Karl opened the door, a photographer, accompanied by a younger woman, stood outside.

"Good afternoon." The woman's eyes widened, as if she was surprised to see him standing before her. "I'm Amanda Bowe from *Capital Eye*," she said. "Can I speak to either Justin or Jenna Lawson?"

Capital Eye was a daily tabloid that specialized in bold, lurid headlines. The thought of Constance being that headline revolted Karl.

"I'm sorry," he said. "Neither my brother or his wife are available to speak to the press."

"Then perhaps you'd like to answer a few questions." The reporter slid her tongue over her teeth in an involuntary flick. Mid-twenties, Karl guessed, chic yet business-like in a black trouser suit and white blouse, the top button undone, a hint of lace at her cleavage. She thrust a small recorder toward Karl. "Is it true that Constance Lawson was not in bed this morning when her mother entered her room?"

"No comment," he replied. Had Constance's friends alerted the media? Everything was moving too fast, like a snowball on a hill, increasing in size with each lurch.

"If your niece is missing, and my source has told me she could be missing since last night, you need exposure and you need it fast," she said. "I can get the details into our evening edition but I'm on a tight deadline so I need information now."

"I've told you, we've nothing to say to the press."

"By saying nothing, you're admitting that Constance is still missing. Tell me otherwise and there's no story."

"Ring the Garda Press Office if you want information. As I've already told you, I've no comment to make."

The photographer raised his camera. In contrast to the journalist's chic appearance, he looked as if he'd slept in his baggy cords and jacket.

"I can always get a statement from the press office," she said. "But if you talk to me, you can make a direct appeal to Constance. I believe you've a special relationship with your niece."

She took a step backward, as if inviting Karl to challenge this statement, and slid her tongue over her teeth again. Was it a nervous gesture, he wondered, though nothing suggested she was uneasy about arriving unannounced on the doorstep.

"No *comment*." He stepped back and prepared to close the door. The photographer was already retreating, walking backward toward the gate, his camera clicking.

"Who was that woman?" Jenna came into the hall.

"A journalist from *Capital Eye*."

"Oh, Jesus!" Jenna banged her fist against her mouth. "Not that rag. What did you say to her?"

"Nothing."

"What does she know?"

"Just that Constance is missing."

"Missing." Jenna gasped, as if the word had punctured her lungs. "Yes, she's missing. She hasn't run away. She's been taken—"

He pulled her into his arms. "Stop it, Jenna. Thinking like that will weaken us. We have to stay focused and concentrate on the most likely explanation. Constance is upset. She's gone off somewhere to sort herself out. It's only a matter of time before she comes back to us."

How long before such platitudes stopped comforting her, he wondered? Even now, they had a hollow ring, but Jenna relaxed against him as if his assurances gave her a brief relief.

✦

By evening time, a search base had been established in the Glenmoore Community Center. Women offered to make sandwiches, soup, tea. It seemed to happen effortlessly, as if there was a prior plan, ready to handle such emergencies. Yet, it made sense. There was always a plan. Even in the midst of war, the recovery strategy was being quietly mapped out. Karl's stomach clenched in a spasm of nausea. He hadn't eaten all day. No wonder he was feeling weak. He leaned against the wall until the nausea passed and he was able to join the volunteers. He drove slowly through the housing estates surrounding Glenmoore Village. Some were recently built but others, like his childhood home on High Strand Crescent, were part of old Glenmoore before it became a built-up suburb. Twilight was settling by the time he returned to the search center. The emotions of the day— the apprehension, false optimism, dread, disbelief and conviction that Constance was just around each corner, beyond each hill—hung over the center as the volunteers made arrangements to meet again tomorrow.

CHAPTER THREE

Nicole was preparing their evening meal when Karl entered the kitchen. She swirled pasta in a saucepan of boiling water, a Bolognese sauce bubbling on the hob. The smell of garlic and tomatoes added normality to an abnormal situation but her anger was obvious when she faced him.

"Jenna told me about that beach party," she said. "I can't believe you never told me about it."

"It was a stupid thing to do," he admitted. "I never thought—"

"It was more than stupid," she interrupted him curtly. "It was highly irresponsible. Constance could be mixed up in some hare-brained challenge that would never have happened if her parents had known what was going on."

Her anger strengthened the images in his head. He imagined Constance spraying graffiti inside a railway tunnel, a train coming fast along the tracks. She could have drunk too much vodka and choked on her own vomit. What if she had jumped from an apartment balcony because someone had challenged her to try magic mushrooms? All his fault...all his fault...

"I made a stupid decision and I've been beating myself

up over it all day," he snapped. "So can we just leave it . . . *please*."

"Keep your voice down." She turned back to the cooker. "Lara and Matthew are sleeping here tonight. They're edgy enough as it is. I don't want you upsetting them any further. Tell them dinner's ready."

The girls were playing with Sasha's collection of dolls in the living room. Lara was a year younger than her cousin, four on her next birthday, but they looked as alike as twins, wispy blond hair and fringes, blue eyes, pert noses, the same smattering of freckles on their cheeks.

"I'm not hungry." Lara's bottom lip quivered when she looked up from their play.

"You have to eat something," said Karl. "There's ice cream afterward. Where's Matthew?"

"In the back garden," Sasha said.

"Okay. I'd better go call him. You two scoot to the bathroom and wash your hands."

Matthew was sitting motionless on Sasha's swing, his toes scuffing the grass.

"Hey, dude, you hungry?" Karl pushed the swing forward but Matthew stopped it with his heels.

"Do you think Constance is coming back?" he asked.

"Of course she is."

"She's *such* a crybaby."

"She was upset last night. But she'll be home soon."

"She never wants to live with us again."

"That was just angry talk, Matthew. Come on inside. Dinner's ready."

Nicole kept up a cheerful patter throughout the meal but avoided looking at Karl. Justin and Jenna arrived to say goodnight to the children, their voices strained when they reassured them all would be well tomorrow. Their house had been searched by the police for clues but they found nothing that could shed light on Constance's whereabouts.

Justin gestured at Karl to join him in the kitchen. "You were specifically asked not to talk to the press," he said.

"I haven't spoken to them."

"How do you explain this, then?" He handed Karl a copy of *Capital Eye*.

Karl shook out the front page of the tabloid and stared at the picture of Constance. A slightly blurry image that looked as if it had been lifted from Instagram or Facebook. The photograph that had been taken of Karl earlier at Justin's front door was positioned in the center of the report. His stance looked aggressive, his expression belligerent.

LOCAL GIRL MISSING FROM GLENMOORE
AMANDA BOWE

A search began this afternoon for a teenager from Glenmoore, a busy suburb on Dublin's east coast. Constance Lawson, 13, was missing when her mother, Jenna Lawson, 35, entered her bedroom this morning. Her parents are uncertain as to what time she left the house but assume it was between midnight and 7 a.m. Her distraught father, Justin, 37, contacted Glenmoore Garda Station and a garda search was launched shortly afterward.

A popular, intelligent and fun-loving schoolgirl, Connie loves music and is a dedicated fan of the disgraced, one-time hard-rock band, Blasted Glass. Her uncle, Karl Lawson, 35, pictured above at his brother's house this afternoon, spoke briefly to Capital Eye. *Editor of the popular music magazine,* Hitz, *he intended bringing Constance and two of her friends to an upcoming Blasted Glass gig, when the band played the Ovid in Temple Bar. Her parents, worried about the band's notorious reputation and the adult content of their lyrics, had refused to allow Connie to attend the gig. A bitter family row is believed to have followed their decision and Connie has not been seen since then.*

Connie Lawson is 5 feet 3 inches in height with brown, shoulder-length hair and hazel eyes. A black leather jacket, Levi jeans ripped at the knees, a blue sweater and black ankle boots are missing from her wardrobe. Her parents believe she is wearing them. The Glenmoore Community Center has been turned into a base for the search and the number of volunteers continues to grow. Gardaí are hopeful that the missing teen will soon be found.

"I never gave that information to the reporter." He handed the tabloid back to Justin.

"How else would she know about the row?"

"She must have contacted Tracey or Gillian."

"I've already checked. Amanda Bowe hasn't been in touch with them and she certainly *wasn't* given that information by the Garda Press Office."

"Why would I tell her anything like that? She must have another source. You believe me, don't you?"

Justin nodded, his shoulders slumping. "Constance tells you everything. Can't you think of anything she said that can help us find her?"

"For Christ's sake, Justin, don't you think I'd tell you if I knew? Look, here's my phone. Read her texts. See for yourself."

Justin skimmed the texts and handed the phone back to him. "How come she never mentions Ben's Shack?"

"We talked about it. I trusted her when she told me she'd left the gang."

"You trusted her?" Justin's eyes flashed. "I wonder how you'd feel if Sasha was a vulnerable teenager and I kept that kind of information from you? If I told you I'd taken her trust at face value?"

Karl tried to imagine his daughter as a teenager, her Dora the Explorer days well behind her. He had no answer to that question and the atmosphere was taut with unspoken accusations when Justin and Jenna left to wait throughout the night for news.

✦

Karl tensed as a sound broke the midnight silence. The sudden thud had come from directly above him but he was unsure what had caused it. He left the bedroom quietly, anxious not to awaken Nicole, who, unlike him, had finally drifted into an exhausted sleep.

The folding ladder leading to the attic had been pulled down and the trapdoor pushed to one side. Last year, he had laid down an attic floor and put built-in cupboards under the sloping eaves. He intended turning the attic into an office so that he could work from home when Nicole was on day shift at the hospital. The cupboards were still unfinished and his intention to replace the folding ladder with a spiral staircase had been put on hold when his bank manager refused to extend his loan.

Someone was up there now. Could it possibly be Constance? Heart thudding, he climbed through the open gap. A bare bulb shone dimly down on him as he looked across the floor. Matthew was standing in front of one of the cupboards, a screwdriver in his hand. Unaware of Karl's arrival, the boy was trying to push the tip of the screwdriver between the frame and the door.

"Matthew, what are you doing?" Karl spoke quietly, afraid the boy was sleepwalking.

Matthew jumped at the sound of his uncle's voice but he looked fully alert when he turned around to face Karl.

"I'm looking for Constance," he said. "She could be hiding up here. It's the only place left."

"Why on earth would Constance be hiding in a cupboard?" Karl crossed the attic and took the screwdriver from him.

"She said she was coming to live with you and Auntie Nicole. She's not downstairs and she's not in the garden so she must be hiding in the attic."

"Look, Matthew, it's empty," said Karl when he had prized the cupboard door open "And it's far too small for Constance to hide inside."

The boy sneezed, dust clogging his nostrils, and rubbed his hand across his nose. "The guards asked me loads of questions about her."

"What did you tell them?"

"I said she likes our house the best."

"Then you told them the truth, Matthew."

"Yeah..." He sneezed again. "You're just our uncle. Constance can't like you more than she likes Daddy."

Karl put his arm around his shoulders. "Your daddy's very special, Matthew. I'd never try to take his place. Constance didn't come here. If she had, I'd have sent her home straight away."

"I want her to come back."

"We all do."

"I'm sorry I said 'shut up' to her last night when she was crying. Do you think that's why she ran away?"

"You'd nothing to do with it, Matthew. And she'll be home soon—"

"I didn't tell the guards that she said your house was better than ours. Was that a lie?"

"Angry talk isn't true, Matthew. Don't worry about the guards. You didn't do anything wrong or tell any lies. Come on back to bed, like a good boy."

They entered the spare bedroom. The duvet on Lara's bunk had slipped to one side, exposing her legs. Her arms were sprawled above her head, as if she had abandoned herself to the realm of dreams. Karl slipped the duvet back over her and settled Matthew into the top bunk.

The rigidity of Nicole's shoulders when he returned to bed suggested she was awake. She kept her back to him as he eased in beside her and switched off his bedside lamp. She remained silent when he slid his arm over her waist. He was unable to decide if she was staring into the darkness or still asleep. He would tell her about Matthew in the morning. To seek the relief of touch and allow his fear to be consumed by sex was an urge that came and went, an abstract emotion without passion, and Nicole's stillness warned him not to come any closer.

It rained during the night. Heavy and persistent, it fell until dawn. Was Constance sheltering somewhere? He longed to leave the house and search for her in the beating rain but recognized the uselessness of such an action. He willed the phone to ring with news from the police but it remained silent.

He had been traveling through Australia when Constance was born. He remembered Justin's jubilation when he rang with the news, forgetting the time difference and awakening Karl in the small hours. Jenna had sounded exhausted but happy. Karl had wanted to be with them in the hospital ward, sharing their joy. Never their terror, never that—but if Constance was not found by tomorrow, what then... what then?

CHAPTER FOUR

Day Two

Did fear have a smell that caught at the back of the throat and make it hard to breathe, Karl wondered when he opened his brother's front door. That was how the house smelled, as if fear was a miasma, seeping from the pores of every room. Jenna, who had spent the night in an armchair, sounded hoarse with surprise that a new day had finally arrived. Justin's eyes were bloodshot from lack of sleep.

They had chosen the photograph they would use for the *Find Constance* poster. Not a smiley one. Wherever Constance was, they knew she was not smiling. Her hazel eyes were her most arresting feature. Find me, they said. Rescue me before it's too late. Karl emailed the photograph and the text for the poster to his deputy editor. Barbara promised to have it printed and the posters couriered to the community center as soon as possible.

The family liaison officer arrived and brought an air of calm into the frenzied atmosphere. Specialist air and water units would be engaged in today's search, Shauna told them. Nicole would look after the children and Karl would join in the search.

Volunteers and guards had already gathered at the

community center, cups of hot coffee in hand. Members from the local civil defense had also offered their services. They looked assured and well trained, but the mood was somber as the searchers were organized into separate groups. Karl set off with his team in the direction of Turnstone Marsh.

He had seen it on television, the wide line of searchers slowly progressing across a rugged terrain, eyes down as they combed the ground for clues. It was always someone else's story before, but now, it belonged to them.

Turnstone Marsh became a flood plain in winter but in the summer children scrambled their mountain bikes over the grassy mounds. When he was a boy Karl had broken his collarbone and cracked his ribs cycling on Toblerone Range, so called because of the serrated chain of humped earth stretching away from the highest peak. Races had been held regularly between the children who played on the marsh and Karl, by the age of ten, had held the record for descending the Toblerone on his bike at the fastest speed. According to Constance, who had tried and failed to beat his time, the record still held.

Last night's rain puddled the ground and the mud splattered the legs of his trousers. The sun cast a hard, metallic sheen on the river as it flowed through the marsh. The volunteers all tensed when something blue and fluttering floated into view. A woman laughed nervously when they realized it was a discarded umbrella, the fabric bloated by the swell of the river. They stopped when they found a rusting fridge, abandoned in a thicket. A young guard stumbled back from the rank smell it released when he forced the door open.

At the end of the marsh, they crossed Orchard Road. The orchard that gave the road its name had become a wilderness since the death of its owner, Isaac Cronin. Karl and his friend, Domo Kelly, used to take turns robbing the orchard when they were teenagers. Climbing the wall, Karl had been agile and quick, his feet planted in Domo's cupped hands, his knees working hard against the rough stone. On reaching the top, he had always experienced a moment of indecision as he looked down at the long drop into the orchard. Then he would jump, landing nimble as a cat, and take a ladder and bucket from Isaac's shed. Once the ladder was propped against the wall and the bucket was full, he would lower it to Domo, who would transfer the apples to another container. This would continue until they had as many apples as they could carry and Mr. Kingston—who drove a fruit and veg-etable van, and never asked questions—would pay them a pittance for the lot.

Isaac Cronin never chased them. Too old and hobbling but, even if he had been fleet of foot, he wouldn't have bothered. Karl's mother used to say Isaac was born with a lazy back-bone. An only child, who grew into a man-child, dependent on his parents until they died. They had successfully worked their orchard but Isaac had been content to fritter away his inheritance in the bookie office. He lay dead in his living room for seven days before his body was discovered.

Karl was living in New York when Domo, or Dominick, as he now preferred to be called, rang with the news. A post-man had raised the alarm when he realized that the same house lights were switched on each time he called. Dominick had been one of the first responders to the scene. A fireman, as he'd always planned. He said it was a grim discovery.

Karl had met Dominick earlier at the community center. He was off duty but anxious to help. Like the civil defense team, he had an air of assurance about him. A man used to facing danger on a regular basis. He had joined the marsh search party and was picking his way carefully through the overgrown grounds surrounding the old house.

Isaac's laziness had extended to dying intestate. No

relations had been found to inherit the property, which had remained empty since his death. Two stories high with gray walls, the house had always been a bleak, functional building. Now it was dilapidated. Roof slates and the front door were missing, the windows smashed.

The volunteers were silent as they approached the house. Graffiti artists had been busy; the gray walls were covered in swirls and loops, hard angles and the occasional expletive. Someone had sprayed an enormous pair of lips around the frame of the missing door. As the volunteers moved toward the entrance, it looked as if they were stepping into the maw of an inanely grinning beast.

They divided into smaller groups to examine the rooms on each floor. Note everything, Sergeant Moran advised them. Anything they saw that aroused the slightest suspicion should be reported and the police would decide its importance.

Karl climbed down the slippery steps to the basement where broken furniture had been dumped over the decades by the Cronin family. The woman beside him gasped and held her nose, the smell of rot and damp almost overpowering her. He sensed something menacing that was, as yet, undefined in this cheerless place. Constance…Constance…Constance… he repeated her name like a mantra. What would he do if he found her here? He shuddered as he thought of Isaac Cronin turning purple, slowly, irrevocably.

A cupboard lying face downwards reminded him of a coffin. Dominick helped him to lift it upright and check that it was empty. Glass from a television screen crunched under their feet. The searchlight illuminated broken bottles and syringes. Karl picked up a bottle. It looked clean. Someone had been drinking here in the recent past. Dominick said it happened regularly. Vagrants drinking red biddy, kids shooting up.

Eventually, the search of the house was called off and they emerged into daylight. The volunteers looked ashen, as if the gray, moldering atmosphere had seeped into their skin. The orchard stretched on either side of the house and around to the rear. Not that it looked like an orchard any more. Ivy clung to the branches and briars snapped at their clothes as the group re-formed and moved through the trees. How anything but weeds could grow in this wilderness he didn't know, but the trees looked healthy and windfall apples from last season's crop rotted in the long grass. The wall Karl had once scaled, hoisted upward by Dominick, still looked as intimidatingly high as it did all those years ago.

Litter had caught in the long grass, tin cans and bleached scraps of paper from a discarded black plastic sack, ripped open by birds. The searchers stopped at a command from Sergeant Moran. She bent over to check something on the ground.

"What's going on?" Karl asked the woman next to him.

She craned her neck, then shrugged. "Can't see. Could be nothing."

But it had to be something significant. Shivers ran over his skin. He wanted to break rank and run toward the policewoman but he waited, like everyone else, when they were told to hold their positions. Trampling grass could destroy vital evidence, Sergeant Moran said. She gestured at Karl to come forward and hunkered over a clump of thistles. A mobile phone cover was caught between the barbs. The sides of the cover were open and splayed like the wings of a speckled butterfly.

"Do you recognize this cover?" she asked Karl.

He was about to kneel to look closer but a curt command from her kept him on his feet.

"No, I've never seen it before," he replied.

"Think carefully. Have you ever seen your niece using it?"

"Never. Her cover is pink and covered in music stickers."

Sergeant Moran pulled on a pair of rubber gloves and carefully transferred the phone cover to a plastic bag. Last night's rain had collected in the grooves and stained the leather surface. The speckles, Karl realized, were small holes, as if the leather had been pecked by birds or scratched by rats. He was unable to read the sergeant's expression but he suspected that recovering fingerprints from it would be difficult, if not impossible.

She walked along the line and spoke quietly to the search team. They must retrace their steps and search for a phone. They turned and painstakingly scanned the grass. They checked between the roots of trees and deep in the tangled undergrowth but all they unearthed were more pockets of litter and rusting tin cans. Finally, the search was called off. They returned to the community center, where the atmosphere was muted, the conversations low. They accepted mugs of tea or coffee and sat down at tables that had been laid with plates of sandwiches.

Justin, who had been talking to a group of volunteers, came over to Karl. "Have you read this?" He flung a copy of *Capital Eye* on the table.

The headline *Connie Come Home* and an enlarged photograph of Karl and Constance seemed to jump out at him from the front page. They had been photographed sitting on the edge of the stage at the end of a concert, spotlights bathing the background in a lurid red. The photograph had obviously been taken on a mobile phone by either Tracey or Gillian. Constance, her arm around his neck, was leaning forward, pouting provocatively at the camera. Karl had no memory of the moment they were photographed but he must have protested because his hands were splayed across his face and only his eyes were visible.

His anxiety grew as he read the caption. *Missing school-girl, Connie Lawson, seen here at a concert with her uncle, Karl Lawson, controversial editor of* Hitz, *the popular music magazine.* How many images had Amanda Bowe viewed on the girls' mobiles before she had chosen that one, he wondered, as he began to read.

CONNIE COME HOME
AMANDA BOWE

A day after gardaí launched a search for missing schoolgirl, Connie Lawson, 13, the mystery remains. Where has she gone? Did she run away from home? Was she lured from her bedroom by someone she trusted? Was she groomed by an anonymous "friend" on social media? These are the hard questions her distraught parents must confront as the search for their daughter continues.

Her close friend, Tracey Broome, wiped tears from her eyes when she spoke about Connie. "She loves horses and training with the Glenmoore Junior Harriers. I hope she comes back to us soon," she said between sobs.

"She's a Blasted Glass fangirl," added Gillian Miller, another close friend. "She was really looking forward to hearing them at the Ovid. She phoned just before I went to sleep and said she'd ask her uncle to sort it out. That's the last time we spoke."

Connie's uncle, Karl Lawson, controversial editor of the popular music magazine Hitz, *enjoys a close relationship with his niece and had promised to bring the girls backstage after the concert to introduce them to the band members.*

The tearful schoolgirls sent out a special plea to their friend. "Please Connie, get in touch. We're so worried about you. We love you, Connie. Please phone and let us know you're safe."

Hopes are high that Connie will soon be reunited with her distraught family. Gardaí intend carrying out door to door enquiries in the Cherrywood area but, as yet, foul play is not suspected.

Foul play…foul play…the expression had a staccato force that stripped away the pretenses, the possibilities and reassurances that came from the brisk busyness of the volunteers. They had formed for only one purpose. To search for a girl who could be the victim of foul play.

"How often do I have to say it?" He raised his hands in an appealing gesture to Justin. "Constance didn't contact me and, if she did, I'd have sent her straight home again. I never take sides with her in a row, as you know. You have to ignore this rubbish."

"How do you propose I do that?" His brother's clothes were rumpled, the same ones he had pulled on yesterday when he realized his daughter's bedroom was empty. "Should I ignore the fact that the reporter is telling the truth?" He jabbed his finger at Karl. "You were forcing Constance to grow up too fast. Turning her into a groupie."

"That's not fair!" Karl protested. "I always keep my eye on her and her friends when I bring them to gigs. All they ever do is look for a few autographs and take some selfies with the bands."

"She's too young to be exposed to that environment. She was into harmless boy-band stuff until you started influencing her—"

"I gave her a few free albums, that's all. Some she hated, some she liked. I never tried to influence her."

A woman approached the table with a teapot and filled Karl's cup. Her hand trembled, as if the intensity of his dread had touched her.

"No, you just play the hipster uncle," Justin said when she left. "Undermining my authority every chance you get."

"That's *not* true."

Justin wheezed and pulled an inhaler from his jacket pocket. "Oh Jesus...Jesus...my little girl...where has she gone?" His cheeks hollowed out as he sucked in two deep inhalations.

"Not far, Justin. She can't be far away." Karl gripped his brother's arms and held on to him as tears coursed down Justin's face.

Shauna arrived at the community center. Enquiries from the press had been coming into the Garda Press Office all day. She was worried that the media would gather on Cherrywood Terrace. Justin and Jenna should go home before that happened. There was nothing more they could do today. She overrode their objections and nodded in agreement when she heard that Matthew and Lara would remain with Karl for another night. They must be protected from the unfolding publicity at all costs.

Television crews had already arrived by the time Karl reached the terrace. Satellite dishes extended from the roofs of two television vans parked outside Justin's house. Photographers had erected cameras on tripods and were photographing Shauna, who had left the house. She ignored the reporters, who clustered around her, microphones and recorders thrust forward. She continued resolutely toward her car and drove away.

"Jenna's just been on the phone." Nicole met him in the hall. "She said you and Justin had a row in front of everyone at the search center?"

"It wasn't a row. Justin was upset over something he read in the paper—"

"I saw it." She had been crying, her eyes red-rimmed, her gaze still angry. "Where did the journalist get that photograph?"

"From one of Constance's friends, obviously."

"It's not a nice image, Karl. You look..."

"What?"

"Nothing."

"Say it."

"It's as if you're trying to hide something. And Constance, the way she's hanging on to you..." She pressed her lips together and shook her head.

"What are you suggesting, Nicole?"

"It's an ugly photograph," she stated flatly. "Lecherous, even. It could give readers the wrong impression."

"I don't believe this—"

"Uncle Karl!" Matthew stood at the living room door, his Game Boy in his hand. "There's a man outside the gate taking photographs of your house."

When Karl rushed into the living room, Lara and Sasha were standing on the sofa under the window, waving at the photographer from *Capital Eye*. Karl ordered them to sit down and swished the curtains closed.

"Why is there a television van outside our house?" Matthew asked. "Is Constance a celebrity now?"

"No. She's still just Constance."

"I'm going to stop this right now." Nicole stormed out to the hall.

"Stay here and don't look out the window again," Karl warned the children before hurrying after her. She had opened the front door and was about to step outside when he grabbed her arm.

"Leave me alone," she snapped. "He's no right to be on our property."

"He's standing on public property outside our gate." Karl slammed the door closed. "There's nothing we can do to stop him photographing the house."

"We'll see about that." She tried to jerk free from him but he held her back.

"Listen to me, Nicole. I know how these stories work. The more you engage with the press, the more complicated it becomes. All he'll do is take your photograph and use it in tomorrow's edition."

"He's still there," Matthew called from the living room.

"I told you to keep away from the window," Karl shouted.

"I'm only peeking," Matthew shouted back. "There's a woman coming in the gate."

"Go back to the children," he whispered to Nicole when the doorbell rang. "Distract them somehow."

Why was he whispering in his own house? Cowering away as if he had something to hide? The doorbell sounded again. This time it was a prolonged blast. Nicole's expression, before she returned to the living room, defied him to continue ignoring it.

On the third ring he opened the door to Amanda Bowe.

"Why are you calling here?" he demanded.

"I just want to ask you some questions. Was Connie in a secret—"

"Her name is *Constance*." He jabbed his finger at her. "She hates being called Connie and none of her *tearful* friends would ever call her by that name. The least you can do is get your facts straight."

"Was Constance in a secret gang?" She appeared unruffled by his fury. "Did you know about her involvement in dangerous rituals? If so, why didn't you alert her parents?" Her brown stare suggested that every answer she received hid a deeper truth, which she was determined to uncover.

"Why is she talking about Constance?" Matthew had pushed past Nicole and was staring up at the journalist.

"You must be Matthew." Her black hair swished over her cheeks when she looked down at him. "Did Constance tell you where she was going before she ran away from home, Matthew?"

Karl gripped his nephew's shoulders and turned him around. "Go back into the living room, Matthew and stay there." He stepped toward Amanda Bowe. "It seems that ethics were never included in your journalistic training. I'm going to report you to the press council for questioning a child without parental permission."

"Why are you trying to prevent me from seeking answers that will help in the search for your niece—?"

He closed the door on her words and pressed his arms against the wall. Where was she getting her information? How would she use it in tomorrow's edition of *Capital Eye*? His skin prickled in a sudden, uncontrollable flush of anxiety.

"I guess it's time for popcorn and hot chocolate." Nicole herded the children into the kitchen. "Come on, Matthew. I'll make your favorite flavor, pecan and butter."

Popcorn rattled furiously against the saucepan lid as the children gathered around the cooker.

Tomorrow, if there was no overnight news about Constance, Nicole would bring them to Grass Haven, a horse shelter in Wicklow run by Jenna's friend Caroline. A visit to Grass Haven was a good idea. Cherrywood Terrace was no longer a safe place for them. The horses would be a distraction from the terror gathering around them as the second day of Constance's disappearance drew to a close.

CHAPTER FIVE

Day Three

The search broadened. Wastelands and fields beyond Glenmoore were being examined, and Karl, having spent the morning on another futile search, drove into Dublin's city center to hand out fliers to passing pedestrians. Some people ignored him, believing he was advertising restaurants or discount deals, but those who accepted the fliers slowed their pace and wished him success in his search for Constance.

His deputy editor rang. Barbara no longer joked about hormonal teenagers. Her tone was somber when she asked for news and deepened with sympathy when she heard there was none.

"Have you seen *Capital Eye*?" she asked.

"Not yet," he replied. "Why?"

"Amanda Bowe is on the front page again. And she's written a profile about you on the inside. She doesn't forgive easily."

"What do you mean?"

"Don't you remember her?" Barbara sounded surprised. "I thought she'd made an indelible impression on you at her interview."

"What interview?"

"You tore her to shreds when we were interviewing for

a features writer. Not that you weren't justified in doing so. She arrived late and hadn't a clue about the magazine."

He cast his mind back to the interviews that had taken place two years previously. He had no memory of interviewing her, nor had her name meant anything to him, yet, as Barbara described the encounter, he vaguely remembered meeting her.

She had been heavier then, her chunky figure in too-tight clothes, her feet squashed into too-high shoes. Had she been wearing glasses, her black hair cropped tight? That would explain why he hadn't recognized her. He recalled how ill-prepared she had been, half-answering his questions and giving the impression that she thought *Hitz* was a down-market musical version of *Hello!* A point of view that had infuriated him. From the brief glance he had taken at her published clippings, he knew she could write, but it was her attitude, her lackluster answers that had annoyed him and made him terminate the interview early.

He entered a newsagents on Grafton Street and checked the shelves. *Did Missing Teen Have Link to Secret Cult?* The headline tore across the front page of *Capital Eye*. He paid for the tabloid and crossed over to St. Stephen's Green. The sky had darkened, bruised charcoal clouds heavy with rain. No one in the park seemed to notice. Children threw bread at the ducks, mothers pushed buggies along the tree-lined paths. People laughed. A leaflet fluttered before a gust of wind and dropped into the duck pond. Constance... Constance floating on the water... lost.

He sat down on a bench and unfolded the tabloid.

A dark cloud hangs over Cherrywood Terrace. Until three days ago it was a place where parents were happy to rear their children in a safe and free environment. But all has changed since Connie Lawson disappeared.

Rumors abound in this close-knit community. It's been alleged that Connie had become involved with a cult where secret rituals were carried out during a member's initiation. These rituals were continued afterward and were seen as evidence of the member's loyalty to the cult. It is also alleged that Connie's uncle, Karl Lawson, 35, controversial editor of the magazine Hitz, *learned about this cult from his missing niece but failed to warn her parents until the teenager's disappearance.*

Gardaí investigating this possibility have searched her phone and laptop. They have been unable to find any information to back up Lawson's assertion but are keeping an open mind about this sensational claim.

Connie's friends deny the existence of such a cult. "What Connie loves most is being in her room with her fluffy toys and her music," said Tracey Broome. "I never heard her mention anything about a secret cult."

In the meantime the heartbreaking search continues. Connie's brother, Matthew, 8, and sister, Lara, 4, had been staying with Karl Lawson and his New York wife, Nicole, 33, since their sister's disappearance. Nicole Lawson has now moved with them and her daughter, Sasha, 5, to a secret location.

Gardaí are still hopeful of finding Connie alive. Her parents will make a televised appeal for her safe return tomorrow if there is no news of the missing teenager by then.

Profile on Karl Lawson on page 6.

Karl stared dully at his photograph. He looked threatening and aggressive, his finger jabbing the air as he stood in his doorway, while Constance's photograph, the one used on the poster campaign, was framed in a small circle beside it.

The journalist must have a source within the police. The coverage in the other papers, broadsheets and tabloids alike, and the regular news broadcasts, never mentioned Karl's connection to his niece. Instead, the reporting focused on the search and appeals to the public for information. Was Amanda Bowe using her pen as a weapon to seek revenge for the *Hitz* interview? It seemed preposterous, yet the ground beneath him felt insecure as he turned the pages of the tabloid. He had only ever felt that way once before. Selina Lee... Arizona... He tried to blank the memory as he began to read his profile but the sensation of being caught in a trap, boxed in on all sides, was, once again, frighteningly familiar.

PROVOCATIVE EDITOR NO STRANGER TO CONTROVERSY

Hitz is a well-known magazine in music circles. Young bands know its power to make or break them. Seasoned musicians, eager to promote their new albums, are only too well aware that a review in Hitz *means an instant spike in sales but a negative review is the kiss of death. Karl Lawson, 35, the magazine's editor, cut his teeth on the famous New York music magazine,* Cannonade, *where he worked as their music critic. Before then, he spent time in Arizona, working in construction. Five years ago he returned to Ireland with his New York wife, Nicole, and their baby daughter, having been headhunted by Lar Richardson, the ebullient magazine mogul, property developer and owner of LR1.*

Shortly afterward, Lawson interviewed the members of the infamous Manchester rock band, Blasted Glass, whose ex-drummer, Ed Stone, had abused an underage fan. Despite denials from band members, it is alleged that they turned a blind eye to Stone's activities. After Stone was found guilty of the charge and imprisoned, Lawson gave the band space to refute the allegation that they had been involved in a cover-up.

Two months later, a letter written by Stone was published in Hitz. The convicted pedophile attempted to exonerate himself from his crime. The Hitz offices were picketed and windows broken when a crowd of protestors attempted to storm the building. Lawson strenuously upheld his right to publish the letter by Stone, insisting it was an attempt by the pedophile to atone for the hurt he had caused his young victim. Stone later committed suicide in his cell.

Now, once again, Lawson is in the public gaze. This time it is more personal and closer to home. Uncle to missing schoolgirl Connie Lawson, 13, he enjoys a close relationship with his niece, and has been actively involved in the search for her...

Unable to continue reading, Karl hunched over the tabloid. How long since he had thought about Ed Stone? An insignificant-looking drummer, always in the background of the band, his dark urges hidden. The court case could have been harrowing but he had pleaded guilty and was quietly dispatched to jail.

The band found a new drummer and radically changed their image and their music. Their new music bored Karl. It lacked challenging rhythms but it attracted a younger audience. Karl gave the band the front cover of *Hitz* and an interview when the first album featuring their new sound was released. Barbara had warned him against publishing Ed Stone's letter of repentance. She forecast a vicious backlash and was proved right. Karl had known there would be hate mail, accusations that he had allowed a pedophile to peddle his depraved opinions in print. Ed had confided to him that he would be dead shortly afterward. Far better a swift death than the beatings and rapes he was enduring in jail. Karl was the last person he phoned. On the day after his letter was published, he slit his radial artery with a shard of glass he had managed to smuggle into his cell. It was a fitting weapon to end his life, symbolic and deadly. Nothing could stop the flow of blood, just as nothing had stopped the hate mail that piled up on Karl's desk. The increased sales of *Hitz* proved the old adage that there was no such thing as bad publicity and Lar Richardson had refused to take any action against his editor.

Amanda Bowe had crafted his profile with care. He closed his eyes. Tiredness was catching up on him. Too little sleep, and what he had managed to catch was riddled with nightmares that were becoming dangerously real. How did she know about Arizona? Was her reference to his time there a throwaway line or a chilling indication that she was investigating that dangerous period of Karl's life; a distant haze of red dust and splintering sunshine that still haunted his dreams?

His mobile rang again. Sergeant Moran sounded as brusque as ever. The police would like to search his house on the off-chance that Constance could have left a clue to her whereabouts there.

"It's purely routine," she said. "As your house appears to be her second home, it could help us in our investigations." She paused, then added, "If you've any objections, I'll organize a search warrant."

"I've no objections," Karl replied. "But I'm in the city handing out leaflets."

"I'm aware of that." Her tone suggested she had full knowledge of his movements. "I suggest you leave now. We'll be waiting for you when you return."

CHAPTER SIX

The sounds from upstairs were intrusive, doors opening, drawers being pulled out, furniture being shifted as the police moved methodically through each room. Was this a routine search, as Sergeant Moran had indicated, or was something more sinister going on? What were they expecting to find? He should have demanded a search warrant and contacted his solicitor before allowing them into his house. But why should he need a solicitor or a search warrant? He was jumping ahead too fast but the jittery suspicion that he was under investigation grew.

Unable to keep still, he carried a mug of tea into the living room. Outside on the pavement, a petite red-haired woman had erected a television camera and was filming two squad cars parked on the road. Other journalists had arrived, including Amanda Bowe and her photographer. She was laughing over something he had said, her head flung back, her stance relaxed as she waited for the police to emerge.

Karl drew the curtains and hunched into an armchair. He was under siege inside and outside his home.

Sergeant Moran came into the living room and sat opposite him.

"Do you recognize this?" She laid a transparent plastic bag between them on the coffee table.

He stared at a fragment of white material inside the bag. Something belonging to Sasha, he thought at first. One of her many hairbands or vests. But the guard's watchful expression warned him that it had nothing to do with his daughter. He recognized the shape. Two small triangles of cotton trimmed with lace, a strap on either side, a row of pink love hearts on the band.

"Do you recognize it?" she repeated.

"It's a bra," he replied.

"Well observed." She waited for him to ask the obvious question.

"Where did you find it?"

"Between the wall and the base of your bed," she said. "Does it belong to your wife?"

He knew nothing about bra sizes but if Nicole had ever fitted into this one it must have been when she was a pubescent teen. She yearned to have the figure of an athlete but her breasts were full and heavy, wonderful to hold.

He shook his head.

"Could it belong to Constance Lawson?"

He was about to say, "She doesn't wear a bra" but how would that sound? What interpretation would Sergeant Moran take from it? He had no idea if Constance wore a bra and, if she did, how it had ended up in his bedroom. Was this a trap? Evidence planted to incriminate him?

"I don't know if it belongs to her. If it does, I've absolutely no idea how it got there."

"Has she ever slept in your bedroom when she stayed over?"

"Never," Karl replied. "She sleeps in the spare room."

"So, can you explain how we found it in your bedroom?"

"I've no idea."

"Don't you think it strange that we should find it there?"

"Of course I do. Maybe she slept there when we were on holidays and forgot it. Justin has a spare key. We come and go from each other's houses all the time."

"You obviously have a close relationship with your brother."

"Yes, I do."

"Yet you didn't think it necessary to warn him about his daughter's reckless behavior on the beach?"

"I know it seems wrong but—"

"Seems?" She clamped her lips and pressed her fingertips together with the same vigor. "She's thirteen. Didn't you have any regard for her safety?"

"I trusted her. She was adamant she'd never do anything stupid like that again."

"Yet you went straight to that cove as soon as you heard she was missing."

"It was a possibility—" He stopped, unsure how to continue.

"That she broke her promise to you?"

"Yes."

"Her father claims you take her regularly into an adult environment."

Her voice, never losing its monotonous tone, stoked his panic. "I get free tickets for concerts all the time. Sometimes, I give them to Constance and her friends when I believe they'll enjoy the band."

"You allow her to roam backstage in an unsupervised environment."

"She's always accompanied by me and her friends."

"Who are just as young as Constance. Are you in the habit of currying favor with thirteen-year-olds, Mr. Lawson?"

"I'm her uncle. We get on well together. Is that a crime?"

"Did I imply it was a crime?"

"No..."

"Then why mention that possibility?"

"It was a turn of phrase."

"Choose your phrases carefully, Mr. Lawson."

His eyes stung as he held her gaze. "If you've any further questions, Sergeant Moran, I'll be contacting my solicitor."

"That may or may not be necessary." She was the first to look away, coiling back and holding off the strike for another time. "It depends on how our investigation proceeds. Thank you for your cooperation, Mr. Lawson."

The number of journalists outside his gate had increased by the time the police left. Karl pulled the curtain slightly to the side and watched as cameras flashed. Sergeant Moran ignored their shouted questions and strode purposefully past the reporters. No wonder the media were gathering. They reminded him of caged panthers as they paced the pavement, clutching takeaway coffees and speaking into their mobiles about the latest curve of the investigation.

He tried to ring Justin and Jenna but their phones remained unanswered.

"How are you holding up?" Barbara rang as he was defrosting his dinner in the microwave.

"With difficulty," Karl replied. "I read *Capital Eye*."

"She's a muckraker, Karl," she replied. "Remember what she wrote when that kid was shot in the inner city last year. She put his family through hell."

"She's obviously determined to put me in the same place."

"What's all this stuff about a secret cult?"

"It's rubbish," he replied. "Constance wasn't in a cult. She was in a clique who liked living on the edge. And, yes, I did keep that information from her parents because I trusted her to stop behaving so foolishly. And, *yes*, Nicole has removed the kids from our house but only to protect them from the media. This stuff Amanda Bowe is writing is inflammatory but she's hanging by her fingernails to the edge of truth. And now my house has been searched by the guards. The media are outside and there's still no sign of Constance."

"I can't imagine what her parents are going through."

"It's hour by torturous hour. They can't look beyond that. How are you managing?"

"The magazine's almost ready to be put to bed..." She hesitated, then continued. "What should I do about the Tin Toy Soldiers review Constance wrote?"

"Oh, *Christ*." He pressed his hand to his forehead. "I'd completely forgotten about it. We obviously can't use it until we find her."

When would that be? Grief welled inside him as he remembered her excitement when he had told her she could write her first music review for *Hitz*. She had called to his house one night when he was putting Sasha to bed.

"Anyone home?" she had shouted after letting herself in.

Sasha, who had been drifting asleep as he read her bedtime story, sat up immediately and shouted, "We're in my bedroom."

Nicole was on night duty at the hospital and Karl had been hoping to do some editing on his laptop once Sasha was asleep. He sighed as Constance bounded up the stairs, knowing that it would be at least an hour before his daughter settled down to sleep again.

Later, Constance had made herbal tea for herself and coffee for him, then curled up on the sofa to listen to tracks from the latest Tin Toy Soldiers album. She had been a fan of the band ever since he'd brought her and her friends to their concert some months previously. He had advised her to listen to the tracks a number of times and then write a review. If it was up to scratch he would publish it. At the front door she had flung her arms around him and promised he would have it in three days. True to her word, she had emailed the review to him on time.

"I can easily fill the slot." Barbara spoke softly. "We'll use it next month when all this is behind us."

"Yes, that's what we'll do." Hope...there had to be hope. Anything else was unthinkable. "Thanks for taking over, Barbara. I appreciate it."

"It's the least I can do."

"Has Lar Richardson said anything? I rang to explain what's going on. He was at a meeting and he hasn't rung back."

"You know Lar." Barbara sighed. "He's so involved with his new television channel, he hardly has time for anything else. I've spoken to him about Constance. He's sympathetic and knows you'll return to work as soon as she's been found."

CHAPTER SEVEN

Day Four

UNNAMED SUSPECT AT CENTER OF
MISSING CONNIE CASE
AMANDA BOWE

The search for missing schoolgirl Connie Lawson, 13, took a sinister turn yesterday afternoon when gardaí searched a house in the Glenmoore area close to her home. They remain tight-lipped as to the reasons for this search but despite this clampdown on media information, Capital Eye *can reveal that a piece of intimate female apparel found in one of the bedrooms was removed from the house and taken away to be forensically examined.*

House to house enquiries will continue today. The Garda Press Office have appealed to anyone with information, no matter how unimportant it may seem, to contact Glenmoore Garda Station where the search for Connie is ongoing. Her parents, Justin and Jenna Lawson, will hold a press conference this afternoon and make a public appeal for help in finding their missing daughter.

Everyone wanted a piece of him and Amanda Bowe
had shown how it could be done. Journalists were shifting
their perspective from the general to the personal, emailing or shoving lists of questions through his letter box. Karl
watched from the living room window as a male reporter
interviewed Maria Barnes, who lived three doors away from
Justin. Maria, after a quick glance over at Karl's house, as
if she guessed he was watching, closed her front door. The
reporter crossed the road and rang his doorbell. When Karl
refused to answer, he shouted through the letter box, intro-
ducing himself as Eric Walker and asking for an interview.
His voice had an urgency that suggested he was approaching a deadline. His brown hair, chiseled with gel, had been
combed into short, aggressive spikes. Eager and competitive, he wrote for the *Daily Orb* and was cut from the same
mold as Amanda Bowe.

Eventually, when his questions remained unanswered, he
shoved a sheet of paper through the letter box and returned
to the cluster of journalists outside the gate. Ignoring the
others, he sat on the garden wall and spoke on his phone.

Karl glanced over the questions. Each one was primed
with suspicion.

- *Can you describe the "close relationship" you have
  with your niece?*
- *Did Constance tell you where she was going on the
  night she disappeared?*
- *Did the closeness of your relationship cause friction
  with her parents?*
- *Was your house searched by gardaí yesterday and a
  "piece of intimate apparel" taken from it?*
- *Does she come regularly to your house when your wife
  is on night duty?*

• *Were you alone with her in your car on one occasion in the early hours of the morning?*

He crumpled the sheet of paper and flung it into the rubbish bin. The last two questions could only have been instigated by something Maria Barnes had said. The Third Eye, Nicole called her. Someone who could always be relied upon to provide the latest update on what was going on in the neighborhood. But why would Maria distort the truth? She was a gossip but not vindictive, or so he had always believed.

Nicole rang shortly afterward. "Was it our house that was searched?" she asked.

"Yes." No sense denying it. "The police have to follow up every eventuality. Constance treats our house like her own so a search was inevitable."

"I feel sick... *sick* at the thought of them rooting through our private possessions," Nicole said. "Female intimate apparel? What's *that* supposed to mean?"

He hesitated too long. The information was now in the public domain and outside his control but he was reluctant to discuss it over the phone. He heard Nicole sigh.

"What did they take away, Karl? *Tell* me."

"They found a bra—"

"They took one of my *bras* from the house?" Her panic exacerbated his own fears.

"It wasn't yours. They don't know who it belongs to."

"Do you?"

"Of course I don't."

"But Amanda Bowe said they found it in one of the bedrooms. Which one was that?"

"Ours."

"*What?*"

"Stuck behind the base, that's what they said. But that doesn't make sense."

"The police must think it belongs to Constance. Why else would they take it away? Do they think she slept in our bed?"

"I don't know what they think, Nicole. They could be trying to frame me—"

"Frame you for what?" Her voice rasped. "You're not making sense."

"None of it makes sense. Have you been reading that rag? The stuff Amanda Bowe is writing—"

"You've just told me they found Constance's bra in our bedroom." She coughed to clear her throat, her breathing hard and fast. "What she's reporting is the truth. Can't you see how that looks? Constance's bra, Karl, in our *bed*."

"Nicole, you can't believe…are you suggesting I should know how it got there?"

"Of course not. But I'm terrified and that terror keeps growing with every hour that passes."

The landline rang. "Hold on a minute," he said. A journalist from Sunrise Radio wanted an interview. Karl told her to contact the Garda Press Office and hung up. The phone rang again, cutting him off in mid-sentence.

"I have to go, Nicole."

"Who's ringing? Are they journalists?"

"Don't worry." He hit the cancel button on the landline. "I'm not going to talk to them."

She was crying when he ended the call. He wanted to be with her, holding her. Not relating facts that made no sense over the phone. Face-to-face, as they had been in New York the first time they met.

✦

She had been crying then, too, sitting close to the wall in a coffee shop on West 20th Street. Dressed in skinny jeans, a short velvet jacket and a black polo, everything about her had been restrained, even her tears. She had dabbed them discreetly with a paper serviette neatly folded in her hand and it seemed as if Karl was the only person in that crowded cafè aware of her distress.

On impulse, he moved to her table and asked if she would like a coffee. She refused at first but then nodded, smiled wanly. When he returned to the table, he noticed a thin, white line on her suntanned ring finger. A broken engagement, she admitted when her tears dried. Her ex-fiancé's father and her own father were partners in an accountancy firm and her decision to cancel the wedding was affecting both families.

Karl had been attracted to her heart-shaped face, the blond, elfin haircut that emphasized her blue eyes. She was beautiful, he thought. Not the wild untrammeled beauty that Selina Lee had possessed but something more subtle, safer. She made Arizona seem farther away. She offered him an escape and he took it gladly.

Now, he longed to leave the house and drive to Grass Haven, make her listen...understand. But understand what? The number of journalists outside his house had increased. He recognized the distinctive gray and red markings of the LR1 television van. Lar Richardson's magazine company and his television station were two separate entities but that did not lessen Karl's anxiety. His boss had not returned his phone calls. Lar had little time for sentimentality and if Karl was perceived as damaging the reputation of *Hitz*, he would take immediate action.

Soon it would be time for the press conference. Somehow, he had to leave the house unnoticed.

He removed a ski jacket from the hall closet and put it on. Royal blue with slashes of yellow, it was colorful enough to galvanize the media when he opened the front door. He closed the door on the flash of cameras and returned to the living room. He allowed the photographers to see him again, crossing in front of the window, then, out of sight, he draped his jacket over a corner of the sofa, which he pushed into view. It was a clumsy subterfuge but he hoped it would work long enough for him to make his escape. He zipped up a hoodie, pulled the hood over his head and left by the back door. A gate at the end of the garden led him to the narrow lane that ran along the rear of the houses on Cherrywood Terrace. As yet, the media had not staked it out and the way was clear for him to enter Cherrywood Avenue and then hurry on foot toward Glenmoore Village.

CHAPTER EIGHT

He entered the hotel room in the Glenmoore Grand where the press conference was being held and eased, unobserved, into the back row. The click of cameras sounded like rain on a tin roof when Jenna and Justin were escorted to a table on a raised dais. Jenna's slim frame looked fragile enough to break as she sat down beside their solicitor, Olga Nicholls. Olga had been her friend since their schooldays and was also Karl's solicitor. Justin, sitting next to her, was flanked by the family liaison officer. Superintendent Breen, the district officer, was also seated at the table, along with a superintendent from the Garda Press Office.

The sense of anticipation intensified among the assembled media when Jenna began to speak. She broke down before she could finish her prepared statement and Olga took over, smoothly reading the final sentences. Justin remained strong throughout his appeal. The harsh lights of the television cameras emphasized his pallor and the deepening lines on his face.

"It's been reported in the media that we had an argument with Constance before she left home," he said. "We don't believe this argument is linked to our daughter's disappearance. All parents and young teenagers argue over house rules. Constance knows that when we make decisions she finds hard to accept, we do so from a desire to keep her safe. We believe you are out there, Constance. But if you are being held against your will, I'm pleading with your abductor. Please, I beg you, send our daughter safely home to us."

The questions began and were fielded by the press officer, then Superintendent Breen wrapped up the conference. The reporters continued shouting for more information as he escorted the small group from the room. Amanda Bowe hurled a final question at Jenna's retreating back. Her carrying voice reached Jenna, who turned, her face blurred with tears, and nodded as if butting the question away.

Karl was leaving the hotel when the journalist caught up with him and held out her recorder.

"Mr. Lawson, can you confirm that a bra belonging to your niece was found in your bed during yesterday's house search?"

"No comment." He lowered his head and walked faster.

"Has your wife removed the Lawson children to an unknown destination to protect them from you?"

He swallowed, bile rising in his throat. "No comment."

"Have you been named as a suspect in your niece's disappearance?"

She had been building toward that question ever since she wrote her first news report. He should have been prepared for the assault, yet it snapped the last reserves of his composure.

"I haven't been named as a suspect in my niece's disappearance." He wasn't aware he was shouting until he saw her step quickly back from him. "If you dare print otherwise, I'll drag you through the libel courts and reduce that fucking rag you represent to pulp."

"Thank you for your cooperation, Mr. Lawson." She smiled and, once again, ran her tongue over her teeth. The burly

photographer loped in front of her, his scuttling sideways movements reminding Karl of a crab. Then they were gone, chasing a
deadline and a scoop he had handed to them on a plate.

Later that evening, the liaison officer called to his house.
She battled her way through the journalists, ignoring the
microphones and recorders that were thrust toward her.
Once inside the door, her shoulders slumped.

"Your reaction to Amanda Bowe has meant some very
unwelcome publicity." She followed Karl into the kitchen.
"Have you seen the latest from *Capital Eye*?"

"No."

"Amanda Bowe managed to file a piece on the press conference for the late edition." She took the tabloid from her
briefcase and handed it to him.

FEARS GROW AS SEARCH FOR CONNIE CONTINUES
AMANDA BOWE

*The Garda Press Office remain tight-lipped over yes-
terday's raid on the home of a local Glenmoore resident. The raid was in connection to the schoolgirl
Connie Lawson (13) who has been missing for four
days. This dramatic development is being played
down by gardaí, who refuse to confirm whether the
piece of intimate apparel that was removed from this
house belongs to the missing schoolgirl.*

*Connie's distraught parents, Justin, 37, and Jenna,
35, held a press conference in the Glenmoore Grand
Hotel this afternoon. In a heart-wrenching statement,
Jenna pleaded with her daughter to return home. "We
love you, Constance," she said. "Please, please come
back to us. We're waiting with open arms to welcome*

you. You're not in trouble. We're not angry. But we are heartbroken." She was unable to continue at this point and was comforted by her husband.

Despite her distress, Jenna kindly took time to cooperate with Capital Eye *and revealed it was her daughter's bra that was removed by gardaí from the searched house.*

The stress of this search has taken a severe toll on those close to Constance. After the press conference, Karl Lawson, the controversial editor of Hitz *magazine and uncle of the missing teen, made this statement. "I haven't been named as a suspect in my niece's disappearance. If you dare to print otherwise, I'll drag you through the libel courts and reduce that f****** rag you represent to pulp."*

Hatred toward the journalist curdled his stomach. He twisted the tabloid into a skein and flung it down on the table.

Shauna ignored the gesture. "Just so you know, Jenna has no memory of speaking to Amanda Bowe at the press conference."

"She nodded when she was asked a question," Karl replied. "That was all she needed. Can you explain to me how I've gone from being Constance's favorite uncle to being a suspect—?"

"You're not a suspect," Shauna interrupted him firmly.

"*Not* a suspect?" His mouth was parched, his throat clamping. No wonder he couldn't swallow. A noose was being tied around his neck and it was tightening by the hour. "My house has been searched by gardaí and that journalist is destroying me."

"She hasn't named you as a suspect. You're the one who responded to her by making that statement. I asked you not to speak to the media."

"I know, I know."

"We're still hopeful that we'll find Constance alive so it's essential that we investigate anything that could be relevant to her disappearance," said Shauna. "Yesterday, you were just helping us—"

"With your enquiries. Yes, I know the jargon. If what I experienced yesterday wasn't an official interrogation then I dread to think what the real thing must be like."

"Believe me, you'll know the difference if that happens." Her polite, professional mask was slipping. Did she have a daughter the same age as Constance? Did she see him as a killer? A monster who invaded the safe perimeters parents built around their children?

"We're searching for your niece but you *are* becoming the story, Karl," she continued. "It's imperative that you don't engage again with her or any other member of the media."

"I'm a prisoner in my own home when all I want to do is search for Constance."

"The search for your niece is in the hands of experts. You're a distraction when the focus needs to be on finding her."

"I must talk to Justin and Jenna. They're not taking my calls."

"Stop ringing them. They'll talk to you when this publicity dies down."

"Why not now? They can't believe—"

"They're too upset. It's understandable, under the circumstances, and Olga Nicholls has invited them to stay with her until Constance has been found."

✦

The solicitor's house, with its Palladian-style pillars and long, elegant windows, had belonged to generations of the Nicholls family. Once, it had sat in its own spacious grounds, but the rolling pastures had been sold in the eighties to a property developer, who built the Cherrywood housing estate on them. The house remained separated from its neighbors by thick walls, sheltering trees and high black gates, operated by remote control. It would offer Jenna and Justin protection from torturous questions and flashing cameras until Constance was found.

Karl had no such protection. Someone was leaking information to Amanda Bowe. The other journalists were just carrion, feeding off the entrails. Even the broadsheets, the language carefully couched. No accusations. Just speculations. Innuendo that he was powerless to battle. His sense of dread increased as he read the latest online edition of the *Daily Orb*.

Constance Influenced by Older Man
Eric Walker

As the search for missing schoolgirl, Constance Lawson, 13, continues, gardaí refuse to comment on whether or not an older man, known to the missing teen, has been questioned about his relationship with her. The removal of a bra belonging to Constance during a house search suggests that she had recently visited him.

"Constance is a very trusting young girl and easily influenced," claimed Maria Barnes, a close family friend. "She used to visit him at what I considered inappropriate times. I saw them parked outside her house once in the early hours. I debated telling her parents but one is reluctant to interfere in other people's business. In the light of what's happened, I'm heartbroken I ignored the warning signs."

CHAPTER NINE

Day Five

Karl checked the clock on the bedside locker. Thirty minutes since the last time he looked. That was how he slept these nights, fitful snatches that never lasted beyond half an hour. Sweat trickled under his arms, ran down his spine. He had been dreaming about Constance, the images vivid as she was crowd-surfed at a rock concert. A tiny speck being passed above the heaving crowd, and Blasted Glass had been playing the hard, unforgiving rock they used to compose. He could still hear the music in his head when he left his bed and looked out the window. Two o'clock in the morning and the media had departed. Only Mr. Shannon's light shone from the upstairs window.

A sudden thought, still linked to his dream, struck him. He gripped the window ledge, his knees weakening. The latest Blasted Glass album—he had intended giving a copy of it to Constance. At his request, the band's promoter had sent it to him and the members of the band had autographed it for her.

He hurried downstairs to the dining-room, which also served as his office when he worked from home. A temporary arrangement, he had believed when he began to convert the attic. Along with crockery and glasses, the mahogany sideboard was used to store general office supplies, and the numerous sample disks that came across his desk every week.

Karl had left the compact disk on the sideboard and had planned on asking Constance to review it. He hadn't thought about it since. When did he bring it home? Was it the day before she disappeared or the same day? He switched on the dining-room light and immediately saw that it was missing. Maybe he had left it in one of the drawers. He rummaged through the disks, taking each one out and studying their covers. Could he have left it on his desk in the *Hitz* office or somewhere else in the house? No, he distinctly remembered putting it on the sideboard. Maybe Sasha or Nicole had moved it... He pressed his fist to his mouth. Was it possible Constance had entered his house that night? She would have expected him to be up late, watching television or listening to his stereo with his earphones on. Had she seen the disk and taken it with her? And, if so, how was he to explain that to the police—or to Justin and Jenna? He needed to talk to someone or he would go crazy.

✦

Dominick Kelly's cottage was easy to miss, obscured by overgrown foliage and a monkey puzzle tree that blocked any natural daylight from the front rooms. His friend's jeep was parked in the driveway and a light shone from behind the drawn curtains in the living room. Dominick didn't answer until Karl rang for the third time. He was walking back down the driveway when the door opened. Barefoot and dressed in a singlet and boxers, Dominick was visible in the spill of light from the naked bulb in the hall.

"What the fuck are you doing out at this hour?" he demanded when he recognized Karl.

Karl knew Dominick had been drinking, even though he seemed sober, starkly so. The air in the living room was rank, trapped between windows that Dominick never opened. He noticed a half-empty bottle of whiskey on the coffee table. Another smell permeated the cottage, a fungal odor that Karl recognized as dry rot. Timber crumbling into dust, like Dominick's marriage, a bitter, acrimonious breakup. Too many unsociable hours and too much team socializing in the pub, Siobhan, his wife, had said when she demanded a divorce.

Dominick had lived with him and Nicole for a month before moving into the cottage, drinking too much whiskey and complaining bitterly about a wife who was unable to appreciate the stress of entering a burning building. Not knowing what would be found within the flames. Not knowing when a ceiling could collapse or an explosion start a conflagration. They were relieved when he left, tired of listening to him bemoaning all he had lost while doing nothing to reclaim it.

This time, Dominick became the listener. He scratched absentmindedly at a mass of black chest hair poking from his singlet, his expression grim.

"That bitch journalist is doing a hatchet job on you, all right." He slapped a heavy hand on his friend's shoulder. "Controversial editor, that's a term she's far too fond of using." He knocked back his drink and raised the bottle. "Will you join me? You look like you could do with a stiff drink."

"No. I'll stay with this." Karl held up the mug of tea he'd made when he entered the cottage. "*Four* days, Dominick. Where is she?"

"She ran away because she was pissed off with her father. Justin was an uptight pain in the arse as a kid and he's not

72 LAURA ELLIOT

much better now. Constance wouldn't be the first kid to do a bunk when things got too tough with the parents."

"I know her. She wouldn't put them through this."

"Is there any truth to the stuff they're writing about her? That cult—"

"It's *not* a cult. It's a gang of kids doing stupid things. Everything's being distorted and now I've discovered—"

"Cool down, cool down." Dominick leaned forward and laid his hand on Karl's knees. "In my line of work I come across tragedy all too often. Even before I reach a fire, I have the sense of it. What's to come, so to speak. All will be forgiven and forgotten when she's home again. There'll be a lot of coverage and speculation until she's found. You need to avoid reading that crap or it will chew you up. Let your solicitor handle it."

"I don't have a solicitor."

Olga Nicholls had rung him after the press conference and told him she would be unable to represent him. A conflict of interest, she said, but refused to elaborate on what that meant.

"Then, my friend, I'd advise you to get another solicitor and do it fast before things get out of control," said Dominick.

"You don't think I've anything to do with her disappearance?"

"Course not." His eyes slid away from Karl and in that shift, that sideways, speculative glance, the atmosphere between them changed. He suspects me, Karl thought, suddenly breathless from the stuffiness in the room. To discuss the missing disk would only add to that suspicion.

Dominick stood up abruptly. The whiskey bottle wobbled when his knee banged against the coffee table. "Whoa!" He grabbed the bottle before it fell and steadied it. "Listen, it's late and I'm wasted. You need to get some sleep."

"I can't sleep."

"I'll give you something." He left the room and came back a few moments later with a sheet of tablets. "Take one of those when you go home. You'll feel better in the morning, more clear-headed and able to cope."

He walked to the front door with Karl, a big man with bulk, all of it solid. Climbing ladders out of forbidden orchards was a far cry from the ladders he climbed these days. He was losing his hair but that just enhanced his masculinity, his sense of knowing his place in the world. A functioning alcoholic, who seemed capable of drinking through the night and turning up for work the following morning, clear-eyed and clear-headed.

Karl drove over the humpback bridge that spanned the marsh river and swerved as he turned too sharply into a bend on the road. The old house where Isaac Cronin had lived was visible in the headlights, the rusting gates once again padlocked. An image came to mind, a laser blast that seemed to explode inside his head. The sense of menace he had experienced in the basement. A feeling so undefined he had forgotten it until this instant. Graffiti sprayed on the raddled walls. Broken glass crunching underfoot. That smell penetrating through the mold and rot. Spray paint, faint fumes trapped in the turgid basement air.

He parked the car and took a torch from the glove compartment. Was he mad, he wondered, as he climbed through the gap in the wall and entered the old house. Apart from his footsteps, the house was steeped in silence. He made his way down the steps into the basement and shone his torch around it. He moved closer to one wall. The graffiti on display was a microcosm of the world outside. Undying vows of love, initials entwined. Hatreds twisted into tight, hard angles. Flourishes that promised to save humanity. Hammer fists that threatened to destroy it. And there, in the midst of this gaudy collage, Karl saw it. Blasted Glass's new logo, the font softer and more curved than the splintered lettering the band had once used. Had Constance sprayed that logo on the wall? His mind seethed with possibilities. Had she broken her promise to him and, angry with her parents, taken on another challenge, lured by the thrill of danger and the secrecy it demanded?

Karl stepped carefully around the debris on the floor and moved closer to the wall. The paint looked fresh compared to the other drawings, the colors still vivid, no streaks of dust and mold. Who was with her when she sprayed that logo on the wall? Who was with her when she left—or was she still here somewhere, imprisoned? Dead?

The word lurched against his heart. He had to build that possibility into his consciousness but he was not prepared to go down that dark path, not yet. He searched the rooms, retracing the steps of the volunteers. They had found nothing so why should he? Yet he kept moving from one room to the next. A rat scurried past and disappeared into a crack in the floor. Stuffing spilled from sagging armchairs and a rusting saddle. A table lay on its side, two legs missing. A piano sounded a note when he hit a broken key. He went outside. Dawn was a sliver on the horizon and the pale moon had yet to fade. Sky graffiti, the symmetry of a pearled circle shining over a wretched house that offered nothing except an explosion of paint blasted against a basement wall.

Had the mobile cover found in a bed of thistles belonged to a secret phone The Fearless used to record their escapades? What cover had been on the phone Constance used when she showed him the video of the shack party? He couldn't remember. He turned suddenly, convinced that someone was hovering on the periphery of his vision. He shone his torch into the tangled undergrowth but was unable to see anyone. He climbed the wall and slumped over the wheel of his car. Was he going crazy? Constance would never have come here. He had spoken to Tracey and Gillian at the community center on the first day of the search. They had been just as bewildered as everyone else by her disappearance. Nothing in the texts they exchanged had suggested that Constance was preparing to do something so reckless. And yet...that logo. The same one she had doodled many times on copybooks and notepads.

The blinds were down on Cherrywood House as he drove past. Justin and Jenna would be sleepless behind them. Their silence was the deepest cut. A wound Karl feared would never heal. What would they think if they knew where he had been? If only she had left her name on the wall—CONSTANCE WAS HERE—in three-dimensional boldness. But that explosion of color he had seen—what did it signify? Nothing. Blasted Glass fans were numerous and the image of shattered glass had been merchandised on T-shirts, posters, mugs, anything with a surface that could be exploited to display the band's symbol. His suspicion would only add to their fears, not their hopes. He was crazy, his imagination in overdrive. He drove past the high security gates of Cherrywood House without stopping.

Reluctant to return to his empty house, he continued driving until the lights of the city came into view.

CHAPTER TEN

Dawn rose above the Daniel O'Connell monument. Pigeons strutted past the bench at its base, ignoring Karl's feet and fearlessly pecking at the night's leftovers. The traffic was sparse, mostly taxis and some early-morning commuters heading across O'Connell Bridge. He dozed on the bench and was jolted awake by pedestrians hurrying past him. The pulse of the city had quickened and the early edition of *Capital Eye* was on the streets. A newspaper vendor walked past. The placard stuck to the front of his orange hi-vis jacket read *Suspicion Grows as Connie Search Continues*.

Karl bought the paper and returned to the bench. Amanda Bowe's report was accompanied by the same photograph of himself and Constance at the Tin Toy Soldiers gig.

Fears grow as each day passes that Connie Lawson, 13, could have been abducted by someone she trusts. Gardaí leading the search for the missing schoolgirl are following a definite line of inquiry. They are appealing once again to the public to come forward if they have any information that can help them to trace the teenager's movements on the night of her disappearance.

He pressed his hand to his forehead and stopped reading. The feeling that he was under observation intensified. Was someone watching him now? People ran for busses, pushed shopping trolleys, lingered in front of shop windows, and some, fugitives from this normality, shuffled by with glazed indifference. But even that could be a subterfuge. To hide among the homeless and addicted was to remain invisible.

"Shocking tragedy." The man sitting beside him was also reading *Capital Eye.* "That poor kid's dead, no doubt about it. I've a daughter that age myself. Jeeze…there's times I want to lock her up in a tower like Rumpelstiltskin."

"Rapunzel," Karl replied.

"Whatever." The man shrugged. "I reckon it's the uncle who done it. Castration, that's the answer. The bleedin' hearts can shout all they want about their civil liberties but that'd take care of them sickos quick enough."

The wafting smell of the man's takeaway breakfast roll turned Karl's stomach. Afraid he would throw up, he walked away without replying. He flagged down a taxi and directed the driver to bring him to Fitzwilliam Square. He desperately needed to talk to a solicitor.

✦

Angelina Ward, Lar Richardson's legal expert, kept him waiting just a short while before he was ushered into her office. They had worked together before on sensitive features he had published in *Hitz* and Karl respected her opinion.

"Can you stop the media writing lies about me?" he asked. "In particular, Amanda Bowe?"

"Lies, yes." Angelina nodded. "But she's careful. What she's writing is highly suggestive but not libelous—yet. I presume the bra found in your bedroom belongs to your niece?"

"Her mother identified it, so yes, it does. Our house is like a second home to Constance but I've no idea how or why her bra was there."

"So, in effect, Amanda Bowe hasn't written anything that's untrue."

"No. It's what she's implying—"

"Freedom of the press has to be protected." Angelina briskly interrupted him. "She's pushing the boundaries but not breaking the laws of libel, or naming you as a suspect. Tell me about your niece and everything that's happened to you since she disappeared."

She interrupted him occasionally as he did so, asking him to elaborate or clarify information. A family photograph sat on her desk: two teenage boys sandwiched between a handsome, dark-haired man and her, their mother, all staring at the camera with confident, white smiles.

"The liaison officer is right," she said when Karl finished speaking. "You need to keep out of the media's way. I'll check everything that's being written about you for libel but you can't prevent them gathering outside your house. If they enter your premises, that's a trespassing matter and I can seek an immediate injunction against the perpetrator."

On entering Cherrywood Terrace, he could see that the media presence had increased since the previous day. Reporters parted to allow him to drive his car into the driveway. He ignored their questions about the search and turned his face away from the cameras as they vied with each other to catch the elusive shot, to record the unthinking quote. Amanda Bowe was not among them. His antennae would have picked her out from a multitude.

He closed the front door and rang Nicole. An automated voice informed him that her number was inaccessible and continued to do so until she finally returned his calls. Her voice broke on his name, then steadied.

"Why did you tell Matthew to lie to the police?" she asked.

"What do you mean?" He frowned, unable to understand a question that sounded more like an accusation. "I never—"

"You did!" He heard her swallow before she continued. "You found him searching for Constance in the attic and told him he'd be in serious trouble if he told anyone she was staying with us until the row with her parents blew over."

"That's ridiculous, Nicole." He tried to remember the conversation he had had with his nephew. It seemed such a long time ago. "Matthew was confused, afraid of the police. I meant to tell you but with all that was going on..." His voice trailed away.

"But you didn't."

"Nicole, you know that Constance never came near our house that night."

"How do I know that?" She spoke slowly, a pause between each word, and in those pauses he could hear the heartbeat of his marriage slowing down. "I was on night duty."

"Are you saying you don't believe me?"

"Her bra was in our bed. What does that signify?"

"It signifies nothing because I don't know how it got there."

"So you keep saying."

"It's the *truth*." How to convince her when the truth was too tangled up in grief and dread to be recognized.

"I'm bringing the children back to Glenmoore tomorrow." Nicole was anxious to finish the call. "I'm staying with them in Olga's house. That journalist tried to question Matthew in the stables. Caroline ran her off but others will come. Don't argue with me about my decision, Karl. You can't expose Sasha to the publicity that's surrounding you."

"Don't do that, please," he begged. "Come home and talk this through with me. I swear to you, if Constance came to our house I knew nothing about it. Are you going to accept my word or the word of a confused and frightened boy?"

"I have to go, Karl. I'll ring you again when I'm not so upset." She was gone before he could respond.

He opened the medicine cabinet where Dominick's sleeping tablets sat, untouched. The relief they would bring. Oblivion. The memory of the last time he had sought such oblivion was sharp and dangerous, but could be forgotten easily if he gave way to temptation. He slammed the door closed and crossed the landing to Sasha's room. Exhaustion swept over him as he collapsed on her bed. He closed his eyes and blocked out the images of Dora the Explorer, Boots and Pablo traveling to distant lands across the wallpaper.

"All I need is a brainwave," he'd said to Nicole last month when he finished wallpapering Sasha's room. "If I could create another Dora, think what we could make on the merchandising."

Nicole had laughed and said, "Relax while you can. Next year she'll want My Little Pony or the Sylvanians."

"One obsession at a time is all I can handle." He had wiped his brow in mock exhaustion and followed her downstairs to the kitchen where lasagne bubbled in the oven and the table was set for three.

✦

He tensed when he heard the doorbell. Edging to the window, he saw a squad car outside. Once again, Sergeant Moran was accompanied by Garda Finnegan. Her usual brusque manner as she entered his house was modified and her request that Karl should consider helping them with their enquiries sounded almost pleasant. He could refuse if he wished, she added. But it could help clear the air if he would accompany them to the police station.

"I've no problem accompanying you," he said. "But, first, I have to contact my solicitor."

"By all means do so," she replied.

He retreated to the kitchen and rang Angelina's number. The receptionist's chirpy voice dropped when she heard who was calling. "I'm afraid Ms. Ward is not available right now," she said.

"Tell her to ring me as soon as she's free."

"She's busy for the afternoon—"

"I'm not interested in her work diary. Tell her I'm heading to Glenmoore Garda Station and she needs to meet me there."

The media swarmed forward when he left the house. Boredom and brief adrenaline-fueled periods of activity; he was familiar with their chorcography. Amanda Bowe was still not among them. Was she skulking outside Grass Haven or driving fast back to the center of activity? She cloyed his skin, like a cobweb he was unable to shake free.

She was waiting with her photographer outside the police station when he arrived.

"Karl, what can you tell us about Connie's disappearance?" She raised her voice as he was ushered past. "Do her parents know you're being questioned by the police? Is it true that you were seen in the vicinity of Cronin's orchard in the early hours of this morning?"

He ignored her questions as he mounted the steps, shoulders hunched, hood up. Already, he was acquiring the posture of the guilty. Heat spread across his neck and chest. His imagination had not been playing tricks on him when he stood in front of the old house and sensed another presence behind him. The police had been following him in the darkness, waiting out of sight until he emerged from Dominick's cottage, then keeping him under observation when he entered Cronin's orchard.

The familiar smell of freshly percolating coffee greeted

him when he entered the station, but this homely aroma did nothing to lessen his apprehension. The interrogation room immediately rocked him back to Arizona. Gray walls, harsh, fluorescent lights overhead, some chairs, a wide table over which secrets were extracted with clinical precision. His nervousness increased when he was left on his own. He was aware of the tactics, the mind games that would be played out in this bleak room.

Two plain clothes detectives entered and sat opposite him. The female detective, who introduced herself as Detective Garda Newton, wore a denim jacket with frayed cuffs and a shapeless pair of jeans. Her fingers were long and slim, short, square-cut nails. In contrast, Detective Garda Hunter's jacket and trousers were sharply tailored, and his round-necked top had a discreet designer logo on the pocket.

"You do understand that you're here in a voluntary capacity to help us with our enquiries?" he said.

Karl nodded. The detectives seemed relaxed, with none of the aggression he had experienced from the police in Arizona; but this was a stage, carefully set. He told them about the night on the beach with Constance, the times she had spent in his house, the concerts they'd attended together. The pressure built slowly. Detective Hunter had a slight twitch in his right eyelid. It was barely perceptible yet Karl found himself watching out for it, having realized that it was always a prelude to a more ominous question.

"Mr. Lawson, can you tell us what were you doing this morning between 3 and 4 a.m.?" he asked. Detective Newton laid on the table some photographs that had been taken with a night camera. Karl was instantly recognizable, walking toward the derelict house.

"I was following up on a hunch that my niece could have met some friends there on the night she disappeared," he said.

"Why would she do that?" Detective Hunter asked.

A logo on a wall of graffiti. How was he to explain his suspicion that Constance had been in that oppressive basement?

"Constance is a fan of the band, Blasted Glass. I wanted to find out if she'd painted their logo on the basement wall as a dare."

"Blasted Glass?" His eyelid twitched. "The band that that paedo...?"

"Yes. But the band has changed—"

"Ed Stone is dead," said Detective Newton. "How can he be connected in any way with your missing niece?"

"I didn't say he was connected. As I've already told you, Constance hangs out with a gang of kids who do crazy things. It was a hunch I thought was worth following up."

"Because you saw some scribbles on a wall?" she asked.

"Not scribbles. Graffiti. She's always drawing their logo on her copybooks." It was important to talk about Constance in the present tense.

"You'd know that, wouldn't you?" Detective Hunter leaned closer, a whiff of garlic on his breath. "Seeing as how you have this 'close relationship' with your niece."

"I love my niece. I'd walk through fire if it helped to find her."

"That's heartening to hear." Their eyes locked. "She phoned one of her friends and told her she was calling to your house. You're a regular fixer, apparently."

"But she didn't call—"

"What about your brother and his wife?" Detective Newton's expression was impassive as she interrupted Karl once again. "They've suffered a lifetime of grief since their daughter disappeared. Right now, you can end their uncertainty by telling us what went on that night between you and Constance."

Karl half-rose, then slumped back in the chair. "Nothing was going on. This is bullshit. I'm entitled to consult my solicitor."

"Why do you need a solicitor if we're taking bullshit?" asked Detective Hunter. "You're not under arrest, Mr. Lawson. You're simply helping us—"

"I demand to speak to my solicitor." He could no longer control his panic. The expression on their faces, the standard disbelief. Was it something they learned in training college?

He continued to answer their questions until Detective Newton pushed back her chair and stood. "You're free to go, Mr. Lawson."

"Free?"

"Until we need you again. If that happens you'd be well advised to have your solicitor with you."

He blinked when he emerged into the sunshine and saw the assembled media. Eric Walker ran alongside him, recorder in hand. The red-haired camerawoman filmed him. He had seen her on a few occasions on Cherrywood Terrace but, now, for the first time, he realized she was working for LR1.

He broke free from the group and ran toward a taxi. Cameras were pointed like guns at the windows. Lips moved but the questions being shouted at him were inaudible.

"You're either a celeb or a crim," the driver said as he accelerated away. "As long as you pay your fare, I don't want to know."

Back home, he made coffee, strong, black. It scalded his tongue. He hardly noticed the pain. Angelina's email was the first one he saw when he switched on his laptop.

I'm sorry, Karl. I've had a meeting with Lar. A tough one, I'm afraid. He reminded me in no uncertain terms that my responsibility is to the Richardson Magazine Group, not to individual staff members. Due to this conflict of interest I'm unable to work with you. As we discussed this morning,

*the media coverage you're receiving is unfortunate and
damaging. I've asked my nephew, Fionn Drury, if he's free
to represent you. You may have someone else in mind but
Fionn's an excellent solicitor. I highly recommend him. His
details are attached if you want to contact him.*

Karl was checking Fionn Drury's website when his
mobile rang. He wasn't surprised to see his employer's name
on the screen. After reading Angelina's email, he had known
it was inevitable that Lar Richardson would make contact.

Lar had once confided to Karl that his youthful ambition had been to play guitar with a rock band. Instead, he
established *Hitz*. Fifteen other magazines followed but *Hitz*
remained his favorite, his indulgence, his nostalgic salute to
dead dreams, flares and mullets. He had always been willing to support Karl whenever he stepped over the editorial
line. But not any longer. *Hitz*'s advertisers were becoming
nervous about the publicity surrounding its editor. Three
major clients had pulled out of their contracts and more were
expected to follow.

"You're fired," Lar said.

Unlike Angelina, he didn't say he was sorry. Why use
three words when two would suffice? And Lar Richardson
never apologized for his decisions.

✦

Amanda Bowe's update on the search for Constance made
the late online edition of *Capital Eye*. The next morning,
Cronin's house and orchard, and the surrounding area,
including Turnstone Marsh, would be cordoned off and systematically searched for evidence that Constance could have
been there on the night of her disappearance.

CHAPTER ELEVEN

Day Six

It was the small hours in Arizona when Selina Lee rang. Her voice was instantly recognizable, the slightly husky tone unchanged, but she spoke more slowly than Karl remembered, as if she pondered the meaning of words before uttering them.

"I had a phone call from an Irish journalist," she said. "She told me Constance is missing. Can this possibly be true, Karl?"

"Yes, it's true," he said. "I'm sorry you had to hear the news from a reporter. I assume it was Amanda Bowe who rang you?"

"Yes, that's her name," Selina replied. "But how terrible for you all. She said Constance has been missing for almost a week?"

"This is the sixth day. We're still hoping she's run away. Otherwise..." He swallowed, his mouth sour and dry. "Did that reporter upset you?"

"She caught me off guard." Selina's voice quavered. "It's difficult when I don't have time to prepare." Her life, like his, had moved on, yet, listening to her, he knew she was still marked by the night that had changed everything.

Still gripped by a fear that could come without warning and swamp her.

"What did she want from you?" He knew the answer already. Amanda Bowe would have dug deep before she made that phone call.

"She asked about that time."

"What did you tell her?"

"The truth. How did she find out about us?"

"I've no idea, Selina. I'm so sorry she contacted you."

"It's not your fault, Karl."

"I wish I could believe that—"

She interrupted him, as she always did in the past when he attempted an apology. "We mustn't have this conversation again. Otherwise, we'll only talk in circles and get nowhere. Are you in trouble?"

"You answered her questions truthfully so, no, I'm not in trouble." He was not going to add to her fears. "How's Finchley Creek?" He deliberately changed the subject. "Jago must be delighted it's still so popular."

"It puts bread on our table." She dismissed his question lightly. "What about you? Still editing *Hitz*?"

"Yes. Still slaving away."

"And your wife?"

"Nicole. She's fine. We have a daughter."

"Sasha. I know. Barney keeps me up to date."

They sounded like polite strangers, their turbulent past veiled by small talk and lies. No sense reigniting memories they had both reduced to dust. They said goodbye and he promised to contact her as soon as Constance was found.

✦

Karl had never planned on moving to Arizona. He had badly wanted to work on *Cannonade* magazine, with its mix of music, film and political coverage, but in New York he was just another wannabe, flipping burgers in McDonald's and paying an exorbitant rent for a tiny studio apartment. The features he submitted to the editor were never acknowledged and seemed to disappear into a black hole. Karl was ready to surrender his dream and return home when Barney O'Reilly phoned to offer him a job in Arizona with his construction crew.

Barney was Karl's father's second cousin, a ruddy-faced Irishman who had left Ireland forty years previously. He lived in a small town outside Phoenix called Winding Falls. Karl could live with him until he found his own accommodation.

The thought of steady work with Barney's crew was too tempting to refuse. Karl would investigate the music scene in the Southwest, write reviews for *Cannonade* and try, by dint of perseverance, to attract the editor's attention. He would return to New York with money in his pocket and a steely resolve to succeed.

Shortly after moving to Winding Falls, he met Selina Lee in a bar. She was at a hen night, or a bachelorette party, as the bride-to-be called it. "Bachelorette" sounded far too sedate for what was taking place on the bar tables. Eight women dancing and being cheered on by Barney's crew, who were slaking their thirst after a day's work in the desert heat.

"That one's trouble," Barney said, nodding toward Selina. "*Big* trouble," he added. "Be warned. I've known her since she was in diapers."

"Bring it on," said Karl and, Selina, knowing they were talking about her, flounced her dress higher. Bare legs, long, tanned and smooth, and a flash of red lace; she had jumped lithely from the table to sit beside Barney.

"Hey, Irish!" she said, flinging her arm across his burly

shoulders. "Aren't you going to introduce me to your new friend?"

"He's a clean-living Dublin lad," said Barney. "Sheath your claws, lass."

"I'm all for clean living," she replied and stretched across him to shake Karl's hand.

She was an actress, a ring girl, a kick-boxer, a waitress, a dancer, a torment—and Karl fell in love with her without a thought for the consequences.

He never knew what she was going to do next. She would burst into song in the middle of a crowded shopping mall, kick-box in the ring like a ballet dancer, waltz him down a busy street, strut around the boxing ring in a red bikini, holding a number sign above her head.

They moved in together before the summer was over and rented a wooden cabin on the outskirts of Winding Falls. The cabin was isolated but the rent was cheap, the rooms cool and spacious. Longspur Peak, a parched hill studded with cacti and stumpy-limbed saguaro, rose behind them. Forest of spruce and juniper fell away in front.

She flew in tandem with him when he skydived for the first time. He learned to wakeboard on the lake near their cabin and purchased a Harley so that he could ride beside her through the Sonoran Desert. Barney muttered about "trouble" every time she turned up at the construction site in a halter top and shorts, her black hair spilling over her shoulders when she took off her motorcycle helmet, the crew going wild, whistling and gyrating as she strode past.

Karl met her parents. Her father worked in oil. Her mother taught first grade. They treated Karl with a gentle indifference, as if they knew his time in their lives was limited.

✦

How had Amanda Bowe found out about her? Karl paced
the kitchen. Speaking to Selina had swept him back into a
maelstrom of forgotten—no, not forgotten, just dormant—
memories. The wide open road, so straight and long. The
monochromatic earth that could suddenly yield to color;
reds and yellows and purples spreading like a rash across
the sand. Red bluffs and boulders, the shuffle of nocturnal
beasts, a swing of black hair. And blood, always blood, dangerously red and spreading through the gorges of his nightmares.

CHAPTER TWELVE

CONTROVERSIAL EDITOR'S NAME LINKED
TO SEXUAL ASSAULT IN ARIZONA
AMANDA BOWE

In a shock revelation, Capital Eye has discovered that Karl Lawson, 35, ex-editor of the controversial magazine Hitz, and uncle to the missing schoolgirl Constance Lawson, 13, was a prime suspect in a case of sexual assault seven years ago in Arizona. The victim, Selina Lee, 33, best known for her role as bad girl Cheryl Storm in the soap Finchley Creek, spoke openly to Capital Eye about her horrendous ordeal.

Ms. Lee had been in a relationship with the suspect for eight months when the ferocious attack occurred. On the night in question, she had asked Lawson to move out of her home. He left in a violent rage and, sometime later, an unnamed assailant entered the cabin they had been sharing and struck Ms. Lee across her head with a baseball bat. She is a trained martial arts expert but the attack was so unexpected that she was unable to defend herself. She was dragged to the floor and savagely raped before being stabbed. She was unconscious and critical when Karl Lawson notified the emergency services. He claimed that her assailant was disturbed by his return and fled the scene of the crime.

Karl Lawson was questioned by the police and charged with rape and assault. Despite the fact that his semen was found inside the victim, and his skin under her nails, he was released from custody after three days due to lack of evidence. The file on the case is still open, according to a source in the Winding Falls Police Department.

Selina Lee suffered a nervous breakdown in the aftermath of the attack and spent a year in therapy. She is the wife of Jago Wells, scriptwriter of the soap, Finchley Creek, *and lives with him in a gated community in Phoenix. She admits that her lifestyle in the suburbs differs widely from her bad-girl screen alter ego, Cheryl Storm, who is fearless in her pursuit of pleasure and revenge. Selina Lee locks doors and won't go upstairs without switching on the burglar alarm. She jumps at sudden sounds and sleeps with the lights on.*

No one else has ever been charged with her rape. Due to attacks of post-traumatic stress each time she relives her vicious assault, she was reluctant to comment on the reasons why her case remains unsolved.

A spokesperson at the Winding Falls police station also refused to comment but admitted that the case remains open.

A police photograph of an unconscious Selina, her face swollen and bruised, was positioned beside Karl's mugshot, which had been taken at the police station in Winding Falls. *Man Charged with Violent Sex Assault* was the reproduced headline from the *Winding Falls Echo*. A grainy shot of the police station where he had been confined was also shown. Shivers ran under his skin when he looked at its gray bleakness. The headline used three days later announcing his release had not been included in Amanda Bowe's latest scoop.

+

Justin had aged in six days. His eyes were sunken, bloodshot, red-rimmed. A shambles of a man who had argued with his daughter and slept that night on his anger. No sleep for him now. He hadn't shaved since Monday. He liked a clean, close shave. Impossible these days with the tremble in his hand. Jenna came with him to Karl's door. They stormed past the journalists, oblivious to cameras and shouted questions, and laid the print edition of *Capital Eye* on the kitchen table.

"It's a total distortion of the truth," Karl tried to fend off their fury. Excusing is losing... excusing is losing... even to his own ears, he sounded as guilty as hell.

"Tell us about this distortion?" Justin looked as if he was about to hurl himself at his brother. To take a razor and cut him open if it helped him to find his daughter. "How come you never told us you'd been arrested?"

"It happened shortly before Mum died. I couldn't talk about it when I came home for her funeral. And, then, Dad's death so soon afterward... I wanted to forget it ever happened. I'd been exonerated—"

"*Why* were you exonerated?"

"Because I was innocent. Do you understand? *Innocent*. Read between the lines. This is nothing but innuendo."

"Then let's do away with innuendo," Jenna cried. "Did you assault that woman?"

Karl hardly recognized her. The fury of her gaze. A Valkyrie, storming into battle with retribution in her blood.

"No. I did not."

"Why should we believe you?"

"It wasn't the police who exonerated me. It was Selina. Why don't you ring her. She'll tell you exactly what happened."

"But it did happen!" Justin yelled. "And now our child is missing. Where is she? What have you done to her?"

Jenna tried to hold him back but he pulled free and lunged forward, slamming his fist into Karl's chin. Karl didn't try to defend himself. He was on his knees, shielding his head, when Jenna pushed between them.

"Do you want the media to break down the door?" she cried. "This isn't going to bring us any closer to finding Constance." She sank to her knees beside Karl. "For Christ's sake, help us... please help us. Just tell us where she is? Why are the police searching Cronin's orchard?"

He stood and pressed his hands against the table. He tried to explain about the graffiti. It didn't matter what he said, how he said it. They had made up their minds. No room for explanations. Suspicion had corroded the truth and made it shapeless. They left as abruptly as they came, their faces blank with hatred. They had crossed a bridge of lies and left him behind on the other side.

✦

Nicole rang. No tears this time. "We're not supposed to have secrets. Wasn't that what we told each other when we first met? No secrets. And now I have to read a newspaper to find out about your past. How could you keep something so important from me?"

He wanted her in his arms. Then he could explain how the need to forget had been stronger than the need to share. Revealing secrets gave them life. They mutated and were transformed once they belonged to someone else and, so, he had stayed silent during those early months when they were together and he still carried the stench of the cell on him. He'd needed to eradicate it. A clean slate and a new beginning. But the longer the delay, the harder it became to confide in her, in anyone. Arizona was so far away. A scorched, red landscape, quivering in a heat haze of horror.

Sasha had been born a year after their marriage. He would watch Nicole feeding her, her nightdress unbuttoned, the curve of her breast visible above their daughter's head, and the urge to tell her about Selina Lee would rise within him. But such horrifying revelations would curdle her milk, he'd think, and the longing would fade until it became a dreamlike sequence gathering dust.

"I'd nothing to hide, Nicole," he pleaded. "*Nothing*. You must listen to me. I know how it sounds but I was innocent. Completely exonerated. Please come home and let me explain what it was like then. And now I'm living in another nightmare. Just when I think it won't get any worse, it does. It's that journalist—she's trying to destroy me—us..." Excusing is losing...excusing is losing...he was unable to stop and Nicole was unable to hear him.

✦

The beginning had been good. Sex and fun and much laughter got them through the first six months of playing house. Karl blasted rock and shuddered under the power of a pneumatic drill. He bought albums by little-known bands and wrote about them. Finally, to his astonishment, one of his reviews was published in *Cannonade*. A second one followed soon afterward. The thrill of seeing his name in print in a magazine he had been reading since he was eleven was spine-tingling. Selina wasn't interested. The numerous auditions she attended had finally paid off and she had landed a small role in a television soap being filmed in Phoenix. She played the role of the "other woman" on the soap, *Finchley Creek*, causing havoc in what had been a stable marriage until she sashayed into it. Her future role was still in the hands of the scriptwriter Jago Wells and Selina was determined that he would grow her character.

Initially, Karl believed her excuses when she rang claiming she was too tired to ride her Harley back to Winding Falls and would stay overnight in a girlfriend's condo. His suspicions grew when her overnight stays in Phoenix increased but the truth only emerged when he arrived back from the construction site one evening and found her making enchiladas in the kitchen. She was wearing a see-through top and nothing else. The top swung loosely over her hips as she turned into his arms but, even as he lifted her on to the table and she linked her strong legs around his waist, he was aware of being manipulated. It was a brief and spontaneous coming together, over in minutes. The enchiladas were still warm when they sat down to eat.

The air in the cabin was humid. He opened a window to allow the night breeze to cool the room and heard a shuffling movement outside. Javelinas, he thought. He had become accustomed to the boar-like animals shuffling past the cabin, often knocking over the bins in their search for food.

Selina advised him to ignore them. Her voice slurred. She had been drinking steadily throughout the meal, finishing a bottle of wine and changing to tequila. At first, when she mentioned Jago Wells, Karl thought she was talking about her role on the soap. As he listened more carefully, he realized she had been with Jago on those nights when she stayed in Phoenix. Jago had ended their relationship that afternoon and Selina, repentant and drunk, wanted absolution from Karl.

He listened to her faltering confession and wondered if she would remember any of it in the morning. He understood the highs of false courage, the reckless abandon of caution, and the comfort of amnesia the following day. He held tightly to that knowledge when the urge to take the bottle from Selina and pour a measure for himself was dangerously tempting.

He demanded to know why she was lying on the sofa with him when it was obvious she preferred the casting couch on *Finchley Creek*. She scratched his face, then sobbed apologies, pleaded with him to forgive her.

He pushed her from him and left the cabin, rode his Harley up Longspur Peak. The sky was black, slashed with stars. He watched them shoot through the glistening firmament until his blood cooled. He would leave tomorrow. He had had enough of the dizzying sun, the breathless heat and scorched riverbeds. Enough of Selina Lee. He wanted wind with a promise of rain and the pulse of New York energizing him.

When he returned to the cabin, the rubbish bin had been upended. The javelinas had vanished and leftover food was strewn across the porch. He straightened the bin and entered the cabin. What remained in the bottle of tequila had formed a pool on the wooden floorboards. A broken glass lay beside it. The see-through top he had pulled so urgently over Selina's head a few hours earlier was also on the floor, the delicate fabric rent from neck to hem. She was lying naked beside it. Blood seeped from her hair, smeared her face, oozed from her mouth. He noticed bruising on her neck, a stab wound on her shoulder. He felt her pulse to check if she was still alive, then covered her with a rug and waited for the emergency services to arrive.

He was arrested on the spot. He had no alibi. If anyone had noticed him on Larkspur Peak, they would only remember a black-clad figure with a visor over his face, riding through the night in a fury.

His skin was removed from under Selina's fingernails, his semen identified. He refused to sign a statement admitting guilt. The cops were tough, determined to get a confession from him.

"Avoid his head," the bigger of the two said when they came into his cell. The beating they gave him was swift and brutal. Winding Falls was a small, closed town. Neighbors knew each other and Selina's parents were pillars of the community. Barney sent his lawyer to look after him when he was charged with rape and assault. A burly man with a pockmarked face and an attitude that suggested he was immune to clients protesting their innocence. A guilty plea would work in Karl's favor, he said. No one, not even Barney, believed in his innocence.

When Selina recovered consciousness and was able to remember the events of that night, she informed the police that Karl was innocent. His only crime had been to leave the back door unlocked when he rushed from the cabin.

Her assailant's features had been distorted under a black nylon stocking. He carried a baseball bat and stunned her before she could retaliate. She remembered the smell of drink on his breath. The stench of rum would never leave her nostrils. He had planned to kill her. He told her so as he raped her and repeated it before he stabbed her. No trace of an Irish accent. He was still talking when she lost consciousness. She had no memory of his escape or Karl's return. He must have heard the Harley and fled from the cabin, taking the condom he had used with him and knocking over the bin as he ran.

The test results when Karl was checked for alcohol and drugs had been negative. He had also grown a beard when he started working with Barney's crew and, although the nylon

stocking had disguised Selina's assailant, the material was
fine enough for her to know he was clean-shaven.

Barney removed Karl's belongings from the cabin and
collected him when he was released from custody. Selina was
discharged from the hospital and moved back to her parents'.
They tried to remain friends, believing they owed that much
to each other. Their bruises and cuts healed. Hers had been
visible and his, so skillfully delivered, were hidden. But the
internal wounds were too deep to allow room for friendship.
Instead, they became a reflection of each other's terror.

Two weeks later, Karl's mother died suddenly from a
brain hemorrhage. Justin rang to break the news and the
shock Karl felt over what had happened to Selina was sub-
sumed into this new grief. Returning for his mother's funeral
offered them a dignified way to say goodbye.

His father was stooped and grieving. A month later, his
death certificate would claim he had died from an aneurism,
but his sons knew his heart had broken. Karl never told him
about Selina Lee. Nor did he tell Justin. Too much history
from the early years between them. Unable to cast off the
roles they played, they remained the perfect son and the
problematic son, who always brought trouble in his wake.

✦

The late news was on television, the volume down. The
newsreader's mouth moved, her expression more nuanced
without the distraction of words. Karl turned up the volume
when Constance's face appeared on the screen. The same
photograph that had been used for the poster campaign.

"We're going live to the scene of the search where journalist Amanda Bowe is ready to bring us the latest developments in the search for the missing schoolgirl." The
newscaster swiveled sideways and smiled at the reporter,

who stood in front of Isaac Cronin's house. She touched her teeth with her tongue a few times but apart from this minor sign of nervousness, she seemed perfectly at ease as she described the ongoing search. The scene moved to the orchard, where the search dog was moving between trees. He would have sniffed Constance's clothes, breathed in the scents her young, delicate skin had exuded.

Amanda was back on camera. The search was being called off for the night but would resume at first light tomorrow. Karl pressed the remote and banished her.

He thought about a tree that grew in the garden he had shared with Selina. Leafy and broad, the palo verde gave them shade in the evenings when the heat of the day cooled and the enveloping darkness chased the wine-red sunset from the hills. But those rustling leaves could fall from the branches without warning. No slow fluttering, no russet flaunting. At the first hint of a drought, they dropped and allowed the tree's energy to survive in the parched earth.

Everything that had sheltered him since he left Arizona had been stripped from him with that same suddenness. The years in between, those safe six years of rebuilding his life, had just been an interlude. An interlude that fooled him into believing nightmares could be left behind in the searing Sonoran Desert.

The urge to sit there in the darkness and let them come for him overwhelmed him. The police with their book of evidence. The media with their sources and suppositions. His family with their broken lives. His chin was swollen, throbbing. He wondered if his neck was dislocated. *Brother Attacks Brother over Daughter's Disappearance.* Would that be her headline tomorrow.

No, too staid. It would probably read *Connie's Distraught Dad Attacks Sex Fiend Brother.*

CHAPTER THIRTEEN

Day Seven

They found Constance's body on the afternoon of the seventh day. Nicole rang to tell him. He knew the search was over before he answered his phone. She broke down when she heard his voice, unable to utter the dreaded truth.

"Tell me," he shouted. "For Christ's sake, tell me."

The liaison officer had arrived at Cherrywood House with the news. The search dog had located human remains, but as yet, the body found on Isaac Cronin's land had not been "publicly" identified.

"Let me talk to Justin," he gasped. "I *need* to talk to him, Nicole."

"He's not taking calls from anyone right now." She coughed, or perhaps she sobbed; the sound was too muffled to decipher.

"I'm not *anyone*, Nicole. I'm his brother. I'm coming over right now."

"No!"

"Nicole—"

"I said *no*. They've just heard the news. They need time—"

"I have to see them. How can they believe I had *anything* to do with this? Nicole, you don't believe it . . . you can't . . ."

Unable to listen to her protests any more, he ended the call. He was about to open the hall door when he remembered the media. He could see them through the stained-glass panels, their presence swelling the pavement outside his house, and keeping watch on the back lane. He leaned his back against the wall and slid to the floor. Dead...gone forever. The last fragment of hope shattered. Where had she been found? Cronin's land, Nicole had said, not inside the house. His hunch had been right but only half-realized. Had Constance been watching him from some distant, ethereal sphere when he had shone his torch on her graffiti? He must talk to Justin. Make him understand that the wedge Amanda Bowe had driven between them was built on words. Carefully constructed words that warped the truth and replaced it with a treacherous perception. Once they came face-to-face, Justin would understand how his suspicions had been manipulated. Together, leaning on each other, they would mourn Constance.

The doorbell rang constantly, as did his phone until he switched it off. He listened to each news bulletin to hear if Constance's name had been released. The longing to storm through the media, force his way through the high black gates of Cherrywood House, gave way to despair. Trapped in a cocoon of suspicion, he switched on his laptop and read the latest online edition of *Capital Eye*.

BODY OF MISSING SCHOOLGIRL IDENTIFIED
AMANDA BOWE

For seven days the community of Glenmoore, and far beyond, have been tireless in their search for missing schoolgirl, Connie Lawson, 13. Now, tragically, this close-knit community must come to terms with

*the horrendous truth that one of their young shining
stars is dead. The frantic search for Connie ended this
afternoon when a crack team of investigators, aided
by search and rescue dog, Midas, discovered her
body in an underground location and broke the cata-
strophic news to her parents, Justin Lawson, 37, and
his wife, Jenna, 35.*

*They had lived in hope that their beloved daugh-
ter was alive. That hope was cruelly dashed when her
remains were located in a buried water tank on land
that had belonged to the late Isaac Cronin.*

*The tank had been drained and closed off after
Cronin, a colorful eccentric, died. It remained buried
on his land, unseen and forgotten until someone with
local knowledge dug through the shallow earth covering it. This person is alleged to have removed the cover,
hidden the schoolgirl's body in this cement chamber
and concealed the recently dug soil with scrub. If not
for the valiant efforts of Midas, who burrowed under
the dead undergrowth and drew the attention of the
searchers to the location, Connie Lawson's young
body would never have been recovered.*

*A Blasted Glass CD was found in the pocket of
her leather jacket. The album, which has not yet been
released, had been autographed by the band members. A local man had been seen by gardaí in the early
hours of Friday morning in the vicinity of Orchard
Road and had been questioned at Glenmoore Garda
Station. An arrest is expected shortly.*

Throughout the day and into the night, he rang Nicole,
Justin, Jenna. His panic grew when he heard their answering
machines and waited in vain for them to return his calls.

He was upstairs in his bedroom when the crash of broken glass alerted him. Shocked but not surprised, he checked the window and saw them in his garden. Youths, he guessed, their hulking shapes indistinguishable in the darkness.

"Fucking paedo…out! Out! Out!" Their voices rose. "Burn the paedo…burn the paedo!"

Had they come from Ben's Shack, high on whatever it took to make their blood race? Secure in numbers, they were in control of chaos, uncaring how it was unleashed. Cameras flashed as the photographers moved around the edge of the riot. Reporters retreated from the pavement to the safety of the road as a flame flared from the mouth of a bottle.

Karl heard another crash and a whoosh as the petrol exploded. He ran down the stairs and grabbed the fire extinguisher from the hall. The petrol bomb had come through the living room window. He aimed the fire extinguisher at the flames spreading across the wooden floor. They were quickly extinguished but the smoke, black, dense and choking, shoved him backward. He closed the door and ran into the kitchen, soaked a tea towel in water. Using it to mask his nose and mouth, he returned to the living room. The floorboards and the curtains were alight. The television screen burst, showering glass into the flames. He struggled to breathe, dizzy and disoriented from the chemical fumes. The fire was out of control, the sofa smoldering as flames licked along the scrolled armrests. He retreated to the hall but he could still hear the roar of fire gaining ground behind the closed door. He had left his phone in the bedroom. He sprinted up the stairs, terrified a second petrol bomb would be flung into the hall and he would be unable to come back down. The electricity blew and he had to scrabble in the darkness for his phone. He hurried downstairs and out into the open air. His throat felt so charred he was unsure if the woman on the emergency line

could understood what he was saying. She kept reassuring
him that the emergency services were already on their way.

Lights had been switched on in neighboring houses.
Doors opened and figures emerged in dressing gowns. The
teenagers had scattered, running from the flames and belch-
ing smoke. Karl gave chase and grappled with a youth who
had taken longer than the others to run. A solidly built phy-
sique, he was probably on the local rugby team, bulked with
creatine and aggression. He struggled to escape, roaring
with pain as Karl punched him repeatedly in the face. His
friends never looked back. Karl had no idea if the youth he
had caught was the one who had flung the petrol bomb, nor
did he care. All he knew, with a chilling certainty, was that
he was capable of hitting this anonymous teenager until he
lay lifeless on the ground.

A siren sounded, the whirring noise almost deafening in
its urgency. The fire brigade entered Cherrywood Terrace.
Hands dragged at Karl, pulled him away.

"Murdering fucking paedo." The youth struggled to his
feet. "What did you do to Constance?" He tried to lunge at
Karl but was held back by the man restraining him.

"That's enough lip out of you." The voice of the man who
had pulled them apart was familiar. "You're under arrest on
a charge of arson," he shouted at the teenager. "Don't make
this any worse for yourself or you'll be cooling your heels
for the night in a cell."

Plain clothes detectives. Karl should have guessed. The
same ones who had interrogated him at the police station.
Before the stunned youth could reply he was clasped in
handcuffs. A squad car had followed the fire brigade and
the handcuffed youth, blood flowing from his nose and a cut
below his eye, was led away. He looked back at Karl before
entering the squad car.

"*Murdering* paedo," he roared. "I'll have you up on an assault charge and you won't get off so easily on that one."

"You stood by and let them burn me out." Karl's voice was too croaky to sound angry or disbelieving as he confronted the two detectives, who must have watched the unfolding scene. The woman looked as disheveled as he remembered, her eyes sunk into tired folds. She shrugged, without replying, and turned to speak to a guard in uniform.

"We've dealt with it. If you've a complaint to make, you're free to do so." The male detective walked away, a tall, imposing figure, illuminated by the fire truck's headlights.

The firefighters had extinguished the blaze in minutes.

"You okay, Karl?" Dominick stopped to speak to him.

Karl rubbed his sleeve across his eyes and tried to focus on his friend. Dominick took off his helmet and ran his hand through his thinning hair.

"How bad is the damage?" Karl asked.

"It's been confined to the living room." The hard lines of Dominick's face were streaked with soot, his eyes red-rimmed. "Detective Newton alerted the emergency services as soon as those yobs lit the petrol bomb so there was no time wasted." His tone was cold and formal. "There'll be smoke damage so you'll need an assessor to give you the full picture. Just as well you were on your own when it happened."

Karl's eyes smarted. Tears chafed his cheeks. Smoke or anguish, what did it matter? Sasha could have been sleeping in her Dora the Explorer bedroom, Nicole in the next room. He staggered, his knees giving way, and reached toward his friend to steady his balance.

"You heard about Constance?" he asked

Dominick stiffened. "I heard," he said. "Heart-breaking."

His disgust, barely concealed, ran like a fine wire along Karl's arm. He was surrounded by people, the media, police, firemen, neighbors. The same neighbors who had gathered in Justin and Jenna's house to help in the search for Constance. He was conscious of a palpable wave of hostility directed at him from all directions. This then, was hell, he thought.

Hell had always been an abstract concept to him, terrifyingly real when he was small, dismissed when he was in his teens, and ignored until now. But it existed, not in some eternal furnace occupied by tormented souls. It was here, in this quiet, suburban terrace where neighbors gathered in each other's houses for parties and book clubs and children's birthday celebrations. Hell was watching the uncertainty on the faces surrounding him. Neighbors who believed he was guilty of a crime that had yet to be determined. Hell was watching the smoldering remains of a living room where he sat in the evenings with Nicole, watching box sets together on the sofa, discussing their day's work, regaling each other with funny Sasha stories after their daughter had gone to bed. Hell was his dead niece whose disappearance had shattered everything he had taken for granted: trust, love, friendship, family bonds.

"Where will you spend the night?" Dominick nodded toward the house. Some of the crew had entered it, checking for danger signs that could ignite another fire.

"What?" Karl tried to concentrate on what his friend was saying.

"It's obvious you can't spend it here."

"But you said it was confined to the living room."

"Look at the place, for Christ's sake. You'd choke from the fumes."

"But I can't leave the house. Those kids could come back..."

"They won't. They've done their worst and they'll be

lying low to avoid the police. Not that they'll avoid them for long. That yob they arrested will sing like a canary."

"Let's go, Dominick," one of the firemen shouted as the crew prepared to leave.

"Are you sure you're all right?" Dominick sounded apologetic, aware that he'd been unable to disguise his involuntary shudder. "Phone me if you need to talk about anything... anything at all." His eagerness to go was painfully obvious as he hurried toward the crew.

Dominick was right. Breathing the air inside the house was impossible. He ignored Maria Barnes when she offered to keep an eye on it in case there was another attack. No one offered Karl a bed for the night.

He packed an overnight case in his bedroom, his breath shallow, his throat clamped against the charred air. His home felt like a shell, devoid of life and memory, when he locked the front door and booked into the Glenmoore Arms for the night.

CHAPTER FOURTEEN

He was arrested just before midnight. The night porter watched curiously as he crossed the foyer to the squad car parked outside the hotel entrance. Always one step ahead, Amanda Bowe was waiting for him at the police station. She shoved past one of the guards as Karl was led toward the entrance.

"Are you being arrested on suspicion of the murder of Connie Lawson?" She held her recorder toward him.

"That's enough now." The guard escorting Karl glared at her. "Out of the way, Miss. You're hindering our progress."

"The public have a right to know." She stared defiantly at Karl. "Did you silence your nephew Matthew with threats to prevent him telling the guards that Connie was going to your house on the night she disappeared?"

She had abbreviated Constance's name into a headline and had eviscerated Karl with the same callous indifference. His hatred had a raw energy, a clarity that shone through the muddied incomprehension of his grief. He would have struck her down if a second guard, sensing trouble, hadn't guided him firmly into the station.

His solicitor had already arrived. Fionn Drury looked

young enough to be smoking behind the bicycle shed in secondary school. A boy who would hardly be old enough to
vote; but his voice was deep enough to reassure Karl that it
had broken some time ago.

"I keep reading about this 'close relationship,'" he said
when Karl was ushered into the small meeting room before
his interrogation. "What exactly is this journalist implying?"

"Do you have nieces or nephews?" Karl asked him.

"Four," he replied. "Two of each."

"How would you describe your relationship with them?"

"It's close." He nodded. "But I'm not the one sitting where
you are. Perception makes a lot of noise and the truth can get
lost in the hubbub. Talk to me. I need to know everything
that's happened to you over the last seven days."

Karl's feet tapped against the floor as he struggled to
piece his week together. Already, it was fragmenting into
moments of clear recollection and long periods of incomprehension. The solicitor took notes, interrupting him occasionally to ask questions.

"Did you coax your nephew to hide relevant information
from the police?" he asked.

"No, I didn't." What exactly had he said to Matthew that
night when he found him in the attic? Something about
angry talk not being true. "Matthew had some notion in his
head that it would reflect badly on his parents if he told them
Constance preferred living at my house. He's only eight.
A kid. He was frightened and bewildered. All I did was
reassure him that Constance never came to my house and
that he didn't have to say anything about her 'angry talk' to
the guards."

"So, you did tell him not to pass that information to them.
Your wife was correct in what she reported to the liaison
officer."

"My wife... what do you mean?"

"She believed the police should be notified about that conversation. Your nephew has now made a new statement, claiming that his sister left her house with the intention of going directly to yours."

"But Nicole knows that's not true."

"She was working when Constance left home and can't offer you an alibi."

"She knows—"

"A CD of Blasted Glass was found in the pocket of Constance's jacket. Your wife claims it was on a sideboard in the dining-room of your house when she left for work that night. Two days ago, you were seen by two detectives at four o'clock in the morning near the site where her body was found. And Arizona... you can see how they are building a case against you."

"None of it is true—"

"I phoned Selina Lee before I came here," said Fionn. "She's preparing a statement and emailing it to me. It should be with me shortly. I've been in touch with the police in Winding Falls. They've agreed to send on your file. It will establish the truth of that case."

"Do you believe me?" Desperation cracked Karl's voice. "I *need* to be believed."

"My personal belief never interferes with my ability to defend my clients."

"Someone *has* to believe me."

Fionn nodded and shoved his notes into a file. "Stay calm when you're being questioned. This is a fishing exercise. They've a long way to go before they can charge you with any involvement in Constance's death."

Confident words that followed Karl along the corridor as he walked toward the interrogation room.

LOCAL MAN CHARGED WITH CONNIE MURDER
AMANDA BOWE

Karl Lawson, 35, with an address at 22 Cherrywood Terrace, Glenmoore, has been charged with the murder of Connie Lawson and remanded in custody to await trial.

Flowers are being laid outside the site where Connie Lawson's body lay undiscovered for seven days. Her friends are receiving counseling and the oratory at Queen of Angels Secondary School has been opened and turned into a shrine of remembrance for a popular and much-loved pupil and friend. A date for Connie's funeral has yet to be decided.

Connie's parents remain in Cherrywood House under the care of their solicitor, Olga Nicholls. They are being comforted by their sister-in-law Nicole Lawson, 33, who will remain in the Nicholls family home until she can return to her own house, which was damaged last night in an arson attack. Her husband, Karl Lawson, was at home at the time of the fire and narrowly avoided serious injury. A local youth, who cannot be named because of his age, has been charged with arson.

PART TWO

CHAPTER FIFTEEN

To look back on Connie Lawson's disappearance as the turning point in Amanda's career seemed cruel. That, however, was the unpalatable truth. Amanda had no memory of sleeping much during those seven days. Karl Lawson was running like a fever through her blood as she trawled through his life story and assembled it for public consumption. She had never experienced anything like that rush. If it should come upon her again, she wouldn't trust it. It made her lose sight of Connie. She was still missing but Amanda was convinced, as were the rest of the media, that he was guilty, and that was the only story she wanted to tell.

She hadn't realized his connection to Connie until he opened the door of his brother's house on the first day of the search. He didn't remember her. Not even a flicker of recognition when he saw her standing outside with Shane.

"No comment," he'd said when she asked him for information about his missing niece. "No comment... *no* comment." Dismissing Amanda with the same condescending glance she remembered from her unfortunate interview in his office. As Shane photographed him in the doorway and they retreated down the garden path, she was recalling that humiliating day in precise, painful detail.

She had begun her career with *Capital Eye* by writing reports on dreary and argumentative county council meetings. That was followed by "Life on the Fringe," a series of columns drawn from interviews she conducted on the steps of the district courts. People's willingness to talk to her about their lives, their chaotic relationships, their drug use, their alcohol abuse, their shoplifting escapades, never failed to amaze her. Some of her colleagues at *Capital Eye* accused her of sensationalism and claimed she exploited her interviewees. As "Life on the Fringe" was one of the most popular pages in the tabloid, Amanda viewed such criticisms as a measure of her success.

Eventually she became bored by these confessions, which were becoming repetitive, and her sympathy toward recidivist shoplifters and welfare cheats was wearing thin. She looked longingly toward the brash, barrel-bellied criminal courts where drug lords from the inner city strutted, unafraid and unashamed; and wife murderers hid between the burly shoulders of the police when they were led away in handcuffs.

Lilian Bond, the crime reporter for *Capital Eye*— embittered as a witch and stooped from the weight of the evil she confronted daily—continued to report on the juicy stories. Amanda willed her to retire or develop some age-related illnesses like arthritis or dementia, but such hopes were punctured when she received an invitation to Lilian's fiftieth birthday celebration. *Fifty.* That meant another fifteen years of Lilian at the crime desk. An eternity. Amanda was considering this fact when she heard that Karl Lawson was looking for a features writer for *Hitz.* Her knowledge of the music industry was scant but she could write a good story. Cocaine, trashed hotel rooms and speed sex with groupies sounded far more alluring than "Life on the Fringe."

On the morning of her interview, as she was about to drive from her apartment car park, she realized she had left her "Life on the Fringe" press clippings behind. When she hurried back to her bedroom, she noticed her fiancé's iPhone on the bedside locker. Graham, who never left the device out of sight for an instant, was in the shower. His voice came to her from the en suite; he was a baritone and not a bad singer. Not a bad lover, either, as Amanda discovered when she checked his texts. They explained a lot. For six months he had been playing with her mind, ridiculing her suspicions and accusing her of being paranoid when he claimed he had to work late or stay overnight on another unexpected business trip.

Later that night, unaware that his lies had been exposed, Graham would phone to apologize for working late yet again and Amanda would stop shredding his shirts long enough to take his call. Afterward, she would continue her campaign of retribution by pouring bleach over his entire wardrobe, but that revenge had to wait until after her *Hitz* interview. She had carried a scream of rage inside her when she sat down in front of Karl Lawson, breathless and distracted when she should have been clear-headed and sharp-witted. She had stammered through her answers and lost the thread of what she wanted to say. His eyes glazed when she spoke about the influences of classical music on rock, the sexual allure of boy bands and the politics of hip hop. The quick glance he exchanged with his deputy editor, Barbara Nelson, told her they had already made up their minds. All Amanda could think about were those texts. Sex texts, clandestine meetings; such smug infidelity. Barbara, who must have gone through a goth phase in her teens and still thought the eye makeup was a good idea, didn't even bother reading Amanda's clippings. Karl Lawson, after a cursory glance at them, handed the file back to her.

Outside his office door, she had leaned against the wall to recover her breath. She overheard their laughter and the comment he tossed at Barbara. "She's a good writer so I have to assume there's a brain somewhere between her ears. But I don't have the time or the patience to search for it. Who's next on the list for interviewing?"

A week later the rejection letter from *Hitz* arrived. He was sorry her application hadn't been successful and wished her every success in what he believed would be a significant career in journalism. A sugar-coated rejection pill that did nothing to alleviate her humiliation.

Shortly after that disastrous interview, Lilian Bond died from an undiagnosed heart condition and Amanda's days on the steps of the district court came to an end.

Lilian's shoes were hard to fill. She had spent her career building up her contacts, crims and constables, as she used to say, and the fact that she had taken those names to her grave didn't help Amanda settle into her new position. She had made some underground contacts from her "Life on the Fringe" column but she needed a wider network of sources close to the criminal drug gangs. On hearing that Lilian had often frequented Rimbles, a late-night members'-only club, situated in the docklands, she had gone there one night in the hope of picking up information on the Shroff drug gang.

The club was quiet that night and she was about to leave when a man sat down at a table near her and ordered a double espresso. She noted his shabby trainers, the frayed ends of his jeans, his well-worn leather jacket. Was he a musician, relaxing after a gig at some nearby club? A doctor seeking a caffeine hit after a twenty-four-hour shift? Or had he spent the night dealing drugs in dark lanes with urine-splattered walls? He seemed oblivious to her presence as he checked his phone and sipped his coffee.

The following week, she saw him again. He sat behind her, his reflection blurring in the steamy window. He was watching her. She sensed rather than saw the tingling run of his eyes between her shoulder blades. Graham's deception had honed her antennae when it came to the opposite sex. She trusted her instincts. What could not be seen had as much, if not more, validity than the evidence before her eyes. A second man entered and stopped to speak to him. Amanda recognized Killian Shroff, one of the three brothers who ran the most notorious gang in the city. Killian, whose name had been abbreviated to Killer as soon as he was old enough to handle a Glock, disappeared into the back of the club and the man sitting behind Amanda left.

She followed him along the quays. The streets were quiet, the nightclubs and music venues emptied out. When he disappeared from view, she was conscious of her aloneness as she hurried toward the Ha'penny Bridge. A car stopped and the driver lowered the window, called out to her. She ignored him and walked faster, her heels clicking too loudly against the pavement. As she passed by a shop doorway, she became aware that someone was standing in the darkened entrance, watching her.

"Why are you following me?" the man from Rimbles asked. Before she could answer, he reached out and pulled her into the doorway.

She should have been frightened. He was standing too close, his hand still on her arm, a light grip that would tighten if she moved. She could be in danger, yet she felt curiously light-headed. The anonymity of their encounter had been set to a preordained course, she believed, and it was now reaching its conclusion.

"I'm Amanda Bowe," she replied, as if the force of her name would stall the violence he threatened. "I'm with—"

"I know who you are." He laughed, abruptly. "I didn't ask for your name. I asked why you're following me."

"I'm hoping you can help with some information."

"What kind of information?"

"The Shroffs, for one."

"Why should I know the Shroffs?"

"I saw you earlier with Killer. I can pay you for information."

"How much?"

"Depends on the importance of the information you give me."

"Okay. Let's see how this goes." The heat of his breath against her neck warned her to stand still. "Here's the first piece of information. Propositioning strange men in cars in the small hours of the morning is a high-risk, criminal activity. Aren't you afraid?"

"No."

"You should be. I could arrest you for soliciting."

"Arrest me?"

"I saw you soliciting a punter just a few minutes ago. You're in the arms of the law, Amanda Bowe."

"I wasn't—oh my *God*, you're a cop." She pressed her hand to his cheek, as if seeking reassurance that he had substance. Stubble rasped against her palm and the giddy skittering of her heart warned her of the consequences that would follow if she didn't step away from him. His fingers tangled in her hair. He drew her head back until she was staring into the murky outline of his face. They were breathing in synch, the clamping pressure low in her stomach intensifying when she realized that he, too, was swept up in the intimacy of that dark encounter.

"Are you going to arrest me or kiss me?" she whispered and he, in reply, opened her lips with his tongue, his knee parting her legs with the same driving force. She gave herself over to the thrust of their desire, unaware of the cold, marbled wall against her back, unaware of everything except the strength of his arms when he lifted her on to him. Beyond the muscular curve of his shoulder, she could see the Liffey; the slow flow of the river reflected the street lamps of the city.

Later, there would be time to talk but, in those few jagged moments, nothing mattered except the splintering satisfaction they demanded from each other.

Over the following months, they often joked about having a top-secret affair. Not that it was a joking matter. There was far too much at stake for them to be seen together in public. Detective Garda Jon Hunter had no intention of jeopardizing his career or his marriage—and Amanda had no intention of jeopardizing an excellent source. His marriage had been a surprise, especially when he told her he had three children, but not enough of a shock for her to end their relationship. He gave her the names of contacts who could help her with information, and educated her on who was who in the criminal underworld.

He liked to live on the edge. Contentment bored him, routine crushed his spirit, and so he took risks with Amanda, while covering their tracks with layers of subterfuge. She, too, enjoyed the hurried, passion-fueled trysts in anonymous hotel bedrooms, the belief that the knowledge he was sharing with her would strengthen her reputation as a serious crime reporter. But it was only when Connie Lawson disappeared that Hunter—convinced of Karl Lawson's guilt and afraid the evidence against him would be too circumstantial to convict—revealed confidential details to her on the ongoing police inquiry. What had been a top-secret affair had become a dangerous liaison.

CHAPTER SIXTEEN

At first, Amanda had been convinced Connie was just a disgruntled teenager who would turn up after a few hungry days on the road and be forgiven by her grateful parents for being a brat. Glenmoore was leafy suburbia. Tennis courts and coffee shops, fashion boutiques and glass-fronted restaurants overlooking the beach. Teenagers did not run away from home or end up dead in ditches for non-payment of small debts to drug gangs. Early on in the search, Hunter had told her about the row over the Blasted Glass gig. The girls who were supposed to attend it with Connie had been willing to talk to Amanda. They showed her the texts they had exchanged the previous night. All fume and bluster about their parents and their inability to remember what it was like to be young. To have fun at concerts and scream until the mass of energy gathered there, full-throated and on the verge of hysteria, became a heave of collective ecstasy. But, after that initial flurry of texts, and a phone call to one of her friends, they had heard nothing further from her. She had left her phone at home, which puzzled them. It puzzled Amanda, also. A teenager going out at night without her phone was akin to a snail leaving the shelter of its protective shell.

Her friends were convinced Karl would know exactly where she was hiding out. They used his name casually, like he was one of them, tuned in to their wavelength and immune from any generational barrier. Thanks to Hunter, Amanda also knew about the beach party challenge. The Fearless? The girls shook their heads. They had never heard of them.

"Constance tells us *everything* and she never said anything about a gang like that." The taller of the two girls, Tracey Broome, blue eyes glistening with unshed tears, was adamant. "We wouldn't keep secrets like that from each other."

Amanda was inclined to believe them. Afterward, she wondered if that was a choice she made and then forgot as she continued to delve further into Karl Lawson's unfolding story. The Fearless sounded like something from an Enid Blyton plot. These sophisticated teenagers lived their lives through their iPhones, not through the pages of an old-fashioned children's book. The photographs on Connie's phone bore this out. Shopping centers and school discos, end-of-term plays, school tours, beach parties on the dunes with the sun, not the moon, shining overhead and, of course, the gigs with Karl Lawson. The girls said he was "cool." All those free tickets and autographs. All those selfies taken with celebrities to show off in class. Amanda had checked the selfies. Some had been taken with the members of Tin Toy Soldiers when they played the Ovid. The band were seasoned musicians, who had been around the block more than once. When Amanda saw how the singer looked at the girls, a lecherous middle-aged rocker checking out young meat, she had wondered whose buttons Karl Lawson was pressing by bringing those kids backstage.

At first, this was just a fleeting thought. Gone and forgotten

as she tried to build a profile of Connie. She had decided early
on to change her name. Constance sounded too out-dated
and prim. It didn't suit the image Amanda had of her. Connie was almost fourteen but looked older, sixteen even, in her
photographs. Something about her mouth, that lustrous bottom lip, inherited from her uncle. On her it had looked sexy-
vulnerable. On him it signified arrogance.

Tracey believed Connie had been in love with him. "No
matter what we were talking about, she'd bring his name
into the conversation," she said.

Gillian disagreed and claimed Lucas O'Malley was the
one Connie *really* fancied.

Lucas O'Malley, when Amanda interviewed him, was
equally dismissive about The Fearless. He was amused by
the idea that she should think he hung around with Connie
and her friends. Fifteen years of age, he had the petulant
allure of a boy-band singer and Amanda had no difficulty
believing Connie was infatuated by him. As the search
continued, she was convinced The Fearless was a figment
of Karl Lawson's imagination and this belief grew as hope
faded.

While Hunter had provided much of the insider information to Amanda during the search, the Arizonian angle
was due to her own tenacity. She was online, checking information on Karl Lawson, when she discovered the features
he had written for *Cannonade* about bands in Arizona: an
obscure hip hop band from Winding Falls, a bluegrass band
from Tucson. He had also taken some brilliant shots of bands
gigging in Phoenix. Ah, Amanda thought. No mention of
Arizona on his website or any of the social media sites he
used. Why not? She checked further and eventually discovered his name in the *Winding Falls Echo*. A short report in
an obscure newspaper.

Selina Lee was reticent when Amanda phoned. The soap star had refused, at first, to speak about her assault. She insisted that Karl Lawson had nothing to do with the horror of that night but Amanda was convinced she was lying. The victim protecting the perpetrator because the truth was harder to handle.

Her own mother had lived under the same code of denial. Imelda Bowe fell down steps, walked into walls, hit her head off the open doors of kitchen cupboards and smacked her daughters for leaving them ajar. Amanda had heard it all, hiding with her sister and their cat in the tiny bedroom they shared. Walls, steps, doors...they never dared contradict Imelda or challenge their father's fury. The truth hidden behind dark glasses, long sleeves and lies.

Selina Lee had invested in Karl Lawson and was too far into denial to change her story. The reporter on the *Winding Falls Echo* confirmed Amanda's suspicion. An unsolved crime. He'd always had his doubts about Karl Lawson and had a cop friend who agreed with him.

The media went into a frenzy after the Arizonian revelations. Amanda was interviewed on radio and television, especially when the story reached its ghastly conclusion. Blunt-force trauma to her head, that was how Connie Lawson died, the pathologist announced. The details had been horrendous, the evidence against Karl Lawson overwhelming, especially the discovery of the Blasted Glass CD in the pocket of Connie's black leather jacket, signed by the band members and dated just before she disappeared. Even without the statements from his wife and nephew, it was obvious that Connie had been in his house that night.

That evidence had been sufficient to remand him in custody to await trial. Each week, Amanda expected to hear that a date had been set for the trial to begin. But government cutbacks were eating into all aspects of public life. The legal system was no exception and a backlog of cases, as well as a shortage of judges, was causing delays. She would forget about him for brief periods. The convulsions of the crime world never slowed down and she had moved on to other stories.

She also had to fend off a police inquiry that was launched shortly afterward to find out how she had acquired so much confidential information. Guards had been interrogated, suspicion spreading like a virus through Glenmoore Garda Station and beyond, even reaching the press office. Hunter said the atmosphere was toxic but no evidence of collusion was found and the inquiry had been quietly shelved.

Amanda had remained calm throughout her own interrogation. She had come a long way from the nervous, young journalist who began her career with *Capital Eye* as a reporter of nail-bitingly boring county council meetings and, in the true spirit of journalism, she would go to jail rather than reveal her source.

Her days were busy, frenetic even, yet she remained conscious of Karl. In the middle of writing up a feature or doing an interview, she would recall his expression as he was escorted into the police station. How he had looked directly into her eyes, as if trying to understand the process that had led them both to that moment. She had turned away, relieved that he would soon be behind bars and unable to vent his fury on her.

At such moments of recollection, she would argue with herself. She was simply a cog in the media wheel. One lone voice among the many who charted those seven frantic days when it seemed as if the nation was holding its collective breath until the heart-breaking news finally broke and they could grieve the loss of such a young life.

+

Her relationship with Hunter was changing. Clandestine meetings had added an extra fuse to their affair but those rushed liaisons seemed tawdry compared to her sister's glowing happiness when Rebecca walked up the aisle on a gloriously sunny day in September. Amanda walked behind her, accompanied by three other bridesmaids, all stepping carefully to the rhythm Rebecca had drilled into them. Hunter should have been sharing the day with her. This thought rasped like a burr on her skin and threatened their affair with self-destruction. She began to ask questions about his wife. Hunter dismissed her as "dumpy." Dumpy and dutiful, devoted to her husband and their three children. In the beginning, that was all Amanda needed to know. She imagined her in sturdy shoes behind the counter of a charity shop, or delivering meals on wheels to the aged. When she questioned Hunter more closely, though, he admitted that his wife worked part-time organizing kids' parties.

"Clowns and magicians?" Amanda asked. "Bouncy castles?"

He nodded. "Something like that. Now, can we *please* change the subject."

Her questions irritated him. They filled a need in each other but she had no illusions about him and suspected he would find someone else to add that extra frisson to his life if he ended their affair.

He lived on the outskirts of Glenmoore in a detached house with two cars in the driveway and a garden riotous with color. Was Mrs. Dumpy green-fingered as well as an organizer of children's parties, Amanda wondered on the morning she parked nearby and waited under the mature trees that shaded the road. She watched as the front door of his house was opened by a tall, blond woman in fluttery clothes, who settled two boys and a small, wispy-haired replica of herself into a silver Porsche that shone with newness and style.

This willowy woman with her silky layers could not possibly be Mrs. Dumpy. Where were the stout shoes and swollen ankles, the oversized bust and mousy hair? Just as Amanda had convinced herself that she was checking out the wrong house, Hunter appeared in the doorway, wearing a T-shirt and boxers. He waved a lunchbox and shouted something. Amanda was unable to hear him but his wife's laughter was audible as she walked back up the driveway and grabbed the lunchbox. He swung her into his arms in a gesture that was all too reminiscent of Amanda's first encounter with him. In the kiss they exchanged, she knew they had made love that morning; even from a distance, she recognized the signs of that shared intimacy. She had driven behind the Porsche. A school drop for the children, then his wife drove toward the city. Amanda lost her at traffic lights but, by then, she had the car's registration.

As soon as she reached her desk, she checked it out. Sylvia Thornton. Hunter's wife had obviously kept her maiden name. From there, it was only a short hop to her website. Mrs. Dumpy did more than organize bouncy castles. She worked as an events organizer and publicist for Lar Richardson.

Amanda had attended the launch of his television station, LR1. A magnificent occasion, hosted by Lar and his wife Rosalind. Top bands, dancers and guest singers had performed in a glittering marquee, all organized by Sylvia Thornton.

The next time she met Hunter in another anonymous hotel room with abstract prints on the walls and too much dry air, she asked him to tell her the *real* truth about his wife.

"That sounds more like an interrogation than a question," he said. "What's going on?"

"Curiosity," she replied. "What does Mrs. Dumpy do when she's not blowing up balloons?"

"Don't call her that," he snapped.

"Why not?" She hated the possessive timbre in her voice, a shrillness she was unable to control. "You do. And if you think she's dumpy, you're either visually impaired or lying. Which is it?"

"Have you been spying on me?"

"No," she replied. "I did it quite openly. You have a lovely house. And such adorable children... not to mention your garden. Love the gladioli."

"How *dare* you intrude on my private life." His tone chilled her. "We agreed in the beginning that my personal space was off-limits."

"Why lie to me about her?"

"You're so competitive." He made it sound like an accusation. "I knew you'd be jealous of her. I was right. Now, you want to change the whole dynamic of our relationship."

"How astute of you," she said. "I didn't realize you were a behavioral as well as a liar."

"I'm not going to argue with you about Sylvia—"

"Who's arguing?" She hated the name. Its sleekness was such a perfect fit for the woman she had seen in his arms. "I'm trying to understand why you stay with someone who makes you so unhappy."

She listened to his blustering excuses and was sickened by them. Sylvia would get custody of their children and the house. Did Amanda want to see him reduced to living in a bedsit with damp walls? His mouth hardened when she suggested he move into her apartment. She offered to take his kids at weekends. If he was too scared to confront his *dumpy* wife, she would talk to Sylvia, explain that they were in love and intended building a new life together.

"Don't threaten me," he shouted, then, realizing they were in a cheap hotel room with thin walls, he lowered his voice. "You knew from the beginning that I'd no intention of leaving my family. What we have in this hotel room is the sum of our relationship. Find another source if this one no longer works for you."

There it was, their relationship grinding toward a halt on petty insults; but it had staggered on until Hunter rang her secret phone one night and asked to meet her. The gravity of his tone convinced her that his wife had finally discovered his infidelity. But nothing prepared her for the shock of hearing Karl Lawson's name on his lips and the revelation that would follow.

CHAPTER SEVENTEEN

Seven days to destroy his world. That was the length of time it took to end his marriage, deprive him of his daughter, his career, his home, his security. He saved his sanity, knowing that to lose it would mean he would never be able to extract revenge; for Karl Lawson, standing in the ruins of his life, staying sane was important.

At first, his only feeling was one of disbelief as the cell door closed behind him. Disbelief was followed by rage. Sometimes he wondered if this rage, white hot and pulsing, would attack his spleen and give him cancer, cells corrosively multiplying each time he thought about Amanda Bowe and all she had unleashed. His rage died in a sudden, exhausted splutter and, as the walls of the prison moved closer around him, he stopped demanding justice, lobbying politicians, the chaplain, the prison governor, anyone who was prepared to listen. The media, who had hung on his every word, captured his every expression, now ignored his frantic letters, his insistence that he was the victim of a miscarriage of justice. His letters to Jenna and Justin also went unanswered.

Fionn Drury visited him regularly. His solicitor was a

fighter, Karl would grant him that. But his efforts to have bail set for Karl had been refused each time. The prosecution considered him a flight risk, who needed to be detained at the State's pleasure until the date of his trial. Karl understood the judge's decision. Of course he was a flight risk. To see Sasha once again, to reason with Nicole; the temptation to follow them to New York would be too great.

Nicole had visited him before she left for New York. He had noticed a new firmness about her mouth as she sat before him, her arms rigid by her sides, avoiding contact with her surroundings as much as possible. Her tears had dried. She needed to go home to support her mother. Teresa Moynihan was becoming confused. A diagnosis of rapid onset Alzheimer's had been made and Nicole was determined that her mother should stay in her own home for as long as possible. Her father was floundering under the strain of looking after his business and his wife.

"Please bring Sasha to see me before you go," Karl had begged her.

"No!" Nicole was vehement. "You can't possibly want her to remember you in a place like this."

"I'm innocent, Nicole." It had been a lone cry in this wilderness of disbelief. "I want her to understand that terrible mistakes can happen. I won't be found guilty. I *can't*. The evidence is circumstantial. It will never stand up in court."

"So you keep saying." She had looked across the prison table and beyond him. "I want to believe you. But the air I breathe in Glenmoore is thick with suspicion. It will choke me if I don't leave."

He had drawn back from her grief and the overpowering shame he saw in her eyes.

"I can't even hide in my own house," she continued. "Those kids who set fire to it piss in the living room. They've broken the windows and painted slogans on the walls. I'm trying to protect Sasha. She doesn't understand why we're living in rented rooms. I can't send her back to school. Can you imagine the names she'd be called? My family need me and I need them."

"I'm your family, Nicole." Even as he spoke, Karl knew this was no longer true. His marriage was over. It had ended when his wife decided that the confused recollections of a frightened, heartbroken boy carried more weight than the word of her husband. "You're running away and taking my daughter with you. It must be wonderful to have an escape route."

"Don't you dare simplify what I'm going through." He had never seen her so enraged, her cheeks flaring as she leaned back as far as possible from him. She was unable to face Jenna and Justin. Guilt by association. Sasha crying at night because her father wasn't there to read her bedtime stories. Crying because she was unable to understand why she could not sleep in her own bedroom, safe under her Dora duvet.

They talked in circles, the circle reducing a little more each time until finally only a dot remained in the middle; an atom filled with the explosive remnants of their failed marriage.

He had spoken to Sasha on the phone before they left for New York. She cried and demanded to know why he wasn't coming with her. Nicole had taken the phone from her and ended the conversation.

Being on remand, he was allowed five phone calls a week. Apart from contacting his solicitor, he used his phone card to ring Sasha. She always broke down in tears during their conversations. Nicole told him to limit his calls. They were preventing Sasha from settling down in her new home.

She confined Karl's calls to one a week and began to make excuses when he rang. Sasha was sleeping. She was at the movies with her grandfather or on a play date with new friends she had made in school.

In his cell, he stared at mindless afternoon chat shows on television. At cookery programs where celebrity chefs demonstrated meals that everyone would admire but never cook. The Teletubbies with their tinny voices unnerved him, yet he stared dully at them as they wriggled their plump bottoms, skipped down hills and watered talking flowers. He knew their names, Tinky Winky, Dipsy, Laa-Laa and Po. It scared him, being able to remember such information. He wondered if he was going insane. He had always imagined madness as a flailing hysteria, subdued only by restraint or drugs. Not this dulled indifference that slowed his footsteps and made even the most basic attempts at conversation impossible.

Tomorrow would be different. Karl made this promise to himself each night before he fell asleep. Tomorrow he would awake energized and deal with his situation; but within a few minutes of opening his eyes he would sink back again into the same mindless puddle.

"You'll come out of it," Fionn reassured him. "Shock can manifest itself in many ways and this is how it's affecting you. Do you want to seek help from the psychiatric services?"

"Why? No one believes I'm innocent."

"I do."

"What makes you different to everyone else?"

"Male intuition and a first-class law degree."

"How can you be so intelligent yet look like you're still too young to vote?" Karl demanded.

"Youth is my secret weapon." The solicitor smiled. "It

disarms the opposition. It's too late for recovery by the time they discover I'm a wolf."

Karl began to keep a journal. When his sanity deserted him, his writings would stand as testament to the fact that he was once stable and lucid. He recorded the daily minutia of prison routine. Time had been shredded of meaning but in his journal, each entry dated, he recorded the clang and clatter of his new life. The shouting voices, the commands of prison officers, the cries and expletives of new arrivals, the intimate sounds of desperation seeking relief. He ended each entry with a doodle, the same cluster of smiley faces he used to draw for Sasha's amusement.

He never wrote about Amanda Bowe. Never stained the pages with her name; yet she was always at the forefront of his thoughts.

"She doesn't forgive easily," Barbara Nelson had said in the throes of the search for Constance and he was still bewildered at how she had trapped him in a Kafkaesque nightmare. A nightmare that had taken everything that was precious from him. No going back, no going forward, eight months slowly, torturously sliding by as he waited for justice to be denied or delivered.

CHAPTER EIGHTEEN

Most days were boringly predictable but this could change with such sudden ferocity that Karl took nothing for granted. He had expected to be attacked by the other prisoners. A child murderer was the most despised member of the prison population; but when the first attack came he was not the intended victim.

It took place while he was walking in the prison yard. The prison officers were unaware of the sudden violent surge, and the prisoners standing nearby swerved away, determined not to add time to their sentences by becoming involved in a brawl. They created an immediate firebreak between themselves and the assailants, who numbered three against one. Karl was caught in that empty space, unable to move. He could go in either direction. Go with the prisoners, who were distancing themselves from the fight, or make the odds two against three. If he went with the former he would be safe but still trapped in that numbed sluggishness. Pain, or even death, could come with the latter. It seemed, in that instant of indecision, that this was the most crucial decision he would ever make.

The prisoner being attacked was Gabby Morgan, an

overweight, pugnacious forger whose pasty complexion was seared with acne scars. Outside those steel bars Gabby was the last person he would have wanted to know, yet, as he charged into the brawl, Karl was filled with a murderous determination to protect him.

The man who was about to kick Gabby's head was Killer Shroff. Killer worked out in the prison gym every day and was one of the most feared prisoners on the block. Karl lunged at him, taking him by surprise so quickly that Killer was shoved off balance. This gave Gabby, who was curled in a fetal position on the ground, time to wriggle out the way before Killer could lift his foot again. His arms protected him against the next kick and Killer's two accomplices turned on Karl. Red stars splattered before his eyes. Pain splintered across his face. He was still struggling when prison officers dragged him away. He ended up in solitary for a week. He had no memory of the fight. His only recollection of those few explosive minutes was the fury that had consumed him as his fists smashed against gristle and bone.

Gabby had been beaten up because his impeccable reputation for forged import documentation had failed to fool a customs official. Something about smuggling drugs inside surfboards; Gabby was vague on detail. The surfboards, which should have been cleared through customs and delivered to a sports shop that served as a legitimate cover for the Shroffs, were checked and their contents discovered. Unfortunately for Gabby, he ended up in the same prison as Killer, who was charged with being the recipient of the surfboards.

"Killer would a kilt me if ya hadn't come along." Gabby was grateful for the intervention when he recovered from his injuries. He made peace with the Shroffs—again he was hazy on facts, but information to the brothers on the location of stashed counterfeit fifty-euro notes was mentioned. This gave Gabby immunity from further attacks and was, at his insistence, extended to protect Karl.

He knew better than to protest his innocence to Gabby. If his own family refused to believe him, what chance had he of convincing him? Here, in this rarefied atmosphere, everyone was a potential innocent.

"This place is the fuckin' miscarriage of justice academy." Gabby agreed with him. "I'm expert on what's fake and what's real, and yer the only fucker what's genuine in here. But not everyone thinks like I do so watch yer back. Don't worry about Killer but there's other fuckers who'd take ya down quick enough, so they would."

Alertness replaced apathy, an animal instinct that made Karl constantly aware of danger. He sensed footsteps before they were audible, sensed an impending threat before it struck, sensed the shapes behind the shadows. Flight or fight, his adrenaline in constant flow.

His doodles in his journal, the smiley faces that had once amused Sasha, grew muscle, bone and fiber. They evolved into tiny boar-like characters with spiked hair and large, round eyes. He gave them magical wings and hooves that knocked sparks from the ground when they ran on two sturdy legs. The knot in his chest only eased when he entered their imaginary world where evil was punished and good triumphed. He was tempted to show his illustrations to Gabby, one artist to another, but he resisted the temptation. Gabby was street-tough. He would sneer and claim that his friend was watching too many episodes of the Teletubbies.

Fionn arrived one afternoon on an unscheduled visit. Raindrops glistened on his hair and on the shoulders of his coat. He brought with him the rhythm of normality, of temperatures rising and falling, the pace of freedom. Although he seemed outwardly calm, Karl knew that something was about to change when Fionn passed a copy of *Capital Eye* across the table to him.

The walls of the visiting room blurred as he began to read. The prison noises, a cacophony that had seemed unendurable when he first arrived, fell away and the only sound to fill the visiting room was the almost unendurable pounding of his heart.

CHAPTER NINETEEN

"There's been an unexpected development in the Karl Lawson case." Hunter was whey-faced when Amanda got into the passenger seat of his car. No anonymous hotel room had been booked on this occasion. Instead, they met in a cul-de-sac at the rear of an industrial estate close to Dublin Airport. The staff had left for the night and the shuttered buildings added to the anonymity of their surroundings. In the distance, lights from the runways twinkled, a galaxy of stars spiraling downwards, and the whine of descending aircraft reached them intermittently.

He opened his laptop and cursed under his breath when he entered an incorrect password. The screen lit up on his second attempt. Images he had managed to download onto a USB flash drive opened before them. Selfies and short videos of teenagers egging the wall of a house. A boy holding a long, thick worm over another boy's open mouth. A girl dropping water balloons from a flyover bridge on to the cars below.

"I've copied this from a phone that was found at the scene of a suicide," Hunter said, as more images appeared on the screen.

Amanda recognized Connie Lawson. The young teenager was kneeling on a bed with Tracey and Gillian, the three of them wearing flimsy briefs, their small breasts bared. They waved their bras like pennants at the photographer, their expressions a mix of defiance and self-consciousness. Young teenagers acting out.

Her hands began to sweat. The air in the car was swampy with fear as she stared at a video Connie had shot at a beach party. Ben's Shack, Amanda whispered, and Hunter nodded. Another video revealed a wall sprayed with graffiti, blurry shots of rough stone and a low, arched roof, lit by torchlight.

"Isaac Cronin's basement." Hunter's voice sounded as heavy as lead.

The video Connie had taken was grainy but it was possible to make out the pale curve of her face, her too-wide smile, her off-focus glance as she boasted that she had taken on the graffiti challenge. A Blasted Glass logo zoomed into view, then disappeared, as if Connie, breathless with nerves or excitement, had jerked the phone. Amanda could see it then, the sheen of paint setting it apart from the older graffiti. The wall behind Connie looked grotesque, a psychedelic backdrop that Karl Lawson had examined one night, watched by the man sitting beside her.

Hunter leaned closer, his knee touching hers. Amanda doubted if he was aware of the contact. His car suddenly seemed too small for both of them. She had no idea what was coming next. She just knew it would be bad. He clicked into another short video Connie had filmed outside the padlocked gate. She must have climbed over the wall and was standing on Orchard Road.

"It took a while, Fearless, but it's done," she'd shouted. The video blurred, as if she had been distracted by something. A kid out of her depth; her hands must have been shaking as she panned the road, then focused back on the gate.

"No one can ever call me chicken again." Amanda heard the relief in the young voice; tiredness too.

"Look carefully at this." Hunter replayed the video, then froze it on the road. A smudge of light on the edge of the screen. Amanda peered closer.

"What is it?" she asked.

"A jeep," he replied.

"How can you tell?"

"The video has been analyzed by forensics."

"And?"

"Constance Lawson died an instant after she took that video."

"Oh, my God! I don't believe you."

"You mean you don't *want* to believe me."

Now that she knew it was a jeep, Amanda could make out the square, solid shape and the aggressive bull-bars that always reminded her of gumshields. But maybe that was only her imagination. An illusion made fact. An opinion solidifying into a perceived truth. She was scrabbling to understand, trying to grasp the enormity of what Hunter was telling her.

"But Karl Lawson—" she began.

"Is innocent," he interrupted her. "The driver of the jeep committed suicide. He left a note confessing everything and put the girl's phone on top of it."

Amanda longed to put her hands over her ears and drown out his voice. His dulled recital of the details that had been established. The driver was an off-duty fireman, driving home on the night Connie stepped out from the dark in front of his jeep. He had swerved to avoid her and would have done so if only she had moved a fraction faster. The

wing mirror barely clipped her but it caused her to fall
backward and hit her head against the edge of a sharp brick
that once formed part of the boundary wall. Blunt-force
trauma—death must have been instantaneous. The autopsy
had proved she died from a head injury but the pathologist
had assumed the cracked ribs had been administered during
what was believed to have been a vicious assault.

The driver had tried to resuscitate her. When he realized
she was beyond help, he had put her in the boot of his jeep.
He had driven to the small cottage where he lived alone and
collected a crowbar and shovel. He knew the whereabouts of
the disused water tank that was still buried on Isaac Cronin's
land.

Split-second decisions were often made for the most
mundane reasons and no one would have blamed Dominick
Kelly if he had been sober that night. Connie was running
wild and accidents happen. But he had too much to lose, his
marriage, his family, his job. The breakup with his wife had
tilted him over the edge and, after drowning his sorrows in
his local pub that night, he had taken a chance on driving
home, believing the road would be clear. Orchard Road was
a lonely place, almost forgotten since the closure of Cronin's
orchard. Connie Lawson was a blur on his horizon when she
stepped out in front of him and ended up dead.

Amanda wanted to cry but tears would only trivialize her
shock.

"What's happening to Karl Lawson?" she asked when
she felt strong enough to cope with Hunter's answer.

"He'll be released as soon as Kelly's confession has been
fully investigated," Hunter replied. "I'm giving you first bite
at the story." He spoke dispassionately. "You can look upon
it as my farewell gift. I don't want you near my house, my
wife or my children ever again. Do you understand?"

He didn't need to be so emphatic. Amanda had no desire to be in his car, sharing her guilt with a man who had led her astray with misinformation. They parted shortly afterward, both of them anxious to create as much space as possible between them.

✦

She spoke to Connie's friends. This time, she didn't allow them to sob in each other's arms. Nor did she allow them to lie glibly about The Fearless, and its leader, Lucas O'Malley. After she had extracted the truth from them, she returned to her desk at *Capital Eye*. She didn't need notes. She knew exactly what she had to write.

✦

INNOCENT MAN STILL ON REMAND
AMANDA BOWE

Eight months ago, Karl Lawson, 36, cut a lonely fig-ure when he was remanded in custody to await trial for the alleged murder of his niece, Constance Law-son, 13. Important new proof has now come to light that not only casts doubt on the evidence submitted by gardaí to the office of the DPP but will exonerate an innocent man.

Based on reliable information, Capital Eye *can reveal that the missing teenager was the victim of a hit and run accident that occurred on Orchard Road. The Garda Press Office refuse to verify or deny the allegation that the panicked driver buried her remains in a water tank rather than face the consequences of his actions. If this proves to be the case, Karl Lawson must be freed without further delay.*

Capital Eye *believes that a local Glenmoore resident had accepted responsibility for the tragic death of the young teen. Now deceased, he is believed to have taken his own life and admitted his guilt in a note found beside his body. A phone, also found at the scene, proves that information received by gardaí from Karl Lawson during the search was accurate. Constance has called out from beyond her grave and laid her handprint on the guilty.*

Her disappearance resulted in a nationwide search. As efforts to find her intensified, gardaí, in a routine house search, discovered a bra belonging to her in the bedroom Lawson shared with his wife. A media presence gathered outside his house and gained momentum as the popular editor of the best-selling music magazine, Hitz, became the chief suspect in his niece's disappearance.

Rumors were rife as the search became more widespread and frantic. Lawson was tireless in his efforts to find his niece until the publicity surrounding him made it impossible for him to leave his home. His wife, Nicole, supported Constance's distraught parents by bringing their children, Matthew, 8, and Lara , 4, to the peaceful horse shelter, Grass Haven, where they were protected from the attentions of the media.

In the grim environment that gripped the pretty village of Glenmoore, suspicion grew that there would be a tragic outcome to the search for the missing schoolgirl. The pressure on Karl Lawson increased when it became public knowledge that he had been the victim of a grave miscarriage of justice in Arizona seven years previously. Once this story was leaked to the Irish media and was widely reported in print and on air, Lawson became the lead suspect in this tragedy.

When Constance's body was discovered in a disused water tank, he was arrested. A file was prepared for the DPP and, as a result of this evidence, which has since proved to be purely circumstantial, Lawson has been remanded in custody awaiting trial ever since.

A tearful Tracey Broome, one of Constance's closest friends, has made the sensational admission that she, Constance and some other friends were members of a gang called The Fearless. Led by a convicted arsonist, who cannot be named because of his age, they used the phone to record themselves undertaking reckless challenges. Photographic evidence shows a group of girls partying in Lawson's house when he and his family were on holidays. This also reveals how Constance's bra was found in their bedroom.

Tragically, the last video taken shows Constance spray-painting the basement wall in the house that belonged to the late Isaac Cronin. The teenagers believed the house was haunted and had drawn lots to see who would visit it at midnight. Constance's name had been picked. When she entered the derelict house on Orchard Road, she was in possession of the gang's secret phone, as was the custom when a member was chosen to undertake the next challenge. Initially, according to Tracey, she had vehemently refused to undertake the challenge because of a promise she had made to Karl Lawson to quit the gang. Far from being a predatory uncle, as he was portrayed by the media, he was protective of his niece.

After rowing with her parents on that fatal night, Constance decided to disregard his advice. Lawson's insistence that he had gone to bed early and was unaware she had entered his house is true. Perhaps, if he had been awake, she would have talked to him, as she always did when she was troubled, and the fatal tragedy could have been averted.

Constance had not informed her friends of her intention, hoping, perhaps, to surprise them with her video evidence. This reckless decision led to her death and the wrongful imprisonment of Karl Lawson.

Was there a rush to judgment, fueled by the media interest he attracted? Why did gardaí not heed the information he gave them about The Fearless? Why did they ignore him when he told them about the graffiti he believed his niece had sprayed in the basement of the house?

Capital Eye has established a petition demanding his immediate release, which readers can sign. It's time the public had full disclosure from the office of the DPP as to why Karl Lawson was unjustly remanded in Danevale Prison to await trial for a crime he did not commit.

CHAPTER TWENTY

As soon as he finished reading the words Amanda Bowe had assembled with such care, Karl returned to the beginning and reread the feature. Even then, he was unable to take it in. What had caused this turnabout? This completely different approach? Even the photography told a different story. He stared at a photograph that had been taken at a black-tie award ceremony two years previously in Berlin, and was captioned *Karl Lawson receiving the prestigious European Music Magazine Awards for his editorial features in* Hitz. He looked confident and self-assured as he accepted the award. Guiltless. A second shot, arranged in juxtaposition beside it, showed him leaving court in handcuffs after his application for bail had been refused. This was captioned *Miscarriage of justice victim, Karl Lawson, leaving the district court after being remanded into custody to await trail.* Unlike the photographs that had appeared in *Capital Eye* throughout the search for Constance, this one showed a man broken by circumstantial evidence.

"A car accident killed Constance." He crossed his arms and hugged them against his chest. "Can this be true?"

Fionn nodded. "I'm here on the assumption that it is. But

none of the other papers or media outlets have reported it. There's obviously been a serious leak within the police or the DPP office. Probably the same source she used before. It's all allegations so far but she couldn't have written with such authority unless she had insider information."

Karl still struggled to understand. The press must be mustering outside Glenmoore Garda Station, demanding confirmation, more information, furious that Amanda Bowe had stolen a march on them once again. What of Justin and Jenna? How were they feeling as they read *Capital Eye*? Had they been warned in advance that such information would be published? He desperately hoped so. Once again, Amanda Bowe was controlling his story. In an effort to deflect attention from her earlier reports, she was shifting blame on to an amorphous group called The Media, who had followed so blindly at her heels. He noted her use of Constance's full name. More gravitas, less tabloid.

"Are you okay?" His solicitor observed him closely. "What you've just read must be difficult to absorb."

"I'm stunned," Karl replied, truthfully. "I still can't figure out where all this is coming from."

"Neither can I," Fionn admitted. "I'm going directly from here to the DPP office to find out exactly what's going on." He tapped the newspaper. "I'll be in touch with you as soon as I've any further information." He slid his arms into his coat and swung his briefcase in a sideways arc. He still looked like a schoolboy aping the adults but Karl trusted the determined slant of his chin.

A local man on Orchard Road after midnight. His mind skittered toward a name and away again. No, that was not possible. And yet... and yet...

After Fionn left, he used his phone card to ring Dominick. An automated voice informed him that his friend was

not available to take his call. That didn't mean anything.
Dominick was probably battling a fire somewhere, his phone
switched off.

   On returning to his cell, he studied Amanda Bowe's feature one last time. Then, carefully, as if he was a child again
and not allowed to play with scissors, he tore the paper along
the folded edges and slid the clipping between the pages of
his journal.

CHAPTER TWENTY-ONE

No guard of honor from the fire brigade saluted Dominick Kelly's coffin as it was wheeled into the church. No red fire truck bore him on his final journey to the crematorium. His widow and two young children did not attend the short ceremony but blood decreed that his mother and siblings participate. The press, confined to the back of the church, had been asked by the parish priest to be discreet and respect the family's grief. Amanda sat beside Eric Walker. They were rivals, closely protecting their own sources, striving to achieve the bigger headline, the most sensational angle. He whispered his congratulations to her on the *Free Karl Lawson* campaign as they watched the small family group follow the coffin up the aisle.

Amanda had expected a reaction to her campaign but nothing like the one she'd received. Signatures, far too many to calculate, had crashed the *Capital Eye* website, snarled up the phone lines and resulted in record sales of the newspaper. Online and in print, Karl Lawson was once again the headline story. The campaign was still ongoing and would continue until he was freed.

Another internal police investigation had been launched

to discover how such sensitive information had been leaked. She had been questioned and threatened with legal proceedings unless she divulged the name of her source. The only proven case against her was that she was a diligent and investigative crime reporter. She had left no fingerprints on her relationship with Hunter. They had never exchanged tokens of affection, love-struck poems or a lingering glance that could be traced back to them.

He had not been in touch with her since that night in the industrial estate. The scoop had, indeed, been his farewell gift to her—and the freedom campaign was her farewell gift to Karl Lawson. She had broken him, then built him up again so seamlessly it was difficult now to understand how he had ever become a suspect in the first place.

She was waiting with Eric outside the church when Dominick Kelly's coffin was wheeled past on a gurney by the undertakers and dispatched without ceremony to the crematorium. Elizabeth Kelly had been the last person to speak with her son before he took his own life. Her sons, knowing the media were curious as to the manner of Dominick's death, formed a human shield around their mother as they entered the small crematorium chapel. Elizabeth looked as frail as a wraith. Amanda reckoned she could soon follow her son.

Two days later, she visited Elizabeth at her home on High Strand Crescent. Situated on a height that gave the bungalows a view of the sea, High Strand Crescent was part of old Glenmoore. The fields at the back stretched as far as Glenmoore Woods and, to the front, the sea rolled toward the horizon.

This was Amanda's second time to visit High Strand Crescent. She had been investigating Karl Lawson's childhood on the last occasion and then, as now, she had wondered what it must have been like to grow up in a green, open space with fields on one side, the pull of tides before him and room to breathe in between. Her childhood home on Raleigh Way had been a cottage with a low roof and windows that never let in enough light. Neighbors were always within eyesight, and earshot too, not that they ever admitted to hearing what went on behind the slatted blinds.

Elizabeth's blinds were still drawn over the windows and Amanda had to ring the doorbell twice before the elderly woman answered. After an initial hesitation, she allowed Amanda into the bungalow, accepting without question that she was a friend of Dominick's and had been abroad at the time of his funeral. Amanda offered her condolences and Elizabeth squeezed her hands in gratitude. She had the polite, slightly bemused expression older people got before they sank into dementia.

She served tea in china cups. Everything about her was delicate, from her trembling hands to her stooped, bony shoulders. She spoke in a low, hurried voice about her son. Such a relief to have someone who wanted to hear what she had to say instead of turning away at the mention of his name. A pariah name that had shamed his family so deeply Elizabeth was afraid to utter it aloud. She showed Amanda the notebook he had left with her before his death. Rambling writings in which he claimed he could hear the voice of God channeling his words through his faithful servant, Dominick. He had written quotes from the Bible and highlighted them in yellow.

"Whoever sheds the blood of man, by man shall his blood be shed, for God made man in his own image."
Genesis 9:6-7

Other quotes, also highlighted, expressed the same grim warnings. Elizabeth described him as being "ecstatic" when he spoke about the day of retribution. When all his sins would be washed away and cleansed in the blood of the Lord. Amanda read the last quote he had written in his notebook.

> *"But as for the cowardly, the faithless, the detestable, as for murderers, the sexually immoral, sorcerers, idolaters, and all liars, their portion will be in the lake that burns with fire and sulfur, which is the second death."*
> Revelation 21:8

A week later, he drank a bottle of whiskey and swallowed enough sleeping pills to ensure he never woke up again. The wrinkles on Elizabeth's tissue-fine skin deepened.

"Poor Karl, what he's suffered," she said. "Those media people. They should be ashamed of themselves the way they hounded him, and he's still not free. What will I say when he comes to see me... what can I say..." She wrung her hands and Amanda stood, anxious to leave before the old woman began to cry.

"He'll be free soon." She spoke with assurance as she embraced Elizabeth Kelly and bade her goodbye. She had another deadline to meet.

CHAPTER TWENTY-TWO

Winter outside the prison walls. The shimmer of ice on bare, knuckled branches, his breath hazing the morning air. The speed of the traffic shocked Karl, everything moving in fast-forward motion, the pavements more congested, the sounds duller than the high-pitched clatter of prison life. Three taxis passed before he felt confident enough to hail one. Fionn had offered to pick him up but he wanted to spend those first few hours of freedom on his own. A miscarriage of justice. False imprisonment but no formal apology. Just an assurance that he was free to go.

Cherrywood Terrace was quiet, the morning rush over, children in school, people at work. A *For Sale* sign stood in Justin's garden. The house had been made presentable to potential buyers, the windowsills and gateposts freshly painted, the garden hedge neatly trimmed. The front door had been painted a bright shade of yellow. The color was out of keeping with the more subtle grape and umber shades of the neighboring doors, but Karl knew that this was a house where sadness needed to be vanquished.

The curtains were closed and Jenna's white car was so caked with dust that some joker had traced *"Gimme a wash!"* on the side.

Karl crossed the road to his own house. His front garden was overgrown, the purple rhododendrons seared of color. Dead leaves had blown into a rank heap against the garden wall. The lawn needed mowing and plaster dust had settled like hoar frost on the grass. He smelled paint fumes when he opened the front door. The insurance claim for the fire damage had been paid into his bank account and he had organized the repairs from prison. The painter had used the same shade of magnolia on all the walls; a bland color that he and Nicole had always avoided. Sasha's bedroom was empty, the wardrobe door open, drawers also, everything thrown out. No more patterned wallpaper for Dora and her intrepid friends to explore. Karl believed he could still smell smoke, imagined it spiraling thinly in nooks and crannies.

A ring on the doorbell startled him. He stood for an instant, uncertain what to do. Every decision, even opening his own front door, had become a considered response. The stained-glass panels in the hall door that Nicole had chosen with such care had been replaced by glazed glass. He could see the shape of a woman standing outside. Jenna. He stopped and half-turned, as if to retreat to his cell. He grabbed the banister rail to steady himself and continued on down to the hall.

"Maria Barnes told me you were back," Jenna said when he opened the door. "She thought I'd like to know."

"Come in." He turned and walked into the kitchen, uncaring whether or not she followed.

She unbuttoned her parka jacket. Its padded bulkiness had disguised her weight loss but it was immediately apparent when she unwound a long scarf from around her neck. The tip of her nose was red from the cold and pointier than he remembered. He had never noticed her nose until now. It had been an unremarkable feature in her face but thinness had pinched its regular shape.

"How are you, Jenna?" He gestured at her to sit at the table and pulled out another chair for himself.

"In hell," she replied. "Some days are worse than others. Today was a bad one until I heard you were here." She coughed, as if smoke clogged her lungs. "Yet, I don't know how to talk to you, Karl. You must hate us so much."

"I don't feel anything," he admitted. "Nothing at all. I want to grieve for Constance. I thought I could but I can't even do that."

"It will come," she said. "Until then, I'll do your grieving for you." She shivered, flexed her hands, as if encouraging the blood to flow to her fingertips. "It's freezing in here. Why don't you turn on the heat?"

"No oil," he said. "Someone siphoned it off. Don't worry. I'll cope until a new delivery arrives."

"How can you expect me not to worry?" Unable to sit still, she filled the kettle and switched it on. "Does Nicole know you've been released?"

"Not yet. Have you been in touch with her?"

"She phones occasionally. But she finds it difficult to talk to us."

"Guilt by association. That's how she sees it."

When the kettle clicked off, Jenna made tea and checked the fridge for milk. She closed the door abruptly when she realized it was empty.

"I'll take it black," Karl said. The tea scalded his lips. In prison, he was used to drinking it tepid. "How is Justin coping?"

"Badly," she said. "He's in Boston at the moment. His company have transferred him to their headquarters. I suppose you saw the *For Sale* sign in our garden?"

He nodded.

"So many decisions to make. It fills the space between us. We'll take Constance's ashes with us. When we're ready to move on we'll let her go."

"Will you ever be ready to do that?"

"Will you ever be ready to forgive us?"

"You're here. We're talking. That's a start."

"No, it's not." She groaned, then pressed her lips to stifle the sound. "It was so real at the time. Like we were possessed, unable to look in any other direction—and now this...I can't take it in, Karl. Dominick Kelly! How could he have put all of us through such agony?"

"I don't know, Jenna." He spread his hands, his bewilderment echoing her own. "He's paid the price yet I'll never believe it's enough. Not *near* enough."

"The coward's way. Such an easy option." She clasped her hands around the mug to stop them trembling. "I can't reach Justin. We should be able to shore each other up but I'm afraid to even mention Constance's name. He goes running when I try and talk about what we're going through. He jogs for hours but he's still the same when he returns. Will you talk to him when he comes back from Boston?"

"I don't know if that's possible, Jenna. Constance is dead because of me. If only I'd told you about the beach—"

"Stop!" She pushed the chair back so hard it almost toppled over. "You've no idea how I torment myself with what if. What if the row hadn't happened? What if I'd gone into her room to make up with her before I went to bed? What if...what if...what fucking *if*...?"

He poured the dregs of his tea into the sink. Adjusting to everything—from the small to the overwhelmingly large—was going to take time.

"We've all lost so much, Karl." Jenna stood and rewound

her scarf. Her fine-boned face was a mask, one she had assembled for a brief, polite period that was now coming to an end. "You and Justin have to make peace with each other before we leave. Promise me you'll try?"

"That's all I can do, Jenna."

She kissed his cheek, then pulled him close to her. "Constance will help us work this out," she said. "Her spirit is with me every minute of the day."

CHAPTER TWENTY-THREE

Unlike her son's funeral, Elizabeth Kelly's was well attended. A packed church, the local choir singing and three priests on the altar concelebrating requiem mass. Amanda sat at the back of the church and took discreet notes. She left before the service ended and stayed out of sight behind a yew tree while Shane photographed Elizabeth's coffin being carried from the church by her sons, grandsons and, bringing up the rear, Karl Lawson.

At first, Amanda wasn't sure it was him. His hair, naturally wavy and blond, used to be long. Not hippie length or rock-star tangles, just enough to set him apart and be noticed. But now he had shaved it off and the slightly darker stubble on his chin added to his gaunt appearance. He reminded her of someone who was terminally ill, his facial bones accentuated, his clothes a size too big for him.

Outside the church, Dominick's brothers slapped his shoulder and stood in an awkward huddle around him as Elizabeth's coffin was placed in the back of the hearse. He spoke to Dominick's wife, who wept when he hugged her. The sound reached Amanda, a faint, jagged wail that bristled the hairs on her arms. She signaled to Shane, who moved unobserved toward the group. Their embrace would perfectly illustrate the ending of this wretched story.

She was still unable to understand Elizabeth's sons' decision to move their mother into a nursing home. Old people needed their familiar surroundings about them; but they had insisted that, as she couldn't be trusted to turn unscrupulous reporters from her door, they were left with no other option. They complained to the editor of *Capital Eye*, claimed that Elizabeth had never intended her conversation with Amanda to be published. Since then, she had been under siege from the press in her own home, terrified to leave in case she was bombarded with questions.

Amanda understood the media. Their interest in Elizabeth would have faded away in a few days and the nursing home was an overreaction, a harsh and unnecessary decision. She had been saddened but not surprised to hear that Elizabeth had died three weeks later.

As the funeral cortège drove from the church grounds, Karl Lawson walked toward the car park. Amanda moved from the shelter of the yew to a nearby grotto where a statue of a pensive Bernadette stared upward at the embracing arms of the Virgin Mary. The grotto gave her a view of the car park. Only a few cars were left and the one he unlocked must have been picked up in a scrapyard.

He turned suddenly, as if he had sensed her presence, and came swiftly across the car park toward the grotto. A wall on one side blocked Amanda's exit. The only other way to leave would place her directly in his path. Her heart grazed her chest; a peculiarly unnerving pain that always reminded her of the consequences of making mistakes. She knelt on a kneeler and, like Bernadette, stared raptly upward at the statue of Mary.

His voice came from behind her. "Vengeance is mine."

He spoke softly but distinctly. "And recompense, for the time when their foot shall slip..." The quote sounded biblical and threatening. Was he reminding her of Dominick Kelly? His religious fervor as he waited for death to claim him? Amanda stood up from the kneeler and turned to face him. She had never noticed the color of his eyes until now. Cloudy green-gray, like the sea before it stormed. He paused, as if allowing the words to settle between them. She remained silent, struggling and failing to find something to say that could connect them. She was the first to look away. He walked back to the car park, folded his long figure into his car and drove away.

Her feature on Elizabeth's funeral, illustrated with an enlarged photograph of Karl Lawson and Siobhan Kelly embracing outside the church, made the late edition of *Capital Eye*.

+

Amanda needed to move on and concentrate on other stories. The Shroff brothers, for one. She was writing a series of features on their criminal activities for *Capital Eye* and had been commissioned by a publisher to follow that with a non-fiction book about the family. Her first book. Thanks to Hunter, she had enough research to fill the pages and more besides. The Shroffs repelled and fascinated her in equal measure. Four generations of pitiless moneylenders, that was how they began their dynasty. Originally, their family name was Cummins but Flab Cummins, the great-grandfather— who had been as famous for his sense of humor as for his brutality—had changed it to Shroff by deed poll when he discovered the word meant an Asian banker or money charger. They had expanded into drugs and the three brothers, now dominating the gang, were ruthless and dangerous enough to terrify Amanda into a burrow, if that was her inclination. It wasn't. She was fearless, verging on reckless. Her days of hiding in her bedroom with Rebecca and a cat were over. In a fortnight's time, five double-page spreads would run in the weekday editions of *Capital Eye,* culminating in an interview with her in *Eye on the Weekend,* the Saturday magazine supplement.

She stayed late at the office, anxious to finish a feature on the Shroffs. The fact that Killer was on remand in Danevale awaiting trial added to the immediacy of the story. Had Karl Lawson come across him? Had they spoken to each other, shared life experiences? Prison must be the ultimate common denominator.

It was after nine when she drove into the Arbutus Complex car park. She picked up her post from the mailbox and entered her apartment. After she had eaten and cleared the dinner dishes into the dishwasher, she poured a cup of decaf coffee and opened her mail. Bills, mostly, apart from a small Jiffy envelope. Unable to see a letter inside, she reached into the bubbled plastic and touched what felt like something solid wrapped in cotton wool. Curious, she pulled the wad from the envelope.

The bullet was layered in such softness that the crude feel of it against Amanda's skin was electrifying. A jolt coursed through her arm, along her spine, and the bullet—hard, cold lead glossed with metal—fell on to her lap. She jumped to her feet and flapped at her skirt as if to douse a flame. The bullet dropped with a dull thud to the floor and rolled a little before lodging against the leg of the table. She rummaged in the envelope and found a card. *The next bullet will be delivered from a gun. Watch your back, Amanda.*

She left the bullet on the floor and stepped out on to the balcony. Five stories up, the noise from the city was a distant hum. The wind shrilled as it blew hard against the glass walls of the complex, flapped the dead patio plants and the stacked sun chairs waiting for summer. *Watch your back, Amanda.* Below her, pedestrians moved to a soundless rhythm. A gray, indistinguishable procession that never looked upward—except for him. He must be down there. Waiting. Watching. His gaze filled with the same hatred she had seen on the night of his arrest and today at the grotto. She shivered and folded her arms across her chest. Her living space had been contaminated so that, despite the cold, she was reluctant to return inside.

Eventually, the wind drove her indoors. In the kitchen, she pulled on a pair of rubber gloves and lifted the bullet from the floor. She studied its slender sheath, the deadly penile tip. She imagined it penetrating her heart. A bull's-eye shot. She replaced it in the envelope.

Vengeance is mine, he had said, standing rigid before her. She Googled the quote on her laptop. It came up immediately.

Vengeance is mine, and recompense, for the time when their foot shall slip; for the day of their calamity is at hand, and their doom comes swiftly.
    Deuteronomy 32:35

CHAPTER TWENTY-FOUR

Elizabeth's burial would be over by now. Kevin Kelly, her eldest son, had invited Karl to join the mourners for lunch. He nodded when Karl made excuses. They both understood the difficulty of making polite conversation when the unspoken words were the only ones that mattered. Dominick's family...he tried to imagine how they must feel, the shame, the guilt, the anger.

Elizabeth had written to Karl shortly after her son's death. Fragile handwriting, as if she could barely hold the pen. She begged him to call and see her but he, knowing he would need to be stronger for such a meeting to take place, had not responded. And now it was too late. Three weeks in a nursing home before she slipped quietly away in her sleep.

He drove from the church to the Glenmoore Shopping Center. The harsh supermarket lighting was welcome. It dispelled shadows, the unseen threat that could come upon him without warning. He stopped in front of the dairy section. So many decisions to make: low-fat, skimmed or fortified super milk, pure butter or low-fat spread, free range, farm fresh or organic eggs? Not so long ago he would have made such choices without thinking. Now, he was alarmed by his indecisiveness as he pushed his shopping trolley to the checkout.

Maria Barnes was sweeping dead leaves from her garden path when he returned to Cherrywood Terrace. He willed her to keep sweeping, her eyes on the ground, but she straightened and came across the road to him.

"I'm glad you're home, Karl," she said.

He nodded without replying and opened the gate.

"Come over to the house and have a cup of tea. You look like you could do with one."

"No, thanks." He swallowed bile at the thought of the interview she had given to the *Daily Orb*.

"Please do, Karl. I've wanted to talk to you ever since... since Constance... I still can't say her name without wanting to cry." Her eyes moistened. "Those comments I made in the *Daily Orb* about her being in your house so often—"

"Maria, I'm not interested."

"That wasn't what I meant at all." She stepped back from his anger. Her discomfort was obvious as she drew the edges of her cardigan over her chest and tried to explain the suspicion that had grown like a cancerous root through this small terrace. "I don't blame you being mad but all I said to that reporter was that your house was home from home to Constance and you'd never harm a hair on her head. It came out different when it was in print. I rang Eric Walker and called him a liar. He said he'd quoted me verbatim and had the recording to prove it, but he only used some of the things I said."

"It's all to do with context, Maria. It doesn't matter now."

"Of course it matters, Karl. I'm ashamed—"

"Then let it go. Talking about it serves no purpose."

She nodded. "I've a pile of letters for you. The postman's been leaving them with me since the fire. Hold on 'til I get them."

Probably junk mail or bills, he thought when she returned with two supermarket bags filled with letters. They could whistle Dixie for the latter, he thought. The rest would be hate mail. Social media hadn't completely obliterated the poison pen letter.

The prospect of wading through them wearied him but a long afternoon stretched before him. As he suspected, some of the letters written after the discovery of Constance's body were vitriolic, but most were recently dated and from supporters. People who claimed they had believed all along in his innocence. They wished him well, offered to pray for him or spilled out personal tragedies that they too had suffered through miscarriages of justice. All of them praised Amanda Bowe for her courage in organizing such a powerful campaign.

Unable to contain the mixed emotions the letters evoked, he left the house and drove to Turnstone Marsh. The suspension in the car was bad, jolting him over every minor bump in the road. It was fifteen years old, and hard-used, but he had picked it up for next to nothing on *Done Deal*. It would do until he could afford something better.

When he reached the marsh, he parked the car at the side of the road and climbed down the grassy embankment. His boots sank into the soggy earth. The sun, fleeting between lowering clouds, glinted off the peaks of Toblerone Range. He used to ride the range with Dominick, the two of them hurtling fearlessly up and down the steep gradients, unafraid of falling off or of the consequences that would follow. The marsh was where they had smoked their first joints, drunk their first beers, kissed their first girlfriends on the bank of the river. Rock climbing, football matches, an unforgettable holiday in Spain to celebrate their Leaving results; they'd had a history spanning three decades. A history that had clearly counted for nothing when it came to Dominick's self-preservation.

He crossed the marsh to Orchard Road and continued walking until he reached the old house. Someone, probably Jenna, had erected a small roadside shrine at the spot where Constance had been knocked down. The brick on which she had struck her head had been removed. A wooden cross, carved with her name, stood in its stead, bunches of fresh flowers beneath it. Karl knelt and bowed his head. No words came to him and, even if they had, they would have been inadequate. He imagined Dominick on his knees that night, probably in the same spot. Like Karl, he would have been unable to pray, ravaged as he was by the need to remove the tell-tale stains from the scene of the crime. Blood was easily wiped away, especially when it was fresh, but guilt had proved impossible to eradicate.

He had seen Amanda Bowe at Elizabeth's funeral, his gaze drawn to her as he carried the coffin into the church. She was sitting in the back pew, inconspicuously dressed in muted tones, her hair flattened in a severe ponytail. Easy to miss among the congregation that had gathered to pay their respects to the quiet, inoffensive woman, whom she had thrust into the headlines. *Monster Teen Killer Finds God*. The front page as usual.

In the grotto she had stared defiantly back at him. She knew, as he did, that her campaign was throwing sand at the truth and proving that the last story written was the one that would be remembered.

CHAPTER TWENTY-FIVE

The phone call came in the early hours. Amanda struggled from sleep and reached out to answer it. An accident, her mother, her sister... her thoughts hurtled from one fearsome scenario to the next. The number was unknown and the voice muffled, covered either by a hand or a scarf.

"What's keeping you up so late, my lovely?" he asked. "Three o'clock in the morning and you still haven't closed your eyes. I'm glad you sleep with your lights on. I want you to recognize me when I come to kill you." She resisted the urge to scream. To demand to know who was calling. No sense adding stupidity to her shock. She resisted, also, the temptation to look out the window. Even if Karl Lawson was standing below in a pool of light in the courtyard of her apartment block, she would be unable to see him.

She cut him off in mid-sentence and switched off her bedroom light. Ringing the police at this stage was useless. His number would be untraceable. He had either rung from a public phone, if such things still existed, or he would have already destroyed his mobile. Her door was securely locked, her apartment fitted with a sophisticated security system.

She tried to sleep but she was unable to drown out his threat: *I want you to recognize me when I come to kill you.*

She had reported the bullet at her local police station. The guard on duty, a heavyset man with an intimidating chin and disconcertingly small, yellow teeth, had recognized her.

"Amanda Bowe," he'd said before she could introduce herself. "That's a mighty fine job you did with your freedom campaign." She thought he was being sarcastic but his compliment had been genuine. So, too, had his shock when she showed him the bullet.

He asked if she had enemies. Take your pick, Amanda wanted to say. If I didn't have enemies, I wouldn't be such a successful journalist.

"Could it be gang-related?" he'd asked. "It's tough when a pretty girl like you has to hang around with the hard men." His tone suggested he had slumbered his way through the feminist and post-feminist eras.

"Hanging around with the hard men is mandatory in my job," she'd replied. She had not mentioned Karl Lawson's name. How could she accuse him of death threats when she was responsible for his freedom? The irony of such an accusation would not be lost on the media, nor would they hesitate to give it front-page prominence. Garda Ryan had promised to be in touch when the bullet had been forensically examined.

Unable to go back to sleep, Amanda entered the kitchen. She felt her way through the darkness, afraid to switch on the light in case he was watching from the back of the apartment complex and would see her fear illuminated. She opened the fridge door. Using the interior bulb to guide her, she poured milk into a cup and heated it in the microwave, adding a dash of nutmeg, as her mother used to do when their nights were disturbed by random violence. Gradually, she relaxed and the urge to ring Hunter receded. Too much was at stake. He had given her the scoop of her career and she would abide by the pact they had made not to contact each other. She could manage this on her own.

When she returned to bed, her dreams were fitful, vivid, repetitive. Karl Lawson featured in each one.

Two days later, she received another dangerous envelope; a Manila one this time, small and innocuous enough to allow her to open it without hesitation. It had been left at *Capital Eye*'s front desk by a courier and Regina on reception had handed it to Amanda when she arrived into work.

Everything in the busy office stilled as white powder spilled over her hands and settled with an inaudible puff on her desk. Anthrax? She had written a feature about it once. The pictures of skins infected by the powder had horrified her. She sat rigidly in her chair, her breath suspended, afraid the force of her breathing would cause the powder to blow across the office and contaminate the air. How strange to think that something so deadly should feel like silk on her fingers.

Regina admitted she had been on the phone when the courier arrived with the envelope. She had noted with disapproval that he failed to remove his helmet but he left before she could chastise him. Later, she would discover that the name he signed in the visitors' book was *Darth Vader*.

The forensic team arrived and sealed off Amanda's office. They believed this was a "low risk" situation, but could not say for definite that she had been the victim of a hoax. She showered in the staff bathroom and put on a track-suit, hastily purchased by Regina in the nearest Penneys. The results would be with her as soon as the samples were tested, an investigator told her. That could take some hours, he warned, and advised her not to worry too much.

"Go home," her editor said. "I'm calling a taxi for you. Do you have someone who can stay with you until the results come through?"

Amanda nodded. As soon as she entered her apartment she showered again. She turned up the thermostat, scrubbing her skin until it was red and wrinkled. After drying off, she rang Rebecca and listened to the message on her sister's answering machine. No sense ringing her mother and scaring her. Imelda's nervousness would only exacerbate Amanda's own fear.

Each ticking second on the clock sounded like a time bomb inside her head. If the results were positive she could be in the hospital by tonight, her skin rupturing in hideous sores, or she could be dead on a slab.

She huddled in a chair by the window. She had to contact Hunter. Their pact no longer mattered. He was the only person who would understand what she was going through. She opened the wardrobe and removed a jacket with a thick faux fur collar, searched for the slit she had made in the fabric for her secret phone. She sent a text to his number, hoping he had not already destroyed his own phone. Her fears were soon confirmed. His number was no longer in service.

A prolonged buzz on the intercom jerked her back to reality. Garda Ryan stood outside. Talcum powder, he said when she opened the door to him. Lily of the valley, a deadly flower in its own right. It was a hoax but, combined with the bullet and an increased number of anonymous phone calls, it had to be taken seriously. Once again he asked if there was someone out there with a grudge against her? Karl Lawson—she bit back his name. How would it look if she accused him without proof? How could she describe his sulfuric gaze at the grotto, his biblical threat? Amanda clenched her hands until it seemed as if her nails would break the skin and draw blood.

At one in the morning she took a sleeping tablet. Tomorrow, she was being interviewed on LR1. Nothing too dramatic, just an afternoon chat show where she would talk about her career as a crime reporter. The upcoming interview had been promoted on LR1 and he would be watching, planning new ways to intimidate her. She would look her best, composed and unconcerned by his dangerous games.

CHAPTER TWENTY-SIX

LR1 was located next door to Richardson Publications. The two buildings took up most of the business park, which also contained a gym, an office block and Quix Cafè. The television station was situated inside a square, utilitarian building, uninspiring from the outside but with a spacious, glitzy interior. In the reception area, a circular glass elevator glittered like a bauble and, for those nervous of stepping inside it, a spiral staircase also led to the upstairs offices. Strains of classical music floated from an invisible sound system. The receptionist sat a little straighter as Karl approached her desk.

"Mr. Richardson is at a meeting and cannot be disturbed." She repeated the same message she had given to Karl each time he rang LR1.

"Yes, he can." Karl ignored her automated response, her frozen Barbie smile. "Tell him I don't intend leaving until he sees me. I'm prepared to wait all day, if necessary. You can order security to throw me out but I'd hate to add assault to the case of unfair dismissal I intend to bring against him."

"Please take a seat, Mr. Lawson." The flick of her spidery eyelashes betrayed her uneasiness as she gestured toward a leather armchair.

He had already spoken on the phone to Barbara, who had been apologetic about stepping so effortlessly into his shoes.

"Truth is, Karl, we're trying to manage *Hitz* on a very tight budget," she'd said when he asked about the possibility of working for her. "Things have changed in the past few months. Lar is focused only on LR1. That's where he spends all his time now and, more worryingly, it's where all the investment is going. We're not taking on new staff at the moment and he's told us—"

"I can do freelance work." He had interrupted her excuses.

"That also applies to freelancing," she admitted. "Lar has closed down two of his magazines and I'm keeping my head down in case he looks in my direction. I'll ring back if the situation changes. I hope things work out for you. I really mean it, Karl. We must have lunch together soon."

"That sounds like a plan," he said. "I'll look forward to it."

How easy it was to break ties with the past, he'd thought as he hung up. To move effortlessly from being friends to being acquaintances, who promised lunch in the knowledge that it would never happen.

"Mr. Richardson will see you now." The receptionist beckoned him to her desk. "His office is on the third floor—"

"Thank you." Karl was already striding toward the elevator.

Lar's office, like the foyer, seemed enormous. A prison cell gave space a new perspective.

"Well, Karl, I hear you're making a statement, as usual." Lar stood and leaned across his desk to shake hands. He had always dressed with flair, flashy ties and bold pinstripe suits, the flourish of a handkerchief in the breast pocket. Now, as a mark of respect to his wife, who had died while Karl was in prison, that flamboyance had been toned down to a gray suit and a black tie.

"I was sorry to hear about Rosalind." Karl gripped the older man's hand. "She was a wonderful woman. I was very fond of her."

"Everyone loved my wife." Lar sat down heavily and tilted his chair back. "Now that you've offered your condolences, would you like to explain why you're threatening my staff?"

"I want a job. I know Barbara has replaced me on *Hitz* but I'll settle for an equivalent position on one of your other magazines."

"You were never a man for small talk," Lar replied. "So, I'll reply in kind. I fully accept that you'd nothing to do with that young girl's death. But the publicity was appalling and our advertisers reacted in an extremely negative way. You know this business, Karl. Advertising is the lifeblood of any magazine, and *Hitz* is no exception. Despite the popularity of Amanda Bowe's freedom campaign, your name has been tainted by that tragedy."

"What do you expect me to do?" Karl asked. "Assume a new identity?"

Lar made a steeple with his index fingers and pressed them against his chin. "Assuming a new identity would be the perfect solution. However, in the real world, perfect solutions seldom present themselves. But you can change direction. Retrain and find a job where your name won't be in the public domain. Come back and see me then. I'll give you names of good contacts who'll be willing to help you start over."

"There is another alternative," said Karl. "I can sue you for unfair dismissal."

"I assume that's meant as a threat?"

"Not a threat, Lar. A fact."

"How long do you think that will take?" The businessman

surveyed Karl over his glasses. "You've already lost eight months of your life. You should be playing catch-up instead of pursuing a case you'll eventually lose. Our defense team will be robust, make no mistake about it." He opened a drawer in his desk and removed a spreadsheet. "It's all here." He slapped his hand against the columns of figures. "Lost revenue, Karl. All of it incurred by Richardson Publications from the bad publicity before and after your arrest. We've already had to downsize and sell off two of our titles as a result. What happened to you was a disgrace but, unfortunately, dominoes only need a finger flick before they collapse. That's what almost happened to my company because of its association with your name."

"My name has been cleared—"

"Of course it has. Justice was delayed but done in the end. All those signatures demanding your release. I signed the petition myself and asked everyone else in the company to do the same." He stared at a photograph on his desk of his late wife and moved it fractionally closer to him. "How we deal with the knocks in our lives is what sets us up for the future."

Rosalind had been the softer side of the Richardson partnership, ambitious for the company but without Lar's ruthlessness. She would have fought for Karl, browbeaten her husband into doing what was right.

"Take my advice and make a fresh start," said Lar. "That's what I did when I was your age and my first company collapsed." He stood up to signal the end of the meeting. "There's so much goodwill toward you out there. Amanda Bowe certainly tapped into it when she petitioned on your behalf."

"I'll see you in court." Karl ignored the proffered handshake and left the office.

The elevator glided to a stop. The shrill timbre of violins grated against his ears as he crossed to the exit. The glass doors opened automatically. A woman, approaching, stopped and waited for him to emerge. She was dressed for the cold in a brown faux fur coat, her trousers tucked into a pair of Uggs.

"Karl," she said and pulled off a glove, held out her hand. "How are you?"

He stared, perplexed, unable to remember her name.

"I'm afraid I don't—" he began.

"I'm Sylvia Thornton." She shook his hand, a warm, firm grasp. "We've met before but only briefly."

Her name chimed faintly in his memory. "Forgive me... how do we know each other?" he asked.

"Lar Richardson introduced us at one of his Christmas parties."

The annual Richardson Publications party was a mix of small talk that inevitably turned to drunken babble as the night wore on. Karl had always left as soon as Lar delivered his motivational speech and thanked his staff for their dedication; words that would ring hollow the following year when some hapless employee was fired for not reaching his projected target.

"I'm sorry I didn't recognize you," he said.

"No need for apologies. I'm always behind the scenes at a Richardson event."

He nodded, placing her now. "You're his publicist."

"My official title is 'dogsbody' but yes, publicity and event organizing is part of my brief." She smiled fleetingly and moved a step closer, her gaze quizzing. "How are you, Karl?"

"I've known better days," he admitted.

"What happened to you was horrendous. I'm so sorry—"

"You weren't to blame."

"Personally, no, but I believe in collective responsibility. The coverage you received . . ." She shook her head.

"It wasn't just the media."

"I'm well aware of that fact." Her polite expression never wavered yet he detected an undercurrent flowing beneath their polite conversation. "What are you hoping to do now?" she asked.

He shrugged. "I'm flying to New York at the weekend to see my family. After that . . . who knows."

"I wish you the best of luck." She smiled again and entered the building.

CHAPTER TWENTY-SEVEN

The interview on LR1 was as smooth as Amanda expected. She spoke knowledgeably about the Shroffs and their strong family bonds, their petty squabbles and murderous feuds, their international criminal links. Cass Green, the presenter, asked about the dangerous line Amanda walked when researching their activities. Did she, as was suspected, have a mole within the gardaí? Amanda gazed into the camera, and shook her head. She was her own sleuth, eyes wide open to find the story under the skin. As the interview drew to a close, Cass congratulated her on the success of her *Free Karl Lawson* campaign. Amanda laughed airily and thanked the public for their support.

"You were good." Eric Walker, who had left the *Daily Orb* and joined the team on LR1's newly introduced investigative program, *Behind the Crime Line*, was waiting for her at reception.

"Good?" Amanda arched her eyebrows, newly threaded.

"Awesome," he amended and stepped back to survey her. "Have you lost weight?"

"Why?" she asked. "Did I look too thin?"

"You looked perfect. Have you time for coffee?"

"A quick one. You must tell me all about your new job."

"Just as well you didn't apply for it," he said as they walked under the archway that led them to Quix Cafè. "It was a tough enough interview process. Four times they called me back. *Four* times. And a different panel each time, apart from Lar Richardson. They psychoanalyzed me so thoroughly they now know me better than I know myself. But hell, I got the gig in the end. What do you think of the program?"

"It's good."

"Good?" Now it was his turn to lift his eyebrows. "You can do better than that, Amanda."

"Good," she repeated. "It's still finding its feet but it will be excellent when the team take on some really tough investigations."

Eric agreed. "We're falling over each other with ideas but still learning to execute them. Why didn't you apply for the job?"

"Too busy," she replied. "Anyway, I'm happy where I am."

"Yeah...but television." He opened the cafè door and stood aside for her to enter. "I would have thought *Behind the Crime Line* was right up your street."

Quix Cafè, all gleaming chrome and hissing coffee machines, was busy. The customers, gathered in huddles around the tables, created an atmosphere of jittery, stressed, argumentative and high-octane creativity. She would have passed triumphantly through those four interviews but she had been caught up in the freedom campaign she instigated on Karl Lawson's behalf. All those letters and emails she had received. The invitations from activist groups to speak at their meetings. The constant pressure she had been under to continue writing about Karl Lawson until he was released from prison and free to terrorize her.

Eric mentioned his name. Had he a direct line to her

thoughts? She blew on her decaf coffee but set it back on the table.

"What did you just say?" She touched her teeth with her tongue, a nervous habit she had conquered—almost.

"You just missed him earlier," he said. "Kicked up a row at reception. Demanded to see Richardson and wouldn't take no for an answer. Got his way in the end, too. Pity you missed him. He'd have been delighted to see you."

She met his gaze and smiled wryly. For an instant she was tempted to swear him to secrecy and confide in him. The thought quickly passed. Their backgrounds were too similar to pretend that the story wasn't more important than the sharing of secrets between friends.

"I'd better head back to the office." Amanda stood. "I've a series to finish. Lots of luck with your new job."

She hurried past Richardson Publications, where Karl Lawson had once interviewed her and found her wanting. "Don't be afraid to dig deep," he had told her during that humiliating interview in his office. "There's always another story under the skin." Easy crumbs of advice tossed from his lofty editorial table. Could he possibly still be lurking around here? The cars in the car park looked glossy and sleek, their registration plates proving they had been purchased in the last few years. Nothing like the clapped-out banger he had driven to Elizabeth Kelly's funeral. She zapped her own car and was about to turn on the ignition when her phone bleeped. No name on the text, just another unfamiliar number.

Explosive interview, Amanda. Why didn't you check under your car. Boom!

A hoax, like the powder, it had to be a hoax. She opened the door and stepped carefully away from her car. Slow,

careful steps, her eyes scanning the car park. Was he watching her? He had to be nearby. Otherwise, how could he have
known when to send the text? Her father used to have that
same menacing watchfulness as he waited for the trigger that
would cause him to strike that first blow. Amanda straightened her shoulders and rang the emergency number Garda
Ryan had told her to call when next she was surrounded by
danger.

The television station was evacuated. The Army Bomb
Disposal Team came and went. The device under her car
was harmless. Another hoax. The police took her phone.
She could reclaim it when they had traced the text. Her car
was declared safe but she was too shocked to drive it away.
She was sitting on the sofa in reception when Lar Richardson stepped from the elevator and walked toward her. She
straightened her shoulders and struggled up from the plush,
enveloping cushions.

"Amanda Bowe. You certainly caused some excitement
today." He shook her hand and sat down beside her.

"I'm mortified over the trouble I've caused." Her cheeks
stung with embarrassment. "I should have guessed it was a
hoax."

"But it might not have been a hoax. And then what?" He
looked younger when he smiled. Power had chiseled his lean
face with authority and his silver hair, brushed back from his
forehead, was still plentiful.

"I didn't realize the army would make everyone evacuate
the business park."

"Inconvenient but necessary," he replied. "How are you?"

"Still shocked." She sipped a glass of water and tried
not to wince when it touched her teeth. According to her
orthodontist the work was almost complete, but her teeth
remained sensitive from the braces she had to wear at night.

"I watched your interview," he said. "You're a courageous reporter. I admire that about you."

"Crime reporting is difficult," she said. "And it doesn't get any easier."

"Have you ever considered moving in a different direction?" he asked.

"Such as?"

"Television?"

Cool, she thought, stay cool and composed. She flicked her tongue against her teeth—she must *stop* doing that—and counted to five before replying. "My job is very fulfilling. I wasn't considering a change."

"But you look like someone who enjoys a new challenge. Why don't you call and see me when you've fully recovered from your ordeal." He handed his business card to her. "This is my private number. Ring me next week and we'll talk again."

He escorted her to the exit. When she glanced back he was still standing where she had left him, his gaze fixed on her.

By lunchtime the following day, Amanda's phone had been returned to her. No luck, she was told by the guard on duty. She had debated changing her phone number when the calls began but that would be inconvenient. Anyway, Karl Lawson could easily discover her new number and taunt her with his knowledge.

CHAPTER TWENTY-EIGHT

Justin's car was parked in his driveway. He was out running, Jenna said when she opened the front door. No more spare keys or treating each other's houses like extensions of their own. Lara greeted Karl with her usual exuberance, demanding to know when Sasha was coming home. She quietened down at a sharp reprimand from Matthew, who had flushed violently as soon as Karl entered the living room.

"Lara!" Jenna called from the kitchen. "Come and help me empty the dishwasher."

Karl sat down beside his nephew as Lara ran from the room.

"How are you, Matthew?" he asked.

"I'm good." His nephew stared steadfastly at the television. He had grown taller, his hair shorn at the sides, a quiff in front.

"We don't have to be cross with each other," Karl said. "I'm not angry with you. Are you angry with me?"

"No." Stiff little shoulders, taut little face. He could have been speaking to a frightened stranger.

"It's okay, Matthew. You can tell me the truth."

The boy shuffled his body deeper into the sofa. "You made me tell lies to the guards."

"How did I do that?"

"I don't know...you just *did*." He folded his arms and pressed them hard against his chest.

"We were going through a terrifying time, Matthew. And now we're going through a very sad time. It's easy for everything that happened to us to become mixed up in our heads."

"Like scrambled eggs," said Matthew.

"What?"

"Scrambled eggs is what my head is like inside."

"That's a *very* good way to describe it. We all miss Constance so much. It's okay to cry buckets when you feel like it. She'll look after you. You know she can do that, don't you?"

Matthew looked directly at him for the first time since Karl entered the room.

"Can you see her?" he asked.

"Yes."

"What does she look like?"

"I see her dancing in a shining green light," said Karl. "She probably comes to you in a different way."

"She's always galloping off on her horse." Matthew nodded. "There's sparks on his hooves. She never lets me catch up with her."

"Some day she will. But not for a long time yet."

"That's when I'll be dead like her, right?"

"Yes," Karl nodded. "But she's here with us in other ways. You can't love someone as much as she loved you and just vanish forever. Talk to her. Tell her your problems. Write them out in a letter to her, if you like. She'll hear you, I guarantee it."

The boy's shoulders relaxed and he leaned his head sideways to rest against Karl's arm. "Words kept getting mixed up in my head when she was lost and when the journalist that made you free from jail came to the stables to ask about Constance—"

"What did she say to you?"

"She said I had to think really hard about what you said that night when I was looking for Constance 'cause it was important to tell the truth to the guards." He blinked hard and rubbed his knuckles into his eyes. "It's just that I don't know what you said or I said or she said and it hurts my head so bad. You went to jail and that's all my fault..."

"Matthew, Matthew—you don't have to cry over that. Jail didn't matter. Are you listening to me? Only the truth matters. And that truth is that you and I did nothing to hurt Constance. I'm not angry with you. I love you as much as I ever did. And Constance didn't stop loving you when she died. She understands all our mistakes and confusions, and the silly things we sometimes do. You talk to her and you'll find she has an answer for everything."

He left the house shortly afterward and drove to North Beach Road. The sun, rimming the clouds, was sinking fast when he parked in the beach car park and cut across the dunes to Ben's Shack. The cove was empty except for the lone figure of his brother sitting motionless, staring at the sea.

"*Karl.*" Justin breathed his name on an exhalation. His face, flushed from running, was grim as he put out his hand to steady himself against the rocks and struggled to his feet.

"Jenna said I'd find you here." Karl moved closer, his gaze fixed on Justin, who had pressed his elbows into his sides as he prepared to run from the cove. "We have to talk—"

"We've nothing to say to each other." Justin's tone was definite.

"We have *everything* to say to each other."

"The time to talk was when Constance was alive." His stance reminded Karl of their teen years, righteous, intractable.

"I realize that. I made one terrible mistake—"

"One terrible omission." Justin's breathing was shallow, fast. "You chose not to tell me my daughter was in danger. Now, when it's too late, you come here thinking a few fucking meaningless words can heal us."

"I know that apologies are useless but how else—"

"Was Constance in your house that night?"

"She must have been. But I didn't know. Justin, you've *got* to believe me."

"How can you expect me to believe you? Or believe you didn't influence Matthew? And Dominick Kelly was your friend. The two of you were fucked up when you were teenagers. The trouble you caused . . . and you thought Constance was made from that same reckless mold."

"For God's sake, Justin, you're not thinking straight—"

"Don't. You. Dare. Tell. Me. How. To. Think!" With each word, Justin jabbed his finger into Karl's shoulder and forced him backward across the sand. "Constance was only a child. It was my duty to protect her. That's what fathers are supposed to do. How can you expect me to forgive you for depriving me of that right?"

"Does it help your grief to blame me?" Karl's anger blistered and broke. "Have you even begun to grieve for Constance? Or does your hatred for me leave room for nothing else? I've lost everything. *Everything.* Is that not enough to balance our scales of suffering?"

"You still have your daughter." Justin began to jog on the spot, frantic, fast movements that kicked sand into the air. "Leave me alone and let me grieve in my own way."

"I came here hoping we could make peace with each other." Karl's anger left him as suddenly as it had ignited. "Obviously, I was wrong. It was never in your nature to forgive."

"I wish I could but I can't . . . *can't.*"

Watching him run across the sand, Karl realized the abyss

between them had grown too wide for hands to reach across.
Guilt, guilt . . . the air was poisoned with it. He stayed in Ben's
Shack until darkness fell. A full moon rose above the dunes.
Close enough to touch. Close enough for the cow to jump its
cratered face and for prisoners to howl.

CHAPTER TWENTY-NINE

Something was wrong. Amanda knew this as soon as she entered her apartment. This awareness was instinctive, the hairs on her arms bristling when she opened the bathroom door. Everything seemed as normal. Shower gel, shampoo and conditioner aligned on the shower tray, an aromatic oil burner positioned dead center on the window ledge, body moisturizing creams and tanning lotions neatly stacked on glass shelves. Nothing had been touched or moved since she left for work that morning, yet the room breathed a warning. An intruder had stood where she was standing and, somehow, had destabilized the harmony she had created in this compact space. It had to be her imagination. An overflow of stress brought about by the knowledge that she was being followed by Karl Lawson.

This morning, an envelope with the warning PHOTOGRAPHS. DO NOT BEND. had been handed to her by Regina when she arrived into work. She had opened the envelope, believing the photographs were from Shane. Usually, he sent them electronically but, sometimes, when the photographs were particularly atmospheric, he gave her prints for her records.

These photographs, black and white, had indeed been atmospheric. A long-range shot, which had been taken through her office window, showed her in profile, sitting at her desk. The second photograph was taken earlier in the week when she was interviewing a retired policewoman in a café on Dawson Street. In others, she was talking to Shane on the steps of the criminal court, driving into her apartment car park, collecting her mother for lunch, shopping on Grafton Street, emerging from a fitting room in Brown Thomas.

She had called in to the police station with the photographs. A different guard was on duty, younger and eager to assist. He whistled sharply between his teeth as he examined the photographs and took details on the latest anonymous phone calls. The deadly threats that warned her that the next time powder spilled from an envelope, it would be the real thing. The next time a real bomb, a real bullet. A different number each time, but the same muffled voice and adenoidal snuffling.

Perspiration trickled coldly under her arms as she hesitated at the entrance to the bathroom. Her gaze swept over the upright toilet seat. Such a bold, masculine statement. How had she not noticed it immediately? She took a step back, tried to stem her panic. Logical thought was needed here. She could have left it up after she scoured the bowl. An easy mistake to make...but it was one she never made. Always down, except when she'd lived with Graham, who had seemed incapable of remembering that small detail. Her father had insisted it must also remain upright; another of his petty tyrannies imposed on a houseful of women.

She walked to the toilet bowl. Someone had urinated into it, a tinge of yellow when the water should be clean and pure. Her legs weakened. She reached toward the basin to steady herself, then pulled her hand back in case her intruder's touch had contaminated the surface. She listened for a sound that would alert her to his presence but the apartment was silent. She should ring Garda Ryan. A toilet seat left up, a toilet bowl unflushed. How would that sound, especially to a man? A common, everyday occurrence, that's what he would say. He would be right—except that in her apartment everything had an unchanging order.

She checked the other rooms. All empty, and none of them projected the unease that had gripped her as soon as she opened the bathroom door.

Her phone rang. Another unfamiliar number, the same voice. "Feeling pissed off, Amanda?" he said. "Next visit, I'll fill your bath with blood."

She held her breath and waited for him to continue. "Not talking?" he asked. "That's unusual for Amanda Bowe. You've such a way with words."

Her mouth pulsed with the need to scream. She forced herself to stay silent and cut off the call. She phoned a locksmith, who promised to be with her within an hour. Even after he finished changing the locks and her security system had been recoded, she was unable to sit still.

She had to contact Hunter and tell him her life was in danger. That he, too, would not escape the wrath of Karl Lawson. She used her secret phone to ring his home number and braced herself when it was answered. The voice was young and male—one of Hunter's sons. She had never asked their names but the deepness of his tone told her he was the eldest boy.

"I'm carrying out a market research survey," she said. "Can I speak to your father, please?"

"He's not here," the boy replied. "Will I get my mother for you?"

"No. It has to be your father. Have you any idea when he'll be back?"

"Tomorrow, I think."

"Who's on the phone, Lewis?"

Amanda's heart jerked when she heard Sylvia Thornton speak for the first time.

"Some woman looking for Dad," he yelled back. Amanda ended the call and threw the phone on to the table. A moment later it rang. Petrified, she stared at the screen. Hunter's home number. Sylvia Thornton was ringing back to check up on her. She ran to the bathroom and flung the phone into the toilet bowl, pressed the flusher. She clasped her hands behind her head and rocked backward as she watched the water gush loudly over the phone and silence it.

Hunter arrived late the following night to her apartment. She knew he must be desperate to have risked such direct contact with her.

"What the hell is going on?" he demanded. "How dare you ring—"

"Shut up and listen," she snapped. "I wouldn't have contacted you unless it was important."

"Important enough to destroy my marriage. Sylvia took down the number."

"When you gave me that phone you assured me the number could never be traced back to me."

"Nor will it," he snapped. "But it was still an incredibly reckless thing to do."

"You needn't worry. I've destroyed the phone." She had retrieved it from the toilet bowl and broken it into tiny pieces before walking to the Liffey wall and flinging it into the river. Untraceable in every way.

"But she suspects—"

"Your wife's suspicions are your problem," she curtly interrupted him. "Karl Lawson is ours."

"What's that supposed to mean?"

"He's threatening me."

His abrupt laugh echoed with disbelief. "That would be one for the books, right enough," he said. "Amanda Bowe threatened by the man she saved from a miscarriage of justice."

"I'm serious, Hunter. He broke into my apartment and left the toilet seat up."

"The toilet seat up? Give me a break, Amanda."

"I never leave it up. Never. *And* he used the toilet to let me know he'd been here."

Hunter was silent as she listed the hoaxes and threats she had endured since Karl Lawson was released from jail.

"How do you know he's the one giving you grief?" he asked when she paused for breath.

"*Grief?* I'm taking about *death* threats."

"What proof do you have that it's him?"

"Who else can it be?"

"I could list the names but I don't have time for a marathon conversation."

"For God's sake, Hunter, *why* aren't you taking this seriously?"

"You destroyed him, Amanda. Then you tried to put him back together again with your self-serving *freedom* campaign, which had nothing to do with his release. Once the legalities were sorted, it was inevitable."

"You destroyed him, too. He has as much reason to hate you. What if he comes after you as well? And your family? He talks about bloodbaths. How many bodies does it take to fill one?"

"If Lawson's playing games, I'll sort him out quickly enough."

"How?"

"That needn't concern you." His expression was grim, as

closed off as the night she had seen him talking to Killer Shroff in Rimbles. He had been incognito then, an undercover cop who straddled the fine line between crime and conformity, and reveled in the risks he took. "Don't contact me again," he warned as he was leaving. "You're still under suspicion and your phone could be tapped. So could mine. Just trust me to take care of things. Okay?"

"Okay."

He departed as abruptly as he had arrived. In the chill of his leaving, his protective rush back to his family, she saw the ashes of what...love? Lust? Mutual usage? They had plundered what they needed from each other and all they had left to do was return without a backward glance to their separate lives.

CHAPTER THIRTY

Karl was awakened at two in the morning by a prolonged blast on the doorbell. He pulled on a pair of joggers and ran down the stairs. The familiar fear kicked in when he recognized Detective Garda Hunter on the doorstep. The detective was dressed in a hoodie and jeans. The hood, pulled up over his head, accentuated his high forehead and broad cheeks. Karl looked beyond him, expecting to see his female partner, and was surprised to discover he was alone.

"What is it, Detective? Come to arrest me again?" His bravado hid his unease and the silence that followed was deliberate, timed to work his pulse rate and set his heart pounding.

"That depends on what you've been doing...or are going to do," the detective eventually answered him. "You're flying to New York tomorrow."

"Yes." He had no idea how the detective had come by that information. The fact that he was aware of his plans increased Karl's anxiety.

"Documentation in order?" Detective Hunter moved closer.

"I assure you, everything is in order."

"You must be looking forward to seeing your daughter."

"I'm sure you haven't come to my house in the small hours to discuss my relationship with my daughter." He resisted the inclination to step back from the man's threatening gaze. The twitch of an eyelid, a muscle spasm so slight as to be imagined, yet Karl saw this involuntary movement in slow motion, or so it seemed, and it increased his fear that anything could happen, no matter how unimaginable, and he would be swept into the vortex. "Why are you here, Detective? If it's to interrogate me, I intend to call my solicitor before continuing this conversation."

"That won't be necessary," the detective replied. "This is an informal call. Advisory, you could say. Are you aware that you're under investigation for breaking and entering, for terrorism, threatening behavior and stalking?"

"*Excuse* me?"

"You heard. Obviously, you were well mentored in jail."

The accusations being outlined were crazy, yet they could be made to fit his crime. Square peg, round hole—that wouldn't matter to the man standing before him.

"*Terrorism*? How am I supposed to have terrorized anyone? And who am I stalking? I demand to know their names."

The detective thrust his head forward until their faces were almost touching. "I'm giving you fair warning before the guards close in on you—"

"I'm calling my solicitor—"

"You don't call anyone." He moved so quickly that Karl had no time to react before his arm was grabbed and lifted above his head. The man's solid bulk pinned him against the doorframe.

"I can make sure you never enter the United States," he said. "Documentation is everything and with a reputation as flawed as yours, it won't be a problem. Do we understand each other?"

"I haven't a clue—"

"I'm doing you a favor, Lawson. If you ever mention one word about tonight, and the fact that I've gone out on a limb to protect you, you'll feel the full weight of the law on your back."

"Detective Hunter, you're here illegally on my property and you're threatening me."

"Advising you. Kids grow up fast these days. Your daughter could be a mother before you see her again. What you've done will put you away for a hell of a long time. And you needn't depend on any freedom campaign to release you next time around. So, to repeat my question. Do we understand each other?"

It came to him then, a blast of awareness that gathered the scattered pieces of a jigsaw puzzle and slotted them into place. Detective Garda Jon Hunter and Amanda Bowe. Finally, it all made sense.

"Yes, Detective Hunter. I understand you perfectly."

"Better get your beauty sleep then." He released Karl's arm and stepped back. "You've an early flight to catch in the morning."

CHAPTER THIRTY-ONE

Sunday lunch in Raleigh Way was a tradition Imelda began after the death of her husband and had continued ever since. This weekly lunch was Amanda's main contact with Rebecca and the sisters used it to keep in touch, knowing they would drift apart if it was not there to anchor them. As children, they had been conjoined by fear, wary of their father's moods, his sudden outbursts of violence. Amanda had learned early to disguise that fear, even when it ripped through her chest and her breath was a bubble that refused to burst. Rebecca could never pretend. She shivered like an aspen when he raised his voice but Amanda, as she grew older, had stared him down, even when it meant the side of his hand on her face.

On this Sunday morning, she rubbed steam from the bathroom mirror and checked her reflection. The skin under her eyes looked bruised, her cheeks too hollowed. She made up her face and applied a lavish amount of blusher. Dark red lipstick, a defiant shade, and she was ready for the afternoon.

Her childhood home was unrecognizable since Rebecca, who had studied interior design, had eradicated all traces of their father from it. Raleigh Way had also changed. What was once an impoverished area had become gentrified as elderly residents died and the cottages were renovated by young couples seeking homes close to the city. The canal had been cleaned and was now inhabited by swans, who swam past Amanda with stately indifference as she parked her car and walked toward her mother's house.

Rebecca and her husband had already arrived. Two months pregnant, Rebecca was afflicted with morning sickness, a misnomer, she claimed, as it also extended into the afternoon, evening and night.

"I saw you on the telly." She lay on the sofa, her bare feet being massaged by Danny.

"You were great," he said as he vigorously worked each toe in a circular movement.

"You made quite an impact." Rebecca turned a wan face toward her sister. "But the powers that be can't have been happy about evacuating the building. LR1 was off the air for ages."

"Don't exaggerate," said Amanda. "And they received massive coverage from the media as a result. Lar Richardson said he could never have managed that amount of free advertising, even in his dreams."

"Who's he?" asked Danny.

"The *power* that be," replied Amanda. His business card was in her wallet, a select card he gave to very few. She had memorized his private number, stroking her finger across the embossed LR1 logo.

She helped Imelda carry the dishes from the kitchen to the dining-room. Roast lamb was on the menu today. Rebecca bolted to the bathroom when the smell wafted toward her and emerged, red-rimmed eyes, ashen cheeks. It was going to be a long pregnancy.

"How come you know so much about the drug gangs?"

Rebecca toyed with a scoop of mashed potato and waved the gravy bowl away.

"It's my job to know about them," Amanda replied.

"When will the articles you're writing about them be published?" Danny asked.

"Next week."

"All this talk about gangs scares me," said Imelda. "What's this city coming to? That's what I want to know."

"Scumbags," agreed Danny. "Let them take each other out and be done with it."

"Is that all you're going to eat?" Imelda looked pointedly at Rebecca's plate. "That wouldn't fill a canary's belly. You have to eat for two, you know?"

"It's plenty, Mum." Rebecca sighed. "Stop fussing."

"This is delicious, Imelda." Danny piled his plate high and coyly patted his wife's non-existent bump. "I'll eat for the three of us."

"I can't keep anything down but you've no excuse for not eating," said Rebecca. "You're too thin, Amanda."

"There's nothing wrong with my weight."

"Of course not, dear." Imelda patted her arm. "But you do look tired. Are you sure you're okay? That terrible bomb—"

"*Mum*, it was a hoax." She was tired of discussing it with her mother, who phoned every few hours to check if she was okay.

"But why would someone do that to you?"

"There's crazies everywhere. I don't want to talk about it any more. When's your next hospital appointment, Rebecca?" Steering the conversation to scans and prenatal yoga, Amanda wondered how soon she could escape.

The swans were resting in the rushes when she left the cottage. She hurried toward her car, which she had left around the corner on Raleigh Lane. A Mercedes was parked in front of it, a silver jeep behind, both empty. She would have difficulty easing out of that space but it could be done. She got into her car—and knew instantly that something was wrong. The warning on her skin. The same itching uneasiness she used to experience before her father came home in one of his moods. Portents of trouble to come . . . and when the back door was whipped open she was terrified but not surprised. Too dazed to move when a hand came from behind to cover her mouth, she heard his voice, so familiar by now, but no longer muffled. "You've kept me waiting a long time, Amanda."

She swiveled her eyes toward the rearview mirror. All she could see was his hulking figure leaning forward from the back seat. His aftershave, expensive and overpowering, was unable to mask the rank sweat oozing from his pores. His nasal twang was more pronounced and he spoke with utter conviction when he told her he would return to kill her if she didn't shred every word she had written about the Shroffs.

"What you've experienced so far is just a taster," he warned. "Can you imagine what we'll do when we come after you for real?"

She tried to nod but his hand had immobilized her. Only her heart moved, frantic kicks against her chest as she realized who was behind her. Billy Shroff, the eldest brother, his features hidden behind a balaclava.

"I'm going to remove my hand from your mouth," he said. "Don't even think of screaming or I'll be very cross with you. Do we understand each other?"

She nodded.

"What are you going to do, Amanda?" he asked.

"I'm going to destroy my features."

"Say it again, only louder this time."

"I'm going to destroy my features."

"Again, Amanda. Again and again and *again*."

Her voice shook but she continued repeating the same assurances until he grew tired of the game.

"You know who I am, don't you?" he said.

"No. *No* . . ."

"No lies, Amanda. Of course you know. Can you remember what you wrote about my daughter's wedding dress?"

"I don't remember—"

"Try."

"Honestly, I *don't*."

"You described it as a meringue whipped from egg whites and cocaine."

"I'm sorry . . ." She was unable to recall those words but they were exactly what she would have written. Careless words, instantly forgotten by her but etched into Billy Shroff's memory.

"You're a cruel bitch when you have a pen in your hand," he said. "And out of your hand too. Just remember this. The Shroffs are a close family. Insult one and you insult us all. New locks won't keep us out when we come for you the next time."

The interior light flashed on when he opened the back door. He walked past the Mercedes and turned the corner into Raleigh Way.

Amanda nudged out of the narrow space. Her hands slipped on the steering wheel once and she thought she would back into the jeep. Eventually, she was free . . . free . . . free.

She opened her laptop as soon as she entered her apartment. Was it her imagination or did the faint smell of aftershave hang in the air? She ran to the bathroom. Everything was as she had left it. She returned to her laptop and systematically deleted the research she had conducted on the

Shroffs, the notes she had so carefully compiled and, finally, her almost-completed features. She felt no regret as she watched her work disappear. She was alive and free from danger as long as she walked that line laid down by Billy Shroff. She should have realized that only the Shroffs had the wherewithal to carry out such an intimidating strategy. Karl Lawson had consumed her thoughts and dulled her objectivity. She should contact Hunter, tell him everything was under control. But what if his wife…if his superiors— no, she could not afford to take that risk.

When she closed her laptop, she knew with absolute certainty that she would no longer write about crime. Let the druggies wipe each other out on Main Street and do their deals in dingy alleyways. She no longer cared about their Spanish hideaways and drug landings on deserted jetties. Men would continue to murder their wives whether or not Amanda reported on their brutality. Children would go missing, thieves would still plunder, and youths maim each other in the mean, small hours.

CHAPTER THIRTY-TWO

Karl picked them out immediately from the waiting crowd in arrivals. Sasha in pink dungarees, leggier than he remembered, and Nicole, skinny jeans tucked into knee-high boots, a streamlined jacket cinched at the waist, her boyish haircut emphasizing her high, angular cheekbones.

Sasha broke free from her hand and charged toward him, shrieking, "Daddy. *Daddy!*"

People smiled indulgently as they moved aside to let her pass. He held her aloft and stared at her face, thinner now, her childish chubbiness gone, her ponytail replaced by a neat bob. She knotted her arms around his neck, and he, crushing her just as tightly, smothered her with kisses.

"Give Daddy a chance to breathe, darling." Nicole smiled too brightly and said, "Welcome to New York, Karl."

He gently prized Sasha loose and lowered her to the ground. "How are you, Nicole?"

"I'm good," she replied. "How was your flight?"

"Long but uneventful."

"You've lost so much weight."

"Gym workouts and a restricted diet over the last eight months."

Her forehead puckered as if rejecting this dash of reality, and Sasha, tugging at her hand, her voice reedy with anxiety, said, "Kiss Daddy, Mom. Kiss him, *now*."

Nicole gave him a quick hug and pressed her lips to his cheek. He breathed in her perfume, a light, lemony fragrance that reminded him of nights when she had turned to him in sleep, the scent still lingering on her skin. Aroused by her warm softness, he would hold her and she, sensing his near-ness, would awaken and sleepily open to him. The memory was as cold as stone. Difficult to believe they had once been happy together, good friends and lovers, contented parents. The life they had known had been pulled apart too savagely to piece back together. Had he ever known her? Had she ever known him? Was it possible to know another person? To even know oneself?

"Are you and Dora still best friends?" he asked Sasha as he rummaged inside a carrier bag.

"Boots is Dora's very best friend but I'm her bestest one after him."

"Then look who's traveled all the way from Dublin to New York to see you."

He removed the Dora doll with a flourish and presented it to her.

"Oh thank you, Daddy! Thank you." She hugged the doll and danced on the spot, red lights flashing from the heels of her trainers. "I missed you over the moon and back again."

He laid his case flat on the trolley and perched her on top of it. Nicole smiled and gave the trolley an extra push. Their hands were close but Karl had no desire to touch her. Sasha was the glue holding them together and her excited chatter filled the awkwardness between them as Nicole drove from the airport.

"How's Jock?" he asked.

"Sasha's given him a new lease of life." She smiled at her daughter through the rearview mirror. "Tell Daddy what Granddad calls you."

"The best girl this side of the Alleghenies," Sasha chirped.

"Looking after Mom was tough on him," said Nicole. "She's looking so much better since she went into the nursing home. The routine suits her. Most days she recognizes us. But everything's changing so fast. It's quite horrendous for all of us, particularly for Dad."

"I've always liked Teresa. I hope I'll have a chance to visit her."

"She liked—" Nicole faltered and blinked back tears. "Likes you too. When I told her you were coming over to see Sasha she asked if you're still writing for *Hitz*. I was amazed she remembered the name of the magazine. But that's the way she is. So clear one day and confused the next. Obviously, I haven't told her anything about...you know?" She stopped at traffic lights and inclined her head toward Sasha.

"Of course." He turned to see Sasha sucking her thumb, the doll clasped in her other arm.

"When did she start that again?" he asked, softly.

"She only sucks it occasionally." Nicole, too, kept her voice low but she sounded defensive as she accelerated away from the lights.

His father-in-law was waiting at the front door to greet them, his sizable girth emphasized by a loud check shirt. Not that there was anything slovenly about Jock's weight. It was solid and arrogant, as was the habitual expression on his fleshy face.

"Welcome, Karl, welcome." He enfolded Karl in a bear hug. "What do you think of this young lady, eh?" Leaning into the back of the car, he unstrapped Sasha and perched her on his shoulders. "Isn't she as pretty as a princess? Who's the best girl this side of the Alleghenies?"

"Me, me." Sasha laughed and gripped his neck, the Dora doll forgotten on the back seat.

The house was exactly as Karl remembered. Teresa Moynihan was a quiet, unassuming woman, who had always dressed in grays and beiges. She had applied the same color scheme to her interior decor. It was tasteful, instantly forgettable and allowed her husband to dominate a room without distraction from his florid personality.

"What are your plans, Karl?" Jock settled back in his leather recliner while Nicole put the finishing touches to a meal she'd prepared earlier. "How long do you intend to stay?"

"As long as it takes," Karl replied.

"What exactly does that mean?" Although Karl had been blameless in Nicole's decision to break off her engagement to his business partner's son, he had always been viewed as an interloper by his father-in-law.

"That's between myself and Nicole."

"Of course…of course." Jock crossed his legs on the footrest and pressed the remote on the television. "Has she told you how seriously her mother's health has deteriorated in recent months?"

"Yes. I'm hoping to visit Teresa while I'm here."

"I'm afraid that won't be possible. Teresa is frightened of strangers. Not that you're a stranger," he added hastily. "But she's not acquainted with you on a daily basis and a visit would destabilize her." He slammed the footrest back into position when Nicole called them into the dining-room to eat.

"I've just been explaining to Karl that visiting Teresa is out of the question," Jock said when they were seated around the table.

"Why?" Nicole asked. "Mom would enjoy a visit from

him. You know how bored she gets sitting in that room on her own."

"Remember what happened when she saw Seth?" Jock's chin jutted forward. "How long did it take before she calmed down again? I don't want a repeat of that experience."

"Then let's not talk about it over dinner." She avoided Karl's gaze as she placed bowls of rice and chicken curry on the table.

"Don't want any." Sasha pouted and pushed her plate away.

"Come on now." Jock tore a slice of naan bread in two and handed one half to her. "No more of this nonsense at mealtime."

"Don't...want...*any*," she repeated and stared defiantly back at him.

"It looks delicious," said Karl. "Why don't we have a race and see who gobbles everything up first?"

She allowed him to coax her into eating a small portion but messed with her food throughout the meal. He, too, had trouble eating. In prison, the food was bland and, now, free to eat whatever he wanted, everything on his plate seemed tasteless. Had he lost his ability to savor the spices Nicole had added to the sauce, to enjoy meals that once made him salivate?

"Seth?" He followed her to the kitchen, where she was setting a tray with dessert dishes and a blueberry pie. "As in Seth Kilbourne?"

"Seth's a family friend." She removed a bowl of ice cream from the freezer.

"He's also your ex-fiancé. I thought he'd moved to California."

"He's back in Highbridge."

"Visiting your mother?"

"Once. It wasn't a good idea. It's so hard to tell with Mom."

210   LAURA ELLIOT

"Does he visit you... and Sasha?"

"Of course not. You mustn't create situations that don't exist, Karl."

A prolonged shriek from the dining-room interrupted their conversation.

"What's up with her now?" Nicole, recognizing the beginnings of a Sasha tantrum, sighed loudly, the tray tilting dangerously when she lifted it.

"Let me." Karl took the tray from her and followed her into the dining-room, where Sasha was standing angrily in front of her grandfather.

"Stop your nonsense at once," Jock shouted. "I've told you before, princesses don't do tantrums."

"I'm not a princess," she shrieked. "I'm Sasha."

"Let me handle this, Dad." Nicole spoke quietly and Jock, responding to the authority in her voice, sat back in his chair.

"Look at the mess she made." He pointed toward an upended plate of curry and a seeping brown stain spreading across the tablecloth. "She did that quite deliberately."

"I hate you." Sasha pushed past him and buried her face in Karl's knees. "Granddad said you're going away again," she sobbed. "He's a big, bad liar."

"Enough of that talk now. That's not what I said, Sasha." Jock tried without success to placate her. "I told you that your daddy will have to go back to Ireland at some stage because that's where he lives."

Karl felt her shudder, her grip on his legs tighten. "Come here to me, darling." He lifted her in his arms. "Daddy's not going anywhere without you."

She rubbed her fists into her eyes and sobbed. "Where's my Dora doll? I *want* my new Dora doll."

She was still sobbing when Nicole returned with the doll. "Why don't you show Daddy your bedroom?" she said.

"He'll read you a bedtime story. Tomorrow he'll be back here again and we'll have a lovely day together."

Karl carried her upstairs and took down a book from her bookshelf. Lulled by the sound of his voice, she was asleep by the time the story came to an end. Jock was watching American football on television when Karl came downstairs.

"Is she asleep?" he asked.

"Yes. She was overexcited."

"She was fine until today," he said, without taking his eyes from the screen. "We'd settled her into a routine but now she doesn't know what's going on."

"What's going on is that her father has come to see her," said Karl. "I've every right to knock her routine out of kilter. That's not what's bothering her and you know it."

Jock shrugged without replying and raised the volume. Karl had forgotten just how much he disliked his father-in-law. Time and distance had softened the memory but, now, looking at the width of his wide neck, his self-assured jowls, he felt the familiar loathing kick in stronger than ever.

Nicole was stacking the dishwasher when Karl entered the kitchen.

"I want to see Sasha on my own tomorrow," he said.

She closed the dishwasher door and wiped down the work-tops, working speedily, efficiently. He had always admired her ability to bring order to a room in minutes. She had used the same skill to restore order to her life when it was in danger of spinning out of control.

"That won't be possible," she replied. "While you're here, you can see Sasha as often as you like. But I insist on being present at all times."

"Why? Are you afraid I'll do what you did and kidnap her?"

"Kidnap? What exactly are you implying?"

"You took our daughter from me without my permission. Do you have another definition for kidnapping?"

"I had no choice. I was needed here."

"Stop lying, Nicole." He wanted her to stay still and listen to him. "You *had* a choice and you decided to leave me. Sasha is the one who had no choice. The impact that's had on her is obvious. I want custody of my daughter. Do you understand?"

"No, I don't understand." She kept her back to him as she stacked a chopping board against the wall. "What exactly do you plan to do with her? Where will she live?"

"Where she's always lived."

"Don't lie to me, Karl. I know the bank is foreclosing on the house and you've already lost your job—"

"I'm aware of what I've lost." Bitterness. It had a taste that sickened him, sour, like vinegar tainting a fine burgundy wine. Finally, Nicole grew still and faced him. Her lips puckered, as if she, too, could taste the sediments of loss.

"I wish I'd been stronger, more trusting," she said. "Everyone seemed to have an opinion on Twitter, Facebook, all those chatrooms—"

"Chatter. That's all it was," he said. "The echo chamber. Sounds *so* harmless, doesn't it?"

She blinked, her eyes lustrous with tears. "Matthew was distraught when he told me about that conversation in the attic. I kept it to myself until they found Constance. Then I couldn't… all that publicity… it had destroyed me." Tears streamed down her cheeks. "I understand why you can't forgive me. But we must still work together to decide what's best for Sasha."

"Nicole's right." Neither of them had heard Jock entering the kitchen.

"Dad, this is between me and Karl," she cried. "Don't interfere."

"I'm not interfering." His wide girth filled the space

between them. "You can make this as easy or as difficult as you want." He spoke directly to Karl. "We'll do our best to facilitate you—"

"Facilitate? I'm not here to be *facilitated*. I'm here to seek custodial rights to my daughter and bring her home."

"Let me remind you of this salient fact," his father-in-law said. "Unlike you, Sasha is a U.S. citizen, as is her mother. Do you honestly believe any judge would allow you to have custody of her under those circumstances?"

"I have rights—"

"We all have rights," Jock agreed. "My daughter had the right to know the truth about your past when you married her. You lied to her about Arizona—"

"I never lied about that."

"No, you didn't," Nicole agreed. "You simply avoided telling me the truth."

"What has Arizona got to do with Sasha?"

"Everything." Arms akimbo, Jock rocked back in his easy slippers, his large feet spread wide. "That investigation is still open. No one has ever been convicted for assaulting that unfortunate woman. Don't you think that's going to have an impact on the judge's decision, especially when your niece's tragic death is public knowledge and the accused was your friend?"

Karl walked to the end of the kitchen and breathed deeply. Ten deep breaths was supposed to calm the nerves and lower blood pressure, but the pounding in his head continued.

"Stop it, Dad." Nicole sounded calm and in control again. "You're *so* out of order. Apologize to Karl immediately."

"I'm a straight talker, always have been," Jock blustered. "I'm only telling you how it will be perceived by a judge."

"He's waiting for your apology, Dad."

"Fuck your apology." Karl resisted the urge to smash his fist into Jock's self-righteous face and loosen his too-white teeth. "I'm taking my daughter back to Ireland with me and there's not a damn thing you can do about it. Challenge me on this and I'll show you what I learned about protecting one's property while I was in jail."

"That's enough." Nicole shoved them apart and hustled her father from the kitchen.

At the kitchen door Jock looked back, confident on his own turf. "I know your status, Karl. If you overstay your visit you'll be in trouble with immigration. Believe me, that's not a sensible idea. Keep your record clean and you can visit us again. But if you make things difficult for Nicole, I'll make sure you're served with a deportation order as soon as your time here is up. Then you'll have to wait till hell freezes over before you see your daughter again."

"How can you stay with him?" he asked Nicole when she drove him to his hotel. "You hated this house when you lived here. Your father was a bully then and he hasn't changed. All he wants is a housekeeper now that your mother isn't around to wait on him hand and foot."

"What he wants and what he'll get are two different things," she replied. "I start nursing in Highbridge Memorial next month and I intend on finding my own place as soon as possible."

Another brick in the wall of her new life, Karl thought. Her father was an obnoxious buffoon but he spoke the truth. Karl had flown to New York on the wings of a fantasy, the longing to see Sasha blinding him to his reality. A savings account that was almost gone. A house that would soon be repossessed. A dole allowance that would barely cover the rent of a bedsit as he searched for work. A name that would forever be associated with Constance's death and the tragedy that had unfolded in Arizona. His time with Sasha would be precious. Gems to collect and take with him when he was forced to say goodbye to her.

PART THREE

CHAPTER THIRTY-THREE

The Years That Followed

Lar Richardson was waiting for her in a seat by the restaurant window. Their first date, he called it. Such an old-fashioned phrase, quaint. But there was an age gap between them that could not be denied. Amanda was accompanied to her table by the maître d', a portly man who effortlessly combined haughtiness and deference toward those who dined in The Amber Door.

Eyes swiveled to observe her. She delighted in their attention and the knowledge that they recognized her. The weight she had lost had made her intriguingly thin without being considered anorexic. Her hair, strong and straight, hadn't needed much attention, apart from a strategic red streak in front. Just the right amount of collagen had been used on her lips and she'd had some minor work done around her eyes. Her teeth were perfect. Nowadays, when she scrutinized herself in the mirror, Amanda loved what she saw. Narcissism, she believed, was part of the human condition. The prime motivator for success. Her narcissism had a function and Lar's gaze proved that her efforts had been worthwhile.

He had steered her in a new direction. Admittedly, *Mandy Meets*, her celebrity chat show, sounded like the title of a pre-teen comic for girls but it was catchy, easy to remember, and Lar was delighted with the rankings. She had reinvented herself and life was good. Four times a week, Tuesday to Friday, a prime afternoon television slot.

"You're a natural," he'd told her when he had interviewed her shortly after the unfortunate bomb hoax. "I've an eye for quality. When that's combined with style, drive and ambition, it's unbeatable." This was a statement, not a compliment, and when she thanked him for his kindness, he said, "I've been called many things, Amanda. Kind is not one of them. You're entering a harsh industry. If I didn't believe you have the toughness to cope, you wouldn't be sitting here in front of me."

Mandy Meets had been an immediate success. A chat show with clout, it reminded Amanda of her "Life on the Fringe" interviews. Only now, instead of the grim district courts, she conducted her interviews at gala openings where celebrities spoke to her in their slinky dresses and stilettoes, their black ties. The red carpet had never been so glittery; but Amanda was not a simpering cipher for guests to promote their egos and latest releases. When she sat in her swivel chair to interview them, she knew where to stick the needle and puncture the celebrity membrane. She would search for the sudden foot-tap, fingers tightening, the jerk of an Adam's apple. Those tell-tale signs told her she had smashed through PR spin and stroked the nerve that made her guests more interesting or defensive—or simply angry enough to walk off her show. All grist to the publicity mill, and Lar's invitation to dine with him in The Amber Door told her he was happy with the direction she had taken.

He ordered oysters for a starter and lobster for his main course. Amanda stayed with the salads and made a pretense of eating the scallops. He talked to her about widowerhood and the difficulties of moving on. She wondered if she should offer him her condolences. It seemed such an intimate thing to do and she had only met Rosalind once at the LR1 launch. Better not. Who needed to be reminded of sorrow when they were smiling?

The Amber Door had been his wife's favorite restaurant, he told her. Tonight was the first time he had dined there since her death. It was rumored at LR1 that he kept Rosalind's ashes in an urn in their bedroom. Such a romantic, foolhardy thing to do. She had been a renowned entrepreneur, who had never wanted children to interfere with her business interests. Together, she and Lar had acquired property, expanded their stable of magazines and, finally, fulfilled their ambition to establish their own television channel.

Tiramisu or Chocolate Heaven? Amanda skimmed the choices on the dessert menu. Not in a thousand years.

"Just black decaf coffee for me." She smiled across the table at Lar.

"You've eaten so little," he protested. "Are you sure you won't indulge?"

"Image is everything," she said. "I can't afford to look ten pounds heavier on screen."

"Even if you indulged in the entire dessert menu, you'd still be flawless." His eyes lingered too long on her midriff and it was there, that jolt of anticipation. An awareness that they both understood how the night could end.

He talked about his magazines and she listened eagerly, flattered to be taken into his confidence. More cutbacks in Richardson Publications. The sales of *Hitz* had dropped. He intended on closing the magazine down. Readers claimed it had lost its hard edge since Karl Lawson left.

"Did Lawson ever thank you for the freedom campaign you ran for him?" Lar asked.

Hearing his name uttered so casually startled her. Was this a sardonic comment, she wondered, but, no, he sounded genuinely interested.

"No. I never asked for thanks," she replied. "He suffered greatly from the media coverage at the time of his niece's disappearance. It was my way of helping him get his life back together again."

She didn't want to talk about Karl Lawson yet he was there at the table, the whiff of homelessness pushing through the smell of lobster thermidor and loin of venison. They were everywhere these days. The nation's disgrace, sleeping in cardboard boxes and damp doorways. How could Karl Lawson possibly have joined their ranks?

She had seen him on the Liffey boardwalk one afternoon when she was returning from the launch of a lingerie collection. He had let his hair grow or, perhaps, just hadn't bothered having it cut, and the wavy, uncombed strands added to his unkempt appearance. His anorak and jeans were clean, and he had a backpack on the bench beside him, a rolled sleeping bag attached to it. He was watching the river as it flowed between the high, gray walls. Amanda turned before he saw her and joined the pedestrians hurrying across the Ha'penny Bridge.

"Did you believe he was guilty?" she asked Lar.

"Whether I did or not was irrelevant," he replied. "The scandal was affecting our advertising revenue."

"Innocent or guilty, it didn't matter to you?"

"Sentiment doesn't increase my bottom line."

"Why didn't you give him back his job when he was released?"

"Mud sticks. You can wash it off as often as you like but a residue remains." He handed the dessert menu back to the waiter and ordered Chocolate Heaven.

Amanda hoped it wouldn't give him indigestion. A long night lay ahead.

"A cigar would be an excellent way to end a wonderful evening," he said when he had ordered a brandy for himself and a glass of Evian water for Amanda. He smiled, deep crinkles around his eyes. How he would enjoy viewing her through a satisfying plume of smoke, Amanda thought… but times had changed, and the air between them was clear and perfect when they left the restaurant. He asked if he should call a taxi to take her home.

"That would be ideal," she replied, holding his gaze, unafraid and certain. "Or, it would be, if that's what you'd like me to do."

When the taxi arrived, he waited until she was seated inside and then joined her. The driver drove through Sandymount and Blackrock, past the lights of Dun Laoghaire Harbor and onwards to the outskirts of Rockfield, where his house stood on the summit of Bayview Heights. An avenue of cypress led to the front entrance, where the name "Shearwater" was carved in granite.

Reminders of Rosalind were everywhere. The elegant wall hangings and paintings had been chosen by her on their trips abroad, said Lar. The photographs that had charted their lives together were still on view and the library, filled with her favorite books, had the dusty stillness of a shrine. Amanda studied her portrait in the hall, the proud tilt of her head, her frozen smile.

They didn't lie on the marital bed. The guest room was bright and impersonal, no memories to distract him, no ashes. The age difference didn't matter. Lar was a robust sixty-year-old with the sexual urgency of a teenager. When Amanda used the bathroom, she saw the tablets he took. He had hidden them in a discreet drawer that also held his blood pressure and cholesterol medication. She would never reveal that she knew how his energy was fueled—or that she had found Rosalind's ashes in the master bedroom when he was downstairs in the kitchen making eggs Benedict. They were in an ornate urn, which had been, Amanda suspected, bought by Rosalind on one of their trips abroad. She touched the urn and smiled.

She had heard that his aggression was more pronounced since her death. Amanda didn't fear his aggression. It had lifted him from the floor whenever he failed, a tougher man each time. She, too, knew what it was like to fall apart and rise again. She hurried back to the spare room to await his return.

Later, he took her hand and led her out on to the balcony to admire the view. Stars splintered like cut glass on Dublin Bay and the city below them was ringed with radiance.

CHAPTER THIRTY-FOUR

Lar was wrong in believing Rosalind had given him everything he desired. He could have asked for more, but never knew he wanted it until Amanda awakened that need in him. Fatherhood at sixty. He had been thrilled. A child to carry his footprint into a new generation.

The word was out in LR1 that she had trapped him. Let them gossip by the water cooler. Amanda didn't care. No one trapped Lar Richardson. He made his own decisions. The gamble she took when she discarded her contraceptive pill had paid off and she was no longer a frivolous dalliance on his arm. She had acquired status. His child's mother. His wife. Touching her belly, tiny feet beating against his hand.

✦

Amanda wasn't too posh to push and Marcus came easily, slip-sliding into his father's waiting arms. She had never been a fan of newborn babies, always finding something vaguely repulsive about their piscine features and slitted eyes. Their thin cries reminded her of kittens scrabbling at the sack before her father drowned them in the canal. Marcus cried the same way. His mouth opened like a goldfish

kissing water. His head was scrunched and there was a purple crease, thick as a matchstick, in the center of his forehead. She thought Rebecca had lost her senses when Josh
was born, all that drooling and nonsensical cooing. She
hadn't realized love could be so savage, so dazzling.

Her arms ached to hold Marcus. She stared at him for
hours. Mesmerized. Her milk was bountiful and she gave it
willingly. Lar said she was a natural mother. That thought
would once have been alien to her but motherhood had filled
a hole within her. She had never realized it was there or that
it needed filling until Marcus curled himself effortlessly into
that waiting space.

At night, she sat by the window and watched the stars.
He tugged at her breasts, his hard, firm gums demanding
sustenance, and she found it almost impossible to believe
she would have considered aborting this tiny life if Lar had
rejected her. Motherhood had turned her on her head and she
wallowed in the joy of it.

Lar moved into the bedroom he had once shared with
Rosalind. Unlike many younger husbands, he didn't feel
threatened by Amanda's all-consuming emotion. Rebecca
was not so fortunate and claimed that her husband had complained bitterly about being left out in the cold after Josh
was born. Amanda suspected that Lar was quite relieved he
didn't have to spend his energies on a passionate wife. He
needed a peaceful night's sleep to tackle the workload that
awaited him every morning. He suggested hiring an au pair
to look after Marcus when Amanda returned to LR1. She
disagreed, vehemently. Marcus would attend a crèche. He
needed other children, not some sultry Spanish au pair who
would steal his affection with her kisses.

✦

Two months after Marcus was born, she returned to work. Older fathers was the theme of *Mandy Meets* that afternoon Three guests appeared on her panel: a retired solicitor, a jaded actor, who would never be able to retire now, and her husband. All entering fatherhood for the first time, and all in their sixties. Lots of jokes about sleep deprivation and pouches under their eyes. Marcus was the only baby who didn't cry in front of the camera. Another natural, like his mother, Lar said afterward.

Amanda thanked her fans for their cards and gifts. She had received a myriad of blue bootees and storks and teddy bears; all reminding her that she had a treasure. But there were always those who resented other people's happiness. She was used to it by now. Not everyone liked what she did on *Mandy Meets*, or what she had written when she was with *Capital Eye*.

One of the cards was black. The white cross painted in the center reminded her of a gravestone, as it was supposed to do. Lar shuddered when he saw it and handed it directly to the police. They would investigate but find nothing. Billy Shroff, of course, just reminding Amanda he was still on her case. She had always been fearless. Many had called her reckless but she had trusted her instincts as she walked that thin line between caution and audaciousness. Now that line had collapsed under the weight of a new responsibility. She rocked Marcus in her arms and knew that she would take on the world to protect her son.

CHAPTER THIRTY-FIVE

On Grafton Street Amanda Bowe carried her baby in a sling, casually, as Nicole had done when Sasha was that age. Like their children were molded from their hipbones. She was accompanied by Lar Richardson, his arm possessively across her shoulders, his eyes fixed proudly on his sleeping child. Karl hid in a doorway, ashamed to be seen. A homeless man of no fixed abode.

The slide had seemed sudden, yet really it had been a slow descent that began after his return from New York. As he had anticipated, his house was soon repossessed by the bank. He handed back the keys and rented a bedsit within walking distance to the city center. He looked for work. The woman at the recruitment agency slid her hand over his résumé and said, "False imprisonment, how unjust." Her smile was thin, her gaze wary. "What kind of job do you have in mind?"

"Anything." He was no longer interested in writing about music. Let others deconstruct, analyze, review, criticize. All he wanted to do was listen to it on his earphones and deaden the voices in his head.

"*Anything?*" She disapproved of such vagueness. She would be in touch with him if anything suitable arose.

Fionn introduced him to a solicitor who specialized in employment law. Sheila Hande agreed that Karl had a case against Richardson Publications but warned him it would take time to bring a case for unfair dismissal to the labor court. Lar Richardson would do everything in his power to delay it. A wily fox who knew how to outfox the system.

As the weeks passed, Karl realized that Lar had been right about one thing. His name was tainted, his face instantly recognizable. No smoke without fire. He knew the maxim, but had never understood its destructive nature until then. Was there anyone in the country who had not followed those seven agonizing days of searching and speculation? Constance's face on the posters, on the television, in the newspapers. People drew back a little, shifting their gaze, when they recognized him. Their tone changed, became more emphatic when they told him the job was taken. Guilt by association, a notorious crime remembered in fragments and colored by the prism of their personal recollections.

His landlady was sympathetic when she told him he had to leave the bedsit. Property prices were rising again and she had a buyer interested in the building. He tried to find another flat. A room with a door that he could close at night. But rents were increasing and the owners, after a quick glance at him, insisted the accommodation had already been let.

Even when he was sleeping in the same room with five other men, who snored, farted, snuffled and moaned their way through the night, he was still unable to accept the reality of homelessness. The hostel was a temporary arrangement. He would pull himself together and find proper accommodation.

After a few nights he stopped noticing the stench of urine from the communal bathroom. It had become absorbed into the fug of humanity hanging over the hostel. When he caught sight of himself in shop windows he was detached from his reflection. The man staring back at him could have been a stranger who bore a faint resemblance to someone he once knew.

He had started drinking after Justin and his family left for Boston. At Dublin Airport, he had watched them walking toward the departure gates. Lara's resemblance to Sasha was so striking that when she bumped into a passenger hurrying in the opposite direction and dropped her carry-on case, Karl had to stop himself from rushing forward to pick it up. Matthew was beside her instantly to check that she was okay. She nodded and held his hand as they pulled their cases behind them, their expressions too solemn for children embarking on a new future.

Justin and Jenna walked closely together. The shock of Constance's death must have changed them profoundly yet, outwardly, they looked the same, an inoffensive, suburban couple, whose lives should have had a preordained ordinariness. But they had been plucked from obscurity and into the headlines by one reckless, unforeseen act. At the departure gates Justin stopped. Karl willed him to turn around and pick his brother out from the hurrying passengers. Was it possible, even at that late moment, for blood to win out and cut through the bitterness, the misunderstandings that made forgiveness impossible? But Justin had gazed straight ahead and was soon out of sight.

Karl had taken a bus to the city and entered a sports bar where six television screens competed with each other for attention. He had watched a wrestler with blond, tumbleweed hair and distended muscles lock his arms around his opponent's neck. On another screen, he followed the flight of a golf ball. Sixteen years on the dry and the taste of his first drink was startlingly familiar, wantonly pleasurable.

The taste of coming home. He had always been reckless around alcohol. At sixteen, he had taken his first drink and was a recovering alcoholic by the time he turned twenty-one. His therapist said he had an addictive personality. Genetic, probably. His maternal grandfather had been an alcoholic, who died from liver failure. Karl would go the same way, his therapist claimed, if he didn't accept responsibility for his addiction. He had taken that warning seriously—until there was no longer any reason to give it credence.

Fear, he realized, had been the staying hand. Afraid to smoke a joint, to take a beer, to enjoy a glass of wine with a meal. Afraid that one slip would hurtle him back into the chaos of his teenage years. Now, freed from fear, he embraced chaos and found it comforting.

He sat most days on the Liffey boardwalk and thought about death, as Dominick must have done in those final weeks. He could easily acquire the tools he needed—a rope, a blade, tablets, a river—but death required energy and planning. He seemed incapable of doing anything that would stir him to action. Loss was a palsy shivering through him. It could not be endured. He took the bottle of whiskey from his backpack and drank from the neck.

Spirals of light embraced the fat-bellied girth of the city and the flow of the jade-green river called out to him, tempting him to take that step closer to the edge.

✦

He saw her again, this time on television. Not just one television but many, all of them displayed along the main aisle of a vast electrical store. Curved screens, flat screens and high definitions, her flawless image on each one. Her face looked thinner than he remembered and her lips, startlingly voluptuous, gave her mouth a generosity it once lacked. A bold red streak highlighted her black hair and her teeth had been straightened, their glossy whiteness visible when she smiled.

The studio set was garish with an artificial afternoon brightness, and the words *Mandy Meets* were illuminated on a white screen behind her. She looked relaxed on a swivel chair, long legs crossed, her skirt sitting primly above her knees. Three men sat on a sofa facing her, sheepish and besotted as they tried to control the babies on their laps. The man in the center was Lar Richardson.

The automatic doors of the electrical store slid open, as if inviting Karl to step inside.

"Can I help you, sir?" The sales assistant smiled warily as Karl moved between her replicated images.

"Just checking the televisions," Karl replied.

The sound was turned down and there was nothing to distract from her presence, her vibrant smile, her luminous eyes, so different to the hawkish gaze that had devoured him. He lifted his foot and slammed the heel of his boot into her face. The television set toppled backward. For an instant he thought it would bring down the next set, and the one after that, dominoes collapsing, as Lar Richardson had said, but it just missed the curved sixty-five-inch model behind it. The screen cracked and her face disappeared.

For an instant, the sales assistant was too shocked to move. That pause gave Karl time to escape. He ducked around a heavyset security man, who tried to grab him, and ran toward the entrance. An alarm sounded. The high-pitched clamor echoed through the store and added to the confusion. Customers and staff looked around, bewildered, as he ran past. The glass doors had parted to allow a customer to enter and she stepped hastily to one side as he came toward her. He sprinted through the open gap, aware of raised, angry voices, footsteps gaining on him.

Outside, traffic was moving slowly along the narrow exit road leading from the retail park. He darted between two cars. The driver of the first car slammed on her brakes and blasted the horn. Karl was across the road by then, sprinting between the parked cars. He reached a high wall behind an island of shrubbery, and ducked down into the bushes, his escape route cut off. Some of the shrubs were thorny, tearing against his clothes, but they grew densely together and there was space underneath to hide. He lay down on the hard earth and wriggled out of sight.

In the bushes at the bottom of his parents' garden, he and Dominick had made a den where they could hide from enemies. Pirates and bank robbers, grizzly bears, dragons, cannibals... the list was long and fearsome, and he had never forgotten the pleasure of being equally thrilled and scared. Sasha had found such a hideout in her new garden. Nicole sent him the video of her waving out at him between the leaves, her childhood replicating his own memories.

Everything gone because of Amanda Bowe. Sasha would grow up without him. Nicole would marry again. Justin, his mouth set tight, would never return to Ireland. The rank smell of dead vegetation, the scum of withered leaves on his skin, Karl bent his head to the earth, overwhelmed by self-loathing and the need for another drink. Cars roared by. People hurried along the pedestrian paths with their boxes and bags. He had planned to buy a one-man tent in the outdoor activities shop, but now all thoughts of purchasing anything that would make his life easier had disappeared. His pursuers had given up the chase but still he didn't move. A blackbird hopped across the ground, a worm dangling from its yellow beak. A glisten of slime, a frantic wriggle to be free before it was swallowed.

✦

He slept in a doorway one night, too drunk to find his way
to the hostel, and was awakened by the hot sting of urine on
his face. The men, three of them on their way home from a
nightclub, were equally drunk but, unlike Karl, they would
stagger through their own front doors, and that distinction
between them was seismic.

The following day he boarded a bus to Glenmoore and
walked from the village terminus to Cronin's orchard. The
windows in the old house had been boarded up, the entrance
closed off by a sheet of metal. The back door was still intact
but a padlock had been placed on it. Karl was able to force
one of the windows open. He could tell by the litter, the
bleached scraps of paper and rusting beer cans that no one
used the house as a refuge any longer. Perhaps those who
once came at night with their syringes and bottles were
afraid of meeting Constance's ghost.

He rolled out his sleeping bag in one of the rooms and
rummaged in his backpack for a bottle of whiskey. In the
morning he would clear away the refuse. He needed so little
to survive now and the house would provide him with shelter
until he was ready to move on again.

Constance came to him in a swirl of green when he slept.
Dancing through eternity, that was how he always saw her.
Death by misadventure had been the coroner's verdict at her
inquest. An accident with fatal consequences. Cold hard fact
explained by a pathologist and analyzed by expert witnesses.
How unsatisfying was that? But she always danced through
his dreams and it was easy to imagine her being light-footed,
wherever she was.

CHAPTER THIRTY-SIX

Amanda had intended to have a small party for Marcus's first birthday. She would invite the children from his crèche and their mothers, whom she met briefly in the mornings. All of them rushing to work and stifling their guilt because the sand of sleep was still in their children's eyes. But Lar calmly overrode her wishes and insisted on a major celebration. He reassured her she had no need to worry over catering or who to invite. Mrs. Morris, their housekeeper, would organize the catering. His publicist would oversee the guest list.

Sylvia Thornton knew the backs he needed to scratch, the hands he needed to shake, the egos he needed to flatter. She had turned Marcus's first birthday into an LR1 corporate event, yet one that was skillfully hidden behind the clamor of children as they twirled on a carousel, bounced on trampolines and were entertained by clowns, fire-eaters and magicians.

Marcus had cried when the one candle on his birthday cake was lit—he was unused to all this attention—but he recovered his good humor when Amanda carried him out to the terrace. Amanda's mother sat down heavily on a chair and fanned her face with her hand.

"It's a wonderful party." She smiled as a group of children chased after a clown on a penny-farthing bike. "Are you happy with Lar?"

Amanda kissed the top of her son's head. "Of course I'm happy. What's not to love?"

Mrs. Morris walked briskly past and spoke to one of the waiters. Giving orders, no doubt, and delighting in the authority she projected. By challenging every decision Amanda made, she refused to lay the ghost of Rosalind to rest. Like Lar, who rebuffed all Amanda's efforts to change anything in the house, she had turned Shearwater into a monument to a dead woman. But Rosalind was rattling an empty cage, and it was Amanda who held the future of Shearwater in her arms.

She watched the clown almost tumble from his penny-farthing bike and ride off in wobbly loops. Children shrieked as they jumped on the bouncy castle. On the far side of the terrace Lar was speaking to Sylvia Thornton, who worked exclusively for him and seemed to come and go from LR1 at times of her own choosing. She was always at ease with him, deferential without ever losing her own authority, and Lar, who fired people on a whim, appeared utterly reliant on her.

Amanda had learned at a young age that it was possible to compartmentalize her life. To love her father when he was in the mood to be attentive to her. To sit down to a family meal and not anticipate his sudden outbursts, the whisk of a tablecloth scattering dishes. Pigeonholes, her mind was crammed with them, and Hunter would have remained in one of them if his wife was not a constant reminder of that night on the quays, and the intimate months that followed. Her presence, however inconspicuous, always sent a shiver along Amanda's spine. Could she possibly suspect? As a publicist, she would have been trained to hold her emotions in check. A disturbing thought, but surely she would be unable to conduct herself so serenely around Amanda if she knew the truth? Her mask would slip, her nails scratch through the polite charade Amanda performed each time they met.

✦

"That went off well." Lar sat down heavily on the sofa when the guests had all left. Marcus was asleep and Mrs. Morris had gone home. "I can always rely on Sylvia to run a successful event." He patted the cushion beside him, his firm, decisive slap against the leather making it seem like a command rather than a desire to hold her close. "Come here, Mandy. You look tired."

He had abbreviated her name and, in doing so, Amanda felt less whole, somehow. She had asked him to stop but he insisted it was a term of endearment. Like the way he had always abbreviated Rosalind to Rosie when they were alone.

She stretched out on the sofa and rested her head in his lap. He glided his fingers through her hair. He told her once that Rosalind had loved having her scalp massaged at the end of a tiring day. She would then massage his shoulders and spine. What else did they do, Amanda wondered. Pick fluff from each other's belly buttons?

She wanted him to stop stroking her scalp. It was irritating enough to make her teeth ache. He talked about rankings. *Mandy Meets* was continuing to build its audience and *Behind the Crime Line* was also performing well. She was pleased for Eric. Coming from the same tabloid background, they understood the reader's need for immediacy, the power of a sensational headline, the lure of sex and crime.

Sometimes, sitting in Quix Cafè listening to him talking about gangland feuds brewing in the inner city, or the links between dissidents and criminals, Amanda would feel a nostalgic urge to leave the red carpet and return to the mean streets.

"Out of the question," Lar had said when she suggested doing an occasional report for *Behind the Crime Line.* "I don't want you receiving bullets in the post or, more importantly, in your head."

"I coped with that kind of pressure when I was with *Capital Eye*," she'd argued.

"Things are different now," he said. "You're my wife, the mother of our child. I'm not arguing with you, Mandy. Your doorstepping days are over. Don't forget what that thug threatened to do if you ever wrote about his family again."

It seemed so long ago, the anonymous calls and the hoax bomb. These days she received goodie bags instead of bullets, invitations to gala openings instead of white powder, and her phone calls, carefully vetted, were usually from some PR executive, inviting her to lunch.

Lar's breathing deepened. "That's enough shop talk for tonight," he said. "I've another more important matter on my mind."

Amanda clenched her teeth—so perfectly aligned now—as he slid her hand downwards, his desire obvious. He was close behind her as they walked up the stairs. She had a sudden yearning to make love to him against the landing wall. The two of them caught in an urgent, mindless union? But she knew, as Lar did, that such acrobatics were beyond him. She stifled a sigh as he opened the door of the bedroom where Rosalind's long shadow did not fall.

Afterward, she eased from his side and checked on Marcus. He had flung his arms above his head, his legs apart, the duvet kicked down. He stirred and murmured in his sleep. She covered his starfish body and stroked his cheek, then slipped quietly back into bed beside her husband.

CHAPTER THIRTY-SEVEN

Karl walked through Cherrywood Terrace and stopped outside the house he had once shared with Nicole. The bank had finally sold it and the new owners were in the process of gutting the interior. He tried to look through a crack in the curtains but was unable to see anything.

"Karl, is that you?" Maria Barnes shouted from her doorway.

He could ignore her, but she would probably ring the police and report a suspicious stranger loitering.

"Yes, it's me." He walked swiftly down the driveway, hoping to avoid talking to her, but she was already crossing the road.

"I'd be hard put to recognize you behind all that hair." She peered at him through the shadowy street lighting. "Where are you living now?"

"Here and there."

"That's as clear as mud," she said. "It certainly won't work as a forwarding address. Remember the letters I gave you when you got out of jail?"

He nodded.

"I missed this one. It fell behind the cupboard in the hall

but you'd disappeared by the time I noticed it. I haven't seen hide nor hair of you since."

"Dump it," he said.

Ignoring his words, Maria thrust the letter into his hand. "It belongs to you, not to me. Dumping it is your decision."

"Thanks. Anything else that comes, get rid of it."

"You're sure you're okay, Karl?"

"Yes, I'm good."

"You don't look good, not from where I'm standing," she said. "Why don't you come into the house for a bowl of soup."

"Another time. I've to meet someone and I'm already late."

"Take care of yourself, Karl."

"You too, Maria."

✦

O'Toole's pub was busy, the clamor of voices and music slamming into him. When a couple rose to leave, he slipped into their seat and took the letter from his anorak pocket. The noise and movement in the pub receded as he stared at the dusty, crumpled airmail envelope, postmarked Arizona.

Selina Lee's handwriting used to be filled with flourishes, as flamboyant as her personality, yet there was nothing familiar about this handwriting, so neat and cramped, as if the sender was afraid a stray stroke could change the meaning of a word. The suffocating sensation of being penned in by bars overwhelmed Karl. Not steel, but bars of memory pressing against his chest, making it difficult to breathe as he opened two thin sheets of airmail paper.

Dear Karl,

How to begin such a letter? The false starts. The "how are you" enquiries. I've crossed them out and

started again, only to end up with the same banal
greeting. How are you, Karl? I know you are grieving
over the passing of your lovely niece but I hope you've
moved on with your life after the appalling injustice
that was visited upon you.

When that journalist rang, I couldn't believe our
story had traveled beyond Winding Falls. I asked how
she had stumbled on it but she was not answering questions, only asking them. She wanted details. I told her
the only detail that counted was the truth. But that was
not her truth. She had found what she believed to be a
gold nugget and would not allow me to tarnish it. I was
appalled, but frightened also, by the utter certainty in
her voice. She believed I was delusional. One of those
women who fall in love with convicted murderers, lured
by the power evil attracts.

I should have hung up but I needed to convince her
she was wrong. She demanded to know why I was protecting you. How I could have been so sure you were
innocent? I told her you loved me. It seemed such an
egocentric thing to say, yet it was true until I stamped
all over your feelings.

After talking to her, I crashed. It's happened in
the past. I thought I'd moved on but when the memory of that night is thrust upon me without warning it
can trigger an attack of post-traumatic stress. I hear
his voice again, smell his breath, feel his knife on my
throat. I can't breathe and the terror is indescribable.

When I discovered you'd been arrested on suspicion
of having murdered your lovely niece, I thought I was
to blame. That I hadn't been convincing enough during
that interview. Self-blame; it's so corrosive, so weakening. I suffered a severe attack of depression and was

admitted to the hospital. I didn't contact you after I was discharged. My recovery was fragile and I wanted to build safety barriers around myself.

I'm okay now, wrung out but stronger. I've seen the freedom campaign she's organized for your release. What changed her mind? Having destroyed you, is she trying to rewrite the past? Does she not realize the past never goes away? It can swing a fist and knock us out with one blow.

My marriage is over. I've set Jago free. We married for the wrong reasons. His was guilt that I almost died on a night when he and I should have been together; would have been together if he hadn't ended our relationship that day. My reason for marrying him was security. The need to feel safe again, and Jago does have broad shoulders. But I wanted to stop being a victim living in a gated community where locks and cameras created the illusion of safety. And he deserves a real relationship, not one based on the roles we both played throughout our marriage.

I've moved to downtown Phoenix and have bought a small apartment. My address is on the business card I've enclosed, if you ever feel the need to contact me.

I hope you've survived your ordeal with the loving support of your family.

Always in my memory,
    Selina

Always in my memory...His hand shook as he finished her letter. What questions had Amanda Bowe asked? Prodding Selina with her harrying voice and refusing to listen to the answers, her mind already forming the narrative she

would create. Karl was unaware that he was crying, unaware
that his tears had soaked the thin airmail paper, unaware of
anything except the memory of the warm desert wind on his
face as he rode his Harley to the summit of Longspur Peak
and Selina was left for dead on the floor of their cabin.

He hurried from the pub and entered a late-night supermarket, brightly lit, with just a few wan-faced customers
buying wine and takeaway food. After scanning bottles of
water and some fruit through the self-service scanner, he
returned to the old house. Anger shook him like an ague
but it had a purpose that was as yet, undefined. That would
come in time and, then, he would be merciless. Already, his
body was craving a drink. Soon, he would lose this clarity,
but the sensation of being awake after a long, nightmarish
sleep filled him with a manic energy as he emptied bottles
of whiskey down the sink. He laid out the bottled water, the
bananas, the juicy satsumas and purple grapes. He rolled out
his sleeping bag and zipped himself into it.

✦

Time passed. He had no sense of its rhythm— an hour, an
afternoon, a night. The room remained dark, only shards
of light penetrating the boards across the window. As his
withdrawal symptoms increased, he saw spiders the size
of his fist scurrying down the walls to crawl over him. He
screamed, whimpered, sweated. Beat at them with his fists
as they swarmed across his skin. In lucid moments he drank
water and shuddered as it settled uneasily on his stomach.
He peeled bananas and sucked feverishly on satsumas. The
fruit was easy to peel, yet his hands shook so much that even
this simple act felt as if he was moving through viscous mud.

This was nothing compared to the last time he had been
weaned slowly and with care in rehab. This was cold turkey

at its rawest. Constance floated across the room in a luminous swerve. Always the same image, whether he was drunk
or sober. Had she come to say goodbye to him or take him
with her into the shade? She was dancing, spinning in a
green pool of sunshine, dazzling him with her brilliance.

She came again. This time she touched him, her hand
cool on his forehead. She spoke but he was unable to hold on
to her words. When she vanished, he thought he had imagined her but knew, also, that she would return. There was
something more substantial about this apparition. Something that was not Constance. A more earthed presence yet
leaf-like, drifting past him in flashbacks that made no sense,
or coming upon him for brief instances that settled his dizzying surroundings to rights.

Once, he imagined she was speaking to him. He was
drinking something that made him shudder. Grass? Liquid
grass? How could he drink grass? He used to smoke it with
Dominick down by the river in the marsh. Justin found them
once and punched Karl so hard he was knocked backward
into the water. Solid, reliable Justin, who did everything by
the book and was rewarded for his efforts with a broken heart.

"Drink this." The voice came to him faintly, yet, insis-
tently. It penetrated the fug in his brain. A figure moved,
ephemeral, a presence that would vanish if he uttered a
wrong word or made a hasty movement.

"I know it tastes vile," she said. "But it will help you
recover."

He swallowed, obediently. A wraith, but not Constance.
Not Nicole, either. Nicole was refusing to take his calls.
Too upsetting for Sasha, she'd insisted the last time he rang,
alarmed by his aggressive demands. She sent him videos
from her phone. Sasha playing with the garden hose, waving
from a carousel and from the treehouse her stepfather had

made for her. Snippets from a life that was slowly stealing
the memory of her father from her.

He had let everything go, a quick sliding that made him
wonder if it was his own will, rather than outside forces, that
had collapsed his life. Had he wanted his marriage to end,
to lose his daughter, his house to be repossessed? That he
could even construct such a thought appalled him yet, like the
edge of a broken tooth, he was unable to leave it alone. Had
he sought out this punishment as an atonement for the loss of
Constance? I should have fought to the death to keep what was
precious to me, he thought, as the longing for another drink
watered his mouth, broke sweat on his forehead. He was going
to throw up again and this apparition, as if anticipating the
spewing, held a basin under his chin. Why didn't she go away?
Even if she was an illusion, he didn't want her witnessing his
humiliation, or his tears, which she wiped with a damp cloth.
Then she was gone, closing the door behind her, the bloated
wood scraping against the floor, a juddering, familiar sound
that, surely, could not be imagined.

He sank back against a pillow that had been placed under
his head. This time there were no spiders, no nightmares,
just a depthless sleep.

Slivers of light had forced their way through the boards
when he awoke. Sandwiches wrapped in cellophane and a flask
of soup had been left beside his sleeping bag. Soup, steamy
and hot, the smell of beef reminding him of Sunday dinners
his mother used to make. He tried to gather his thoughts as
he poured the soup into the beaker and raised it to his lips.
His hands shook. Hot soup dribbled down his chin but he was
hardly aware of anything except the need to nourish his body.

She had left two supermarket shopping bags propped
against the wall. He slathered butter on bread rolls, filled
them with cheese and ham. This was real. He was filling his

stomach with food he didn't buy. She must exist. A guardian angel, not a wraith, but a flesh and blood angel, who did supermarket shopping and did not step back from the ugliness of vomit when it stained her clothes, or turn her head away when he cried.

He put on fresh clothes, brushed his hair and tied it back in a ponytail. He made his way to the portable toilet he had purchased soon after he moved into the house. The light hurt his eyes and he staggered, an invalid finding his feet after a long illness. Golden sun, not green, as he had imagined. Fighting the temptation to return to the house and cocoon himself in his sleeping bag, he approached the water barrel. The water was icy cold, silvery droplets splattering as he washed his face. The chatter of starlings drowned all other sounds but activity, inaudible yet pulsing, was all around him.

The dilapidation of his surroundings bore down on him. He walked through the rooms, noting the mold on the walls, the rotting floorboards and cracked ceiling. He emptied out his tent and washed out his sleeping bag, spread it over a bush to dry.

She came as darkness was falling. This time she knocked on the door, a visitor calling and waiting to be admitted. The door snagged as he pulled it open and he saw her properly for the first time. Pale skin, a splash of freckles on her cheeks, blond hair drawn back from her forehead.

"I'm glad to see you on your feet again," Sylvia Thornton said as she lowered another supermarket bag to the floor and sat down on one of the camping chairs, seemingly unconcerned by the squalor surrounding her. "You've been on quite a journey."

"I appreciate your help but I'm ashamed you had to witness…" He paused, his face taut with embarrassment. He must have held her hand, gripped it tight in case he drowned.

Had he raved at her, spilled out his self-loathing, his fury? Had she been repelled by him? The ugliness of what he remembered shamed him but, even worse and more painful, was what he couldn't remember. "How did you know I was here?"

"I followed you from the supermarket," she said. "I knew something was wrong but I was afraid to intrude. Next day in work I kept thinking about you. I became convinced you were going to harm yourself, or worse. You were in the middle of a delirium when I came here. I tried to help as best I could."

"I'm so ashamed you had to see—"

"Whatever you feel, it should not be shame." She stood abruptly and walked to the boarded-up window. "Tomorrow morning, you must let some light in here."

"I intend to."

"You called me Constance," she said. "You asked her to keep dancing, and for her forgiveness. Why her forgiveness, Karl? Is that what all this is about?" She gestured at the decaying room.

"She's dead because I didn't allow her parents to take care of her...and that night she disappeared..." He swallowed, his mouth dry. The need for a drink sickened him. He had known the urge would still be there but had forgotten its ferocity. "She would have told me what was bothering her but I was asleep when she came and that changed everything."

"Perhaps Constance is asking you to forgive yourself so that she can dance forever without being burdened by your guilt," Sylvia said.

The image she conjured was comforting. Constance in a swirl of green, dancing through eternity.

"So many people were affected by her death." She spoke with her back to him. "My husband is Detective Garda Hunter."

"Ah." The name sent a shockwave through him.

"Jon was doing his job," she continued. "But, sometimes, terrible mistakes happen."

He was doing more than his job. Karl bit down on the words. What good would it do to vent his bitterness on her? Did she know the truth about her husband? His unholy alliance with Amanda Bowe? Impossible to tell from her tone. A woman who knew how to keep secrets. Otherwise, she would not be working so closely with Lar Richardson.

"Is that why you're here?" he asked.

She shook her head and faced him again. "I'm here because I care what happens to you. Not as some kind of recompense for Jon's decisions. You need to get out of here and bring some normality back to your life."

"How would you define normality?"

"Not this." She picked up an empty whiskey bottle that had rolled under a camping chair. "Staying here is not the solution but you know that already. Otherwise, you would not be sober."

She left soon afterward, hurrying home to a fickle husband and children who would still be awake, waiting for her to hold them and say goodnight.

The air in the room was stuffy, the silence even more unbearable. He pushed open the back door and walked under the trees until he came to the clearing of rubble. Weeds and patchy grass marked the water tank. He collapsed to his knees beside it. He had no idea if he was praying. The words he uttered did not belong to any childhood prayer he had learned by rote but they had a rhythm that consoled him. And when Constance came to him, a fleeting vision that could have been the drift of moonlight or something more ethereal, he held on to the peace that followed. Maybe, in time, normality would come but, for now, he would stay in the shade of her passing.

CHAPTER THIRTY-EIGHT

Amanda seemed destined to live her life on a tightrope. No wobbles allowed. No safety net. Meeting Hunter with his wife was bound to happen sooner or later. She had braced herself for such an encounter—but when she saw him as she was about to enter The Amber Door for Sunday lunch, she stumbled on the steps of the restaurant and would have fallen except for Lar's firm grip on her arm.

Hunter's daughter was perched like a trophy on his shoulders. His two boys ran before him and Sylvia, cool in a white linen dress and a wide-brimmed sun hat, strolled at his side. They looked like an idealized family in an advertising campaign for happy living. Lar, recognizing Sylvia, shouted her name and waved. He hugged her so enthusiastically he knocked her sunglasses sideways. She laughed as she adjusted them and called on the boys, who were flushed and disheveled from playing in St. Stephen's Green, to wait.

Hunter's neck looked broader than Amanda remembered. Soon, he would have jowls. Too much junk food and sitting in cars waiting for someone to make a wrong move.

"My husband, Jonathan Hunter," Sylvia introduced him, then added that everyone called him Jon.

His dumbstruck expression reminded Amanda of a rabbit caught in headlights. When Lar heard they were on their way to McDonald's, he insisted on inviting them to lunch in The Amber Door instead. He strode purposefully ahead into the restaurant and spoke to the maître d', who whisked away a reserved sign from a circular table with space for eight. Marcus's cheeks flushed with excitement when he was seated next to the little girl. Ella, slight and fey, blond hair flying each time she swung her head, was determined to bedazzle him.

The adults talked about holidays, weird and horrendous experiences they'd had in other countries. Amanda called him "Hunter" once and slid her tongue over her teeth. No one seemed to notice except him, but his glacial stare warned her to be careful. The boys kicked their heels, bored with the slow service and food that came on plates instead of cardboard cartons labeled Happy Meal.

They spoke briefly when Lar and Sylvia brought the children to the dessert trolley to view the array of cakes and puddings on display.

"How are you, Amanda?" Hunter shifted in his seat, pulled himself into a more upright position.

"As you can see, I'm very well."

"Nice kid, Marcus. Well-mannered, unlike my mob."

"Yes. He's wonderful. Children keep a marriage together. I can understand why you never wanted to leave Mrs. Dumpy."

"Stop it." He grabbed her wrist under the table, a vise-like grip, and she winced, wondering how this man had once moved her to passion. She wished he was someone's else's shame, someone else's story.

"Stop what? I'm merely passing an observation. And issuing an apology for assuming it would have been easy for you to walk away from your marriage."

A waiter handed the dessert menus to them

"Lar always chooses Chocolate Heaven," Amanda said. "He says it's aptly named."

"Not for me. I've to watch the calories these days."

"I noticed."

"There's nothing much escapes you, Amanda. Just don't fuck up my marriage, okay?" He exhaled heavily as Marcus ran toward them, followed by Ella, who demanded triple dollops of ice cream.

"Me too, me too," shouted Marcus and the boys, livening up, demanded chocolate brownies.

Sylvia checked her phone. A message had arrived. She must answer it immediately. As she hurried toward the entrance, she tilted her hat over her forehead to shield her face from the sun.

CHAPTER THIRTY-NINE

"Karl Lawson," said Eric. "I don't suppose you've any idea where I can find him?" He had joined Amanda in Quix Cafè for a coffee after *Mandy Meets*, and, as always, she was disconcerted by the unexpected mention of Karl's name.

"Whatever for?" she asked. "Surely he's yesterday's news."

"He was in Danevale Prison with Killer Shroff," said Eric. "I heard they had a fight. Both were in a bad way afterward. That must have been a first for Killer. Very few men would have the nerve to take that thug on. I'd like to find out how Lawson mixed in with the hard men and survived. But I haven't been able to trace him."

"What makes you think I'd know where he is?"

"You ran his campaign. I thought he might have kept in touch with you."

"He didn't."

"What's wrong?" Eric's glance was perceptive. "Don't you think interviewing him is a good idea? You were fascinated by him at the time."

"Everyone in the media was."

"Not everyone," he said. "Some reporters had a different view."

"I don't remember anyone holding back, especially you."

"But I never got the scoops," he said and leaned closer. "I was always curious about your source. I don't suppose you'd care to whisper his name in my ear?"

"I could, but I'd have to kill you afterward."

"Ruthless as ever." He laughed and ran his finger along her arm. Danger signals that had sneaked up on her and were becoming increasingly difficult to ignore.

He returned to his office to finish a report that was going out that evening on Killer Shroff's release from Danevale.

"Stick to the facts," Amanda advised him before he left. "And don't mention wedding dresses."

She had broken the story of Killer's arrest when she was with *Capital Eye*. Surfboards, she remembered, crammed with cocaine, discovered because of a glitch in the import documentation. Thanks to Hunter she had had the story before anyone else. Now Killer and the forger of the documents had been released from jail on a legal technicality.

"A successful appeal," Killer's barrister had claimed on the steps of the criminal courts, but Eric called it, "An almighty cock-up."

She collected Marcus from his crèche and strapped him into his car seat. He was full of chatter as she drove home but she answered him absentmindedly, her thoughts returning to Eric and then, unpleasantly, to Karl Lawson, who refused all her efforts to pigeonhole him. Was he still homeless? She watched out for him every time she walked the Liffey boardwalk but, apart from that initial sighting, she had never seen him again. Over dinner one evening, Lar had mentioned an unfair dismissal case Karl's solicitor had brought against Richardson Publications. An outrageous claim, Lar insisted, and bothersome, which was why he finally agreed to settle it.

She watched *Behind the Crime Line* when it aired at

nine-thirty. Nothing earth-shatteringly new on the Shroffs, she thought, just the usual regurgitation of established facts about the family and their notorious activities. Afterward, she watched a books program and spoke on the phone to Lar, who was entertaining potential investors in the Shelbourne Hotel. He would be late home and would sleep in the master bedroom.

"See you in the morning, then." Amanda kept her tone neutral. Lar had an uncanny knack, even over the phone, of picking up on her responses, so she masked her relief carefully as they said goodbye.

Old hound dog, young bitch, a dangerous combination, he had said when Amanda told him she was pregnant with Marcus. If they married, her fidelity must be absolute. Her husband was calculating and ruthless in business but when it came to sexual mores, he had a Calvinistic morality that was intolerant of transgressions. She asked him once if he had ever been unfaithful to Rosalind.

"Not once," he'd replied, emphatically. "Nor was I ever tempted to dishonor the marriage vows we took."

"And Rosalind?"

"Of course she was faithful to me." He stared at her over his reading glasses. "Why would you even ask such a question?"

It was idle curiosity on her part and his anger had startled her. "It happens in marriage—"

"Not in mine," he stated, flatly. "Not then, not now. Infidelity is something I'd never tolerate."

His threats should not frighten her. But they did. To lose custody of Marcus…the idea was unendurable. Like Caesar's wife, Amanda must be above suspicion and, so, she ignored the prickling rush of pleasure on her skin when she was with Eric and their knees brushed under the table in Quix

Café, or their elbows touched accidentally— deliberately? She could no longer tell or pretend to be unaware of the tantalizing but unspoken question hanging between them.

The book being reviewed was the latest thriller by Jackson Barr. Amanda turned up the sound. Her producer had tried unsuccessfully to persuade the crime writer to appear on *Mandy Meets*. His refusal wasn't personal, his publicist apologized. The author was a recluse, who shunned the media yet, somehow, managed to produce two best-selling crime novels every year. He had moved to Ireland after three decades with the New York Police Department and lived in isolation on the summit of Howth Head. His new book received a scathing review on the show but that wouldn't make a whit of difference, Amanda thought, as she switched off the television. It was already number one on the best-seller list.

She lay in bed and thought about Eric. Such fantasies were dangerous, yet she closed her eyes and imagined them disheveled on the floor, against a wall, on the kitchen table…in a field of red poppies—anywhere but in the second-best bedroom with the curtains dutifully drawn and Lar's labored breathing in her ears. The risks with Eric were too high; but this decision only strengthened that clamping excitement, the careless rapture that could be satisfied so easily until it was forbidden. Then it became a thorn that must only be lanced in secret. And indulged in the dusk of her imagination.

CHAPTER FORTY

"What do you expect me to do?" Karl had asked Lar Richardson when he was trying to pick up the pieces of his shattered life. "Assume a new identity?"

"Assuming a new identity would be the perfect solution," Lar had replied. "However, in the real world, perfect solutions seldom present themselves."

As it turned out, Lar was wrong. But it was a drug addict, hardly out of his teens, well-spoken and dangerous with the strength of desperation, who attacked Karl on Temple Bar and made this transition possible.

His attacker came from behind and struck with such ferocity that Karl had no time to react before he was dragged into the shell of a derelict site and forced against a wall.

"Drop the bag or I'll slice your fucking face in two," he yelled and slammed his arm against Karl's neck, pressed the tip of a knife to his cheek.

It would have been easy to hand over his backpack. Most of the contents were replaceable. The drop-in shelters would provide him with the necessities he needed for life on the street. But the drawings in his journal were irreplaceable. His attacker would fling them away without a second thought, interested only in Karl's phone or money.

"Drop your bag immediately," the youth repeated.

The knife cut into Karl's face. Blood trickled down his cheek in a hot, ticklish flow. Outside this derelict building, traffic flowed by, and pedestrians hurrying along the pavement, averted their faces. Two thugs fighting: best avoided. He heard a woman talking, a busker singing, laughter. Could they be the last sounds he would ever hear? A tree had rooted in the cracks on the wall, its branches waving like a benedictory hand above victim and attacker. Death was coming, spitting saliva into his face, bad teeth and fetid breath, yet Karl refused to give in. Recovering his wits, he slammed his knee into his attacker's groin with such force that the youth's legs jack-knifed and he collapsed, his knife clattering on the cement floor

Karl staggered through Crown Alley and across the Ha'penny Bridge. On the boardwalk, he slumped on to a bench, the pain in his face taking over. The cut was deep, blood running over his throat, staining his anorak. He pulled tissues from his backpack, frightened by the loss of blood, and tried to stem the flow. His legs buckled when he swung his backpack on to his back but he managed to make his way to the Mater Hospital. The doctor in the emergency department had seen too much to even pretend sympathy. "Count yourself lucky," he said as he stitched the wound. "Much closer and it could have been your eye that was taken out. There'll be a scar but you're strong enough to survive it. There's always plastic surgery to be considered. Just watch your back in the future."

He left the hospital and entered a pharmacy where he bought painkillers. People passing by gave him a wide berth when they noticed his bloodstained anorak, the dressing on his face. He turned down a side street, his stomach churning. Nausea bent him double and he vomited against the wall. A couple hurried past, the woman uttering little shrieks of disgust. He wiped his mouth with his sleeve and sank to his hunkers, his hands hanging limply between his knees. Finally, he found the strength to rise to his feet and make his way to the Glenmoore bus stop.

"Hey, man!" a voice shouted. "Hang on there a sec." Gabby Morgan, dressed in jeans and a brown donkey jacket, hurried to catch up with him. He stared astonished at Karl and said, "Jaysus, man, ya look like someone took a scimitar to yer face."

"Near enough." Hard to smile when one half of his bottom lip refused to move. "When did you get out of prison?"

"We won an appeal. Some aggro over the book a' evidence and I was out on me arse before I knew wha' end of me were up. Me and that effer, Killer." He surveyed Karl, his eyes narrowing. "I heard ya was livin' rough. Where're ya hangin out?"

"I found a squat."

Gabby grabbed his arm and pulled him close. "Ger yerself a proper roof, man. The street's no place for the likes a' you."

"It's no place for anyone."

"There's some can hack it. Others end up bleedin' dead in a doorway. Is that wha' ya want?"

"I don't know what I want any more, Gabby."

"Make up yer mind fast. I can see yer bleedin' ribs from here. There's me address." He fished in the pocket of his donkey jacket and handed Karl a business card with *Morgan Engravings* printed on the front. "I'd ask ya to stay in me gaff, only there isn't room to swing a cat since me ma took her stroke. But yer more an' welcome to call round for a bite anytime, mate."

"Thanks, Gabby."

"See ya then."

The pain in his face was intense, his lip throbbing, when Karl reached the old house. Why had the stealing of his backpack mattered so much when he had lost everything else that was precious to him? Was it because he had a choice? A choice to fight to his death on that derelict site rather than give up his last possession. He pulled out his journal and studied the drawings that had made prison endurable. He had given the creatures a name. Plinks. Sasha's word for pink when she was learning to talk, demanding her plink T-shirt, her plink sandals, a plink cupcake.

✦

The floor of the old house was covered with drawings of the plinks. Responding to years of being trapped in his imagination, they ran, leaped, climbed, swam and flew across the paper. Their colors changed depending on his mood, sometimes primary, sometimes pastel.

They developed characteristics and first names: Super, Bravo, Plucky, Hero, Derring-Do, Ace and Gutsy.

As he had expected, the wound healed but left an angry red scar running down his cheek to his lips. His bottom lip sagged and pulled his mouth to one side. He touched his good cheek. He felt insubstantial, as if the slightest breath of wind would blow him away and leave a stranger in his place.

He cut his hair, shaved the sides and spiked the top, dyed it black. The difference was startling; his eyes seemed greener, his skin tone paler. He bought a pair of glasses, plain lenses with a blue tint and square black frames. A style had evolved from his haphazard searching in charity shops. Eclectic, mismatching pieces he would never have worn in the past. When does an idea become a plan, he wondered; a plan turn to action and gain an irreversible thrust? Like a snake, he was shedding his old skin, and feeling lighter with each sloughing.

✦

Sheila Hande rang. Finally, his claim for unfair dismissal from Richardson Publications had been settled out of court.

"I fought as hard as I could to persuade Lar Richardson to increase the amount," Sheila said. "That's his limit, I'm afraid. If we go to court, a judge will award a higher settlement. I've no idea how long that will take. This way, the money is yours as soon as you sign the settlement form. Do you need it now or can you afford to wait?" They both knew this was a rhetorical question.

He signed the form and demanded the settlement in cash. When this arrived at Sheila's office, he transferred it to the post office box he had been using since he became homeless. His mind was clear at last. No more muddied incomprehension, self-loathing, self-destructive urges. No more yearning for everything he had lost. The present was all that mattered.

Documentation would be necessary to make a fresh start: a bank account, utility bills, a passport, a PPS number. A month later, when Gabby Morgan passed over the forged documents, the last remnants of the snakeskin lay withered on the floor of the old house.

He rented an apartment. It had been built during the property boom and the wooden frontage was already discolored and rotting. He had thought it would be difficult to live among people again, but he soon realized that this anonymous complex was as lonely as a prison cell.

For months he worked tirelessly on his laptop, experimenting, improvising, researching the tools he would need to move forward. His fingers flew rapidly over the keyboard as he prepared for the tempest that was to come.

CHAPTER FORTY-ONE

The buskers were out in force on Saturday morning, musicians, acrobats and pavement artists. Marcus was fascinated by the living statues, who winked their eyes or moved their little fingers in acknowledgment when he dropped coins into their buckets. He was two years of age and Amanda had brought him into the city to have his feet measured for new shoes. Afterward, they would have lunch in the Children's Cave.

At the top of Grafton Street, a group of children had gathered around a pavement artist. Unlike the other artists, he was not drawing saints and angels in gaudy hues, and children pulled at their parents' hands, demanding that they stop to look at his work. Marcus hunkered down to his level and stared at the colorful, pig-like creatures. Upright and balanced on two sturdy trotters, they appeared to move across the pavement, their velvety pelts gleaming in a myriad of hues. Each creature wore or carried an item that defined their activities: mountain boots, goggles, trainers, a propeller, tap shoes, a kayak and a skateboard.

The artist leaned forward and began to draw again. A few more strokes and another squat little creature appeared. This one was swimming and the children jerked back, as if they

expected the waves the artist was drawing to splash over
their feet. Amanda understood their reaction. These were
static figures yet, somehow, it seemed as if the pavement was
swirling with dizzying, three-dimensional effects.

Marcus went down on all fours and crawled closer to the
drawings.

"What are they?" Amanda asked.

"Plinks," the artist replied.

"What are plinks?" She liked the name, succinct and
easy for children to remember.

"Adventurers. Rescuers. Explorers." He held up a chalked
thumb in thanks as a little girl giggled and threw coins into
his basket. "Warriors of retribution."

Dressed in bright red trousers and neon braces studded
with flashing lights, he looked almost as surreal as his characters. His purple T-shirt had a plink printed on the front
and his floppy hat, a paper flower stuck in the brim, was
hand-painted with similar images. His fun appearance was
offset by an angry red scar puckering his cheek. It looked as
if a knife had swerved downwards from below his left eye
and slashed through his lips, distorting his mouth. The children were so mesmerized by his drawings and odd, colorful
clothes that they didn't seem to notice his face—or, if they
did, they weren't bothered by it.

She asked how the plinks originated. They had evolved
from a doodle, he said, which sounded intriguing, yet he
made no further effort to elaborate.

"Have you written stories for them?" Amanda could visu-
alize them in a book, the captivating illustrations enhanced
by simple words.

"Why should they need stories?" He waved his hand at
the drawings. "A picture is worth a thousand words and the
pavement is all I need for a canvas."

"And a shower of rain will wash all your hard work away." She imagined the illustrations blurring, rivulets of color running into the gutter. "You could do so much more with them."

"You don't think this is enough?" He sat back on his heels and tapped the creatures with his chalk. She heard a twang of New York in his accent, too faint to be authentic. He was probably a returned emigrant, down on his luck. His glasses were square and blue-tinted, so it was impossible to see his eyes. Disconcerting. She was unable to tell if he was looking at her or at the children.

"Of course it is," she replied. "But if you want my advice, and I've some experience in this area, you should get off your knees and bring them to the next stage." She smiled encouragingly at him, then looked away in case he thought she was staring at his scar. A smaller scar ran at an angle from the main one and created a pronged pucker above his upper lip. A street fight, probably, and vicious.

"Actually, I am working on something." He rummaged in his backpack and tore a sheet of paper from a sketch pad. The creature he drew on it was similar to the ones on the pavement but the face that emerged belonged to Marcus, his cropped black hair, his rosebud mouth, his cheeks still baby-plump.

Marcus told him his name and he wrote *To Marcus from Ben Carroll* below the drawing. "I'll send you a copy of my book when it's done." This time Amanda knew he was staring directly at her. "You'll have to tell me your name and where you live."

She gave him her business card. He glanced at it but it was obvious her name meant nothing to him. That didn't surprise her. She figured he passed celebrity culture by without a glance. She dropped a ten-euro note into his basket.

The ugly scar furrowed his cheek when he forced his lips into a contorted smile and gave her a thumbs-up.

✦

The Plinks Say Hi was delivered to Amanda's desk two months later. She smiled as she read the attached note.

> *Dear Amanda,*
>   *You asked me to do something meaningful with the plinks and this is my first attempt. Please give* The Plinks Say Hi *to Marcus with my regards.*
>   *Ben Carroll*

She was surprised by the quality of his book. The pages were thick and easy for small hands to turn. Each plink had an individual color and their pelts had a tactile feel; grainy, fluffy, coarse, smooth and velvety fabrics for children to stroke. Their eyes shone, their trotters moved. They spoke their names when their mouths were pressed and, amazingly, scratching their snouts released different smells: chocolate, gingerbread, oranges, freshly baked brownies. Technically, this was an amazing achievement. Obviously Ben Carroll, who had dedicated the book to her, was more than just a street artist. She smiled when she read his dedication. *To Amanda Bowe. Thank you for rising me to my feet.*

She was still examining the book when Eric entered her office. She showed him the dedication and how the pages worked. He flicked through them dismissively. A kids' book, who cared? How she had changed. Before Marcus was born, she would have dropped this book into the litter bin without even opening it.

"Tonight?" Eric asked softy before he left her office. "Is everything okay?"

She nodded and avoided looking at him. Discretion, even when they were alone, was essential. This building had ears and eyes, and gossip was stirred daily in its cauldron. The boss's wife and the crime correspondent—what would they make of that?

✦

The earth does move. This was not a cliché, nor an illusion. It shook to its foundations on the night she drove to Eric's apartment, then steadied slowly in the drowsy aftermath. Dawn was framing the new day in a soft-focus lens when she drove back to her dream home.

Shearwater had never seemed so vast, so empty. Lar was abroad and Marcus was on a sleepover with Josh. Her footsteps echoed in the long hall where Rosalind's portrait hung in proprietorial arrogance. She sank to the floor in her bedroom, her body in spasm as she recalled the slow probe of Eric's tongue as he explored her curves and musky hollows, and how, after they had rested for a short while, they made love again with that same frantic elation. She was undone by desire, dangerously defenseless as she resisted the urge to ring him, just to hear him breathing.

Until that final moment, she had convinced herself they were meeting at his apartment to discuss the sources she used during her time with *Capital Eye*. Contacts that would help Eric do a *Behind the Crime Line* investigation into the drug empire the Shroffs controlled. But that flimsy excuse was soon seen for what it was and, after that first night, there was no going back.

They stole their hours with care. She lay awake at night, coiled away from Lar, afraid to move in case he would stir and fumble toward her in sleep. What was once endurable had become repugnant to her. Did he have any idea where she fixed her mind as he pummeled her body with his chemically fueled desire? He would fall asleep immediately afterward but, even then, there was something watchful about him, as if he was determined to penetrate not just her body but the desire that drove her at every opportunity into her lover's arms.

She could leave him. She thought about it as she lay restlessly in their "second-best" bedroom. She had despised Imelda for not leaving her husband, unable, as a teenager, to appreciate her mother's helplessness, her dependence on the meager allowance he gave her every week. Never enough to manage, yet he refused to allow her to work outside their home. So she stayed and scrimped enough money to educate her two daughters. To make them strong and independent. Maternal love, that's what it was called. Amanda had to wait until Marcus was born to understand its brutal power.

CHAPTER FORTY-TWO

Karl entered Quix Cafè and sat down at an empty table. Staff from the television studio and Richardson Publications came and went. He recognized some of them from his days with *Hitz* but they passed him by without a second glance. He had learned to blend against walls, eyes down, shoulders stooped. The atmosphere was relaxed as they talked shop, ate wraps and checked their mobiles. He sensed a subtle shift in the atmosphere when Amanda Bowe entered and sat at a table near him. No one stopped to speak to her but she seemed unconcerned by her isolation as she messaged on her phone.

Grafton Street had proved to be the perfect canvas to test the plinks. Children had gathered around him, as he had hoped they would, shy and curious to see what he would draw next. Meeting her on that Saturday afternoon had been fortuitous but unplanned. The odds that she would walk past were too slim to consider and Karl had intended contacting her only when he published his first book. But there, in the throng, the boy had hunkered down to examine his drawings and Karl, looking up, had seen her standing protectively over her son.

He watched as Eric Walker entered the cafè and joined her. They spoke briefly before he left. Only a few words were exchanged, yet Karl was so attuned to Amanda Bowe that he instantly understood the stealth of their body language.

She was leaving the cafè when he called her name.

"My goodness! Ben Carroll." She stopped, surprised. "What are you doing here?"

"I was hoping to have a word with you," he said. "Have you time for coffee?"

"I've to collect Marcus..." She glanced at her watch, then sat down opposite him. "I've a few minutes to spare. Black coffee, no sugar."

"A muffin?"

"No, thank you." She made a slight moue of distaste.

She was slim and fit, with a thinness that suggested gym-workouts and rigorous dieting; yet on television she always looked the perfect weight.

"I wanted to send you a thank-you card for your book but I'd no address," she said when he returned with two mugs of coffee. "Marcus adores it. He came home from crèche the other day with a plink drawing. It was a scribble, I'm afraid, but he insisted it was Super Plink. All the children had drawn their favorite plinks, so your characters are becoming very popular."

"Sales are excellent," he replied. "I've just published a second book." He drew a book from his backpack and handed it to her. "I hope Marcus enjoys this one as much."

"I know he will." She picked up her coffee, then set it down again untouched. "What can I do for you, Ben?"

"I'd like to put the plinks on television," he said. "I've written a pitch for Kathy Birch but I'm not sure if she's the right producer to approach."

"She's in charge of children's programming so, yes, you need to contact her."

Her eyebrows rose, thick, dark and perfectly sculpted. "From the pavement to television is an ambitious leap."

"Think of the Teletubbies, how successful they are," he argued. "Handled properly, the plinks could be equally popular. Would you consider reading my pitch before I submit it to her?"

"Of course."

He removed a sheet of paper from his backpack and handed it to her.

"Intriguing," she said when she'd finished reading it. "I like the idea of Plinkertown Hall and all those magical rooms. Also, it's aimed at the right age profile. Marcus would love it. You mention a narrator who will tell the stories and draw the pictures. Who will that be?"

"Me," he replied.

Her eyelids flickered when he tried to smile and he knew she was repelled by his mouth.

"Really?" She leaned across the table and lightly touched his scar. "Don't you think that this could be difficult for young viewers?"

The intimacy of her action startled him. How could she not feel his hatred, sense it by osmosis? He sat motionless before her, the lights in the café glinting off his dark-blue glasses. She blushed, as if aware that she had stepped over an invisible line, but her gaze never wavered as she waited for his reply.

"I would appear in the persona of Super Plink." He pointed to one of the characters on the front of the book. "My scar wouldn't be visible."

"That could work," she agreed. "The drawings are amazing and you have an attractive voice, very compelling. Where are you from?"

"Dublin. But I lived abroad for years, mainly in New York."

"I figured that from your accent. I love New York. Such a vibrant city. What did you do there?"

"Tossed burgers."

"Oh?"

"Things didn't work out as planned."

"How come?"

"The usual story."

"As in . . . *drugs*?" She hazarded a guess, her gaze shrewd as she studied him.

"Some drugs but my problem was drink," he replied. "I'm a recovering alcoholic."

"That must be tough?"

"Not as long as I stay sober." Laughter chafed his throat. He patted his new book. "You're right about the jump. It's ambitious but I'm convinced the plinks can take off if they get the right exposure, which is what I hope will happen on LR1."

"Leave it with me." She checked her watch again and stood. "I'd better rush or I'll be late for Marcus. Thanks for the coffee."

"I owed you one for the free advice."

"Which was?"

"To get off my knees and do something significant with my life."

"Sounds brutal." She laughed abruptly. "But I'm glad you took it. Kathy Birch will be in touch soon."

"What makes you so sure?"

She laughed and tossed a red streak of hair back from her forehead. "I'm Amanda Bowe, that's why."

He watched her go. That confident stride, almost a strut. A person of consequence who knew how to get things done. Her hard, brown gaze had once rested on his world and shattered it. Now, when she looked at him, all she saw was a person she had helped to rise from his knees.

CHAPTER FORTY-THREE

Amanda's gut instinct about the characters had been right and the plinks struck an immediate chord with LR1's young viewers. Ben Carroll had transferred the magic of his pavement artistry to the small screen and held his audience spellbound.

He worked in collaboration with Kathy Birch to create the Plinkertown Hall set. The format he devised was simple. Dressed as Super Plink, he set his stories in the rooms of Plinkertown Hall and illustrated each scene with his fast, mesmerizing sketches. He had designed his own costume. Lightweight fabric, supple and breathable, it gave the impression he was covered in a tawny pelt that glistened under the studio lights. Kathy was delighted with the feedback from parents, and the fact that teachers were using the program as an aid in their art classes.

Amanda watched, amused, as Marcus's fascination with the plinks grew. His attachment to Ben, who drove a colorful plink van and always came to the studio in costume, was touching. He never addressed him as Ben and seemed unaware, or uncaring, that the Super Plink character was a real person.

As the months passed, and Ben's third book was launched at an open-air event in Temple Bar, crammed with Super Plink fans, Amanda's interest in the plink concept widened. She envisaged plink dolls, chairs, jigsaws, musical instruments, water bottles, schoolbags, pencil cases, mugs, lampshades, plink images printed on clothes and shoes, on curtains and duvets. The merchandising potential was staggering. Lar's eyes lit up as she outlined her proposal to him. Like her, he was envisaging the aisles of toyshops lined with plinks, their accessories packaged in plastic. They could reproduce Plinkertown Hall, its furnishings and the plink dolls by Christmas.

Ben Carroll was the only problem. Amanda heard panic in his voice when she rang to discuss her ideas. He refused to attend a meeting with Lar in LR1's boardroom and declared that he had no intention of turning the plinks into a corporate brand. From pavement to screen had been a gamble and it had worked. Why jeopardize a good idea and overkill it?

"I'm an illustrator and a storyteller, not a business executive," he said, his tone flat and vehement. "A partnership with you and your husband doesn't interest me."

Amanda was undaunted by his reaction. Time was on her side. She had powers of persuasion and, in the end, Ben Carroll would see the bigger picture, as she did. She was cresting on certainty, as heady as she had been on the night she stood on the balcony of Shearwater with Lar and knew what she would do to claim it as her own. Like the instant on the deserted quays when she spun into Hunter's arms... and, now, Eric and this dangerous passion that terrified and thrilled her.

Finally, an agreement was reached. Instead of a partnership, she and Lar would buy the merchandising rights from Ben and establish a company called Plink Inc.

"We agree upon a fee that's acceptable to you," Amanda promised when she rang with their proposal. "We take the risks while you continue doing what you do best and become extremely wealthy in the process."

"You think that's possible?"

He was still hesitant, suspicious, playing his cards close to his chest. She imagined his mouth puckering, the pronged scar pulling his cheek to one side. No wonder he never wanted to step out of character.

"I know it is. You have to think big, Ben. The plinks could go global, become an animated series—"

"*Animation*? You can't be serious?" Any progress she had made was suddenly halted. "The success of my program is the interaction between Super Plink and the children," he reminded her. "No! I can't agree to any of this."

She was suddenly weary of small minds grappling with small issues. Ben Carroll had the technical expertise to produce amazing books for children but he would always be a pavement artist at heart.

He signed in the end, as she had known he would; signed on the dotted line. He proved to be a tough negotiator. Lar complained that they had paid over the odds for the merchandising and electronic rights. Their investment in manufacturing and production was also significant but they both knew it would be well worth the outlay. Production would begin immediately.

Lar's respect for her business acumen had grown throughout her negotiations with Ben. The portrait of Rosalind disappeared from the hall. He hired decorators to paint the master bedroom and commissioned Rebecca to change the decor in the downstairs rooms. Finally, he said goodbye to his late wife. The sky was clear when he lifted the urn containing her ashes and leaned over the side of his yacht.

The thin gray stream floated like Chinese ribbons past the stern. They rounded the curve of Dublin Bay and the wind took her away. The sun rested its reflection on the water and the waves danced, as if jigging to invisible golden strings.

The plinks grounded her. They controlled her dizzying excitement, the heat on her skin when Eric was near. They kept her from arranging dangerous trysts until Lar flew to Hong Kong for a plink meeting with investors. Marcus was asleep on the night Eric arrived to Shearwater. The breeze was balmy, silky with promise when they slipped from the house and climbed down the beach path to the strand below. The tide was about to turn when they stripped and ran into the water. The shock of the cold, the exhilaration as Eric swam behind her, knowing he would catch her and carry her back to the rug they had left on the sand.

Suddenly, like a warning beacon, headlights flared across the sea. The boom of a car horn sounded like the song of a lighthouse. A car, driven on to the beach, came close to the water's edge. The windows were down, hard metal rock blasting, young men in the front and back. Probably joy-riders, Amanda thought, as the driver swerved, sand aqua-planing from the wheels; and there, in the dazzling glare, she spotted Marcus running across the beach. The driver swerved and narrowly missed him, the young man leaning from the window, his arm waving Marcus out of the way. She was screaming as she ran toward her son, sweeping him up in her arms and drying his tears. He clung to her, his thin frame shivering. The car left the beach, plunging them back into darkness, and she vowed that night, as Eric hid from view behind the rocks, that it was over...over...*over*. The thought of Marcus searching the house for her and then making his perilous way down the beach path horrified her. She wrapped a towel around her nakedness and carried him

back to Shearwater. She lay on his bed beside him and read
his plink books until he stopped shivering and fell asleep.

✦

Amanda didn't cry on the morning Marcus started school,
although, inwardly, she grieved over the sundering that was
about to take place. She used to cry in front of her father,
until she learned that tears only exacerbated his anger.
Action, not tears, achieved results, and she remained dry-
eyed as she approached the entrance to St. Bede's Junior
Academy with the other mothers, some weeping openly, others dabbing their eyes as their children were weaned from
them. Fathers, too, equally emotional, as Lar had been when
they stood together with Marcus—looking so grown-up
in his new school uniform—to be photographed by Mrs.
Morris. He was photographed again with Josh, the two of
them with their arms around each other, outside the school.
Amanda was still unsure how Rebecca felt about Lar's offer
to pay Josh's school fees. The journey to St. Bede's was longer than the journey to Josh's local primary school but the
opportunity of being educated at the exclusive academy had
proved impossible for his parents to turn down. The boys
were inseparable and St. Bede's would offer Josh a fantastic
start in life. Rebecca wasn't crying either when they waved
goodbye to their sons. Hard training pays off.

Amanda drove directly to LR1. The journey was short,
ten minutes if the traffic was light, fifteen at peak. She
dropped into Lar's office to tell him the transition to St.
Bede's had gone smoothly. His phone kept ringing and she
left him when a call came through from a film company in
Hong Kong, who were interested in buying Asian rights to
the animated plinks.

Marcus had been upset when the Plinkertown set was

dismantled. He hated the animated plinks and refused to watch them. Rebecca said he was "a credulous child." She made it sound like an accusation, albeit an indulgent one. She believed Marcus, unlike Josh, who was already accompanying his father to football matches, was "given to too many flights of fancy." The plinks, for instance, all those dolls at the bottom of his bed and the posters on the walls of his bedroom.

✦

On his fourth birthday, Marcus had refused to consider a magician, a clown or a bouncy castle. He wanted Super Plink to entertain the children, who would come to his party dressed as their favorite plink. He had his way in the end and the guests arrived to Shearwater in their costumes—Gutsy, Hero and the others. Such excitement when Super Plink drove into the courtyard in his magical van! They ran behind him as he led them through the trees at the end of the garden, weaving in and out of the shrubbery, disappearing from view then re-emerging. All he needed was a flute, Amanda thought. The Piped Piper of the plinks.

Later, when the children had been collected by their parents, and Marcus was in bed, exhausted from the afternoon's activities, she had invited Ben to stay for dinner.

"I've other arrangements made," he said. "But thanks for the invitation."

What other arrangements, Amanda wondered. Was there a woman in his life? She had checked his address in Lar's files. An apartment in a north inner city complex. She was surprised he hadn't moved somewhere more upmarket, yet, she thought, the anonymity of his living space tied in with his closed-off personality.

He had removed his costume as soon as Marcus went

upstairs. He looked pale, sickly, his long, black hair lank from the heat of his exertions. His scar seemed rawer than usual against his ashen complexion. He dropped hints occasionally about his life before they met. The scarring was the result of a street fight, sudden and unprovoked. Had he ever considered plastic surgery, she asked him once. She could recommend names if he was interested.

"Maybe in the future," he'd said. "For now, it's a reminder of what it's like to lose everything."

"You must have been terrified when you were attacked," she said.

"Not terrified." He shook his head. "Diminished. I realized I could be killed and no one would even notice I was missing."

In Quix Café, her finger had tingled when she touched his cheek. At the time she wondered if she had struck a nerve, as she did so often with her guests . . . or caused a brief sexual frisson to flare between them. She was wrong on both counts. What she had stirred in Ben Carroll was much more intangible. She had given him a future. Encouraged him to look up from the pavement to a broader canvas. His gratitude took them beyond sex or friendship, and could even be a cause for resentment. Who wanted their soul to be in hock to another? Certainly not Ben Carroll, with a troubled past that had left him wary of affection and only able to express it when he assumed another identity. Touching his scar had been an invasion that went beyond the surface of his skin; as if she had touched something sulfuric in him and ignited sparks.

CHAPTER FORTY-FOUR

Each time they met, Karl had expected her to draw back in shocked recognition. It never happened. She had imprinted her first impression of Ben Carroll on the retina of her eye, and saw only an eccentric street artist with chalk dust on his hands. A busker she would have passed without a second glance if motherhood had not softened her vision.

After he had signed the contract with Plink Inc., he drove up Bayview Heights and stood outside her house with its gilded gates and electronic security system. Other houses similar to Shearwater—perched like eyries above the sea—were steeped in the secluded privacy that great wealth allows. She had tried but failed to persuade him to appear on *Mandy Meets*. Viewers loved a rags-to-riches story, she said, and Ben Carroll ticked all the boxes. A pavement artist who had struck gold. She looked him straight in the eye when she said that. Shrewd eyes, staring at the main chance. Her single-mindedness; he had to admire that about her. The climb upward from a cottage on Raleigh Way to that pile on the summit of Bayview Heights.

A car had ascended the steep road leading to the entrance. He moved out of sight when her silver Saab came into view. The boy in the back seat was visible for an instant before the double gates automatically separated and she drove into the grounds. The gates closed behind her with a clang that catapulted rooks from the trees, noisily scolding and mapping the evening sky with their agitated wings. Their clamor filled his head as he walked away.

Her son was now four years old. On the day the boy celebrated his Plink-themed birthday party, Karl had returned to his rented apartment and showered. The water was hot, almost unbearable, but he had endured it. To find his face again. The cast of his body. To recognize the timbre of his natural voice. It wouldn't be easy. Like trying on a neglected overcoat that no longer fitted his once-familiar frame.

He had rung Sasha. The yearning to see his daughter had never eased but, while he was trapped in alcohol, then trapped in another skin, she had been sliding away from him. Her accent had changed. She sounded more like Nicole where, once, she'd sounded like him. Their relationship was shifting. He was becoming her friend, someone she could confide in, offload her anxieties and grumbles about her mother and Seth, her stepfather.

When the call ended, he had shaved off his hair. He swept up the ratty black clumps from the floor and moved his hands over the smooth contours of his scalp. His face felt vulnerable, his eyes exposed without the shield of tinted glass.

Over the following weeks, he had experimented with makeup concealers, testing one product after another on his scarred face. He searched for one that would blend the redness of the wound into his natural complexion but his scarred face was impossible to disguise under the patina of makeup. Gubby Morgan came to his aid and provided him with prosthetic patches of the kind used by actors and, Karl suspected, by the criminal fraternity. It would carry him past the most sharp-eyed security official, Gabby assured him.

His hair had grown again and his mouth, the twisted groove
that a nameless youth had carved into his lip, was hidden under
a beard when he flew from Dublin Airport. He had taken nothing to the rented apartment when he moved into it and he took
nothing away with him when he closed the door for the last time.
All traces of his presence had been scoured from the cell-like
rooms, the laptop on which he had created his books destroyed.

On the flight to Arizona, he maintained his composure as he
was photographed at security and when his passport was scrutinized. He was aware of the scar, could imagine it pulsing angrily
beneath the patch. As the plane approached Phoenix, he examined his reflection in the cramped toilet, terrified he would fall at
the last fence. His pallor had a sickly sheen; but his disguise was
holding. He barely contained his terror as he passed through
the gauntlets of heavy-hipped, armed security officers, who
demanded that Karl Lawson list his reasons for visiting Arizona.

Selina... Selina... He repeated her name, the sound of
the syllables beating time with his heart.

Outside the terminal, the heat smacked his face. He had
forgotten the ferocity of the sun, its bleached splendor. In the
bedroom of an anonymous hotel, he removed the prosthetic
patch and tilted a Panama hat over his damaged cheek.

A red sundress, flat red sandals; he picked her out immediately from the crowd in the foyer.

"Karl." She kissed his cheek, her sedate greeting setting
the tone for their reunion.

"It's good to see you again, Selina." He took his cue from
her and made polite conversation about his flight when they
left the hotel and walked toward her car. The air conditioning blew coolly around them as she drove on to the highway.

"How are you?" he asked.

"I'm good," she replied. "Very good."

She didn't fool him. He understood the hollowness that followed the ending of a marriage. The struggle to begin again. Her apartment was close to the theaters and art galleries. Closer to danger than the gated community where she had lived with Jago. At her insistence, Cheryl Storm had been written out of *Finchley Creek*, and she was concentrating on theater. Small parts that she hoped would obliterate the character she had created.

"Hard to live down the bitch reputation." She smiled wryly. "I could wear a burka and the audience would still see only Cheryl Storm."

"It's difficult to move beyond a name," he agreed. "Theater suits you. You look wonderful."

Only when they veered off at the junction to Winding Falls did he become aware of her nervousness.

"Is this your first time returning to the cabin?" he asked.

Her fingers fluttered to her mouth, then became still. "I never thought I'd stand inside it again," she admitted. "I wanted to tear up your letter when I received it but you are right. It's time to confront the past."

"You can still change your mind."

"No. I have to do this. I tried once with Jago. I couldn't bring myself to walk through the door. I'm ready now."

The cabin had been repainted, some repairs done to the roof, the garden tamed. A jojoba bush had replaced the palo verde tree and a small gazebo offered shade from the sun. Selina found the key under a terra-cotta plant holder and unlocked the front door. Karl held her hand and drew her over the threshold.

The sofa where they had made love so many times was missing from the main room, but everything else was as they remembered. He wheeled his case into one of the bedrooms. The bed was neatly made, no frilly cushions or pillow shams to suggest a feminine touch. It was obvious from the layout of the room that he would be sleeping on his own.

He showered and shaved off his beard, dressed in fresh

clothes. She had prepared a beef casserole with baked potatoes for their evening meal. Outside, the sun was setting, the quickening twilight chasing burgundy clouds across Longspur Peak. Candlelight flickered on the scoured wooden table where past tenants had carved their names. They, too, had left their mark on the wood, carving their initials inside a heart after a night of rapturous passion. This small cabin was laden with memories, blissful and horrendous.

The following morning, she drove him to a plastic surgery clinic, private and discreet, that was used by members of the *Finchley Creek* cast. She stayed with him until he was wheeled away for surgery and was waiting when he emerged from the operating theater.

Two days later, she returned to Phoenix to attend rehearsals. He remained alone in the cabin, his scars gradually healing. The desert closed around him. The high saguaros with their stumpy arms and cruciform shapes, the dried-up gorges and sandstone bluffs, the gray scrubby bushes, so very different to the green landscape he had left behind.

When he was ready to move on she returned and drove him to the airport. He flew to New York to see his family. Sasha, so skinny, awkward and beautiful. Nicole, so brittle when he embraced her then let her go. And Justin…his wounded heart finally able to make peace with himself. His wounded eyes finally able to envisage a future without Constance. Selina had talked about moving to New York. New beginnings were possible. Karl had sensed it in the yielding promise of her body when she kissed him goodbye at the airport. Was it possible to go forward without looking back, he wondered. But the backward pull was too strong. Skin-deep wounds could be healed by a surgeon's hands but the invisible ones—the septic, festering and invisible wounds—could only be cured through the balm of revenge.

PART FOUR

CHAPTER FORTY-FIVE

Day One

It begins with a phone call.

"Don't answer," Eric whispers in her ear. "The world can wait its turn for your attention." Face-to-face on his bed, they cling to the remains of spent pleasure. He lifts her hands above her head and kisses her throat, kisses her breasts until she, unable any longer to ignore the persistent ring, wriggles free. She reaches across him toward the bedside locker but the phone is lost in the clutter or, perhaps, hidden in the folds of the duvet they pushed to the floor when they tumbled on to the rumpled sheets. The caller gives up before Amanda can locate the phone but the sleepy afterglow is fading. She is aware of time stealing toward her as she turns her back to him and continues to search for her phone.

"If it's that important, they'll ring back." Eric traces his finger along the curve of her spine. "In the meantime, *we've* more important things to do." He's insatiable, it seems, at times like this, and Amanda forgets the phone, forgets everything that has meaning outside these four walls.

It's hot in his apartment. This small bedroom, crammed with his possessions, has become her oasis. For this reason, she tolerates his untidiness. He makes an effort to clear up when he's expecting her, or so he claims, but she's constantly tripping over his books, battery chargers, his laptop and Xbox, his shoes, mountain boots and unwashed shirts.

She strokes the hard length of him and he is inside her again, moving more urgently now, and he groans aloud when the phone rings once more. She pulls away from him and slides to the floor, searching around the bed, impatient now, and filled with a sudden anxiety when the ringing stops. She locates the phone under the duvet and stands, twists free when Eric reaches for her. Rebecca's name is visible on the screen. Both calls are from her and she has left a breathless message on the answering machine.

"Ring me at once," the message says. "It's about Marcus."

"What is it?" Eric rises and stands beside her. "Is something wrong?"

"I don't know," she replies. "It's Rebecca. I asked her to pick Marcus up from school." Even as she speaks, her phone rings and the walls of his small, stuffy bedroom seem to expand outwards and reverberate with alarm.

"Marcus is *missing*." Rebecca is sobbing, whooping, loud sobs that sound too unreal to be taken seriously.

"Missing?" Amanda believes she has misheard her sister. "What are you talking about?"

"I picked him up from school as you asked." Rebecca coughs to clear her throat, her voice thick with mucus. "He ran ahead with Josh and then disappeared. I can't find him anywhere."

"What do you mean? He can't *disappear*. Is this some kind of joke? Where are you?"

"At the school. Everyone's searching for him. The principal has called the police and—"

"The *police*?" Amanda shrieks and Eric jerks away from the piercing sound. "Is this a joke, Rebecca? If it is—"

"Stop shouting and listen to me, Amanda. He was with Josh and then he wasn't. He simply disappeared into thin air. Come quickly. You need to be here."

"I'm on my way." Amanda ends the call and sinks to her knees, presses her hands to her mouth.

"Tell me what's wrong," Eric demands.

He sounds far away, his question irrelevant. She chokes back a scream. What Rebecca said doesn't make sense. Marcus was running with Josh, running in front of her eyes. How could he disappear in full view of parents and children, all of them streaming down Rockfield Road in that manic fifteen minutes when school was over?

She dresses quickly. Her leather skirt is too short, too tight. She wore it deliberately to tease Eric and it belongs only to this bedroom. The zip jams when she tries to pull it up. He persuades her to sit down on the bed and explain to him what is going on. He shakes his head and insists that small boys can't just disappear in a crowd. That sounds reassuringly sane. Marcus has simply been swept up in the crush, forced forward even as he tried to turn back to find Josh. Rebecca is overreacting. Marcus will be waiting for her when she arrives at his school. Eric frees the zip at the back of her skirt and assures her that she doesn't look like a prostitute. No one will guess she's wearing a black lace thong and a bra that plunges to her nipples. He holds her for an instant, but then she's free and heading toward the elevator.

Outside, the wind gusts in from the sea and stings the tears on her cheeks. If only she was a bird and could fly directly over the waves to Rockfield. A direct route, instead of the long drive ahead. Should she take the M50 and veer off at Junction 16? Should she take the short-cut to the city through the M1 port tunnel? The latter is probably a better option but, either way, it's going to take at least an hour to reach Rockfield, no matter how fast she drives.

Traffic is light as she leaves Skerries but the traffic lights flash red…red…*red* at every junction. How could Rebecca have taken her eyes off Marcus? Amanda's fury grows, then subsides back into dread. She waits for her sister to ring and tell her Marcus has been found but her phone remains silent. Her skirt rides up over her thighs. She smells of sex, the pungent scent of Eric still on her fingers. She switches on the air conditioning but it hangs in the ether, the heady odor of illicit pleasure. When she opens the window, the rushing wind cools her down and the noise from the traffic vibrates through the car.

Marcus must have taken a wrong turning at the corner into Rockfield Avenue and wandered into someone's back garden. At four years of age, he's still tempted by an open gate, always determined to explore the forbidden.

She has reached the M1 when Rebecca rings. "The police have arrived," she says. "Why are you taking so long? You should have been here ages ago."

"I'm not at the studio."

"But you said you were working—"

"I was…*am*. I'll explain later. The traffic's atrocious. I'm driving as fast as I can."

"Hold on," she says. "A guard wants to speak to you."

"Mrs. Richardson, I'm Garda Browne." His voice sounds young but authoritative. "Are you driving right now?"

"Yes. But I'm on hands-free."

"I want your full attention. Pull in as soon as it's safe to do so and ring back this number."

She follows a sign for a service station and takes the turn-off leading into it.

"Are you okay to continue driving?" Garda Browne asks when she contacts him.

"Yes, I'm fine."

"We can send a squad car to collect you. Where are you right now?"

"A squad car isn't necessary." Her knuckles whiten on the steering wheel. "I'll be with you as soon as I can."

"Does Marcus have any friends who live in the vicinity of the school? Would he have had a play date in one of their houses today?"

"No. He only started school in September."

"Is he inclined to stray?"

"Sometimes he'll run into a garden."

"Strangers' gardens?"

"Yes. It's just curiosity—"

"So, he *is* in the habit of straying away from you."

What is he suggesting? She steadies her breathing, forces herself to remain still. "I wouldn't call it straying. I'm always right behind him."

"How long before you arrive?" he asks. "We were under the impression you were coming directly from LR1."

"I had to make an unexpected journey." She hates him already. "Work-related," she adds.

She wants to ring Lar and breathe her panic into his ear. The name of the conference or the hotel where it is being held didn't register when he told her. All she knows is that he was due to address the conference in the morning. She tries to calculate the time in New York. He could be speaking to his audience right now, his phone on silent. There is no reason to disturb him. Marcus will be found by the time she reaches Rockfield.

She is driving on the M1 toward the port tunnel when she finally pays attention to the flashing signs by the side of the motorway. The tunnel is closed due to an electrical failure. That means driving through Drumcondra, which is always a bottleneck. A foretaste of the traffic she'll encounter as she approaches the city center.

Drumcondra is as busy as she expected. Roadworks add to the chaos. She resists the urge to blow the horn repeatedly as she drives slowly toward the quays. The traffic eases when she crosses the Liffey and heads southwards.

A tall ship with its magnificent riggings lies at anchor on the river, its proud flags fluttering. This is the last day the ship will spend in Dublin before heading to the high seas again. She'd planned to bring Marcus to visit it this afternoon. They'd Googled it together last night before he went to bed and, afterward, she'd promised they'd go to McDonald's for a Happy Meal. This morning when Eric rang her unexpectedly at work, back a day early from Spain and luring her from her office, from her promise to Marcus, she had convinced herself that her son wouldn't mind. There was always another day, another treat.

The traffic stalls again. Her palms sweat. What explanation can she offer for being an hour and a half late? *I was with my lover, falling over his clutter, tearing at buttons and zips, our bodies already fused before we collapsed on to his bed.* Impossible yearnings that could never be explained. Never be understood by anyone outside their orbit.

The schoolyard is empty when she finally arrives and finds a parking space on Rockfield Road. Two squad cars are parked outside the school gates and a policeman stands at the front entrance. The SUVs and cars that normally obstruct the road during the periods when the younger and older pupils finish school have dispersed, and been replaced by three television vans. She sees the distinctive gray and red markings of the LR1 van, the satellite dish on top. A fist clenches the air from her lungs. What are the LR1 crew doing here? And the journalists waiting outside the school railings? Surely the presence of the media can have nothing to do with Marcus?

She pulls down her skirt and steps from her car. The journalists watch as she approaches. They are about to lunge toward her when they recognize her as one of their own. They slump back into waiting positions. She is familiar with this wait, the passive faces, the impatience that's alleviated with banter, gossip and coffee. She runs from them, tottering in heels that are too high, too unstable to hold her upright, and she slides over on one ankle, wincing from the pain, but she keeps going, distancing herself from the media, hoping they will not realize she is the story that has brought them together. She senses the change in the atmosphere, can almost hear their collective intake of breath when they see that she's not going to join them.

She's almost at the school gates. Once she's inside she'll be protected from their questions. The policeman on duty at the entrance leaves his position and unlocks the gates. A red-haired camerawoman in front of the LR1 jeep presses her hand over her mouth as it dawns on her that this missing child is not just any boy. He could be Lar Richardson's son. A photographer catches up with Amanda and lifts his camera. She recognizes Shane from *Capital Eye*. His merciless lens has only one person in its sights. A journalist, whose name she knows but can't remember, runs beside him.

"Is your son missing?" she shouts.

This clarion call rushes the others forward. Microphones with their identifiable media tags are thrust toward Amanda. They demand a comment that can become their headline story. Shane continues to mark her, clicking- -clicking— and a television camera swallows her disheveled appearance, her frantic expression, her efforts to outrun the media in her ridiculous fetish shoes that should only be worn from car to restaurant . . . or car to bedroom.

The guard ushers her through the gates. Sarah, the principal, stands at the entrance with Rebecca, whose skin is mottled with tears. And behind them, the voices continue calling:

"Amanda! Is your son missing?"

"Amanda! What took you so long to get here?"

"Amanda! Do you think your son has been kidnapped?"

"Amanda, Amanda, Amanda…speak to us, tell us, tell us…"

CHAPTER FORTY-SIX

Their secret. No one else knows. The secret has been a tickle in Marcus's tummy for so long but he pushed it way way down and watched the sky every day. Sometimes it was blue with candyfloss clouds. Sometimes the clouds were bossy and raced past the sun when it tried to shine. Today, the sky is just like Super Plink promised. All glossy with bubbles and Marcus knows it's the right time.

He stares at the cars outside his school and sees the secret signal. A little plink painted on the door of a silver car. He thinks it's Gutsy but he changes his mind when he gets close. It's Ace, the pilot plink.

The back door opens. Super is inside the car, just like he said. All the bubbles are bursting against the glass and the wipers are going *swish...swish...swish* really fast when he drives away.

Staring is rude so no one looks at them. Even if they did, they wouldn't be able to see through the special glass. It's just like the windows in Daddy's big car. Marcus can see Josh jumping as high as a kangaroo to catch the bubbles between his hands. He can't see Auntie Rebecca anywhere and Lollipop Jessie is staring at the bubbles so hard she forgets to stop the cars with her big lollipop.

It's nice in the back seat. Marcus listens to the plink songs and eats popcorn. He thinks about his birthday party when Super did magic tricks and told stories and made a secret with Marcus that no one, not his mammy nor his daddy, not even Josh—who says the plinks are "brill"—knew.

Super laughs and slaps the steering wheel with his magic hand. "Hold on to your hair, little man," he shouts. "We're going to rock this car all the way to Plinkertown Hall."

CHAPTER FORTY-SEVEN

SON OF MEDIA MOGUL AND CHAT SHOW
PRESENTER MISSING

Barbara Nelson

A widespread Garda search is underway to find missing schoolboy, Marcus Richardson, 4. Marcus disappeared shortly after he left St. Bede's Junior Academy on Rockfield Road this afternoon. He is the only child of media mogul, Lar Richardson, 64, and his wife, Amanda Bowe, 32, the well-known presenter of the celebrity chat show, Mandy Meets.

Arriving at her son's exclusive private school an hour and thirty minutes after she had been notified of his disappearance, Amanda Bowe was too distressed to answer questions. Marcus had been picked up from school by his aunt, Rebecca Dowling.

"I always collect him when Amanda is busy at work," Marcus's distraught aunt admitted shortly after her nephew disappeared. "Marcus was expecting to have what he calls his 'Monday Mammy day'

with Amanda and was very upset when she wasn't
there to meet him. After I'd comforted him, he ran
on ahead with my son, Josh. I could see them in the
distance but lost sight of Marcus when the bubbles
started." Fighting back her tears, Rebecca Dowling
admitted, "Amanda's work takes first priority and,
although she only collects Marcus on the days she's
not on air, this is not the first time I've had to step in
at short notice and collect him from school. I'll never
forgive myself if something terrible has happened to
the poor little boy."

Capital Eye has gained access to footage that
shows Marcus at the school entrance. He appears to
be visibly distressed when he finds his aunt instead of
his mother waiting for him. After going through the
school gates with his cousin, Josh Dowling, 5, he is
soon out of camera range.

Gardaí have been unable to confirm if there is any
connection between Marcus's disappearance and an
explosion of bubbles that blew over Rockfield Road at
the same time as school ended.

Marcus was wearing his St. Bede's uniform, a navy
blazer with red trim, charcoal gray trousers and shoes,
a red tie and socks. Under his shirt he was wearing a
Super Plink T-shirt.

Lar Richardson is on his way home from New York
where he was a guest speaker at the conference Digital Media Development—The Next Stage.

As yet, gardaí have no reason to suspect foul play. A
twenty-four-hour information hotline has been opened
and they have appealed to the public for information,
especially all those who were in the vicinity of Rockfield Road when Marcus Richardson went missing.

+

The residents on Rockfield Road and the adjoining avenues
and drives have already searched their gardens, front and
back. They've checked their sheds, their garages and their
houses, in case Marcus found an open door and fell asleep
under a table or in a bedroom.

There were bubbles, thousands of them, according to
Rebecca. An explosion of bubbles that shimmered in rainbow
hues, wobbling and elongated, as big as balloons. Children had
jumped to catch them, to burst them with their fingers, to blow
them higher, and still they'd erupted from a hidden space that
caused no one to wonder because bubbles are fun. Innocent, joy-
ful fun for children and parents alike. And, somewhere, in that
crush and heave, in that instant of distraction, her son was taken.

Taken. Amanda has said it aloud, set the word free. The
police haven't contradicted her. Nor do they deny it. They
simply don't know. They are waiting for something to happen. A ransom demand that will move the investigation in a
certain direction—but, so far, this is a search without clues
to guide them. The lollipop lady claims she didn't notice anything unusual when she allowed the cars to pass. Amanda
doesn't believe her. She's human, after all. An explosion of
bubbles. Of course she'd looked upward and smiled as the
sky was obscured by a dazzling prism.

"He just disappeared into thin air." Rebecca keeps repeating this statement, as if sheer repetition will make it feasible
and remove the burden of guilt from her. Amanda refuses to
listen. Thin air doesn't exist. It's a fallacy, an excuse without
meaning. Someone took her son's hand and led him away
without anyone on that crowded road noticing.

She's unmoved by her sister's tears. Rebecca has to remember something. *Anything* that will give the police a lead. How

far can a small boy stray without being noticed? Unless
a car door opened and a hand reached out to grab him. A
hand belonging to a stranger with the low brow and the tat-
tooed arms of a criminal. A Shroff henchman. How could
Rebecca and all those wary, watchful parents miss something so earth-shattering? Amanda wants to shake the words
from her sister, demand that she remember, remember—
remember.

Lar is on his way home. He has managed to change his
flight and will land in the early hours. At first, when she
made contact with him, he refused to believe her. What did
he think she was doing? Playing some cruel, malevolent
joke? Lighting flames beneath their already shaky marriage?

She is interviewed by Garda Browne and an older woman,
who introduces herself as Sergeant Moran. She has a brisk
handshake and a short haircut that emphasizes her broad
neck. A woman who will command any space she occupies.
She looks familiar but Amanda's terror is too strong to take
in features, names or information.

Sergeant Moran asks if she and Lar have enemies. A
rhetorical question. Of course they have enemies. Amanda
receives enough hate mail and social media abuse to verify
that fact. As for Lar, he hasn't risen to his heights without
stepping hard on too many toes along the way. But to take
their son...how much hate can one person harbor toward
another?

Later, when she is leaving the school, she understands
why the sergeant looks familiar. She had been involved in
the search for Connie Lawson. She must have transferred
from Glenmoore to Rockfield. It's clear from her steady
gaze that she also remembers Amanda and the publicity surrounding that investigation.

Now, as then, *Capital Eye* is the first to carry the story

in their late-afternoon edition. Barbara Nelson, another face from the past, her goth hair tamed with highlights, and a softer palette around her eyes. She moved to *Capital Eye* when *Hitz* folded and now she's chasing scoops, as Amanda used to do. The fact that Amanda was once a prized member of staff obviously means nothing when it comes to exploiting an angle. How could Shane do this to her after all the years they worked together? How demented she looked in his photos, as demented as any mother would be under such circumstances.

Marcus is on the evening news. The television channels use the photograph from his first day in school. He looks so solemn in his St. Bede's uniform, nervous yet excited. She watches the footage of her arriving that afternoon. The bloom of guilt on her cheeks as she ran past the school railings, staggering on her heels, her leather skirt rucked too high over her thighs.

The LR1 news desk reports only on Marcus's disappearance. Shaming the boss's wife in public is not a good idea for those who wish to keep their jobs.

Marcus's room has been tidied by Mrs. Morris. His Super Plink doll lies on the bed, waiting for his arrival home. Usually, he takes it with him in his schoolbag but he forgot it today or, perhaps, he deliberately left it behind. A big boy now, too grown-up to play with toys, unwilling to be teased and called a "baby" by the other pupils. But he is a baby, she thinks. The baby she loves with such fierce, protective passion . . . all forgotten on the whim of another, dangerous passion

This morning with Eric has the shimmer of a dream that glistened briefly and was soon forgotten. She cannot think about it as she smooths the plink's soft pelt. The eyes shine with a startling green light. Of the seven dolls Ben Carroll created, Super Plink is Marcus's favorite and would have brought him some comfort, wherever he is. She hugs the plink to her chest as if, somehow, this can convey her love to her son and transmit to him the courage he will need in the hours ahead. The plink portrait stares at her from the wall. Ben Carroll had drawn her son with just a few strokes, yet he'd captured Marcus's rapt expression, his trusting, inquisitive gaze.

✦

The full moon shines above the trees, a voluptuous, orange belly that fills her vision as she steals through the grounds of Shearwater to ring Eric.

"Why didn't you return my calls?" he whispers, as if he, like her, is afraid they can be overheard. "I've been going out of my mind with worry. What's happening? Is there any word on Marcus?"

"Nothing yet. I can't bear it. I *can't* . . . what if Billy Shroff organized—or Killer . . . ?" The familiar nickname catches against her throat and she's unable to continue.

"Why would they—" Eric begins.

"Why *wouldn't* they? You're doing a story on them. You know what they did to me before."

"But they've no idea I'm working on anything out of the ordinary," he says. "I've a good source, who'd warn me if they had any suspicions about the investigation."

"Your source is a *criminal*. A liar, a murderer, even. You can't possibly give credence to anything he tells you? They must have found out why you were in Spain—" She stops, her voice shaking on this possibility. "I let Marcus down," she says, flatly. "This is my punishment. I should never have listened to you."

"Amanda, *stop*. What happened between us today has

nothing to do with Marcus. How could it? No one knew we were meeting except us—and you didn't know until I rang you this morning."

Eric sounds grim and certain, but he is plucking suppositions out of thin air—*thin* air... what does he know, he or anyone else?

"The Shroffs have no reason to take Marcus," he continues. "He'll be found soon. Someone is bound to have noticed any unusual behavior. It's just taking time for the pieces to come together."

She forces herself to listen to him. To run shrieking into the wilderness of her imagination will not help Marcus, yet she's trapped there, her mind on fast-forward, speeding her toward terrifying conclusions.

"Check with your source," she whispers.

"That's what I'm going to do," he replies, "All my instincts tell me this has nothing to do with the Shroffs. But if there's the slightest hint that this is gang-related, I'll contact the police immediately." He pauses, lowers his voice. "What will you tell Lar if he asks where you were this afternoon?" He, who exposes ruthlessly, now fears being exposed.

She's incapable of thinking straight, yet she feels the kernel of self-survival hardening within her. Her marriage is over if Lar discovers the truth. He will claim custody of Marcus and ensure that in the eyes of the law she is an unfit mother, who could not even keep her son safe, and Marcus must be—has to be—safe.

"I'll tell him I drove to Howth to persuade Jackson Barr to appear on my show." The journey from the crime writer's secluded house to Rockfield would take roughly the same time as it took her to drive from Eric's apartment.

"But everyone knows Barr doesn't do interviews—"

"That's why I decided to speak to him personally." She

won't tolerate Eric's uncertainty. "I hadn't realized he was out of the country until I arrived at his house." She needs to end their conversation. It's a distraction when Marcus's return is all that matters. "Have you a better idea?" Her breath shudders. "If so, let me hear it."

"It could work." He knows how keen she was to interview the crime writer. "Who's going to be able to prove otherwise?"

She returns to the house where Imelda is already on first-name terms with the guards who come and go. She has insisted on staying with Amanda until Lar arrives home but Rebecca decided it was wiser to keep away. She claimed she'd been talking off the record to *Capital Eye* and had no idea her comments would be quoted. What she said had been distorted, taken out of context. She never meant to imply that Amanda was a negligent mother. The lone howl of the misquoted. Amanda is only too familiar with it.

She waits for Lar, wills his bulky frame to fill the doorway and take control. If only a ransom demand would be made. A gruff anonymous voice ordering them not to contact the police but deliver the money to an arranged location. No matter what the demand, Lar will pay it. Their son is priceless. A payment made and they will be together again, a united family.

CHAPTER FORTY-EIGHT

Bedtime. Super Plink gives him a piggyback to Sleepy Nook. The bed is soft and the plink duvet warm and snuggly. Super has a bed beside the other wall so that he's able to watch over Marcus at night and scare the bad dreams away. The stars on the ceiling wink down on Marcus and all the toy plinks sit at the bottom of his bed, just like at home. The real plinks are on Mars and on mountains and at the bottom of the sea. Some are looking after lost children and saving them from falling out of windows and off their bikes.

Super fluffs the pillow and Marcus rests his head on it. He's tired now. The stars are dancing on the ceiling and the stereo is playing his favorite plink song. Super takes another pillow from a drawer and leans over the bed. Marcus can no longer see the stars because the pillow is in the way. When it comes closer, he can see a picture of Plucky on the front. She's the best plink for fighting monsters who scare children with nightmares.

"This will be more comfortable," says Super and tucks it under Marcus's head. "Sleep tight little man and if the bugs bite squash 'em tight."

✦

The boy is asleep at last, contently so. No tears for his mother or father. They will come later. He'll suffer separation anxiety; but, for now, he is still caught in the excitement of his plink fantasy and, hopefully, will sleep until morning.

She made the headlines on the evening news and will continue to do so until the search is over. He watches her on television, tottering on her heels, her short skirt riding too high over her skinny legs, the swing of her hair with its dramatic red highlight.

Pain tightens his temples. He massages them with his fingers, tries to ease the pressure. The migraines started soon after his arrest. In prison, Gabby Morgan had shown him how to ease the pain through massage. Pressure points were important, up the spine to the base of the skull, between thumb and index finger, under the eyebrow ridge. He can no longer remember the other points but Gabby, suffering as he does from reoccurring headaches, knows them all. Not surprising, his knowledge of migraine. Having his head kicked in by Killer Shroff was bound to make an abiding impression on anyone.

He hears a cry from the bedroom and hurries toward the boy. Marcus is half-awake, scrabbling for his plink doll, which has fallen from the bed. He hands it back to the boy, who cradles it to his chest and sinks into a deeper sleep.

CHAPTER FORTY-NINE

Day Two

MYSTERY OF MISSING BOY DEEPENS
BARBARA NELSON

Overnight searches have failed to find missing school-boy, Marcus Richardson, 4. Marcus is the son of chat show presenter, Amanda Bowe, 32, and her husband, the powerful media guru, Lar Richardson, 64.

Gardaí can now confirm that the explosion of bub-bles on Rockfield Road was a deliberate attempt to draw attention away from the boy at the crucial moment of his abduction. An empty bubble machine on an automatic timer, discovered behind the wall of a vacant house close to the school, is being forensically examined.

As the search for the missing boy becomes nation-wide, ports, airports and railway stations remain on full alert in case an effort is made to smuggle Marcus out of the country. Dredging has begun on all local waterways in the Rockfield area and underwater divers are on hand to offer assistance.

"Marcus is a popular and outgoing little boy," Sarah Hodges, principal of St. Bede's Junior Academy, told

Capital Eye. *"His disappearance has been deeply upsetting for our pupils, who will pray for his safe return into the arms of his loving parents. We have organized appropriate counseling for the children who need it."*

The Garda Press Office refuses to confirm or deny if a ransom demand for Marcus's safe return has been received.

✦

Fog lies over Dublin Bay and the sun shines palely behind the haze when Lar flies into Dublin Airport. Sylvia Thornton is waiting in arrivals. She ushers him through the waiting media, past the television cameras and microphones. Amanda, watching him on the morning news, notes his streamlined figure in his bespoke tailored suit. A solid and respectable businessman in sensible brogues.

His chin is rough. The gray stubble scratches her cheek when she runs into his arms. They cling to each other, unable to tell who is holding who upright.

"Have courage," Imelda tells them. She makes it sound like a choice. "Trust in God. Marcus will be found safe and well." She'd watched with Amanda throughout the night, hoping for a phone call, new information from the police or a knock on the door by a kindly stranger, holding the hand of a lost little boy, his ordeal over.

"Thanks for being here, Imelda." Lar sighs and hugs her. Amanda knows he hasn't heard a word her mother said.

"Are you sure you're okay to drive home?" she asks when Imelda is leaving. "You can leave your car here and I'll call a taxi."

"I'll be fine." Imelda pushes her hands nervously together. "Don't be so cross with Rebecca. We all know how much you love Marcus."

"I'm not cross," Amanda lies. "Tell her she's not to speak to anyone from the media. Make sure she understands. I don't want to see her name in print again."

"You took so long to get there, Amanda." The morning light shines harshly on Imelda's strained face. "Everyone was searching for Marcus and Rebecca didn't realize she was talking to reporters. You can't blame her for—"

"Mum, *please* go home. I'll phone you as soon as I hear anything."

"You'll have news soon. I'm sure of it."

Why pretend? Amanda chokes back the question, afraid it'll turn to a scream if uttered. Why is everyone insisting there's a rational explanation to her son's disappearance? His life is in danger and clichés undermine this reality.

Sylvia Thornton doesn't do clichés. When Lar is in the drawing-room talking to the police, she opens the morning newspapers and lays them before Amanda on the breakfast bar.

"I suppose you've seen the coverage?" she says. "And the televised news bulletins?"

"Yes, I've seen them."

"We need to kill the speculation." Sylvia points at one of Shane's photographs. "You must tell me the truth about where you were yesterday."

Amanda nods. No sense pretending she doesn't understand. She speaks with conviction about Jackson Barr. She describes her journey to the summit of Howth Head where she left her car to speak to a woman walking her dog along the quiet road. The dog walker told her the author was in the States, probably signing a lucrative contract for another book or film option. The calls from Rebecca came while she and the dog walker, a fan of the author, were discussing Jackson's latest novel. She hadn't realized Rebecca was trying to contact her until she returned to her car and saw her phone, but the journey across a city blighted with roadworks and malfunctioning traffic lights had been horrendous. That last part, at least, was true.

Her story sounds convincing, yet it rings hollow to her ears. She has no idea if Sylvia believes her; as always, LR1's publicist remains inscrutable. Being in Sylvia's company is always stressful, but today it's unendurable.

"I'll issue a press release with that information," she says. "We need to keep the media's full attention on Marcus and your high profile could be a distraction."

She drives away, speeding home to her children, all three of them watched over by their father, the recently promoted Detective Sergeant Jon Hunter. Amanda rests her elbows on the breakfast bar and sinks her head to her arms. So many secrets at a time when truth is everything.

She sets up a Facebook page and trawls the online newspapers on her laptop. She skims the headline and opening paragraph of *Capital Eye*'s latest online report. Barbara Nelson claims that when the media gathered outside the school yesterday and waited for Amanda to appear, a rumor that she was the victim of a "tiger-style" kidnapping spread like a rash through them. Otherwise, why such a delay? What *utter* rubbish. Amanda controls her anger over the journalist's efforts to focus once again on her late arrival. And those photographs…why does *Capital Eye* keep reproducing them? Such a silly question. She would have done exactly the same if Shane had sent them through to her. Sylvia's statement about Jackson Barr is used in Barbara's report but it is the speculation that drives Amanda's fear.

As the wait for news continues, Marcus's parents must deal with the possibility that their only son has been

abducted by criminals. The Garda Press Office has
neither confirmed nor denied reports that members of
a criminal gang are being questioned about the miss-
ing boy's whereabouts. Lar Richardson has offered a
substantial reward for his safe return and a press con-
ference has been organized for tomorrow, if Marcus is
still missing.

"You were covering their activities in *Capital Eye* for
years." Lar joins her in the kitchen and reads Barbara's
report. "Getting high on their adrenaline until Billy Shroff
stopped your gallop." His skin has a yellowish tinge, due to
shock and his long flight from New York.

Lar is blaming her. He, who fires people without a second thought, closes down his magazines without warning,
rejoices in deals that destroy his competitors—he thinks
she's responsible for provoking hatred. What a pair they are;
so well matched. How did they ever succeed in producing
such a sweet, gentle boy?

"That was years ago," she protests. "What about the
investigation *Behind the Crime Line* are doing on their
Spanish links? What if they've found out about it?"

He nods. "I've already discussed this possibility with
Sergeant Moran. She's trying to contact Eric Walker but he
must be in the air. She'll interview him as soon as he returns
from Spain." He stares at the photograph of her arrival at the
school, then, as if unable to endure the sight, he closes her
laptop. "What the fuck were you hoping to do with Jackson
Barr?" he asks. "Seduce that pretentious prick?"

"I was hoping to persuade him to appear on my show."
She must not sound defensive. "You know how anxious I've
been to interview him."

"Did that involve dressing like a tart?"

"I wasn't—" She swallows hard. "How dare you speak to me like that? I was distraught when I arrived at the school and you, more than anyone, know how images can be manipulated." To alleviate her husband's suspicions, she must lie with utter conviction.

The clock on the wall proves that time will always move on, no matter how ridiculous that seems, and the wait for news stretches into hours. Amanda wants to organize a poster campaign but that's already under control, Lar tells her. When she tries to join the search party, Sergeant Moran vetoes it.

"You'll be a distraction." She echoes the fear Sylvia expressed earlier. "The media can't be allowed to turn you into the story." She fixes her hard gaze on Amanda. "It happens," she says. "But, then, who am I telling?"

News bulletins keep regurgitating the same details. How did the media know so quickly that a child was missing? This question nags her constantly. The police would not have alerted them. Reporters outside the school, churning out information before facts were established, was the last thing they would have wanted. So much to think about, when only one thought matters. Where is her boy?

Lucy Knight, the social diarist from the *Daily Orb,* bypassing Sylvia Thornton and the Garda Press Office, rings her. Amanda refuses to comment and switches off her phone. Lucy's gossip column "Knight on the Tiles" is as titillating as the busty, trout-lipped models in thongs and braces that form the beating heart of the tabloid.

Undaunted by Amanda's refusal to talk, Lucy emails questions, which Amanda deletes. She phones Sylvia to complain about being harassed. The publicist, surprised that any journalist has broken through the protective barriers she has formed around Amanda and Lar, agrees to contact her.

Night draws in. Impossible as it seems, another day without Marcus has passed. In the long, sleepless hours, it's possible to believe that her son has been lifted by magic and floated away on a constellation of bubbles.

This is her punishment, retribution for neglecting him. Guilt and dread do battle with each other as she thinks about the night she invited Eric to Shearwater. What madness had possessed them to take such a risk?

She had lied to her son. Dismissed what he had seen— a robber chasing her in the water—as an illusion; and she was shamed by the lie. And shamed even more when, a week later, she had broken her vow and driven across the city once again to Eric's apartment.

✦

Marcus's tummy growls.

"Time to eat," says Super. He makes spaghetti Bolognese in the Chow-Chow Room. They slurp spaghetti between their teeth and make vampire faces. When dinner is over and all the dishes are washed, Super toasts marshmallows over the fire in the Snuggle-Up Room. They're hot and squishy. Marcus eats six. He has a bath in the Sudsy Room and plays with Derring-Do, who's a water plink and rides on the back of a whale. Derring-Do saves children from drowning if they swim too far from shore.

He thinks about the night he dreamed he was a bird flying over the ocean. Then he fell from the sky. He shouted because he was going to drown in the waves. When he woke up the shout was inside his head, not outside, and Mammy couldn't hear. He cuddled Super Plink against his chest and shouted, "Mammy...Mammy!" but she didn't come.

He pushed down the duvet and wriggled from his bed. Mammy's room was dark. Marcus was too small to reach the switch but the landing light was on and he could see her duvet, all neat and straight, just like the pillows. He heard the gongs on the clock and counted to ten.

Downstairs, all was quiet. He checked the conservatory, the kitchen, the drawing-room and her home office. He ran into the dining-room, even though she never went there except when they had Important People to dinner.

He sat on the bottom step of the stairs and tried not to cry. Daddy was away on Important Business and being alone in the house was as scary as falling from the sky. He kissed Super Plink and stroked his fur. It felt like teddy fur but not as rough. More like soap in the bath, when it was smooth and slippery between Marcus's hands.

Outside in the garden, the sky was black. He could see stars. The terrace was cold and the grass wet like a sponge between his toes. The gate to the beach was open. He went down the steps and saw Mammy in the water. He was afraid because she was so far away. Had she fallen into the sea, like he did in his dream? She swam real fast, even faster than the robber who was chasing her and laughing like a monster. Their arms made sudsy bubbles on the water. Then the car came and did spins. The driver shouted curses out the window at him. The F word, and Marcus cried because the sand was in his eyes. When Mammy stood up, she was white like a ghost and he hid his eyes because she'd forgotten to put on her bikini. She must have heard him crying because she kept shouting, "Marcus...*Marcus!* What are you doing out of bed?"

When he looked between his fingers she had a big towel wrapped around her. She said he had a wild imagination and all he saw was a rock. Things looked different in the moonlight and Marcus must put tonight out of his head.

"Silly boy," she scolded him, then hugged him even

tighter. "Rocks can't laugh. That's only the sea sighing because the tide is turning. Dry your eyes and we'll make hot chocolate with lots of marshmallows on top."

Super comes back into the Sudsy Room and holds out a towel. "You'll grow fins if you stay in the bath much longer," he says.

The towel has a picture of Plucky Plink and it's soft, like the towel Mammy uses when she gives him a bath. The sad feeling comes and makes him cry, but just for a little while. Super says it's okay to be sad and that, sometimes when the moon is full and playing tricks, it's easy to believe rocks are laughing. When Marcus is dressed in his PJs and dressing gown, Super puts on the recording of Mammy in her big chair. She always lets Marcus spin on it when he goes into her studio. That's where she talks to the Invited Guests.

He watches the recording with Super and they laugh and clap when Mammy says funny things and, sometimes, very rude things to the Invited Guests. When the video is over Super carries him to Sleepy Nook and reads *Plucky's Magic Torch*. He leaves the light on so that Marcus can watch the stars shining above him.

Super Plink is the best...

CHAPTER FIFTY

Day Three

WHERE WAS AMANDA ON FATEFUL AFTERNOON?
LUCY KNIGHT

Amanda knows that a question mark at the end of a headline suggests ambiguity. A tease to cover the fact that there are *no* facts. An admittance that what has been written is devoid of information and the question mark has been planted to create controversy, alarm, speculation.

> *Telly babe, Amanda Bowe, mother of missing school-boy, Marcus Richardson, is never far from the head-lines these days. Her refusal to explain why she arrived so late to her son's exclusive, private school on the afternoon of his disappearance has led to much speculation among her peers.*
>
> *PR guru, Sylvia Thornton, claims Amanda had hoped to meet with Jackson Barr, the millionaire author, whose disdain for the media is as legendary as his pulp fiction. But CCTV footage seen by the* Daily Orb *has failed to find any evidence of the glamourous telly babe arriving or leaving the reclusive author's premises.*

Did she get lost among the heather and the cliff walks on Howth Head? Or can there be another reason why she is so secretive about her behavior on that tragic afternoon? Perhaps, Amanda, who has never been a shrinking violet when it comes to following a story, will enlighten us as to why, for once, she shunned the camera when she arrived at the luxurious home of Jackson Barr . . .

Unable to read any more, Amanda crumples the tabloid and flings it on the floor. Lar picks it up and lays it on his desk, smooths out the creases. They are in his home office checking out the morning papers Sylvia had brought with her.

The photographer from the *Daily Orb* had photographed Amanda from behind as she ran toward the school. The stretch top she pulled on with such haste in Eric's bedroom is inside out, the label clearly visible, the fabric puckered. She sees a slash of skin at her waist and, in that gap, the black strap of her thong is visible.

"What the hell does she mean about you not being on camera?" Lar demands.

"I never entered Jackson's premises or came within camera range. This is contemptible reporting." The lie may choke her but it is her lifeline. She will cling on to it until it snaps. After that, it won't matter. She raises her voice at Sylvia, who had moved discreetly to the window while Lar was reading the paper. "You have to put a stop to this kind of sensationalism. Marcus is missing and she's writing about me. Why? *Why?*"

A ring on the doorbell distracts them. A garda car is outside. Mrs. Morris escorts two guards into the living room. If they are aware of tension, they show no sign of it in their fixed expressions and they report... what? Amanda filters through what they are saying and knows that nothing has changed.

She leaves them talking to Lar and opens the French doors leading to the terrace. It's chilly this morning but the breeze is fresh and carries the tang of seaweed on its breath. She sits on a wrought-iron chair, the cold surface penetrating the thin material of her skirt.

Sylvia joins her shortly afterward. "We need to talk." She speaks softly, almost conspiratorially, as if she fears Lar's formidable presence is too close for comfort. "Have you told me the truth about Jackson Barr?"

"Of course I have." Amanda pulls her pashmina tighter around her shoulders. "Why would I lie?"

"To protect your marriage."

"My marriage doesn't need protection."

"But my reputation does," Sylvia replies, coolly. "I'm trying to handle a highly charged situation and need to use every avenue at my disposal to encourage the media to concentrate only on Marcus. But I keep being broadsided by journalists with other angles."

"What angles?"

"Your relationship with Eric Walker." She drops his name like a grenade and waits for Amanda to reply.

"He's my work colleague. Who dares to suggest otherwise?"

"Lucy Knight, for one."

"She's a gossipmonger. No one pays any attention to the rubbish she writes for that rag."

"You're part of the media, Amanda. I don't have to explain how it works. All I need is confirmation that you've told me the truth about the afternoon Marcus disappeared."

"Absolutely." Her voice rings with confidence. Each time

she repeats the lie, it becomes more solidified. Soon, it will morph into a fragile truth. "I've no reason to lie to you or anyone else."

In the distance, a ferry moves imperceptibly across the horizon. Seagulls screech as they swoop downwards to feast on festering scraps. Sylvia buttons her coat as the wind scurries leaves across the terrace. Russet and yellow, they lie in deep drifts that Marcus loves to toss. Amanda has a savage impulse to throw back her head and howl. An indulgence. She needs to be in control as she prepares for the press conference.

The last time she attended such a conference, she was on the other side of the green baize table. The Lawson parents were in a trance of fear as they struggled to articulate their message: help us—please help us...and all the time their daughter was dead. She won't go there, can't go there; she must concentrate on one thing only. Plead, beg, implore the Shroffs to deliver her son safely back to her.

✦

Cameras on tripods, on shoulders, clicking, flashing, rolling. The sound is as deafening as ball bearings rattling; so familiar that Amanda has never noticed it until now. Even the journalists are using their mobile phones to photograph her as she takes her seat in front of them. The atmosphere is taut with anticipation. This is no ordinary disappearance. This is a celebrity story and rumors about a criminal link have given it an extra edge.

She sits beside Lar, their hands clasped. Amanda is flanked by Sylvia Thornton, who will fend off dangerous questions, and a superintendent, whose name she's already forgotten. Lar stays on script and speaks directly to the camera. She must do the same. As media people, they understand the importance of the message. Hands are raised. Questions are directed at the superintendent. The Shroff link? Is it fact? Have the members of the Dublin gang taken in for questioning revealed anything that will help the search? The superintendent fobs off their questions. The press refuse to drop that angle. How many ways can the same question be asked, Amanda wonders, the same answer given.

A journalist, whom she doesn't recognize, asks if she made an enemy of Billy Shroff by once writing an opinion piece for *Capital Eye* about his daughter's wedding dress? Barbara Nelson weighs in with a reminder that Amanda once doorstepped Killer Shroff after his daughter's First Communion service and asked if the gifts of money she would receive from her relatives were drug-tainted. And wasn't that question asked in front of the little girl and her school friends?

Before she can reply, Sylvia smoothly intervenes. "This conference was organized to help us find Marcus and make an appeal for his safe return. Will you please respect the wishes of his parents and confine your questions to that end?"

Delia Wright raises her hand. She is an influential blogger who, having reared and home-schooled her four children, uses her blog to encourage mothers to shun the workplace. *The Wright Path* has an enormous readership, who either like or loathe her.

"On behalf of the assembled media, I'd like to offer Mr. and Mrs. Richardson our support at this difficult time," she says. "Our sincerest hope is that their son will soon be returned to them and their horrifying ordeal brought to an end." She pauses to allow her sympathy to be noted, then adds, "If I could address a question to *Mrs.* Richardson?"

Amanda notes the emphasis on her marital status and

braces herself. Delia's sweetness disguises a steely intoler-
ance. "If you had collected your son from school on Monday, as you'd promised to do, isn't it highly probable that he
would have been holding your hand as you walked down
Rockfield Road?"

How is she supposed to answer that question? The blogger might as well punch Amanda in the face and be done
with it. She tries to respond but the words are trapped in
guilt. "Marcus likes to run ahead—"

"Not when you collect him." Delia will not tolerate
vagueness. "And *that*'s only once a week. A novelty for him
and he was looking forward to being with his mother instead
of being foisted on a childminder at short notice."

"That's an absolutely disgraceful assumption to make!"
Lynn Masterson, an old-school feminist, jumps to her feet.
Sixty plus and still battling stereotypes, Lynn glares at the
younger woman. "What happened to Marcus has nothing to
do with the fact that his mother was delayed at work."

"My point is that this tragedy could have been avoided."
Delia's reasoned tone never wavers. "The demands made on
today's working mothers are putting our schoolchildren at
risk—"

"No one is denying a mother the right to remain at home
and rear her family," Lynn shouts back. "But women must
be allowed that same tolerance when they make a different
choice!"

Two opinionated women have taken over the press conference. They are so certain, so assured that their particular view is the right one, the right path . . . why did Marcus
stray from the right path and disappear into thin air . . . thin
air doesn't exist—can't exist—not a feasible explanation, but
what explanation is there? Sylvia interrupts the journalists
and forces them into silence. The cameras click relentlessly

as the superintendent draws the conference to a close and
they file wearily from the hotel room.

She tenses as Sylvia accidentally brushes against her arm.
It is becoming more difficult, almost impossible, to be so
close to her. They drive directly from the hotel to the search
center but, even there, Amanda is approached by reporters
demanding to know how she feels.

How do they think she feels? Does she have to shriek the
answer at them? *My heart is rent in two.*

※

The press conference makes the evening news. How grave
they look behind the green baize table. Amanda should have
cried. Her responses are too mechanical, words learned by
rote. She is staring coldly at Delia Wright and nodding in
agreement with Lynn. She has no memory of doing either.
Why hasn't that section been edited out? It has nothing to
do with Marcus. But it was confrontational, good enter-
tainment, and Delia Wright has only one agenda, one blog.
There it is, *The Wright Path* blogged large across the screen
of Amanda's laptop.

MISSING CHILD—WHO IS TO BLAME?

*On Monday morning, Marcus Richardson was a happy-
go-lucky little schoolboy. He was looking forward to
spending the afternoon with his mother, the celebrity
hostess of* Mandy Meets.

*When Amanda Bowe's demanding work schedule
meant she was unable to collect him from school as
arranged, Marcus threw a tantrum, as small boys do
when they are bitterly disappointed. Then, somewhere*

on that fateful journey from the school gates of St. Bede's to the car belonging to his aunt, Rebecca Dowling, he vanished.

At the press conference, his father, wealthy businessman, Lar Richardson, made a heartfelt appeal for his son's safe return. The elderly father spoke movingly to the assembled media about his joy on becoming a first-time parent at the age of 60.

"My son is my world," he said. "Please bring him safely home to us."

This tragedy pinpoints an issue that The Wright Path has long highlighted. Today's young mother thinks she can have it all. A demanding career, motherhood and a hectic social life. It takes a tragedy like this one for them to realize the importance of their place in the family home during their children's formative years.

Why did Amanda Bowe disappoint her son? The tyranny of the office desk or, in her case, the television studio, was responsible. If she had kept her promise to her son, would he have felt that urge to run violently into the crowd and disappear from his aunt's sight?

Gardaí still don't know if he was the intended target or if this was just a random abduction. A child in the wrong place at the wrong time. A child whose mother arrived nearly an hour and a half late after being informed her son was missing.

While our deepest sympathy must go to the Richardson parents, this tragic case should allow us to pause and consider the rights of children over a dictatorial workplace that makes no concessions to women whose mothering functions are constantly challenged by this dual responsibility.

"She has a point," Lar says when he finishes reading the blog. "You should have been with Marcus, not chasing some fucking celebrity who wasn't even in the country."

"That's unfair—"

I'll tell you what's unfair, he shouts. A vein swells dangerously in his right temple. "It's unfair that our son is missing. It's unfair that you couldn't be bothered keeping your promise to him. It's unfair that he could be in the hands of a murderous criminal gang."

"You've spoken to Eric Walker. He's confirmed that the Shroffs aren't involved."

"How the fuck does Eric know?" Lar pushes her away when she tries to hold him. "He was out of the country at the time. No one knows *anything*. You should have been at the school to pick Marcus up as you promised." He storms from the drawing-room and slams the door behind him.

Delia's followers are quick to comment. The fundamentalist trolls castigate Amanda and insist that Marcus, if found, should be placed in foster care. The crazies believe he's been abducted by aliens. The internet is a web that displays the calcified flies, never the spider, and such comments are signed by people with monikers like Stigmata Joan, Lily Lips, Silky Mum or, simply, Anon. All that spleen directed at her. All stirred into life by the writings of another. This thread will run for a few more hours, another day at most, then the conversation will move on to something else. But it is there, that shift against Amanda, implicit in those responses that insist a mother's first responsibility is to hold her son's hand and guide him safely through the throng.

✦

Apples on the ground. Some are ripe and some have holes with worms living inside them. Some apples are up high on the trees. Marcus can see them when he looks really hard. First one, then another and another. Red like the apple in the Snow White book. His mammy and daddy are in a Big Apple where houses are made with glass and look like Lego. Not like the rainbow rooms in Plinkertown Hall.

He does lessons and songs in the How-To-Do Room. He can sing "Supercalifragilisticexpialidocious" all on his own now. He plays with magnets in the Wow-Wagon and hears the sea roaring in shells and examines the spiderwebs Super sticks on paper. They're real webs, not like the internet web. All the knowledge in the world is there, Daddy says when he's looking at his phone. And Mammy too, in case she misses any of the knowledge on Facebook.

Super plays DVDs of *Plinkertown Hall* when it used to be real, not cartoons. Marcus had cried when *Plinkertown Hall* disappeared. One day it was there and then, like magic, it vanished. Daddy had said he must dry his tears. The plinks were going global. Super has a globe in the How-To-Do Room. He shows Marcus Ireland on it, all squiggly and green, and lots of other places but, no matter how hard Marcus stares, he can't find Plinkertown Hall anywhere on it.

CHAPTER FIFTY-ONE

No breaking story on the news tonight. No small body has been found on wasteland or dragged from a riverbed. No small boy has been spotted leaving the country, although the police must be dealing with numerous claims of sightings. Marcus Richardson doesn't have any defining feature that would separate him from other black-haired, blue-eyed four-year-olds with a belief in the power of magic.

He watches the press conference on the evening news. Haggard and desperate, Lar Richardson cuts a more sympathetic figure than his wife, who casts her gaze about as if unable to comprehend why she is not seated on the other side of the table with her peers.

The media are edging toward the Shroff connection. *Capital Eye*, as always, will be first off the block. The others will follow. The links are obvious. Amanda Bowe has reinvented herself as a chat show presenter but the reputation she gained as a crime reporter has not been forgotten. Killer Shroff claimed she'd stuck her knife, or, literally speaking, her pen into his family with the "crap" she wrote about the family business. He'd heard other stories from the prisoners about her ruthlessness when he was in prison. Blame was the name of the game there. Like a blight, it consumed them, cast them down, roused them to a frenzy, controlled them.

The boy's bouts of homesickness have been easily assuaged so far. Recordings of *Mandy Meets* are surely a poor substitute for his mother's arms but he seems content to watch them and be satisfied. The weather, being surprisingly mild for late October, allows a certain amount of time outdoors but he is like quicksilver, difficult to contain in a constrained environment. Amusing him is bound to become more demanding. So far, he's still enjoying all that Plinkertown Hall has to offer. Each day has a purpose. One that will lead them to the ultimate goal.

CHAPTER FIFTY-TWO

Day Four

MISSING BOY LINK TO NOTORIOUS CRIMINAL GANG?
BARBARA NELSON

Sylvia slips off her coat and sits on the sofa between Amanda and Lar. She dismisses the newspapers one by one, until she comes to *Capital Eye*. A revenge kidnapping? Amanda huddles away from the chilling possibilities this question mark suggests. She wants to curl into a ball, as hedgehogs do when predators are near.

> *Despite robust denials from Superintendent Burns at yesterday's press conference that no link has been established between the disappearance of missing schoolboy, Marcus Richardson, 4, and the notorious Shroff gang,* Capital Eye *has received information that suggests otherwise. It has emerged that the boy's father, media mogul Lar Richardson, 64, is planning to feature an in-depth investigative report on the gang's drug activities on LR1's popular* Behind the Crime Line *program.*
>
> *A source close to the gang believes that LR1's*

*chief crime correspondent, Eric Walker, 33, has been
involved in a covert surveillance of the gang's Spanish
activities.*

When approached by Capital Eye, *Walker was not
available to comment about his recent trip to Spain.
Flight details acquired by this newspaper verify his
presence in Malaga at the same time as members of
the Shroff family were together at their luxurious villa
overlooking the Mediterranean coast.*

*But Walker arrived home from Spain a day earlier
than planned. Did the Shroffs become aware of his
location? Did their tentacles stretch from the Costa
del Sol to Dublin and is it possible that an innocent
child has been taken in a revenge kidnapping?*

Lar presses his hand against his chest, his breathing short
and loud. "It would make sense if the Shroffs demanded
Marcus's release in exchange for us dropping the investigation," he says. "But, if that's the case, we should have
heard from them by now." He frowns, puzzled, and turns to
Amanda. "I wasn't aware that Walker came home a day earlier than planned. Were you?"

"No, I wasn't." She needs to kill his suspicion before it
has a chance to seed. "Knowing Eric's work ethic, I'm sure
he'd a good reason for doing so. We've no proof if any of this
is true. Insinuations, that's how *Capital Eye* develop their
stories."

"You speak from experience, of course." Sylvia crosses
her slender legs and taps her fingers against the front page.
For an instant, it's out there in the open, the hostility Amanda
believes lurks beneath the publicist's composure. It flares her
nostrils, ripples lines across her forehead that quickly vanish
and could have been imagined. Amanda stands, unable to

bear such close proximity to her. Shades of the past are a distraction when all her energy has to be centered on one thing. Can this story possibly be true? She's spoken twice to Eric since Marcus's disappearance. Factual conversations about his contact with his Shroff source. Each time he was adamant that the gang had nothing to do with Marcus disappearing. But Barbara Nelson knew about his investigations into their activities. Somehow, she has acquired his flight details. Amanda moans aloud as she imagines Marcus in a basement, bound and gagged by Billy Shroff or one of his brothers.

"Name your enemies," said Sergeant Moran on the day Marcus disappeared. Amanda had told her about the bullet, the talcum powder, the threatening voice that warned her she was always within eye range. Her encounter with Billy Shroff in her car. The card with the white cross and the sensation that can suddenly come over her, as if someone is behind her, watching her back, waiting for her footsteps to falter.

"I'll ring Walker now." Lar picks up his phone and hits Eric's number. "Find out what the hell is going on."

When Sylvia leaves, Amanda enters her home office and switches on her laptop. Names she hasn't thought about in years appear on her screen. What was her impact on their lives? Had she been a fleeting irritant or an open abscess? Nathan Travers? A politician with an illegal offshore bank account, his political aspirations wrecked by black ink and a brash headline above Amanda's byline. She recognizes another name. A wife who blamed her for the heart attack her husband suffered after Amanda doorstepped him at his son's graduation to ask why he was laundering money for a terrorist organization. She looks at the photograph Shane took of Killer Shroff outside a church. Surrounded by little

girls in white dresses and parasols, Killer was holding his
daughter's plump hand. Her other hand hid her face, as if she
already knew that every occasion in her young life would
be blighted by either press or police. Elizabeth Kelly...the
photograph Shane snatched of her following her son's coffin
from the church. And, at her own funeral such a short time
later, the photograph of Karl Lawson embracing Dominick's
wife.

She stares at Selina Lee's beautiful, battered face.
Amanda, who had spent her childhood witnessing violence,
should have been shocked by the brutality inflicted on her.
Instead, she had been in a fever, demanding information on
Karl Lawson, convinced she was on the edge of breaking
the most important story of her career. She failed to hear, or
chose not to hear, the tremor in Selina's voice. It has taken
her until now to understand that terror has no circumfer-
ence, no time limit. And Constance's parents—oh Jesus,
what must they have endured? And him also... *Vengeance is
mine*, he had said at Elizabeth's funeral; and with that quote
comes a thought that is too preposterous to even consider.
But all these names must be considered as potential enemies
and handed to the police.

Lar opens the door and closes it quietly behind him.

"Did you find out why Eric came home early?" Amanda
clenches her feet to prevent them tapping against the floor.

"His father was unwell," Lar replies. "Seems he suffers
from angina. Eric reckoned he'd enough research gathered
to move the investigation on to the next stage." Nothing in
his tone suggests disbelief. He's convinced the report in
Capital Eye is pure speculation. Apparently, the Shroffs had
no idea he was investigating them or that we are planning
an exposé on their operations. Now that they know, Eric is
terrified they're going to come after him.

She understands what that means. Eric will have to handle his own fears. Her nightmare allows no room for passengers. Shearwater is under siege. More reporters will soon arrive, lured by the sweetness of the Shroff angle; honey to a bee.

Lar stands behind her and massages her shoulders. "I've been harsh with you," he says. "I'm sorry."

He is not used to apologizing and, although it is a small effort, she stores it for comfort.

"We need to be strong for Marcus," he says as he digs deeper into her flesh, trying to unknot the tension from her neck.

"And for each other," she replies.

The police come and go, both plain clothes and in uniform. Amanda can tell by their stances, their blank expressions and gentle politeness, that they fear the worst. Nothing has changed since yesterday. People are still searching, divers still diving. All leads are being followed, insists Caroline, the family liaison officer, when Lar rages at her and accuses the guards of sitting on their hands. His tolerance, always low when things are not working to his satisfaction, is barely contained as the hours pass without word and his sense of helplessness increases.

Soon afterward, he leaves to visit the search center that neighbors, along with parents from Marcus's school, organized in the Rockfield town hall. Mrs. Morris makes coffee and sandwiches and carries a tray into Amanda's office.

"You have to keep up your strength," she says.

The thought of swallowing anything solid clamps Amanda's throat. She is being destroyed by inactivity. The urge to slash through forests of undergrowth, break down the doors of houses, strangle suspects so that they are compelled to spill their secrets into the open, that is all she wants to do.

She waits for the police to phone or call, and Mrs. Morris, who says Amanda must call her Alice, consoles her with stories of children who were lost and then found.

Lar looks defeated when he returns from the search center. And old, *so* old. The evening news comes on. Marcus's school photograph is used and, once again, footage of her arrival at St. Bede's rolls across the screen. LR1 is the only television station to illustrate their news item with film recorded from the press conference.

Another day draws to a close. Lar takes a sleeping tablet and hands one to her. They lie together, a chaste embrace as they wait for oblivion to claim them. And then, on the instant her body relaxes, Karl Lawson's voice flows effortlessly through her mind: *vengeance is mine…mine…mine…*

◆

It's dark outside when Marcus wakes up. He's warm and cozy in bed but he needs to pee. The light shines on the plink at the bottom of his bed. He sleeps with a different one every night. So far, he's slept with Plucky, Ace and Derring-Do. It's Bravo's turn tonight.

He opens the bedroom door. Rainbows shine above him. In the Sudsy Room, Super has left a box in front of the toilet so Marcus can stand on it to pee and another bigger box at the basin so that he can wash his hands afterward. The window is open. He can see the moon. It's like the pumpkin head they made today. They took out all the squishy bits in the middle and cut out eyes and a nose and a mouth. Super put a candle inside it and it looked like the pumpkin head was on fire.

He stands on his tippy-toes and looks down into the apple garden. The trees are like monsters with wavy arms. There's a light shining brighter than the moon, only it's on the ground. Marcus sees a man standing in front of the light. A car is parked on the grass. The man is a robber and he's got Super's car. He's trying really hard to lift something off the ground. A cloud covers the moon and the man isn't there any more. It's like the night Mammy went swimming and Marcus thought the robber was chasing her.

He has to tell Super. He creeps quiet in case the robber comes into Plinkertown Hall. Super is not in the Chow-Chow Room or the Wow-Wagon or in Sleepy Nook. Marcus is afraid to cry in case the robber hears. He wants Mammy but she's still in a Big Apple with Daddy. He's fed up playing the recording of Mammy in the swingy chair. He wants her arms around him. To smell her special smell, like flowers in the garden. He goes back to bed and pulls the duvet over his head. Then it's okay to cry really loud.

"What's the matter, little man?" Super comes into Sleepy Nook and wipes Marcus's tears away. He's breathing heavy, like Mammy does when she goes jogging. He sits on the edge of the bed and tells Marcus not to be frightened. He's chased the robber from the apple garden with a big stick and he'll never come back again to frighten Marcus.

"Did you box him *really* hard?" Marcus asks.

"As hard as I could," says Super. "Right in the middle of his fat, rubbery nose."

Marcus laughs so loud that the tears come again. But they're okay tears because Super is safe and the robber didn't take his car away.

"I want to be Bravo tomorrow," he says and Super nods, like that's a really good decision. Tomorrow is Hallowe'en and they're going to a special fancy-dress party.

"Now, go back to sleep," says Super. "And if the bugs bite…"

"Squash 'em tight," says Marcus.

CHAPTER FIFTY-THREE

Day Five

Telly Babe Caught on CCTV
Lucy Knight

Sensational information has come to light regarding the mysterious behavior of telly babe, Amanda Bowe, on the afternoon of her son's disappearance. The Daily Orb can now reveal that she was caught on CCTV driving into a service station off the M1 to take a phone call from a guard, who intended sending a squad car to collect her. What was she doing on the M1 when, from Howth, she should have been driving on a completely different route? This raises the question once again…who did Mandy meet on that fateful afternoon?

Was her late arrival at her son's exclusive, private school linked to handsome telly hunk, Eric Walker? LR1's poster boy crime reporter arrived home a day earlier than planned from Spain where he had been tracking the movements of the notorious Shroff family as they strutted around the swimming pools and discos of the Costa del Crime. Is it possible that he was

*discussing tactical maneuvers with Bowe in his Sker-
ries apartment when her son went missing and her
elderly husband, LR1's flamboyant owner, Lar Richardson, was in New York? Your fans want answers,
Amanda. Why did you lie about your whereabouts on
that afternoon when you were questioned by gardaí?
Why do you refuse to answer questions from a con-
cerned media, who want to report the truth and assist
in the desperate search for your little boy?*

Her bedroom door is locked when Lar bangs his fist
against it and demands admittance. He's hoarse, choleric
with rage. If she lets him in, he'll beat her up. How can he
not? Her father never needed a reason and Imelda never
knew how to deflect his fury—not until the day she took the
iron she was using on his shirts and pressed it to his face. Her
daughters had left home by then and she no longer needed to
deflect his anger from anyone but herself. She walked away
from his screams and never spoke to him again.

Lar runs at the door and slams his shoulder against it.
He'll have a heart attack if he continues doing that. Amanda
imagines him collapsing to the floor, grasping his chest as
his heart crashes into stillness. What a solution that would
be. No more trying to hold their shattered marriage together.
No more yearning for...for what? Had she ever known what
she wanted until Marcus came and turned her upside down?

She opens the door and waits for Lar to enter. His forehead is beaded with sweat, his complexion dangerously
flushed. He has her father's face, the flint in his eyes, brutality hardening his mouth. She holds herself steady, waits for
the blow that will floor her.

He sinks to the edge of the bed and covers his face. The
noise a man makes when he cries is ugly. It goes against his

instincts, gushed from an internal reservoir with broken walls. She heard her father cry once. He was dying in a hospital ward and wanted his wife's forgiveness. Nothing she or Rebecca said could persuade Imelda to visit him. Forgiveness was in her gift to give but she refused to allow him that relief. As her father wept, Amanda turned away, repulsed by an atonement that was only possible when his impending death had stripped his anger to the core.

"Were you with him?" Loud, racking sobs have withered the strong lines of Lar's face. "Please don't lie to me at this terrible time."

She kneels before him, forces him to look at her. "I'm so sorry you had to be subjected to those lies. Yes, I was with Eric but it's not what you think."

"You've no idea what I'm thinking," he answers, wearily.

"Yes, I do And I don't blame you for being suspicious. I've been advising Eric, passing on the names of the sources I used when I was a crime reporter. He rang me that morning looking for confidential information about Billy Shroff. I was nervous discussing it over the phone and detoured to his place on my way to Howth—"

"Get off your knees, Amanda." He has stopped abbreviating her name and the hard snap of vowels and consonants sound like a curse. When he pushes her away from him, his contemptuous expression disguises his pain. "There's only one reason why you kneel before a man and it's not to offer repentance."

His unrelenting stare is petrifying but she finds the words to pacify him, dredges them from the depths of her heart, which is shredded but still capable of pumping all that is necessary to survive this ordeal. Gradually his set expression, so terse and judgmental, eases. Grief and dread have dazed him, dulled his usual sharpness. All that matters is

Marcus...Marcus...Marcus, and it is the power of their son's name that brings him back to her. Under normal circumstances, he would not tolerate such a betrayal, but there is no longer any normality in their lives. They are being tossed like flotsam from hour to hour, waiting for a call, a demand, a clue, anything to release them from this interminable wait. And so Lar stands and nods, puts his index finger to her lips to silence her torrent of lies. Their acceptance that their marriage has ended is an unspoken acknowledgment but, for now, they will be together for Marcus.

She will be penniless and unemployable. Lar will see to that. Amanda doesn't fear beginning again but without Marcus it will be meaningless. Eric will move as far as possible from her husband's clutches. The Shroffs he can handle. As a crime reporter, he accepts the risk of retaliation. But Lar Richardson is a different matter. Eric is right to fear him.

✦

Lar drives to LR1 in the afternoon. The newsroom is floundering, unsure how to continue covering a story that has the owner and his erring wife at its center. He is still at the meeting when the police come to Shearwater.

"Unfortunately, there have been no new developments this morning." Sergeant Moran is quick to dampen Amanda's expectations. She shakes her head when Mrs. Morris offers to make coffee, and settles heavily into an armchair. Garda Browne remains standing, notebook and pen in hand. Amanda's nervousness grows. They've arrived unannounced, claiming they have nothing new to tell her, yet there is something about the sergeant's tone, a quickening that's slight enough to be imagined; but Amanda is attuned to her every nuance and expression.

"What is it?" she asks.

"An anonymous tip-off," Sergeant Moran replies.

"Regarding Marcus?"

"It's too soon to know if our information has any credibility . . ." The sergeant pauses then continues, "but we're hopeful that with your cooperation—"

"Of course you have my cooperation."

"Our inquiry is not related to Marcus, at least not at this juncture. Whether or not there is a link depends . . ." Again, she pauses and Garda Browne, still standing, says, "It concerns the late Constance Lawson."

Amanda draws back from a name that still has the power to quicken her heartbeat.

"I don't understand." She appeals directly to Sergeant Moran.

"I know that Marcus is all you can think about right now but we have to check if this information has any validity." She sounds apologetic, sympathetic, even, which just fuels Amanda's anxiety. "I need to know if you were receiving confidential information from anyone in Glenmoore Garda Station, the Garda Press Office, or any other member of An Garda Siochána at the time of Constance Lawson's disappearance?"

The question impacts like a fist against her chin. That night in Hunter's car. The two of them alone in the industrial estate. Planes flying low overhead and the suffocating sensation that came over her when she heard that Karl Lawson was not guilty—*not* guilty . . .

Garda Browne waits, pen poised in hand, to record her response, and Amanda feels it again; that same gagging feeling of being caught out in the wrong.

"No. I certainly was not receiving that kind of information from anyone on the force." Deny, deny, deny. Hunter had drilled that one word into her when the investigation into their activities was taking place. That same advice must hold true now.

"Our tip-off suggests otherwise," says Garda Browne.

"Why would you pay attention to an anonymous tip-off?"

"It could be malicious," Sergeant Moran admits, then continues, "but we have to investigate it, especially when it concerns you. It implies that during our search for that unfortunate young girl, you used confidential information known only to gardaí and reproduced it in *Capital Eye*."

"Correction, Sergeant Moran. I researched my facts, made phone calls, established what I believed to be the truth." Amanda holds herself steady, braced against the next blow. Fear is weakness. To show it is advantageous to the accuser. "As a reporter that was my duty. The information I used was in the public domain. It was simply a case of unearthing it. I didn't need sources in the gardaí to help me."

"The tip-off we received suggests you were in an intimate relationship with a member of the force during that period," says the sergeant. "It also infers that you remained in touch with your source until shortly after Karl Lawson was released from custody. The information on his impending release could only have come from a garda source. Is there any truth to that allegation?"

"Absolutely not." Bile fills her mouth. She swallows, struggles to remain still. Body language, they can read it like a book. "Why are you following up on an anonymous tip-off that is totally untrue when you should be out searching for my son?"

Garda Browne scribbles furiously in his notebook and asks, "Can you tell us why you suddenly switched from your belief that Karl Lawson was guilty of his niece's—"

"I never claimed he was guilty, nor did I name him. I simply reported on the investigation. I was doing—"

"As you're aware, the implications of what you wrote had

far-reaching effects on his life, " Sergeant Moran smoothly intervenes. "Why did you suddenly change from your *perceived* notion that he was guilty to your belief that he was innocent and worthy of a campaign that demanded his immediate release?"

"He was the victim of a miscarriage of justice. I investigated the truth and helped him gain his freedom."

"For that reason he should be grateful to you. Why list him among your possible enemies?"

"Because of the media frenzy surrounding—"

"A frenzy you were responsible for starting," the sergeant curtly interrupts her. "What we're trying to do now is establish whether or not the tip-off we received is connected to your son's disappearance and worth investigating."

Amanda moans and rocks backward, forwards. The wall facing her is invisible, yet she feels as if her head is thudding against it, like she used to do when she was a child alone in her room, seeking courage from the pain. This new pain is inflamed with a terrible truth. Gangsters have nothing to do with Marcus's disappearance. They are professionals. Like Lar, they look at the bottom line. A ransom note would have arrived by now. Not an anonymous tip-off. Somehow, in the middle of a crowded road, Karl Lawson grasped her son's hand and led him away. He is manipulating the media, feeding them information drip by drip, destroying her as she destroyed him. It's not only Amanda Bowe he wants to punish. It's Eric and Lar, all culpable; and, now, Hunter—

"Karl Lawson has Marcus." She states this fact with absolute conviction. "It's his way of punishing me for reporting on his guilt."

"You've just told us you never claimed he was guilty." Garda Browne sounds like a smug schoolboy who has tripped her up in the schoolyard.

"The media picked up on his relationship with those young girls. Those concerts . . ." She bites hard on her lip, her conviction growing. Memories surge forward and demand to be examined. Not that they've ever gone away but, until now, she's always been able to contain them. She recalls Eric's bravado as he banged on the front door of Lawson's house, shoved his questions through the letter box, all the emails he sent, the phone calls, the chase.

"Before we go, I'd like to confirm what you've told us." Sergeant Moran prepares to leave. "At no time during the search for Constance Lawson, or on any other occasion before and afterward, did you receive confidential information from any member of An Garda Siochána."

Has Hunter been questioned? Has he been strong enough to deny any knowledge of their relationship? Amanda has to believe in him.

"I've never received such information at any time," she replies.

Garda Browne snaps his notebook closed.

"Should you think of anything that will help us to further our investigations, don't hesitate to contact us." The sergeant tightens the belt on her hi-vis jacket. Solid brawn, she is a poker-faced harridan, Amanda thinks, who is trying to destroy her. "We'll be in touch again as soon as there is anything new to report in our search for Marcus."

"What about Karl Lawson? Aren't you going to bring him in for questioning?" Her knees shake. She presses them together, aware of Garda Browne's scrutiny. "He told me once he'd get his revenge. He quoted the Bible at me—vengeance is mine, and recompense, for the time when their foot shall slip—"

"You think a biblical quote is sufficient evidence to take him in for questioning?" Sergeant Moran asks. "We're a garda force, Mrs. Richardson. Like you, we're professionals when it comes to obtaining results. We base our success on more than a knowledge of Deuteronomy."

Bolts of electricity: Amanda can feel them shooting through her body. The police have departed and the information they left behind has jolted her from the stupor of bewilderment and terror that has imprisoned her since Marcus went missing. Somewhere, beyond the gates of Shearwater, Karl Lawson is waiting for her to find her son.

She leaves Shearwater, drives past the journalists, who move rapidly out of the way, uncaring whether or not they follow as she heads toward the M50, her foot hard on the accelerator.

✦

Spiderwebs and skeletons hang from the windows in Cherrywood Terrace. Tombstones lean at dangerous angles in front gardens, pumpkin heads glimmer in porches. Soon, the little ones will emerge, shy witches and devils clinging to their parents' hands, as Marcus did last year when he dressed as a plink and Amanda called with him to their neighbors on Bayview Heights.

She brakes outside the house where Karl Lawson used to live. The garden has the tufty greenness of fake grass, and a white, mop-headed bichon frise eyes her suspiciously from the living room windowsill. The dog's high-pitched bark sounds faintly through the glass when she rings the doorbell.

"Karl Lawson?" The man who answers the door grabs the dog's collar as she tries to escape into the garden. "I know he lived here years ago but I've had no dealings with him."

"What about his post? Do you have a forwarding address?"

"Afraid not." He shouts above the dog's barking. "Check

with Maria Barnes. If anyone can give you an update, it's her." He drags the dog back from the open door and closes it.

Maria Barnes is waiting at her gate when Amanda crosses the road. "I thought I recognized you." Her gaze is sympathetic. "I'm so sorry about your boy. I pray to God you find him soon. The waiting must be agony." She doesn't pretend a false optimism. She knows how such searches can end.

"Thank you."

"Are you looking for Karl?"

"Yes." She winces, knowing Maria can barely contain her curiosity. "Do you have an address for him?"

"Not since he left here."

"Have you any idea where I can find him?"

"Not a clue, love."

"Do you have an address or a phone number for his wife?"

"Ex-wife, you mean. Nicole married again."

"Who told you that?"

"I phone Jenna Lawson occasionally. Sasha was Nicole's flower girl. Gorgeous kid. Karl adored the ground she walked on."

"Do you have Jenna's phone number?"

"She's changed it. Last time I rang she'd gone ex-directory." She shrugs. "Pity. We were friends when she lived here but people move on with their lives."

"I have to find Karl. Any information, anything—please Maria . . . *think*."

"I've no idea. Even that plea from his brother on *Eavesdrop* didn't turn up anything."

"*Eavesdrop*?"

"The phone-in radio program in the afternoon. Justin and Matthew came on looking for information on his whereabouts. Far as I know, they'd no luck finding him. Karl looked rough the last time I saw him, like he was homeless. But don't ask me where he was staying."

"You must have *some* idea where I can find him." Amanda wants to shake information from her. "You knew enough about him when Connie disappeared."

"You mean Constance?" Maria tilts her chin, narrows her eyes. "Call the child by her proper name. I hated the way you always shortened it."

Amanda shakes her head, attempts an apology. "I didn't mean that to sound the way it came out..."

"It doesn't matter. You should ring *Eavesdrop*. Maybe they can help."

Maria is still standing at her gate when Amanda drives from the terrace.

She parks by the side of Turnstone Marsh and rings the producer of *Eavesdrop*. He is apologetic but unable to help. Justin Lawson and his son's appeal for information yielded no results, but he texts Amanda a link to the program.

She listens to the recording on her phone, afraid to fast forward in case she misses a vital clue that will help her to locate him. Justin Lawson sounds emotional when he asks the listeners if they can help him trace his brother's whereabouts. His son also speaks. Matthew, a teenager now, or near enough, repeats his father's plea for information. Amanda remembers interviewing him on a farm—no, not a farm, a horse shelter in Wicklow. She found him mucking out stables, the smell of horse on his clothes. He was fearful, shying from her questions, hiding information out of some misguided loyalty to his uncle, or so she had believed. By the time she drove back to Glenmoore, Karl Lawson had been taken in for questioning and she had decided to run with the Selina Lee story instead.

A group of teenagers carrying planks of wood and old tires pass by. They clamber up the embankment into the marsh.

A bonfire will blaze there tonight. Amanda is filled
with an impulse to visit the girl's grave. Not that it really
is her grave, of course, but it's where she always imagines
Connie—*Constance* to be.

Six years ago, she'd watched from a distance as a digger sank teeth deep into the earth and guards in boiler suits
made their fatal discovery. She must have felt sad at the time.
She wants to recall that emotion, yet all that comes to mind
is the adrenaline rush that thrust her forward into the center
of the story.

The pull to return to the site is so strong that she turns
on to Orchard Road. The dour exterior of the old house
looks like a perfect location for a Hallowe'en celebration of
ghouls and lost souls. A new gate has been erected outside
it. Solid steel and high, it hides the grim house beyond it.
The boundary wall has been repaired, the brick that crushed
the life from Constance long removed. What is she supposed
to do here? Stand above an empty water tank and pray for
the young girl's soul? Amanda doesn't believe in the soul.
Death is final. The idea of a fluttering dove rising above her
mortal body was comforting when she was a child but not
now. Constance Lawson is ash, scattered across an American landscape. She drives away without looking back.

✦

The wind is sharp on the Liffey boardwalk. No one is relaxing on the benches overlooking the river apart from a young
man in an anorak, who stares at the photograph of Karl Lawson with the zoned-out gaze of a drug addict.

"What ya' say his name is?" he asks her for the third time.

"Karl Lawson."

She printed the photograph from her Constance Lawson
file. It was taken when he was on his way into Glenmoore

Garda Station for questioning. She has others. The one Shane took on that first morning when he opened the door of his brother's house and dismissed her with a glance. Seven days later he looked unrecognizable, shoulders hunched, his eyes wasted as he was ushered past her into the police station.

"Na, never seen 'im." The man scratches at a pimple on his cheek. He looks so young, a teenager, his features hardened with street knowledge.

"Look at him again," Amanda begs.

"Is he yer ould man?"

"No, he's not my husband," she replies. "Please think carefully. It's important. Have you seen him around here recently?"

"Why? Wha's he done den? Are ya a bleedin' cop?"

"No." She transfers a twenty-euro note from her wallet to the empty carton on the bench beside him. He immediately shoves it into the pocket of his anorak.

He slides his hand over one half of the face and squints at the image. "Could be Scarface 'cept for da hair. He's black."

"Scarface?"

"Yeah...like in the film. Haven't seen him in ages. He's okay, not like some o' the fuckers dat hangs around here. Have ya checked the hostels?"

"Yes. No one's been able to help me."

"If I see him I'll ger him to ring ya. What's yer number?"

"It's okay. Forget it." Time is of the essence and she is wasting it.

"Suit yerself, missus." He shuffles off, heading for a hostel or a fix.

The river is choppy as it runs toward Dublin Bay. A woman begging on the arch of the Ha'penny Bridge, her face raddled from drink and the open air, glances at the photograph and says, "Feic off, luv. He'll be home when he's good'n ready. Give us a few euros for a bed."

"Have you seen him, please? It's very important that I find him."

"Yeah, I knows him." The woman's gaze fastens on the twenty-euro note in Amanda's hand. "But it's ages since I seen him 'round here. Heard he headed to Belfast... or was it Galway? Jaysus, me head's all over the place deze days." She plucks the money from Amanda's hand and holds it out for inspection. "Hope ya find him, luv. Give him a cuddle from me when ya do."

Alms for information, yet nothing she hears brings her any nearer to Karl Lawson. She's exhausted when she enters a cafè and finds an empty table. A man sitting opposite her reads the late edition of *Capital Eye*. The paper hides his face but Amanda can see the headlines. A warning from the fire services about the dangers of Hallowe'en bonfires. A hurricane is causing havoc in the Pacific Ocean. Ben Carroll is launching his fourth book tonight in the Browse Awhile bookshop. Tears rush to her eyes at the sight of his name. Browse Awhile was where she planned to bring Marcus on Hallowe'en... but the plink author is quickly forgotten as she reads the headline above Barbara Nelson's byline: *Constance Lawson—Tragic Link to Missing Boy*. She's unaware that she has cried out until he lowers the paper and asks if she's okay.

She nods at her cup. "Coffee's too hot."

"Take it slowly," he says and continues reading.

"Can I borrow it?" She reaches toward his paper. "I'll only be a minute."

"Take it," he says. "I'm leaving now."

Sensational information has come to light regarding the disappearance of Marcus Richardson, 4. Earlier rumors that he had been kidnapped by the notorious Shroff crime

*gang have now been ruled out by gardaí. An undisclosed
number of men, believed to belong to the gang, were
taken into garda custody for questioning. All have been
released without charge. Now, an anonymous tip-off to
gardaí alleges that Marcus Richardson was abducted
by someone he trusted. It also claims that there is a link
between the boy's disappearance and the tragic death of
Constance Lawson, whose body was recovered from a
disused water tank after an extensive seven-day search.*

*Six years ago, Marcus's mother, chat show presenter,
Amanda Bowe, 32, dominated the media coverage
throughout that tragic week with her headline-grabbing
features and knowledge of the on-going garda investigation. Without naming Karl Lawson, uncle of the missing teenager, as a suspect she, nonetheless, created an
atmosphere of suspicion around him.*

*In the aftermath of Lawson's arrest, an investigation
was launched by gardaí to find out if confidential information had been leaked to Bowe by a mole within the
gardaí. This was dropped due to lack of evidence. It has
now been reopened. Questioned today at Shearwater,
her luxurious home on the summit of Bayview Head,
Bowe insisted she has never received confidential information from a member of—*

Unable to read any more, Amanda closes the paper and
half-stands. Her legs refuse to support her and she collapses
back into the chair, causing it to slide against the tiled floor.

A woman sitting opposite her says, "Oh, my God, you're
Mandy Meets."

Her voice carries across the café. Conversation stops. The
silence that follows is heavy with sympathy. It lifts Amanda
to her feet. As she hurries from the café, she glimpses her

reflection in the window. Her hair is lank. She can't remember when she last washed it. Oh, yes, she can. The morning of the day she met Eric. When all that mattered was wringing pleasure from stolen hours.

Three red devils with horns and tridents, and a monstrous green hulk, pass by on their way to a Hallowe'en party. One of the devils waves his trident in her face and shouts, "Be a bad angel and come with us."

Green lights under the Ha'penny Bridge reflect on the river. Love locks are padlocked to the railings. The custom is forbidden by the city council but who would pay attention to a rule that attempts to stifle love?

✦

"We need to talk." Hunter rings as she's about to start her car. He sounds as if he's on a marathon with no finishing tape in sight. "Can you meet me tonight?"

"Are you mad? The police—"

"We can't discuss this on the phone," he interrupts, his breath loud in her ear. "I'll be waiting at the old boatyard belonging to your husband."

"I can't. For God's sake, Hunter, it's too risky."

"We *have* to talk. I'll see you there," he says and hangs up.

✦

When she returns to Shearwater, the whiskey bottle on the occasional table is half empty and Lar looks as if he has every intention of finishing it.

"As usual, you're at the center of the storm, Amanda," he says. "Who was your source?" His unrelenting stare challenges her to continue lying.

"I didn't have a source." Deny, deny, deny. "But, even if I did, how can you expect me to reveal the name?"

"You're my wife. I expect an honest answer to the questions I ask you." He refills his glass and slams the bottle down on the marble tabletop. "Fool, that I am," he adds, bitterly.

"Being your wife does not negate my responsibility as a journalist," she replies. "Why are we even arguing about this? It's a distraction from Marcus, nothing else."

"You're a skilled liar, Amanda. Don't forget, I know your depths. Tell me his name."

"He doesn't have a name because he doesn't exist. But Karl Lawson does. He's taken Marcus."

"Karl Lawson? Are you mad?"

"I spent hours searching for him today. He's gone to ground. There's only one reason why. He's holding Marcus prisoner—that's if he hasn't already—" She stops, afraid to say the words out loud. Lar waits for her to continue. "We're arguing about something that's unimportant when all the time our son could be dead."

"Don't say that." His color deepens to a dangerous puce. "Don't you dare even think that about my son."

"He's my son, too."

"You weren't thinking about that the day he was taken. Marcus was the last thing on your mind then. Was it worth it, *bitch*? A few minutes' heat for a lifetime of regret." He is spoiling for another row; anything to assuage his anger, the unrelenting tension that holds them together even when it's forcing them apart. "It's all your fault. All your *fucking* fault."

"Karl Lawson—"

"Has nothing to do with this!" he roars.

"You fired him when he was innocent of any wrongdoing."

"I fire people all the time. Do you expect me to list every one of them as my enemy? I paid him off after he claimed unfair dismissal—"

"You boasted that it was a pittance compared to what a court case would have cost you."

He remembers Karl Lawson only as an editor who never wore a tie and liked to tackle controversial issues. He hadn't seen him enter a police station; being led from a courtroom; following a coffin down the steps of a church, his harsh gaze fixed on Amanda. Recompense. She is haunted by images no one else can see.

"I *don't* boast, Amanda, especially over such a trivial matter." Lar is still shouting. "How can you possibly believe he has anything to do with Marcus?"

Would he prefer it to be the Shroffs who have their son? To Lar, that would make sense. A deal done, no matter how high the price. But to believe that the kidnapper is a man shattered by Amanda, and the other reporters, who wove their stories from a frayed fabric? Someone he dismissed because his advertising revenue was more important than his employee's innocence?

✦

Marcus jumps when he hears a bang on the How-To-Do Room's window. So does Super, like he would after sitting down on a big, sharp thorn. They go outside into the apple garden. A dead bird lies on the grass. It's got shiny feathers and eyes like glass. Super says it's a dove that didn't know the window was there. He wraps the dove in a plastic bag and puts it in the freezer. Tomorrow they will have a funeral for the dove, but not now because it's time for Marcus to be Bravo.

His costume feels soft like skin. It fits just right. It's funny being Bravo. He sits behind Super in the car and they go round and round to the top of the car park. Super lifts him on his shoulders and they ride down in the elevator. A girl is dressed like a witch. She shakes her broomstick at Marcus. On the next floor they have to crush up tight because a vampire and a fairy squeeze in beside them with their mammies and daddies. The vampire looks at Marcus and says, "That's Bravo, Mum," as if he's seen a real plink, and Marcus knows he has the best costume of all.

Super says, "Enjoy the Hallowe'en party, children," when the elevator stops and they go out into the street.

The bookshop has balloons like a rainbow over the door and is full of pretend plinks. Some have real costumes and others have masks that the woman in the shop gives them. She shakes Super's hand and says, "The kids are so excited. They're looking forward to hearing you reading from your new book."

Super holds Marcus's hand tight so he doesn't get lost. Emma from school is here. Marcus wants to say "Hi" but Super whispers that the secret has to last *just* a little while longer. Emma puts on a Plucky mask. When Marcus looks again he can't make her out from the other Pluckys.

Super reads his new book. It's *brill*. A man with big glasses shouts, "Let's hear it for Super Plink," and the children clap and jump and scream.

This is Super's last plink book. That's a secret so he can't tell Emma or all the other children in case they get sad. It makes Marcus sad too. But Super says books live forever, especially favorite books, that they live on and on, even after their authors grow old and die.

A girl points at Marcus and laughs when Super lifts him up on his shoulders again and says, "Time to go home to Plinkertown Hall."

A big fire is burning in a field. Marcus can see the flames from the car window. Monsters are jumping around the flames. Last year Mammy bought white stuff and made him a ghost costume but Marcus said, "No! No! No! I'm Super Plink!"

He wants to see the fire. They climb up a hill into the field and there's a river and a mountain and bushes that look like trolls. A monster with bug eyes and a guitar stops playing music and shouts, "Wow! That's some Spiderman threads you and your son are wearing, my man."

The monsters are still jumping and shouting when they go home to Plinkertown Hall. Marcus takes off his Bravo costume. He has hot chocolate with marshmallows and cleans his teeth before going to bed. Hero will sleep with him tonight. Tomorrow night it will be Gutsy's turn, then Super's. But Marcus is not sure he'll still be in Plinkertown Hall then because Super, the real super plink, says seven days will end it all.

He looks out the window after Super hugs him goodnight. There's no robber in the apple garden. Just Super, staring at the sky. It's red. Like all the flames of the bonfire are burning in the clouds.

+

Fireworks explode and set the dogs barking. Bonfires blaze, sirens shriek, the sound faint but insistent. Children, demanding tricks or treats, don't call at Shearwater. That's where the real horror lies and only the police have access to the tragedy within.

Lar is sleeping, drugged with whiskey and a sleeping tablet, when Amanda leaves the house by the back door. She climbs down to the private path that wends its way to the beach below and serves as a short-cut to the harbor. Soon, the waves will wash away her footprints, but it is not enough, not nearly enough. There is a rip tide gathering and it's going to pull her under.

Lar bought the boatyard at the height of the property boom and had planned to build apartments on the site. Luxurious apartments with a view of the sea, they would have fetched a prime price. Then the crash came and the boatyard has been derelict ever since.

Hunter is waiting for her. Impossible to believe she once enjoyed hiding with him in shadows. The abandoned hull of a boat cradles the night and the moon glows over a rusting anchor that lies outside the empty boatyard offices. The interior light flashes on when he opens the passenger door.

"The last thing we should do is meet like this." Amanda slides in beside him. "Why are you exposing me to such a risk?"

"I had to talk to you and the phone is too risky." His fingernails sound like castanets against the steering wheel. "What have you told the guards?"

"Nothing. You?"

He draws in his breath, then exhales loudly. "I've been questioned but I'm in the clear. No one in the force has any reason to associate us. That's the way it will stay, as long as you don't break. You've very vulnerable—"

"*Vulnerable?*" she cries. "I'm distraught! My son is missing, I've no idea if he's alive or dead and all you care about is your own skin. Have you any information about this tip-off—can you tell me *anything*?"

"From what I've been able to find out, it was a text. Untraceable."

"It came from Karl Lawson."

"*What?*"

"You heard me."

"That's ridiculous!"

"He's taken my son. I'm sure it's him."

"Why would he—"

"He must have discovered you were my source. He's been

planting information about me in the media and that anonymous tip-off is his doing."

"You're not making sense, Amanda. Last I heard, he was
wasted. Homeless. How could he possibly take your son and
hide him. There's nothing in the investigation to suggest—"

"There's nothing in the investigation *period*." She begins
to wail, hands to her head like a madwoman who knows no
one is listening to her.

"Stop it, Amanda. Stop it." He grabs her arms, shakes her
into silence. "You're obsessed with that man. You believed
he was responsible for those hoaxes—"

"It's *him*. Marcus is missing for a reason." Why does he
not recognize the obvious? "Revenge. It makes sense. We
all played our part in ruining him. This is his way of getting
back at us and you—"

"*Us?*" His heated denial silences her. "Speak for yourself. I'd good reason to suspect Lawson was guilty—"

He is startled by a flash outside the car window. It comes
again. Lightning-fast. Hunter curses and covers his face.
It's too late. They hear it then: thunder roaring—or is it the
exhaust on a motorbike gaining thrust? The sound is already
fading into the dark and Amanda's hand is unsteady as she
fumbles for the door handle. The car has become too small
for both of them. As the interior light switches on again, she
observes his stunned expression.

"Sylvia mustn't know." He grabs her arm again, grinds
the words at her. "If the worst happens, admit we had some
contact during the Constance Lawson search but admit
nothing else."

Without replying, she tears herself from him and runs
across the beach. The rocks are slippery, strewn with seaweed that squelches underfoot like flatulent frogspawn. Her
feet sink into wet sand. She is awake, yet in the grip of a

familiar nightmare. The one that traps her in slow motion as she tries to move forward and push herself toward safety. But this is not a dream and she is able to move swiftly across the empty beach.

How can she deny the evidence of the camera? It never lies. Except that, of course, is the greatest lie of all.

She doesn't close her eyes throughout the night. She takes no sleeping tablets to dull her wits as she waits for the *coup de grâce*. Which one of the morning newspapers will deliver it? She knows how much patience is needed to organize the type of exposé that took place at the boatyard. The level of information necessary to ensure that everything works according to plan. Shane is versed in night photography. She'd been with him in the past, waiting patiently to capture such a moment. Together, they shared the exquisite relief when it succeeded. Her arms around his waist as he shifted gears on his motorbike and they were gone before those they'd stalked realized their souls had been stolen.

CHAPTER FIFTY-FOUR

The weather has remained mild and bonfires are blazing across the country. Faintly, he hears a fire truck's siren. A bonfire is out of control somewhere nearby. Hallowe'en is a dangerous night, filled with folklore and superstition; he shivers, though his disguise is light and breathable. Spider-man threads. He remembers the guitarist's comment and smiles. He would take it off but Marcus is on high alert in case evil should enter Plinkertown Hall. He needs to be careful. The boy wandering at night is not a good idea. What had he seen when he looked out the window? A robber, he'd said, sobbing and clinging to Super Plink. Leader of the plinks, sworn to protect small children from danger.

He was okay today, his excitement building as the time came to leave Plinkertown Hall in his Bravo costume. The crowd at the book launch had been larger than expected. Small bodies heaving to get close to him. He'd almost lost Marcus in the crush. Still they kept coming to meet Super Plink until Margaret, the owner of Browse Awhile, locked the door and organized an orderly queue outside.

"The children miss you on television," one of the mothers told him when he was signing her daughter's book with his plink fingerprint. "The animated series doesn't have the same appeal as the original. They felt they were part of the story's creation when they drew the pictures with you."

That day on Grafton Street when he'd sketched the boy, Amanda Bowe had asked him how the plinks originated. He had muttered something about doodles, and there they are in his journal. The journey of the plinks. An idea that originated in a prison cell had outgrown him, or so she'd claimed when she insisted the rankings were dropping. Children had stopped watching his program and, as he was no longer needed at the LR1 studio, he had removed the cumbersome Plinkertown set to its new location.

His skin feels tight, a throbbing sensation in his upper lip. A phantom pain, now. But pressure is building, as it did so often in the past. As it did when she leaned toward him in a coffee bar and touched his scar. As it did when he saw her and her husband on the front cover of *Business Font*, a Richardson publication read by corporate tycoons. A two-page feature on the inside had outlined their investment in the plinks and their future plans to develop the brand.

When does wealth satisfy, he'd wondered as he read the article. Does it reach a plateau or become an unassailable mountain? And what is its value against the life of a child?

Revenge has a strange taste, not sweet, nor nasty, just unpalatable, like prison food.

CHAPTER FIFTY-FIVE

Day Six

The sun rises. Clouds trail across the sky, red and blood-ied as opened veins. The digital editions have gone online. A fireman was seriously injured by a flying bottle while he was extinguishing an out-of-control bonfire last night. A stabbing took place at a fancy-dress party and a young man is critical in hospital. On the front page, there's a photograph of all the plinks in the Browse Awhile book-shop, waving at cameras and holding up Ben Carroll's new book. Then, there is the *Daily Orb*. Any hope Amanda had nurtured that the story would have been pulled for the sake of Marcus and all she is enduring is immediately quashed.

Their faces are slightly blurred but recognizable through the front window, as is Hunter's car registration. In the sec-ond photograph, Amanda is reaching toward the passenger door. Her expression reminds her of how her mother's face used to freeze in that lurching instant before she was struck by a fist.

COLLUSION BETWEEN COP AND TELLY BABE
LUCY KNIGHT

*As the hunt for Marcus Richardson, the missing
schoolboy, enters its sixth day, startling information
has come to light regarding collusion between his
mother, telly babe, Amanda Bowe, 32, and Detective
Sergeant Jonathan Hunter, 43, one of the chief investigating officers into the disappearance of Constance
Lawson six years ago.*

*After the tragic discovery of the schoolgirl's body, a
garda inquiry was launched into the leaking of confidential information to Bowe, who was a crime reporter
with Capital Eye at that time. Hunter, who is stationed
at Glenmoore Garda Station, has always strenuously
denied knowing her. He repeated this claim yesterday
during an official garda investigation, instigated by
an anonymous tip-off that claimed there was a link
between the missing schoolboy and the disappearance
of Constance Lawson.*

*Despite this denial, the highly respected and newly
promoted detective sergeant was caught on camera last
night in his car with Bowe. "Knight on the Tiles" has
been reliably informed that he will be suspended from
the force pending further investigations.*

*Gardaí have yet to discover if these two disappear-
ances are connected and the search for Marcus Richardson continues. The substantial reward offered by
Lar Richardson for the safe return of his only child
has failed to cast any further light on the boy's whereabouts. Apart from the anonymous tip-off that claims
this is a revenge kidnapping, the disappearance of
Marcus appears to be a crime without a motive.*

She switches off her laptop. Karl Lawson is Lucy Knight's source. He's been hacking into Amanda's phone since long before Marcus disappeared. She was right when she suspected he was always hiding behind her. His watchful gaze on her back. There can be no other explanation. When she turned suddenly, he was there, not in person but in spirit, tracking her footsteps, planning how to strike at her heart. He eavesdropped on Hunter's desperate plea for a meeting and staged today's exposé with the precision of a trained assassin. Can he be so monstrous, so devoid of human emotion, that he is punishing her child for the sins of the mother? And if he is a monster, why would he spare Marcus? Her legs buckle. How much longer will she be tormented by him? She doesn't want to know the answer but the truth is slowly dawning. Seven days. Seven wrenching, heartbreaking days before she will know the fate of her son.

Lar is still sleeping off the effects of last night's drinking when a car enters the courtyard. She crosses to the window. Sylvia Thornton, punctual as usual. Did she confront her husband before she came here? She must have read the report or received a phone call, a text, a message on Viber or WhatsApp. Why aren't her tires scorching the courtyard? Amanda watches her long-legged stride as she approaches the house. Her hat is wide-brimmed, low over her forehead, and her red, high-waisted coat swings over black boots. She should be wearing armor and carrying a dagger, instead of a briefcase. Her expression is inscrutable as she enters the drawing-room. Is she a robot, programed to withstand emotion? Amanda thinks about the bleach she poured over Graham's clothes when she discovered he was cheating on her. The shirts she shredded. She left chaos behind her in that apartment where they had once planned their future together. Sylvia had made a future with Hunter. They pledged fidelity to each other and walked down the aisle, arm in arm. Yet, last night, Amanda was with him, both of them huddled like fugitives as they discussed how a lie could be shaped into a truth.

"Sylvia, I'm so glad you're here." Amanda sounds composed, but not apologetic. Apologetic equates to culpability and Sylvia must not hear the tremor of guilt in her voice. "I've just seen the online edition of the *Orb*. It's appalling. You have to allow me to explain."

"Why?" Sylvia asks. "What can you tell me that I don't already know?"

"What do you know?"

"That you'll lie to me, as you've been doing ever since your son disappeared."

"I'm not lying, Sylvia. What they've printed is scandalous, manipulated…"

Sylvia is wearing a citrus perfume, a light, fresh scent that imbues but does not dominate the air; yet it is forcing Amanda to breathe shallowly, to speak faster. "I denied knowing Hunter for obvious reasons. He did help me on a few, a very *few* occasions, with some confidential information during the search for that girl. He believed, as I did, that her uncle was guilty and the police were ignoring his findings. We were wrong, horribly wrong, as it turned out. But our relationship was never anything other than professional."

Grubby encounters in unmemorable hotel rooms. The tawdriness of what was once exciting. Those torrid months she'd spent with Hunter have taken on the quality of a dream, or an ancient story told to her by someone else.

"We used each other, that I'll admit," she continues. "Both of us wanted to further our careers. But Hunter never, at any time, betrayed you. That's the truth, Sylvia. We met last night to talk about the reopened investigation.

He was frightened, afraid he would come under suspicion. He needed to know I'd be strong for him. And I would have been... I'd have gone to jail rather than reveal my source. But someone tipped off Lucy Knight and her photographer. I know who it was—oh *Christ*, I know who sent her—"

"I tipped off Lucy Knight." Sylvia speaks distinctly, coldly.

"*What?*"

"I tipped her off," she repeats. "I told her where to find you." She has drawn her shoulders together, as if she needs a barrier between herself and Amanda. No flicker of emotion crosses her face as she calmly admits to ruining her own husband's career and destroying their marriage.

"I don't believe you..." Amanda reels back from the shock of her admission.

"Your belief or otherwise is a matter of complete indifference to me," Sylvia replies.

"Why would you do—?" Amanda slides her tongue over her teeth. She's doing it all the time now. It soothes her, this childhood habit that the pupils in her class used to mock, calling her "Buckteeth Bowe," until she fought the ringleader, loosening one of the girl's own front teeth in the brawl.

"What is your question?" Sylvia spreads out the papers, as she has done every morning since Marcus was taken.

"Why would you destroy your marriage?"

"Since when has that been a concern of yours?"

Amanda's shock is abating, as is her guilt. "You're right. All I care about is finding Marcus. Karl Lawson was your source. He hacked into my phone—"

"My source was anonymous."

"You know it's him. He has my son. Do you understand? He's never forgiven me—"

"Why should he forgive you?" For the first time since Sylvia entered the room her voice shakes, if only slightly; she pauses to steady her words. "You never counted the cost when you and my husband decided to wreck his life."

"We believed he was guilty..." It's warm in the drawing-room, the heating turned up full, but Amanda is unable to stop shivering.

"And now you believe he has your son."

"I *know* he has my son."

"You *knew* he took Constance. You were wrong then. Just as you're wrong now."

"Please help me...*please*."

"I can't, Amanda. The person who has your son is not Karl Lawson."

There is something hidden at the heart of what she has just said. Something that should alert Amanda...would alert her if she was in her studio or investigating a story for *Capital Eye*. Something she should reconfigure, grasp, yet it eludes her. Sylvia Thornton is right. Losing everything that makes life worthwhile has to change a person. But it does not make him invisible. He is somewhere out there and Sylvia, too, is punishing her.

"Sylvia, if you've received any information..." Amanda searches her face for compassion, understanding, relief from her turmoil. "If you know anything that can help the police to find Marcus, *please tell* me."

"The only information I received was from an anonymous source, who claimed you are a liar and a cheat," Sylvia replies. "That was simply a verification of a truth I've known for some time."

"Whatever you're thinking about me, it's wrong—*wrong*."

"Don't patronize me, Amanda. For a detective, my husband was amazingly clumsy when it came to covering his own tracks. You were his first. Did you know that? You left no signs but I sensed your presence. The ones who followed behind you left clues. The back of an earring on the floor of his car. Sand on the soles of his shoes. Unexplained phone calls—"

"I never . . . you're wrong."

"Jon had explanations for everything." Sylvia ignores the interruption. "Explanations I chose to believe. Sounds like a cliché, doesn't it? We all make sacrifices for our children. I chose denial until I was ready to handle the truth." She coughs, an audible rasp, as if her mouth is dry. "You called him 'Hunter' in The Amber Door. I saw him grip your wrist. It was a threatening gesture, not a loving one, but it told me everything. I realized he'd been your source—and much more than that."

"No! That's all he was. My source. I swear to you on my father's grave, there was nothing else going on between us."

Another lie. Cremated and dispersed to the four winds; that's what they did with her father's remains. At his funeral they shook hands with the mourners and agreed that he was, indeed, a devoted husband and father. She leans toward Sylvia, leans so close that she can see the indentation of pain on her skin, faint traces that will, in time, mar her perfect complexion.

"You have to help me, Sylvia. Marcus has nothing to do with any of this. He's a child, scared out of his wits—that's if he's not already . . . *dead*." She whispers the last word, afraid of its force if she speaks it aloud. "You have to tell the police you've been passing information from Karl Lawson to the media. They'll be able to trace his calls to you."

"What can I tell them that they don't already know?" As if Amanda's breath has tarnished her, Sylvia steps back and brushes her hand across her cheek. "They, too, have received an anonymous tip-off but are no nearer to finding your son."

"You know it's him. Where is he, you merciless bitch? Tell me . . . *tell* me."

Sylvia winces when Amanda grabs her shoulders, her head lolling forward in shock and then arching back as she breaks free. "Why should you expect me to reveal my source when you would go to jail rather than reveal yours? If the police want to ask questions, they know where to find me."

She removes an envelope from her briefcase and places it on top of the newspapers. "My letter of resignation. Pass it on to your husband. You and I have nothing more to say to each other."

She leaves as quietly as she entered the room. So many questions still unanswered; but Amanda no longer cares about Sylvia Thornton's dysfunctional marriage, her twisted morals. She outstared Amanda before she left. In her eyes, Amanda saw a glimmer of what she believes was pity— and it adds to her terror.

✦

Lar's hair seems thinner and has turned from silver to an old man's white. He replaces Sylvia's letter of resignation in the envelope and picks up the *Daily Orb*. She waits for him to raise his hand and call her a liar. She would welcome the sting. Anything to relieve the strain on his face as he reads "Knight on the Tiles."

"Karl Lawson is feeding information to the police, to Sylvia, and to the press." She speaks flatly and with certainty. "Seven days, that's how long it took them to recover Constance Lawson's body. He'll kill our son if the police don't find him before then."

He glares at her, his bloodshot eyes filled with contempt. "I've been reading back over your coverage from that time. You destroyed him. You and your *source*."

"Finding Marcus is all that matters, Lar. We must persuade the police to take this search seriously. It's our only hope of finding him alive."

Battle-weary, he is weakening by the hour, but he's finally listening to her.

The guards arrive soon afterward. Is she imagining a new purposefulness about them? Sergeant Moran warns Amanda that she could be charged with obstruction of justice for lying about her relationship with Detective Sergeant Jon Hunter. But, for now, Marcus's whereabouts is their only consideration. They are still following other lines of inquiry, but a full-scale search for Karl Lawson is underway.

✦

Once again, she drives away from Shearwater. Cameras are lifted, mouths move as reporters scatter before her.

Rebecca answers the door. "Come in." She draws Amanda by her hands into her kitchen. "Mam's already here."

She has changed the kitchen decor since the last time Amanda visited. A retro fifties design: baby-pink cupboards, checkerboard flooring, tubular chairs and feel-good mottos on the wall. They advise Amanda to dance if she stumbles. To live the life she loves.

Imelda is scalding a teapot and the table is set with willow-pattern china. "Oh, my poor darling," she says. "Those terrible things they're writing about you. How can they be so cruel when your poor heart is breaking." She speaks as if Marcus is dead.

Amanda sinks into a chair and waits while her mother pours tea. Imelda's hands shake and Amanda is reminded of Elizabeth Kelly, her desperate efforts to be polite while she quivered with grief over her dead son.

"Were you with Eric Walker that afternoon?" Rebecca

stands, arms folded. Ignoring Imelda's *tut-tut* warning, she stares directly at her sister. "Did you ask me to collect your son from school so that you could lie in another man's bed?"

Danny enters the kitchen and pauses, caught in the middle of an awkward silence. A civil defense volunteer, he has been active in the search for Marcus. So, too, has Rebecca, along with Imelda, who manages the tea and coffee urns at the town hall. Amanda wants to ask them how much hope the volunteers still carry within them, but is afraid of their reply. Danny mutters an excuse about a phone call he has to make and retreats from the tension.

"Tell us the truth, Amanda." Imelda holds her hands. "That's all we're asking."

They once lived in a house that breathed danger over the truth. Where it was hidden behind Venetian blinds and silenced behind closed doors. Constant fear exposed them to shame. Rebecca wet the bed until she was ten. Amanda banged her head off the bedroom wall to drown out their father's rage. He died shortly after Imelda had branded him with an iron and closed the front door on his agony. A stroke followed. Suppressed fury can do that. His high blood pressure took care of the rest. Did she kill him, Amanda's wilting mother, who had endured the unendurable until her children were strong enough to walk away?

The tea scalds Amanda's lips and the cup clinks against the saucer when she sets it down. The tears come without warning. A sluice gate opening. She throws her head back and howls, blinds her eyes with salt. She never wants to stop. Imelda dabs at her face with tissues and tries to quieten her, suspecting, perhaps, that she wants to bang her head against the wall again. The truth flutters in her throat. Like wings trapped for so long that the bird has forgotten how to fly. She spits out the lies she has told and waits for redemption. Does redemption have a form, a lightness? Something she can hold on to when the grieving becomes too great? Tomorrow is All Souls' Day and the end of everything has yet to come.

✦

Plinkertown Hall is quiet. The phones don't ring here but Marcus sees Super texting and then throwing his phone into the water barrel. He doesn't know Marcus is watching. When Marcus pulls over a bucket to stand on so he can see into the barrel, Super's phone has disappeared.

"Whoa, there," says Super and grabs him. "Be careful. I don't want to fish out a wet plink."

They eat spare ribs with their fingers in the Chow-Chow Room and Super says the adventure in Plinkertown Hall will soon be over. Mammy and Daddy will be home from a Big Apple. Feeling sad and happy together makes a funny feeling in Marcus's tummy. He really wants to see them again but he won't be able to do adventures any more in Plinkertown Hall, or play football and hide-and-seek with Super in the apple garden.

Super takes the dove from the freezer and lies him down in a little box. The dove is cold as ice and hard like the ornaments on Mammy's mantelpiece. He takes a big spade from the garden shed and gives Marcus a little spade so he can help dig the grave. They march across the apple garden with their spades over their shoulders and Super sings the song about Ace, the pilot plink, who makes holes in clouds for dead doves to fly straight up to heaven.

CHAPTER FIFTY-SIX

Day Seven

The morning air is heavy with a charred, dangerous mist that blurs the ferries on the horizon, and the shriek of seagulls has a muffled harshness. Amanda reads through the morning online editions Nothing. No scoops, exposés, front-page headlines with question marks. Her son has become yesterday's news.

Eventually, the mist clears. The hours pass without any further information from the police. She accompanies Lar to Rockfield Town Hall. The volunteers accept her thanks and murmur quiet words of sympathy.

The reporters outside Shearwater have followed them to the town hall. Questions are shouted at her. Eric's name, Hunter's name; too many fists coming at her. Was that how it was for Karl Lawson as he felt his reality sliding from him? Coming here was a mistake. She nods to Lar, who follows her to his car. The journalists stay with them. She recognizes Shane. He looks more ruffled than ever; heavier too. She has always thought of him as being on her side. But he was only ever on the side of the picture.

A text comes through to her phone as Lar drives away. Another journalist, another question—she will ignore it. A second text arrives, and then another, the repetitive bleeps demanding she pay attention. No name on the screen, just an unknown number. The same message in each text, and it touches the nadir of her fear.

For in six days the LORD made the heavens and the earth, the sea, and all that is in them, but he rested on the seventh day.

Seven days … seven days—finally she has the information she needs. Karl Lawson is resting today, his work done. She screams. Lar's arm jerks at the wheel. The car swerves, then steadies, as he indicates and brakes at the side of the road.

"What is it?" he shouts. "Show me."

His mouth stretches in a rictus as he reads the text. He orders her to stop screaming. "I can't think … can't *think*," he repeats.

"Karl Lawson sent those texts." She needs to be understood, believed.

"A *biblical* quote." Lar is dismissing her already.

"It's a warning. He's killed Marcus. That's why he's resting."

"That's a crazy assumption to make." His fury heaves toward her.

"Don't you understand?" She will scream again if he doesn't listen. "Constance Lawson was found on the seventh day. He's punishing me—oh *Jesus*, I know where he's buried Marcus. We have to go to Cronin's orchard … search the water—"

"You're hysterical." He shakes her into silence, then pushes her away, distancing himself from information he can't bear to hear. "You know nothing. In all probability this is just a stupid hoax …"

He is unable to continue. Perspiration beads his forehead as he calls Sergeant Moran on his Bluetooth. Their conversation is short and terse.

"We have to bring your phone straight to the police station and let them handle it," he says when the call ends. "They want to trace the number."

"There's nothing to trace. He'll have destroyed his phone by now." Amanda imagines him bringing the heel of his boot down on the screen, crushing its memory, destroying evidence they so desperately need.

"Even if he's destroyed it, they have ways of tracing his call." Lar indicates and pulls out into the traffic. "We can't handle this on our own."

Cronin's orchard . . . she must go there and tear at the earth with her bare hands. Then her boy, her darling boy, won't be alone any longer. She opens the passenger door. The road blurs as she prepares to jump from the car. Lar yells and pulls her back with his free hand.

"What the hell do you think you're doing?" he roars as the car skids to a halt.

"Karl Lawson's phone is probably at the bottom of a river. Why won't you *listen*? Marcus is buried in that same water tank where Constance Lawson's body was found."

He slaps her face. She doesn't care if he strikes her again and again. If he knocks her senseless into the middle of next week. Her father's favorite remark when Imelda upset him. Amanda wants her now, her mother's arms around her as they lift her child back into the light. Lar rubs his hands together, then strokes her reddening cheek.

"We'll go there now," he says. His eyes remind her of pebbles, washed by tides until they are lusterless.

Rain begins to fall as he drives along the M50. His car, as sturdy as an armored tank, rocks in a sudden gust of wind. It will take at least forty minutes to reach Glenmoore. Amanda should be alarmed by the cars in front; water is aquaplaning from their wheels as the rain increases, yet Lar does not slow down.

Sergeant Moran contacts them again.

"Amanda believes Marcus is—" Lar's voice cracks and he coughs, unable to continue.

"Karl Lawson has buried him in the water tank where Constance Lawson was found," Amanda cries.

"That's a huge assumption to make, Mrs. Richardson." The sergeant's usually abrupt tone has softened and become speculative.

"What else can it mean?" Amanda slumps back in the passenger seat. Which is more horrifying? Being believed or not believed?

"Go home." The sergeant barks the order at them. "We need your phone, Mrs. Richardson. Let the gardaí do their work. We'll notify the Glenmoore station of your suspicions and they—"

Lar cuts her off in mid-sentence and disables his phone without decreasing his speed.

The traffic is light as they veer off the M50 at the Glenmoore junction. Withered leaves, bedraggled and torn from the trees, rush past the window. By tomorrow the branches will be bare, the desolation of winter upon them.

As if anticipating their arrival, the gates of the old house are open. The front door has been replaced, the windows repaired. The blinds are closed.

Three squad cars from Glenmoore Garda Station have arrived and are parked under the trees. Lar brakes behind them and grabs Amanda's hand as they run toward the orchard. They are drenched within seconds. Rotting fruit squelches under her feet. Her stomach heaves at the sound. A guard in a hi-vis jacket approaches and holds out her hands to prevent them moving nearer.

Amanda remembers her face but not her name. She was part of the team who stood on that same patch of ground on the day Constance's body was discovered. The scene behind her is terrifyingly similar. The digger and the mound of earth. Young guards in boiler suits plying the lid off the water tank.

"You can't be here." The woman speaks with implacable authority. "You must let us do our work."

"No!" Amanda could move a mountain with her fist—with the force of her anxiety. She remembers the policewoman's name: Detective Garda Newton, Hunter's partner. When Amanda tries to shove her aside, the detective holds her in a surprisingly powerful grip and turns her away from the yawning chasm.

The police look down, their solid backs blocking Amanda's view. An early darkness has followed the rain and the natural light is fading from the orchard. Somewhere among the dripping branches a crow caws, an ugly, discordant refrain. She hears the grunt of a guard descending into the tank. A voice calls for the searchlight to be brought closer. Lar's face is wet with rain, or it could be tears that drip from his chin. They hold on to each other as the detective, with a stern warning not to move any closer, joins the team of diggers.

"Be brave," Lar whispers. He shakes as if a palsy has settled on him.

Amanda can see the lid lying on its side, the crowbar alongside it. A ladder has been inserted into the tank. The mound of earth has turned to sludge and is already oozing back into the opening. Lightning streaks across the sky. Sullen clouds roll out their thunder. It seems as if the elements are echoing her howl of loss as the guard lifts her son's small body from the tank and lays him gently on the ground.

Her father beat her once. Amanda couldn't remember it happening. Rebecca said she watched from behind the sofa as Amanda lay unconscious on the floor. Amanda's only recollection was stars spinning and then turning into a black, bottomless hole … and it is that same sensation again, only this time Lar is holding her upright until the blackness clears from her eyes.

Marcus has been buried in a hoodie—no, not a hoodie, a sleek, illuminated wetsuit. A mask covers his face. This is beyond horror. Beyond wailing, beyond gnashing of teeth. The man who lifted him free from the water tank utters a curse, four letters shattering the dumbed hush. He roughly turns her son over on to his stomach. He is treating Marcus like a piece of jetsam that he has fetched from the deep. How dare he show such irreverence for his small, broken body?

Amanda covers her eyes when she hears the glide of a zip being pulled downwards. She wants to be blinded forever so that she doesn't have to witness what follows. Voices mutter, exclaim, shout. Lar utters a startled expletive, then orders her to listen to him and stop wailing. This is not their son. Nor is this flaccid object human at all—or animal.

She is allowed to draw nearer. When she dares to look, the back of the wetsuit is open, only it's not a wetsuit, as she'd thought. It is supple and rippling, a woven, tufted fabric with a velvety pile, like the coat of a sleek, upright creature—like a plink. Inside, it is stuffed with what looks like coarse horsehair that could have come from inside an old mattress and there are newspapers shoved underneath. Detective Newton deftly transfers a copy of *Capital Eye* into a plastic bag but not before Amanda sees the headline, her bold byline and the profile picture that the editor had always used for her features. The detective continues removing newspapers. Seven days of headlines that destroyed Karl Lawson. More recent *Capital Eye* editions follow, as well as the *Daily Orb* and the other newspapers that have charted the days of Marcus's disappearance. Features that have destroyed Amanda's marriage and lost her her son—for Marcus is surely dead by now. Murdered by Karl Lawson, who has finally exacted his revenge.

A second guard climbs back up the ladder. He carries a transparent plastic bag filled with what looks like a collection of small dead animals, squirrels or rabbits, perhaps. Detective Garda Newton holds out the bag for Amanda's inspection. In the beam of the searchlight, she realizes these are not dead animals. They are Marcus's favorite toys. At home, in his silent bedroom, similar toys line the bottom of his bed, awaiting his return. Even his favorite toys…Karl Lawson knows everything about her son.

"Plinks." The name is dry on her lips.

"What did you say?" the detective asks.

"Marcus loves the plinks."

The guard who'd fetched the plinks from the deep, who is probably a father, nods, as if he understands how children would find these fantasy creatures so captivating. He removes a second transparent bag from the tank. This one contains a copy of *Business Font*. Lar's face is on the cover, his gaze arresting, triumphant. A man at the zenith of a successful business deal. Amanda is standing beside him, equally assured. Inside, on the center page, will be the double-spread feature outlining the deal they'd signed with Ben Carroll. The glowing references to their business acumen mask the fact that this had been a shady transaction.

They had pulled the wool over Ben's inexperienced eyes and deprived him of the potential to make a fortune from his fantasy creation. Amanda had felt uneasy when she read that feature. Such deals were done all the time. She had convinced herself that entrepreneurs took risks and needed recompense for their investments. Ben had been a pavement artist, who would have remained on the fringes of street life if she hadn't lifted him up off his knees.

The lid is being replaced on the water tank. The digger growls as the claws sink once again into the mound of mud. Soon, all will be as it was when the police arrived. Her feet sink into the sodden terrain. The grotesque creation that she'd believed to be her son's body has been deflated. A guard is preparing to bag it. A forensic photographer is at work; but this is not a crime scene. It is a tease, a torment. A new puzzle that they must piece together.

The magazine is being bagged and, now that she's seen it in these surreal surroundings, Amanda's agitation increases. Something is eluding her, something she needs to understand . . . and when she realizes the truth—when she finally allows it space to grow—it strikes her with the force of a thunderbolt.

Scarface, that's what the homeless boy on the boardwalk called him. Scarface, like in the film. But . . . Karl Lawson's face is not scarred. When she saw him at Elizabeth's funeral, he still had those long, bony cheeks and arrogant mouth.

"He's black," the boy had said, referring to Scarface's hair and not, as Amanda now realizes, to his skin color.

She digs her nails into her palms as she recalls that haunting sense of awareness she experienced on the few occasions she had seen Ben Carroll without his costume. His pallor emphasized by that matt, black sweep of hair falling over his forehead. His face disfigured by that scar and those glasses, the blue hue obscuring the clarity of his eyes. His accent, the drawling vowels and soft T's reminding her of New York, so that it was his accent, not his voice, she always heard.

This is a preposterous thought, impossible. The raucous crow, as if sensing her outrage, flies above her head in a flurry of wet feathers.

CHAPTER FIFTY-SEVEN

Lar is speaking to Detective Garda Newton when Amanda runs toward the old house. The rain has stopped but the trees are still weeping. The door knocker shines with brassy newness. She bangs it repeatedly. The sound that echoes back belongs to empty spaces.

At the back of the house, the blinds are drawn and she is unable to see inside. She rattles the handle on the door. To her surprise, it's unlocked. She steps into a spacious kitchen with white walls and modern, built-in cupboards. The marble surfaces are bare and gleaming. The cupboards are empty and spotless, not even a crumb or a spill to suggest they'd ever held food. She moves through the downstairs rooms. Sterile, impersonal surroundings, no photographs or bric-a-brac to give them a sense of ownership. One room has a child's desk with two bright red chairs, the only splash of color in this stark, white space. Another room is clearly used for sleeping and has two beds, both stripped of bedlinen. Upstairs, the rooms are spotless but empty, the walls also painted white.

She returns to the bedroom. Marcus has been here. She feels this certainty on her skin, tingling. In her heart, pounding. In her brain, spinning. She kneels beside the nearest bed and closes her eyes. *Come to me…come to me*, she calls to him from the depths of her soul—yes, her soul, that only he has ever managed to unearth and touch. He is so close. She can smell his sleepy muskiness, feel his dewy warmth when he awakens in the mornings. She opens her eyes and sees it—a sliver of amber between the mattress and the wooden base of the bed. She thinks about the sliver of her flesh captured on camera as she ran from her car to his school. It revealed everything, laid bare her guilt…and this, now, this sliver of evidence is within her grasp.

She slides her hand under the mattress and draws out the crumpled piece of fabric that carries her son's sweat, carries the imprint of his body. The Super Plink T-shirt he was wearing under his uniform on the afternoon he disappeared.

Someone knocks at the front door, the sound urgent, demanding. Lar is outside with the police, a huddle of them searching for her, drawn to the house by the lights. Wordlessly, she holds Marcus's top out to Lar, but it is taken from her by Detective Newton and bagged as evidence before he can touch it.

In Glenmoore Garda Station, she sips hot tea and shivers under a blanket someone has found for her. Facts have come to light. The house belongs to Ben Carroll, who had located Isaac Cronin's next-of-kin and bought it shortly after he signed away his rights to all plink merchandise. Burned out fragments from the set of Plinkertown Hall have been discovered in the orchard. A new investigation is beginning and, once again, Amanda can do nothing but wait.

✦

Back at Shearwater, she switches on her laptop and studies photographs of Karl Lawson. He is angry in each one. That was what she'd always thought until now. Angry and aggressive, guilty too. But, now, she sees his fear, his bewilderment.

His struggle to grasp what was to come. She searches for photographs of Ben Carroll and finds only a few. They have been taken mostly from oblique angles, so that his face is shadowed or the brim of his hat shades his eyes. She studies his angular cheeks, the disfigurement of what was once an arrogant mouth, and knows that her suspicion is right.

Lar acts as if she has taken leave of her senses when she insists that Karl Lawson and Ben Carroll are one and the same. His eyes bulge with disbelief; in the midst of his terror, he now also has to deal with a crazed wife. Everything has changed with the discovery that Ben Carroll is responsible. When Lar thinks it through, he understands why. Resentment over a business deal. He has been there many times in the past, when those who believed he'd pulled the wool over their eyes raged and threatened legal action against him. None had dared to do what Ben Carroll did—Lar is prepared to accept that fact—but to suggest he's been hoodwinked by a man with a double identity is ludicrous.

They are still arguing when Amanda's phone rings. An unknown number appears on her screen. A woman speaks her name.

"Mrs. Richardson, is your husband with you?"

"Yes, he's with me. What do you want?"

"Please put your phone on speaker," she says. "And listen carefully to what I have to tell you."

✦

Super makes pancakes with Nutella for breakfast. Marcus eats three and Super says, "Whoa there, little man. If you eat any more you'll never fit into your Bravo costume." He laughs real loud when Marcus sticks out his tummy like a kangaroo but then his face is sad again, like when he told Marcus that their Plinkertown adventure was over.

After breakfast, Marcus puts on his Bravo costume. Super was wrong. It zips up real easy.

The rain is still falling when they reach the big city. Super shelters Marcus under an umbrella and they run all the way to the Children's Cave so they don't get wet.

Marcus loves the Children's Cave. It has trampolines and slides and a swimming pool and a stage with lots of little chairs in front and a place with buns and cakes and crisps. A plink poster is on the wall outside the acting cave. Super reads the words out loud. *Final Performance of* PLINKER-TOWN HALL.

He brings Marcus to the front row and says, "You're a very special boy, Marcus. I'll never forget you." He gives Marcus a plink lollipop and popcorn and goes behind the curtains on the stage.

The plinks come out and shout hello to the boys and girls. Super looks smaller than he does in Plinkertown Hall. His voice sounds different when he shouts, "Have we any children here from Dublin? Have we any children here from Cork? Have we any children here from Galway?"

Marcus puts his hands to his ears to shut out the *YES* screams from the children. Then everyone stops shouting and the plinks do adventures.

Afterward, Marcus jumps on the trampoline. He takes his banana and nuts and grapes from his plink backpack and drinks his orange juice.

But still Super doesn't come for him. When the woman with the Children's Cave banner on her dress says, "Oh dear! Do you know who's collecting you, Bravo?" he takes out the plink card that Super gave him with Mammy's phone number on it and says, "My name is Marcus Richardson. Can you phone my mammy, please?"

Her name is Candy and he cries when she tries to take off

his costume. She lets him leave it on and lifts him up on a
high stool at the desk where people pay money and popcorn
pops. Marcus colors with pencils and the popcorn is pop-
ping when the policemen come in big cars with lights and
sirens. And Mammy, too, running all round the Children's
Cave like someone is chasing her, and she keeps crying.
She doesn't know Marcus. All she keeps saying is *where's
my son*, *where's my son*… and Daddy's here too, shouting
like he has snots in his nose, and no one knows it's Marcus
because he's Bravo.

Candy lifts him up in her arms and says, "It's time to be
Marcus again. Your mammy and daddy have come to bring
you home."

CHAPTER FIFTY-EIGHT

The television cameras and press arrive right on cue for the breaking story and the country rejoices. Amanda carries her son from the Children's Cave, her head averted from the questions being hurled at her. The media quieten when Lar delivers a brief statement. He thanks the police and the volunteers for the unstinting efforts they made to find his son. He asks for privacy so that he and his family can recover from their ordeal. His expression hardens when a reporter asks if Marcus was kidnapped by Ben Carroll, the creator of the plinks. And isn't it true, another reporter shouts, that he and his wife concluded a business deal that cheated Ben Carroll of potential earnings from his creation?

+

The days pass. In the bath, Marcus sings "Supercalifragilisticexpialidocious" and plays with the water plink. He holds shells to his ears and tells Amanda he can hear Super speaking to him. Her skin crawls when she sees him staring at the sky, searching the horizon for bubbles. At night, he refuses to sleep until she reads his plink books to him. He throws a tantrum when she tries to remove the dolls from his bed.

They remain there, still sitting in the same position, staring at her with those flittering eyes that seem to follow her around the room. He wants stars on the ceiling and rainbow arches above the doors. In effect, he wants to turn Shearwater into Plinkertown Hall.

According to the child psychologist, who counseled him after his release, his childish belief in fantasy, and his unique exposure to it, will have helped to promote his personality and social interaction skills. He believes it will encourage Marcus to explore complex issues later in life and view them through an imaginative and creative prism. Amanda has paid a handsome fee to listen to such psychobabble.

Accompanied by his parents and the police, he returns to the old house. He stares at the white, antiseptic walls and stamps his foot, bewildered, and says, "No...no...*no*. It's not Plinkertown Hall."

She holds tightly to his hand as they descend the stairs to the basement. Here, also, the walls are pristine. No graffiti, no clutter, except for a broken saddle, the horsehair stuffing removed from its interior.

He recognizes the apple trees and leads them to a small mound of mud where a bird is buried. The grave is exhumed and the bird taken away by the forensic team in the vain hope that it will provide them with a clue as to the disappearance of Ben Carroll.

"You're crazed," Lar says whenever she tries to discuss his double identity. "You're crazed," he says when she shows him a copy of a birth certificate with Karl Benedict Lawson written on it.

"Crazed" is an innocuous term. Not as defined as "mad," and suggesting that soon, when her shock has abated, she will become rational again. Marcus has been returned to them. For now, nothing else matters. Their marriage, and the question as to whether it can be healed or ended, must wait until the police have flushed Ben Carroll from his lair. Lar is convinced it's bound to happen soon.

Marcus returns to school. Each morning Amanda escorts him to his classroom. She is waiting outside when school ends. Strictly speaking, parents are only allowed as far as the reception area, but she is a mother crazed over her son's security. Parents and teachers hover at a distance. They know too much about her to be comfortable in her presence.

Mandy Meets has been taken off the air. She accepts the corporate decision. How can she conduct interviews with celebrities when she is too jittery to walk a straight line along the red carpet?

He is watching her, she is sure of that, yet the police admit they are no closer to finding Ben Carroll. As for Karl Lawson's whereabouts? Sergeant Moran is firm with Amanda. They have absolutely no evidence to link him to Marcus's disappearance. Ben Carroll is their only suspect. Vengeance and resentment were his motives. They have a trail of evidence that will put him behind bars for a long time. The sergeant's hostility is hidden behind a thin veneer of politeness. It's obvious she blames Amanda for shattering the life of Jon Hunter, who is under investigation for releasing unauthorized information to the media, and whose wife has ordered him from the family home. His phone records, as well as Amanda's, are being checked for evidence but all the police have traced is the one phone call Hunter made to meet her in the boatyard. A phone call Sylvia overheard. Lar has spoken to her. No anonymous tip-off from Karl Lawson on this occasion. Just a wife, tired of her husband's infidelities, seeking retribution.

Circumstantial evidence. Journalists are feasting on it, and yet they shy like startled horses when Amanda contacts them about Karl Lawson. Those who are willing to speak to her demand to know what evidence she has to back up her preposterous claim. She destroyed Karl Lawson once, then campaigned for his release; and now, for reasons that make no sense, she wants to lay waste to him once more.

Plans to feature a Shroff exposure on *Behind the Crime Line* have been put on hold. Eric has moved to France, or, maybe, he's in Germany. No one seems certain where he is hiding. Amanda has no desire to contact him, even if she could rouse herself to passion. All she can think about is the story under the skin.

Sometimes, she believes she has the pieces in place. But the fit is never right. Had she found him on his knees on Grafton Street or had he found her? Had she and Lar manipulated him or had they walked heedlessly into his web?

A month after Marcus had been returned to them, children searching for crabs on Glenmoore Strand find a full-sized plink costume wedged in rocks. Ragged and discolored, devoid of DNA and other incriminating evidence, it has held tight through the ebb and flow of the tides. Their parents call the police, who remove it for analysis. Amanda knows it will be deemed useless for furthering the investigation. She insists it is a red herring but Lar rages that Ben Carroll took his own life rather than face justice. This possibility maddens him. He wants his day in court, full retribution. Not only did he endure the terror of losing his son but the media have turned the plinks into a toxic brand. Parents have banished them from the playroom. Retailers have removed them from the toy shelves and all plink books have been pulped. Their investment has been lost and they own the merchandising rights to a monster. But Marcus can only fantasize about Super Plink. Mother and father and friend rolled into one.

"You're crazed," Lar repeats when Amanda insists that finding the plink costume among the rocks is another taunt, another stunt. Perhaps, if this was a less enlightened era, he would lock her away in an attic or confine her to an asylum for crazed wives who talk too much. But these are modern times and Amanda is free to roam the city streets searching for a phantom.

"Scarface," she says to the homeless and the dazed. She shows them the two photographs she carries everywhere with her. "Scarface, Scarface, Scarface." The youth who used that moniker has vanished. Is he dead or saved? Everything matters now. The air she breathes is clammy, the ground beneath her feet constantly shifting—until the day she sees him leaning against the wall of the Liffey boardwalk.

"Amanda," he says, straightening. "I believe you're looking for me." His lush, arrogant mouth softens in a smile. His hair, the color of wheat, is ruffled by the wind. That same wind chills her. She searches his face for a scar, but apart from some lines around his eyes, his tanned skin is smooth.

"Coffee?" he says and when she nods he purchases two cups from a nearby kiosk. The coffee is bitter. Amanda doesn't add sugar. Nothing will sweeten this conversation.

"How did you know I was searching for you?" she asks.

He shrugs. "One hears things on the street."

"Like the fact that you kidnapped my son?"

"I'd like to ignore the rumor mill." He sips the steaming coffee, his fingers circling the cup. "But your supposition interests me. Why on earth would I kidnap your son and damage him for life?"

"You didn't damage—" She stops, knowing he is toying with her. The story she wove around him changed the pattern of his life and he, seeking vengeance, wove a spell around her son, bewitched him with an elaborate and enchanting subterfuge. He must be aware, as she is, that Marcus was enthralled rather than damaged by his experience.

"I *know* you're Ben Carroll. Don't try to deny it." She meets his challenging eyes. No tinted lens to hide them now but his gaze is just as opaque.

"The rogue author? What an extraordinary suggestion." His voice lilts with amusement. "I presume you've discussed your theory with the police?"

"Marcus has told us enough to unmask you. It's just a matter of time before you're arrested. This time you'll never be released."

"Amanda, it's well established that you and the truth have a rocky relationship." He watches a boat glide by on the river. "Why on earth should anyone, particularly the police, believe what you tell them?"

"Deny it, then. Look me in the face and tell me I'm lying."

He returns his attention to her and says, "Why don't you come with me to Glenmoore Garda Station and make your accusation there? I presented myself for questioning when I realized you were involving me in your son's disappearance. I'm happy to return there for another interrogation. But they will turn me away, as they did last week, and the week before."

"You're responsible—"

"You make a lot of accusations about me. I suffered them once, but not for a second time. So, let me offer you some free advice. Beginning again when you have lost everything is painful. Mistakes are easy to make. I allowed my mistakes to drag me down into a very dark place. Don't go there, Amanda. You have the grit to take—"

Furiously, she interrupts him. "You stole my son and you have the nerve to patronize me with advice."

"Amanda, Amanda, surely you've read the papers?" He

makes it sound like a question, not a taunt. "Ben Carroll took your son on an adventure. You should allow Marcus to live with his memories of Plinkertown Hall until time takes them from him." Before she can move, he presses his finger to her bottom lip, touching her as she once, impulsively, touched his scar. "Deprive him of those memories and he will never stop yearning to return to his fantasy world. If that is the case, who can tell what will happen? Maybe, one day, he'll find it again."

She jerks away from him but she has felt the pressure of his warning. An overpowering sense of the truth slipping through her fingers adds to her helplessness. The wall between them is invisible, yet she senses its width, its height, the solidness of its bricks. Banging her head against it will do no good when violence is only a tremble away.

I know it's you...I'll prove it's you... She doesn't say the words out loud but, in the silence that falls between them, he hears her threat.

"Goodbye, Amanda," he says in the voice that once dismissed her from his office and now dismisses her as someone of little consequence. "It's unlikely we'll meet again. I'm flying to the States tomorrow. I don't think I'll be returning for some time. Just remember that appearances can be deceptive, as can the written word. And scars can hide a multitude of losses. Good luck with your search for Ben Carroll. No one is untraceable. If he's out there, and not at the bottom of the sea, he will be found and brought to justice."

He drains his coffee and crushes the cardboard cup in his hand. His shadow stretches before him, threatening and invincible. His shoulders are strong as he walks away from her. He is wrong, deliberately so. He knows, as Amanda knows, that the search for Ben Carroll will end in failure. He never existed. Just as Plinkertown Hall no longer exists, except in a small boy's wondrous imagination.

AUTHOR'S LETTER

Dear Reader,

"Fake news" is a term that's much bandied about these days. But this new definition of so-called "reality" had yet to dawn when I first sat down to write *Guilty*. As with all my novels, *Guilty* is a work of imagination, it is also a mix of personal observations and experiences diluted into fiction. I began with only the slimmest synopsis to map my way forward. But, as the story developed its own energy, I realized I was drawing together three distinct strands that have marked my career as a writer and merging them together to create the narrative.

Good timing has never been one of my strongest virtues and when I first decided to write I did so in tandem with tending to the needs of a newborn baby and two older children. When that ambition was abandoned and "The Great Novel" was packed away in a deep, dark drawer, never to be revived, I began to write newspaper features. I was lucky enough to attract the attention of a helpful editor, who was interested in my work and commissioned me to write on many different subjects. Without making a conscious decision, journalism gradually became my full-time career and my ambition to write a novel seemed like someone else's dream.

Years later, after much soul searching, I took a career break with the intention of finally writing fiction. The story that flowed from me was not for adults, as I'd planned, but for children. Looking back to that era, it wasn't a surprising development as my "baby"—then aged twelve—was constantly challenging my imagination with requests for stories. And there they were, a host of them just waiting to be written down. Over the following years I wrote many books and short stories for that age group, and also enjoyed writing radio and television scripts for preschool children.

When the issues I wanted to explore became too challenging to sit within the confines of children's literature, I moved seamlessly into writing my first novel for adults. But I've never forgotten the enjoyment of stirring young people's imagination and luring them into the depths of a fantasy kingdom. Nor have I forgotten the buzz of journalism, the excitement of chasing information and piecing it together for an investigative feature. *Guilty* allowed me to combine those two elements into my novel, which was both a challenge and a joy to write.

At the end of a book, I feel lonesome when I wave goodbye to my characters but I'm also relieved to see them enter that long tunnel which, hopefully, has a reader at the end of it. You are that reader and I'm deeply grateful to you for choosing to read *Guilty*. If you enjoyed my book and would like to leave a review, I would be very appreciative. If you'd like to keep up-to-date with all my latest releases, just sign up at the following link. Your email address will never be shared and you can unsubscribe at any time.

www.bookouture.com/laura-elliot

With warmest regards,
Laura Elliot

ACKNOWLEDGMENTS

Firstly, I must thank Sean, my husband. You showed amazing patience and tolerance as I plotted my way through each stage of *Guilty* during those Friday evenings in our local pub. To my son, Tony, my daughters Ciara and Michelle, their spouses and partners, Roddy, Louise and Harry, many thanks. You have supported me over the years with advice, much-needed tech assistance and many comforting dinners. To my wonderful grandchildren, Romy and Ava, whose visits on Tuesday afternoons are a wonderful incentive to switch off my laptop and head to the beach.

A special thank you to Peter Brunton for his patience and advice when I was writing *Guilty*.

My friends are very important to me. If I name them individually I could accidentally leave someone out. Even if they are willing to forgive my short-term memory lapse, I'd never forgive myself. So, to my collective friends, north and south of the Liffey, and far beyond, thank you for the lunches, the early birds, and the coffee catch-up conversations. A special thank you to the novelist Patricia O'Reilly for her ever-attentive and critical listening ear during our discussions on our works in progress.

I'm grateful to my editor, Claire Bord, whose sensitive editing always challenges me to dig deeper into my imagination. To Kim Nash for her enthusiasm and promotional skills, Lauren Finger and Hannah Todd for their patience and attention to detail, and Alex Crow, who will be marketing my newest book. I'm deeply appreciative to everyone in team Bookouture who helped with its editing and production. Special thanks to Emma Graves for a wonderful cover, and to Laoise O'Callaghan, who is the narrator of *Guilty*.

To all the reviewers and bloggers who have taken the time to review my books, many, many thanks. I'm deeply grateful to you all.

ABOUT THE AUTHOR

LAURA ELLIOT was born in Dublin, Ireland. She lives in Malahide, a picturesque, coastal town on the north side of Dublin. Writing as June Considine, she has twelve books for children and young adults. Her short stories have appeared in several teenage anthologies and have also been broadcast on the radio. She has also worked as a journalist and magazine editor.

For more information you can visit:

LauraElliotAuthor.com
Twitter @Elliot_Laura
Facebook.com/LauraElliotAuthor